A Half Forgotten Song

Katherine Webb

An Orion paperback

First published in Great Britain in 2012
by Orion
This paperback edition published in 2012
by Orion Books Ltd,
Orion House, 5 Upper St Martin's Lane,
London WC2H 9EA

An Hachette UK company

1 3 5 7 9 10 8 6 4 2

A CIP catalogue record for this book
is available from the British Library.

ISBN 978-1-4091-3589-0

Typeset at The Spartan Press Ltd,
Lymington, Hants

Printed and bound in Great Britain by Clays Ltd,
St Ives plc

The Orion Publishing Group's policy is to use papers
that are natural, renewable and recyclable products and
made from wood grown in sustainable forests. The logging
and manufacturing processes are expected to conform to
the environmental regulations of the country of origin.

www.orionbooks.co.uk

To Pea

I

The wind was so strong that she felt herself pulled between two worlds; caught in a waking dream so vivid that the edges blurred, and then vanished. The gale tore around the corners of the cottage, humming down the chimney, crashing in the trees outside. But louder than any of that was the sea, beating against the stony shore, breaking over the rocks at the bottom of the cliff. A bass roar that she seemed to feel in her chest, thumping up through her bones from the ground beneath her feet.

She'd been dozing in her chair by the remnants of the fire. Too old and tired to rise, to take herself upstairs to bed. But now the wind had wrenched the kitchen window open and was flinging it wide against its hinges, hard enough that the next bang might be its last. The window frame was rotten; it had been years since it was held shut by anything more than a wedge of folded paper. The sound came into her dream, and woke her, and she hovered on the verge of sleep as the cold night air poured in, pooling at her feet like the rising tide. She had to get up and wedge the window shut before the pane smashed. She opened her eyes, and could see the grey outlines of the room well enough. Through the window the moon raced across the sky, clouds streaking past it.

Shivering, she made her way to the kitchen window where the storm was caking the glass with salt. The bones of her feet ached as they pushed through her skin. Sleeping in the chair made her hips and back stiffen up like swollen wood, and it was an effort to push the joints into movement.

The wind coming in lifted her hair and made her shiver, but she shut her eyes to sniff at it because the smell of the sea was so dear, so familiar. It was the smell of everything she knew; the smell of her home, and her prison; the smell of her own self. When she opened her eyes she gasped.

Celeste was there. Out there on the cliffs, standing with her back to the cottage, facing out to sea, cast in silver by the moonlight. The surface of the Channel heaved and churned, spindrift whipped from white crests and flung stinging against the shore. She felt tiny flecks of it land on her face, hard and corrosive. How could Celeste be there? After so many long years, after she vanished so completely? But it was her, for certain. That long, familiar back, a supple spine descending into the voluptuous curves of her hips; arms straight by her sides with her fingers spread. *I like the touch of the wind, running through my hands.* Her words seemed to whisper through the window, with that strange guttural accent of hers. Long hair and long, shapeless dress, rippling out behind her; the fabric pressed against the contours of her thighs and waist and shoulders. Then came a sudden clear image – of him, sketching Celeste, his eyes flicking up with that frightening intensity, that unbreakable concentration. She shut her eyes again, and held them tight. The memory was both beloved and unbearable.

When she opened her eyes she was still in her chair and the window was still banging, the wind still blowing in. Did she not get up at all, then? Did she not go to the window, and see Celeste? She couldn't tell if that was real and this now a dream, or if it were the other way around. Her heart pounded at the thought – that Celeste had come back; that Celeste had discovered what had happened, and who was to blame. The woman's fierce, angry glare flashed before her mind's eye, seeing everything, seeing right through her; and suddenly she knew. *A premonition*, she heard her mother's voice say, breathing sourly in her ear; so clearly that she looked around to see if Valentina was really there. Shadows lay in the corners of the room, and stared back at her. Her mother had sometimes claimed to have the gift, and had always searched for signs of it in her daughter. Fostered any inkling of inner sight. Perhaps, finally, this was what Valentina had hoped for, because just then she *knew* that change was coming. As sure as the sea was deep. After all the many long years, change was coming. *Somebody* was coming. Fear wrapped its heavy arms around her.

Early morning sunshine poured in through the gallery's tall front windows, bouncing up from the floor, dazzling. Late summer sun that was still warm, and promised a fine day, but when Zach opened the front door there was a stony coolness to the air that hadn't been there even a week ago. A damp tang that spoke of autumn. Zach took a deep breath and turned his face to the sun for a moment. Autumn. The turning of the season, the end of the happy hiatus he'd been enjoying; of pretending that everything would stay the same. Today was the last day, and Elise was leaving.

He cast a look along the street in either direction. It was only just eight o'clock and not a single person was walking along his particular street in Bath. The Gilchrist Gallery sat on a narrow side street, just a hundred yards or so from Great Pulteney Street, a main thoroughfare. Close enough to be easy to find, he'd thought. Close enough that people would see his sign when they were walking past and happened to glance up the street. And the sign was clearly visible – he'd checked to make sure. It was just that surprisingly few people happened to glance to either side as they walked along Great Pulteney Street. It was too early for shoppers yet anyway, he reassured himself. The steady streams of people criss-crossing the bottom of the road had the smart, hurried look of people going to work. The muffled sound of their footsteps carried through the still air, tunnelling towards him through stark black shadows and blinding patches of sunlight. The sound seemed to make the silence at Zach's door ring out sadly. A gallery shouldn't rely on footfall, or passing trade, he reminded himself. A gallery was something the right people should seek out. He sighed, and went inside.

Zach's gallery had been a jeweller's shop before he'd taken over the lease four years previously. When it was refitted, tiny metal links and clasps turned up underneath the counter and behind the skirting; scraps of gold and silver wire. He even found a jewel one day, tucked behind a shelf where there was a narrow crack between wood and wall. It fell onto his foot with a solid little tap when he took the shelf down. A small, sparkling, perfectly clear stone which might be a diamond. Zach kept it, and took it as a good sign. Perhaps it had cursed him instead, he mused. Perhaps he should have sought out the erstwhile jeweller and given it back to him. The shop's aspect was perfect, sitting on a slight slope with its huge windows turned south-eastwards, capturing all this morning sunshine but directing it to the floor of the shop, not onto the walls where the perishable artworks hung. Even on dark days, it seemed bright inside; and just big enough to step back to admire the larger pieces from a suitable distance.

Not that there were many large pieces up, at that moment. He'd finally sold the Waterman landscape the week before; a piece by one of his contemporary, local artists. It had hung in the window long enough for Nick Waterman to start fretting about the colours fading, and the sale had come just in time to stop the artist moving his whole collection elsewhere. *His whole collection*, Zach snorted softly. Three cityscapes of the Bath skyline from various vantage points on the surrounding hills, and a slightly mawkish beach scene of a girl walking a red setter. Only the colour of this dog had made him take the piece. A fabulous coppery red, a blaze of life in an otherwise stagnant scene. The price of the painting, split evenly between gallery and artist, had given Zach enough money to tax his car and get it back on the road. Just in time to take Elise further afield, on some proper daytrips. They'd been to the caves at Cheddar; to Longleat; for a picnic in Savernake Forest. He turned slowly on his heels and looked at the rest of the stock, eyes sliding over some small but nice pieces by various twentieth-century artists, and a few recent watercolours by local artists, and then alighting on the stuttering heart of the collection: three drawings by Charles Aubrey.

He'd hung them together carefully, on the best-lit wall, at the perfect height. The first was a rough pencil sketch, called *Mitzy Picking*. The subject was squatting inelegantly, with her back to the artist and her knees wide apart, the fabric of a plain skirt draped over them. Her blouse was tucked carelessly into her waistband, and had come out at the back, riding up so that a fragment of skin was showing. It was a drawing of outlines and hasty shading, and yet this small section of her back, the indentation of her spine, was so beautifully rendered that Zach always wanted to put out his hand, brush his thumb along the groove and feel the smooth skin, the hard muscles underneath it. The slight dampness of sweat where the sun warmed her. The girl was apparently sorting some kind of foliage into a wicker basket on the ground between her knees; and as if she felt the viewer's scrutiny, as if she was half anticipating this un-invited touch on her back, she had inclined her face towards her shoulder so that her ear and the outline of her cheek were visible. Nothing could be seen of her eye except the smallest hint of the lashes beyond the curve of a cheekbone, and yet Zach could feel her awareness, feel how alert she was to whoever was behind her. The viewer, all these years later, or the artist, at the time? The drawing was signed and dated 1938.

The next piece was in black and white chalks on buff-coloured paper. It was a portrait of Celeste, Charles Aubrey's mistress. Celeste – there seemed to be no record of the woman's surname anywhere – was of French Moroccan descent, and had a honeyed complexion under masses of black hair. The drawing was just of her head and neck, halting at her collarbones, and in that small space it had encapsulated the woman's anger so intensely that Zach often saw people recoil slightly when they first saw it, as if they expected to be reprimanded for daring to look. Zach often wondered what had put her in such a violent mood, but the fire in her eyes told him that the artist had been on thin ice when he'd chosen that precise moment to draw her. Celeste was beautiful. All of Aubrey's women had been beautiful, and even when they weren't conventionally so, he still captured the essence of their allure in his portraits. But there was no ambiguity about Celeste, with her perfectly oval face, huge almond eyes and swathes of inky hair. Her face, her expression, were bold, fearless, utterly captivating. Small wonder that she managed to captivate Charles Aubrey for as long as she did. Longer than any other mistress he had.

The third Aubrey picture was always the one he looked at last, so that he could look at it the longest. *Delphine, 1938*. The artist's daughter, aged thirteen at the time. He had drawn her from the knees upwards, in pencil again, and she stood with her hands clasped in front of her, wearing a blouse with a sailor collar and her curly hair caught back in a ponytail. She was standing three-quarters turned towards the artist with her shoulders stiff and set, as if she had just been told to stand up straight. It was like a school photograph, posed for uncomfortably; but the trace of a nervous smile played around the girl's mouth as if she was startled by the attention, and unexpectedly pleased by it. There was sunlight in her eyes and on her hair, and with a few tiny highlights Aubrey had managed to convey the girl's uncertainty so clearly that she looked ready to break her pose in the next instant, cover her smile with her hand and turn her face away shyly. She was diffident, unsure of herself, obedient; Zach loved her with a bewildering force that was partly paternal, protective, and partly something more. Her face was still that of a child, but her expression, her eyes, held traces of the woman she would grow into. She was the very embodiment of adolescence, of a promise newly made, spring waiting to blossom. Zach had spent hours staring at her portrait, wishing he could have known her.

It was a valuable drawing, and if he would only be willing to sell it the wolves might have been held from the door for a while. He even knew to whom he could sell it, the very next day if he decided to. Philip Hart, a fellow Aubrey enthusiast. Zach had outbid him for the drawing at a London auction three years ago, and Philip had been to visit it two or three times a year since then, to see if Zach was ready to sell. But Zach never was. He thought he never would be. Hart had offered him seventeen thousand pounds on his last visit, and for the first time ever, Zach had wavered. Lovely as they were, he'd have taken half that amount for the drawings of Celeste or Mitzy, the other remnants of his ever-shrinking Aubrey stock. But he couldn't bring himself to part with *Delphine*. In other sketches of her – and there weren't many – she was a bony child, a background figure, overshadowed by the sparkling presence of her sister Élodie, or by bold Celeste. But in this one sketch she was her own self; alive, and on the cusp of everything that was to come. Whatever that may have been. This was the last surviving picture of her that Aubrey had drawn before his catastrophic decision to go and fight on the Continent during the Second World War.

Zach stood and stared at her now, her beautifully rendered hands with the short, blunt nails; the creases in the ribbon holding back her hair. He imagined her as a tomboy; imagined a brush dragged hastily, painfully through that unruly hair. *She had been out along the cliffs that morning, looking for feathers or flowers or anything else worth finding. Not a tomboy, but not a girl who particularly cared to be pretty, either. The wind had whipped her hair into knots that would take days to work free, and Celeste had berated her for not wearing a scarf over it. Élodie was sitting on a chair behind their father as he sketched, kicking her legs to and fro, sulking in a jealous rage. Delphine's heart was full to bursting with pride and love for her father; and as he sketched with a frown, she said prayer after silent prayer that she would not disappoint.* In the bright light of the gallery, Zach's reflection stared back from the glass, just as visible as the pencil lines behind it. If he concentrated, he could see both at once – his expression overlaying hers, her eyes looking out of his face. He didn't like what he saw – suddenly his own absorbed, wistful expression made him look older than his thirty-five years; and just as suddenly, he felt it as well. He hadn't combed his hair yet and it stood up in tufts, and he badly needed a shave. The shadows under his eyes he could do less about. He'd been sleeping badly for weeks, since he'd found out about Elise.

There was a thumping of footsteps and Elise came bustling down the stairs into the gallery from the flat above, swinging through the door on its handle, her face alight, long strands of brown hair flying out behind her.

'Hey! I've told you not to swing on the door like that!

You're too big, Els. You'll pull it off its hinges,' said Zach, catching her up and lifting her away from the door.

'Yes, Dad,' said Elise, any hint of contrition ruined by a wide grin and the shadow of laughter, creeping up on the words. 'Can we have breakfast now? I'm just *so* hungry.'

'Just *so* hungry? Well, that is serious. OK. Give me one second.'

'One!' Elise shouted, and then clattered down the remaining steps to the main shop floor, where there was enough space to twirl, arms wide, feet threatening to tangle with one another. Zach watched her for a second, and felt his throat tighten. She had been with him for four weeks now, and he wasn't sure how he was going to cope without her. Elise was six years old, sturdy, healthy, vibrant. She had Zach's exact shade of brown eyes, but hers were bigger and brighter, the whites whiter, the shape of them in a constant state of flux from wide with amazement or outrage to narrow with laughter or sleep. On Elise, the brown eyes were beautiful. She was wearing purple jeans, torn through at the knees, with a lightweight green blouse open over a pink T-shirt on which a photograph of Gemini, her favourite pony from her riding school, was emblazoned. It was a photo Elise had taken herself, and it wasn't very good. Gemini had raised his nose towards the camera and laid back his ears, and the flash had caused a lurid flare in one of his eyes, so that, to Zach, he looked bad-tempered, oddly elongated and possibly evil to boot. But Elise loved the T-shirt as much as she loved the pony. The outfit was finished with a bright yellow plastic handbag; mismatched clothes that made Elise look gaudy and delicious, like a multicoloured boiled sweet. Ali would not approve of the outfit, which Elise had assembled herself, but Zach was damned if he was going to have an argument and make her get changed on their last morning together.

'Snazzy outfit, Els,' he called down to her.

'Thanks!' she replied, breathlessly, still spinning.

Zach realised he was staring at her. Trying to notice everything about her. Knowing that the next time he saw her, myriad subtle changes would have taken place. She might even have outgrown the T-shirt with the ugly grey pony on it, or just gone off the creature, although that seemed unlikely. At the moment she seemed as upset about leaving the pony as she was about leaving her friends, her school. Her father. Time would tell, he supposed. He was about to find out if his daughter was an out of sight, out of mind kind of person, or one for whom absence made the heart grow fonder. He hoped to God she was the latter. Zach downed the last of his coffee, shut the front door and flipped the lock closed, then grabbed his daughter around her ribs to make her squeal with laughter.

Breakfast was eaten at a tatty pine table in the kitchen of the flat above the gallery, to the strains of Miley Cyrus on the CD player. Zach sighed slightly as his least favourite song by the saccharine pop star came around again, and realised to his horror that he had, gradually and against his will, learnt all the words. Elise bobbed her shoulders up and down as she ate her cereal, in a kind of seated dance, and Zach sang a line of the chorus in a high falsetto which made her choke, and spray milk onto her chin.

'Are you excited about the trip?' he asked, carefully, once Miley had faded into blessed silence. Elise nodded but said nothing, chasing the last few flakes of cereal around in her bowl, dipping them out of the milk like fishing for tadpoles. 'This time tomorrow you'll be on an aeroplane, high up in the sky. It's going to be fun, isn't it?' he pressed, hating himself because he could see that Elise wasn't sure how she should answer. He knew she was excited, scared, looking forward to it, sad to be leaving. A mixture of emotions she was too young to have to deal with, let alone express.

'I think you should come too, Dad,' she said at last, pushing her bowl away and leaning back, swinging her legs awkwardly.

'Well, I'm not sure that's such a good idea. But I'll see you in the holidays, and I'll come and visit lots,' he said, automatically, and then cursed himself in case he couldn't. Transatlantic flights didn't come cheap.

'Promise?' Elise looked up at him and held his gaze, as if hearing the hollowness of the words. Zach's stomach twisted, and when he spoke he found it hard to make his voice sound normal.

'I promise.'

They had to go before the end of the summer holidays, Ali had argued, so that Elise would have a chance to settle in for a couple of weeks before starting her new school. Her new school in Hingham, near Boston. Zach had never been to New England, but he pictured colonial architecture, wide open beaches and rows of pristine white yachts moored along bleached wooden jetties. It was these beaches and boats that Elise was most excited about. Lowell had a sailing boat. Lowell was going to teach Ali and Elise to sail. They were going to sail up the coast, and have picnics. Let him see one picture of Elise near a boat without a life jacket on, thought Zach, and he would be over there in a flash to knock Lowell's smug head off his shoulders. He sighed inwardly at the petty thought. Lowell was a nice guy. Lowell would never let a child near a boat without a life jacket, least of all somebody else's child. Lowell wasn't trying to be Elise's father – he appreciated that she already had a father. Lowell was so damn friendly and reasonable, when Zach wanted so badly to be able to hate him.

He packed Elise's things into her *Happy Feet* rolling cabin case, making a sweep of the flat and the gallery for glittery hairclips, Ahlberg books and the numerous small plastic objects that seemed to pay out behind his daughter wherever she went. A breadcrumb trail, for if ever he lost her. He took Miley Cyrus out of the stereo then picked up her other CDs – readings of fairy tales and rhyming songs, more cheesy pop music and an obscure set of German folktales sent by one of Ali's aunts. He picked up Elise's favourite – the *Tales of Beatrix Potter*, and considered keeping it. They had listened to it in the car on all their day trips during the past week, and the sound of Elise speaking along with the narrator, trying to mimic the voices, and then parroting lines for the rest of the day, had become the soundtrack to the last days of summer. *Give me some fish, Hunca Munca! Quack said Jemima Puddle-Duck!* He thought for a moment that he might play it to himself, and imagine her rendition once she was gone, but the idea of a grown man listening to children's stories, all alone, was too tragic for words. He packed the CD away with the rest.

At eleven o'clock sharp, Ali arrived and leaned on the bell for just a couple of seconds too long, so that it sounded impatient, insistent. Through the glass in the door Zach saw her blonde hair. It was cut into a short bob these days; the sun glancing off it so that it glowed. She had sunglasses hiding her eyes and wore a striped blue and white cotton jumper that skimmed her willowy frame. When he opened the door he managed to smile a little, and noticed that the familiar spike of emotion she usually brought with her was blunter than before, shrinking all the time. What had been helpless love and pain and anger and desperation was now more like nostalgia; a faint ache like old grief. A feeling more softly empty, and quieter than before. Did that mean he was no longer in love with her? He supposed so. But how could that be – how could that love go and not leave a gaping hole inside him, like a tumour carved out? Ali smiled tightly, and

Zach leaned down to kiss her cheek. She proffered it to him, but did not kiss him back.

'Zach. How's everything?' she asked, still with that tight-lipped smile. She'd taken a deep breath before speaking, and kept most of it in, pent up, swelling her chest. She thought there was going to be another row, Zach realised. She was braced for it.

'Everything is great, thanks. How are you? All packed? Come in.' He stepped back and held the door for her. Once inside, Ali took off her glasses and surveyed the virtually empty walls of the gallery. Her eyes were a little bloodshot, a sign of fatigue. She turned to Zach, examined him swiftly with a look of pity and exasperation, but bit back whatever she had been about to say.

'You look . . . well,' she said. She was being polite, Zach realised. They had regressed from being able to say anything to each other to being polite. There was a short pause, slightly awkward as this final transition in their relationship settled. Six years of marriage, two years of divorce, back to being strangers. 'Still hanging on to *Delphine*, I see,' Ali said.

'You know I'd never sell that picture.'

'But isn't that what a gallery does? Buys and sells . . .'

'And exhibits. She's my permanent exhibit.' Zach smiled slightly.

'She'd buy a lot of flights to visit Elise.'

'She shouldn't have to,' Zach snapped, his voice hard. Ali looked away, folding her arms.

'Zach, don't . . .' she said.

'No, let's not. No last-minute change of heart then?'

'Where is Elise?' Ali asked, ignoring the question.

'Upstairs, watching something loud and tacky on TV,' he said. Ali shot him an impatient look.

'Well, I hope you've been doing more with her all these weeks than just plonking her down in front of—'

'Oh, give it a rest, Ali. I really don't need parenting lessons from you.' He said it calmly, half amusedly. Ali took another deep breath and held it. 'I'm sure Elise will tell you what we've been up to. Els! Mummy's here!' He put his head through the door to the stairs and shouted this up to her. He had been dreading her departure for so many weeks, since Ali had told him about the move and all the rowing and discussing and rowing again had changed nothing at all. Now the dread of it had grown almost unbearable, and since the time had come, he wanted it over with. Do it quickly, make it hurt less.

Ali put her hand on his arm.

'Hang on, before you call her. Don't you want to talk about . . .' she trailed off, shrugged and splayed her fingers, searching for words.

'Exactly,' said Zach. 'We've talked and talked, and you've told me what you want, and I've told you what I want, and the upshot is you're going to do what you want, and I can go hang. So just do it, Ali,' he said, suddenly bone weary. His eyes were aching, and he rubbed them with his thumbs.

'This is a chance for a completely new start for Elise and me. A new life . . . we'll be happier. She can forget all about . . .'

'All about me?'

'All about all the . . . upheaval. The stress of the divorce.'

'I'm never going to think it's a good idea that you take her away from me, so there's no point you trying to convince me. I'm always going to think it's unfair. I never contested custody because . . . because I didn't want to make things worse. Make them harder, for her and for us. And this is how you thank me for that. You move her three thousand miles away, and turn me into some guy who sees her two or three times a year and sends her presents she doesn't like because he's so far out of touch with what she *does* like . . .'

'It wasn't about that. It wasn't about you . . .' Ali's eyes flashed angrily, and Zach saw the guilt there too; saw that she'd struggled with the decision. Oddly, it made him feel no better that she had.

'How would you feel, Ali? How would you feel in my place?' he asked, intently. For a horrifying second, he thought he might cry. But he didn't. He held Ali's gaze and made her see; and some emotion caused her cheeks to flush, her eyes to grow bright and desperate. What that emotion was, Zach could no longer read, and just at that moment Elise came rushing downstairs and flew into her mother's arms.

When they left, Zach hugged Elise and tried to keep smiling, tried to reassure her that she didn't need to feel guilty. But when Elise started to cry he couldn't keep it up – his smile became a grimace and tears blurred his last view of her, so in the end he stopped trying to pretend it was all right. Elise gulped and sobbed and scrubbed at her eyes with her knuckles, and Zach held her at arm's length, and wiped her face for her.

'I love you very much, Els. And I'll see you very soon,' he said, giving the statements no ambiguity, no hint of a maybe. She nodded, taking huge, hitching breaths. 'Come on. One last smile for your dad, before you go.' She gave it a good try, her small, round mouth curling up at the corners even as sobs shook her chest. Zach kissed her and stood up.

'Go on,' he said to Ali, brutally. 'Go on now.' Ali reached down for Elise's hand and towed her away along the pavement to where her car was parked. Elise turned and waved from the back seat. Waved until the car was out of sight down the hill and around the corner. And when it was, Zach felt something switch off inside him. He couldn't tell what it was, but he knew it was vital. Numb, he sank down onto the front step of the gallery, and sat there for a long time.

For the next few days Zach went through the motions of his everyday life, opening the gallery, trying to fill his time with odd jobs, reading auction catalogues, closing the gallery again; all with this same numbness dogging his every step. There was an emptiness to everything he did. Without Elise there to wake him up, to need breakfast, to need entertaining and impressing and scolding, there seemed little point to any of the other things he did. For a while now he had thought that losing Ali was the worst thing that would happen to him. Now he knew that losing Elise was going to be much, much worse.

'You haven't lost her. You'll always be her dad,' said his friend Ian, over a curry the following week.

'An absentee father. Not the kind of father I wanted to be,' Zach replied, morosely. Ian said nothing for a moment. He was obviously finding it hard to find comforting things to say; he was finding Zach's company hard. Zach felt bad about that, but he couldn't help it. He had no bravado left; he felt neither brave, nor tough, nor resilient. When Ian tentatively suggested that the move to the States might prove liberating for Zach, might give him a fresh start too, Zach looked up at him bleakly, and his friend fell into awkward silence. 'Sorry, Ian. Crap company, aren't I?' he apologised, eventually.

'Terrible,' Ian agreed. 'Thank God they do a good *karai* here, or I'd have left after the first ten minutes.'

'Sorry. I just . . . I miss her already.'

'I know. How's business?'

'Going under.'

'Not seriously?'

'Quite possibly.' Zach smiled at the horrified expression on Ian's face. Ian's own company – organising one-off adventures of a lifetime for people – was expanding all the time.

'You can't let that happen, mate. There must be something you can do?'

'Like what? I can't force people to buy art. They either want to buy it, or they don't.' In truth, there was more he should be doing. He should be dealing in smaller, more affordable pictures and increasing his stock that way. He should be getting up to London more; calling other dealers and past customers to remind them of his existence. Booking a stand at the London Art Fair. Anything to get the gallery some clients. It was what he'd done in the year before officially opening, and the year after that. Now the very thought tired him. It seemed to require more energy than he had left.

'What about those Charles Aubrey pictures? You must be able to sell them? Buy in some new stock instead, get things moving and shaking . . .' Ian suggested.

'I could . . . I could put two of them up for auction,' Zach conceded. *But not* Delphine, he thought. 'But once they're gone . . . that's it. That's the heart of the gallery gone. Who knows when – or if – I'd be able to afford to buy any more of his work? I'm meant to *specialise* in Aubrey. I'm an Aubrey expert, remember?'

'Yes, but . . . needs must, Zach. It's business. Try not to make it so personal.'

Ian was right, but it was personal to Zach; probably far too personal. He'd known of Charles Aubrey for a very long time, since he was a small boy. On every strained, too-quiet visit to his grandparents, he would spend time standing next to his grandma, staring at the picture that hung in her dressing room. It would have hung in pride of place in the living room, his grandma told him, but Grandpa did not approve. When he asked why not, Zach was told, *I was one of Aubrey's women.* The old woman always had a sparkle in her eye and a pleased smile pulling at her creased lips when she said these words. One time, Zach's father heard her say it and put his head around the door to scowl at her. *Don't go filling the boy's head with that nonsense*, he muttered. When they went back downstairs, Zach's father was staring at Grandpa, but the older man seemed unwilling to meet his gaze. One more of those tense, hung moments that Zach hadn't understood at the time; that had made him half dread visiting his grandparents, and half dread the black mood his father would be in for days afterwards.

The Aubrey print in his grandma's dressing room was a scene of rocky cliffs and a churning silver sea, the clifftops vibrant with long grass smoothed flat beneath the wind. A woman was walking along the cliff path with one hand clamped onto her hat and the other held slightly away from her, as if for balance. It was slightly impressionistic, the brushwork quick and impulsive, and yet the whole scene was alive. Looking at it, Zach expected to hear gulls, and feel the touch of salt spray on his face. You could smell the wet rocks, hear the wind buffeting in your ears. *That's me*, his grandma told him proudly, on more than one occasion. When she looked at the picture, it was clear she was looking into the past. Her eyes fell out of focus, drifted away to distant times and places. And yet, Zach had always thought there was something slightly uneasy about the picture. It was the way the figure looked so vulnerable, on the clifftop. Walking all alone, and holding one hand out to steady herself, as if the wind wasn't blowing in off the sea but off the land instead, and threatening to pull her over the edge into the choppy water below. If he looked at it for long enough, the picture sometimes gave Zach that spongy feeling in his knees that he got at the top of a ladder.

She had in fact been feeling dizzy that morning, slightly unsure of her own feet, and her ability to keep them. The strength of the new feelings gripping her made everything else seem flimsy and false. The walk along the cliffs towards Aubrey's house was a little over a mile, and with every step her heart beat faster, harder. She didn't see him up ahead, sketching with oils. She paused at the top of the long rise in the path, to catch her breath. The wind seemed to blow right into her lungs, buoying her up so that she might be whisked away like a loose kite. The thought of getting closer, the joy of seeing him soon. He showed her the picture afterwards, and her skin tingled – to think that he had been watching her unawares. Seeing her own body rendered in paint by his hand made her ache inside.

By the time his grandpa died, and his grandma, frail and frightened, agreed to move into a sheltered flat, the print had faded so badly that it went into the skip, along with many more of their possessions that were too old, worn and battered to be of use to anybody. *It's too big to hang in that new flat of yours, anyway,* Zach's father had said, gruffly. His grandma had stared from the living-room window, stared out at the skip until the last possible moment before leaving. The original painting was in the Tate, and Zach went to see it whenever he was up in London. He felt nostalgic each time he looked at it. It took him back to his childhood, in the same way the smells of burnt toast and Polo mints and cigarillo smoke did; and at the same time he could now see it through adult eyes, through an artist's eyes. But perhaps it was time he stopped thinking of himself as an artist. It had been years since he'd finished a piece, even longer since he'd finished anything worth showing to anybody else. He really wanted the figure in the Aubrey painting to be his grandmother, and he often searched the figure for familiar characteristics. Tiny shoulders, comparatively large breasts. A diminutive figure with a smudge of light, tawny hair. It could have been her. The painting was dated 1939. That year, his grandma whispered to him as they stood in front of the print, she and his grandpa took a holiday in Dorset, near where Aubrey had his summer house; and they had met the artist whilst out walking.

Only later in life did the implications of all this begin to dawn on Zach. He never dared to ask his grandma outright about that summer, but he was willing to bet she would have given a little laugh and an evasive shrug if he had, and that there would have been that sparkle in her eye as she looked away, and a small smile lingering on her mouth. Her expression when she looked at the picture, Zach could see in hindsight, was that of an infatuated girl, still in the grip of young love over seventy years later. It got him thinking, but Zach's father, maddeningly, bore no physical resemblance whatsoever to either Charles Aubrey or to Zach's grandpa. But nobody in Zach's family had ever picked up a paintbrush or a sketchbook until Zach did. None of his official forebears had any kind of artistic bent whatsoever. When he was ten, he presented his grandpa with his best ever drawing of his BMX bike. It was good; he knew it was good. He thought his grandpa would be pleased, impressed; but the old man had frowned at the picture instead of smiling, and had handed it back to Zach with a dismissive remark. *Not bad, son.*

Another day in the gallery passed with barely any customers. An elderly lady spent twenty minutes turning the wire rack of postcards around and around before deciding not to buy any. How he hated that revolving wire rack. Postcards of art – last chance saloon for any serious gallery, and he couldn't even sell them, thought Zach. He noticed that there was dust on the white wires of the rack. Tiny little banks of it on each and every horizontal. He wiped at a few with his cuff, but soon gave up and thought instead about Ian's last question to him over their recent meal: *So, what are you going to do?*

Something like panic gripped him then, and gave his gut a nasty little jolt; because he really had no idea. The future stretched out shapelessly in front of him, and in it he couldn't find one thing to aim for, one thing that would clearly be a good idea, or that he could afford to do. And looking back was no help either. His one best thing, his greatest achievement, was now thousands of miles away in Massachusetts, probably developing an American accent and forgetting him already. And when he looked behind him, everything he thought he had been building turned out to have been transient, and had crumbled into nothing when he wasn't watching. His career as an artist; his marriage; his gallery. He genuinely wasn't sure how it had happened – if there had been signs he'd missed, or some fundamental flaw in his approach to life. He thought he'd done all the right things; he thought he'd worked hard. But now he was divorced, just like his parents. Just like his grandparents had longed to be; held together only by the conventions of their generation. Having witnessed the bloody battleground of his parents' separation, Zach had vowed that it would never happen to him. He had been sure, before he wed, that he would do right whatever it was they had done wrong. Staring into space, he followed the thread of his life back, right back, searching for all the times and places he'd gone wrong.

The sun sank below the rooftops outside, and shadows stretched long and deep across the gallery floor. Earlier every day, these shadows descended. Pooling in the narrow streets where pale Bath stone façades stretched up on either side like canyon walls. In the heat of summer they were a blissful escape from the glaring sun, from the heat and the sticky press of crowding people. Now they seemed oppressive, foreboding. Zach went back to his desk and sank into the chair, suddenly cold, and tired. He would give every last scant thing he possessed in an instant, he decided, to the first person who could tell him clearly and precisely what he should do next. He didn't think he could stand even one more day trapped in the silence of the gallery, smothered by the sound of an absent daughter, a long-gone wife and no clients, no customers. He had just decided to get horribly, pointlessly drunk when two things happened within the space of five minutes. Firstly, he found a new drawing by Charles Aubrey for sale by auction in the Christie's catalogue, and then he got a phone call.

He was staring at the description of the drawing as he picked up the phone, distractedly, not really interested in the call.

'Gilchrist Gallery?' he said.

'Zach? It's David.' Clipped words in a smooth, unfathomable voice.

'Oh, hello David,' Zach replied, dragging his eyes from the catalogue and trying to place the name, the voice. He had a sudden nagging feeling that he should pay attention. There was a nonplussed grunt at the end of the line.

'David Fellows, at Haverley?'

'Yes, of course. How are you, David?' Zach said, too quickly. Guilt made his fingertips tingle, just like they had at school when the question about his missing homework was asked.

'I'm very well, thank you. Look, it's been a while since I've heard from you. In truth, it's been over eighteen months. I know you said you needed more time to get the manuscript to me, and we did agree to that, but there does come a point when a publisher starts to wonder if a book is ever going to appear . . .'

'Yes, look, I am sorry for the delay . . . I've been . . . well . . .'

'Zach, you're a scholar. Books take as long as they take, I am well aware. The reason I'm calling today is to let you know that somebody else has come to us with an outline for a work on Charles Aubrey . . .'

'Who?'

'Perhaps it might be more politic if I didn't say. But it's a strong proposal, he's shown us half the manuscript and hopes to finish in four to five months. It would coincide very nicely with next year's exhibition at the National Portrait Gallery . . . Anyway, I've been told by the powers that be to chase you up, not to put too fine a point on it. We want to go ahead with a major new work on the artist, and we want to publish next summer. That means we would need a manuscript from you by January or February at the latest. How does that sound?'

With the receiver pressed hard to his ear, Zach stared at the Aubrey drawing in the catalogue. It was of a young man with a faraway expression; straight, fair hair falling into his eyes, fine features, a sharp nose and chin. Wholesome, slightly raffish. A face that conjured up images of boys' school cricket matches; mischief in the dorm room; pilfered sandwiches and midnight feasts. *Dennis*, it was called, and dated 1937. The third drawing of the young man Zach had seen by Aubrey, and with this one, more strongly than ever, he knew that something was wrong. It was like hearing a cracked bell chime. Something was off key, flawed.

'How does that sound?' Zach echoed, clearing his throat. *Impossible. Out of the question.* He hadn't even looked at his half-constructed manuscript, his reams of notes, for over six months.

'Yes, how does it sound? Are you all right, Zach?'

'I'm fine, yes . . . I'm . . .' He trailed into silence. He had abandoned the book – one more project that had petered to nothing – because it was turning out just like every other book about Aubrey he had ever read. He'd wanted to write something new about the man and his work, something that would show a unique insight, possibly the kind of insight only a relative, a secret grandson, would be able to give. Halfway through he'd realised he had no such insight. The text was predictable, and covered well-trodden ground. His love for Aubrey and his work was all too obvious, but that was not enough. He had all the knowledge, all the notes. He had his passion for the subject. But he didn't have an angle. He should just tell David Fellows that and have done with it, he thought. Let this other Aubrey man get his book published. With a pang, Zach realised he'd probably have to pay back the publication advance, modest as it was. He wondered where on earth he might pull that money back from, and almost laughed out loud.

But the picture on the page in front of him kept pulling at his attention. *Dennis*. What was that expression, on the young man's face? It was so hard to pin down. One minute he looked wistful, the next mischievous, and then he looked sad, full of regret. It shifted like the light on a windy day, as if the artist couldn't quite capture it, couldn't quite commit the mood to paper. And that was what Charles Aubrey did, that was where his genius lay. He could pin an emotion to paper like nobody else; catch a fleeting thought, a personality. Portray it with such clarity and skill that his subjects came to life on the paper. And even when the expression was ambiguous, it was because the mood of the sitter had been the same. Ambiguity itself was something he could draw.

But this was different. Wholly different. This looked as though the artist couldn't decipher, couldn't recapture the sitter's mood. It seemed impossible to Zach that Charles Aubrey would produce such an incomplete picture, and yet the pencil strokes, the shading, were like a signature in themselves . . . But then there was the question of the date, as well. The date was all wrong.

'I'll do it,' he said, suddenly, startling himself. Tension made his voice abrupt.

'You will?' David Fellows sounded surprised, and not quite convinced.

'Yes. I'll get it to you early next year. As soon as I can.'

'Right . . . great. Fantastic to hear, Zach. I'll admit, I'd rather thought you'd hit a wall of some kind with it. You'd sounded so sure you had something really fresh on the subject, but then time started to tick along . . .'

'Yes, I know. Sorry. But I will finish it.'

'Well, all right then. Great stuff. I shall tell the powers that be that my faith in you was entirely justified,' said David, and behind the words Zach heard the slight misgiving, the gentle warning.

'Yes. It was,' Zach said, his mind churning furiously.

'Well then, I had better get on. And, if I may be so bold, so had you.'

In the lull after the call ended, Zach cleared his dry throat and listened to his mind racing, and almost laughed aloud again. Where on earth could he start? There was one obvious answer, and only one. He looked back at the catalogue, and down the page to the provenance of the drawing of Dennis. *From a private collection in Dorset*. The seller with no name again, just as before. Three pictures of Dennis had now emerged from this mysterious collection, and two of Mitzy as well. All in the last six years. All apparently studies for final paintings that nobody had ever seen. And there was only one place in Dorset that Zach could think to start looking for the source of them. He got to his feet and went upstairs to pack.

2

In the bed that had been her mother's, and still sagged where Valentina's body once lay, she was visited. Since the night she saw Celeste her dreams had been populous, bustling with the long gone, and the long dead. They waited for her to shut her eyes and then they edged closer, on silent feet, flitting out of distant hiding places and announcing themselves only with the hint of a scent, a murmured word or an expression they often wore. Celeste's fierce eyes; Charles's hands, flecked with paint; the quizzical tilt of Delphine's brows; Élodie stamping her foot. Her own mother, breathing fire. And with them came feelings, each one washing over her like a wave, making it hard to breathe. They towed her far from land, so she couldn't put her feet down, couldn't rest or be safe. Fighting not to drown. An enveloping sea of remembered faces and voices, swirling and surging so that she woke with her stomach churning and her head so full she couldn't remember the time, or the place. They had questions for her, each and every one of them. Questions only she could answer. They wanted the truth; they wanted her reasons; they wanted retribution.

And once her eyes were used to the dark, and could pick out the pale outlines of the window and the familiar furniture, the crescendo lulled a little and the foreboding came back. The feeling that somebody was coming, and that because of this stranger everyone she had lost, and everyone she feared, would come to lurk in the dark corners of the house and wait, just out of sight, for the chance to make their demands. They would demand truths she had hidden for decades; hidden from everybody, sometimes even from herself. Their demands would get louder, she realised. Panic quivered in her gut. They would get stronger, unless she found some way to hold them off. Wide awake she lay, humming softly so that she wouldn't hear them, and strove to discern if the one who was coming would be friend to her, or foe.

The village of Blacknowle lay in a fold of the rolling Dorset coastline to the east of the villages of Kimmeridge and Tyneham – that strange ghost village appropriated by the War Office in 1943 as a training ground for troops and then never returned to its residents. Zach's parents had taken him to the village as a child, as part of an August bank holiday break in the area. Zach most clearly remembered Lulworth Cove, because there'd been an ice cream – much hankered after but rarely had – and the beach's perfect, round crescent had seemed so unreal, almost like something from another country. He'd filled his pockets with the smooth white pebbles until the lining split, and cried when his mother made him empty them out before getting back into the car. *You can keep one*, his dad had said, shooting his fractious mother a thunderous look. Now Zach wondered how he'd failed to realise how unhappy they were. In Blacknowle itself, his father had wandered the short streets with an expectant look on his face, as if he was sure of finding something, or someone. Whatever it was, by the end of the holiday the look was gone; replaced by a settled sadness, and disappointment. There'd been disappointment of another kind on his mother's face.

Zach followed a lane so narrow that dusty lengths of cow parsley whipped his wing mirrors on either side. On the back seat were a hastily packed suitcase and a cardboard box containing all the notes he had accumulated for his book on

Charles Aubrey. There were more than he remembered. The box's handles had sagged dangerously when he'd heaved it out from under his bed. His laptop was zipped up in its bag next to the box, full of pictures of Elise and ways of contacting her; and that was all he had with him. *No*, he corrected himself ruefully. *That's all I have.* He came to the village around the next bend, but the road carried on south, towards where the land dipped and then disappeared into the sea, and Zach was suddenly unwilling to arrive. He had so little idea of what he would do when he did that he felt uneasy, almost afraid. He accelerated again, and carried on through the village, another mile or so, till the lane ended at a small, weed-strewn parking area. There was a faded orange and white life buoy, an abrupt sign warning of tides and submerged rocks, and a crumbling lip of land beneath which the grey sea rolled in, choppy and restless.

Zach considered his next move. He knew for a fact that the house Charles Aubrey had rented as his summer house was no more – other people had tried to visit it, but it had burnt down at some point in the 1950s, and not even the foundations were visible any more. The exact spot had been built over in the 1960s, by the council road that formed a large loop to the south-west of the village. He watched the white froth of the sea for a few minutes. The water looked cold and hostile as it broke over the rocky shore, constantly moving, seething. He could hear it grumbling beneath the higher sound the wind made, parting around his car. This sound, and the flat grey light, suddenly seemed desolate; seemed to echo around the emptiness inside him, magnifying it unbearably. He felt as though he barely existed, and he fought the feeling, thinking hard.

Blacknowle was where it had all started. The rift between his grandparents, the distance between his father and his grandpa that had hurt his father so. This was where Aubrey had cast his spell over Zach's family, and this was where the man's memory still held thrall. Where pictures that both had to be and couldn't be by Aubrey were quietly emerging for sale from some hiding place. Zach opened the car door. He'd thought it would be cold; had pulled his shoulders up in anticipation, ready to shiver. Tensed against an onslaught which didn't come. The breeze was warm and moist, and now it was in his ears it sounded excited, enthusiastic. An ebullient, thrumming sound, not a moan at all. Minute speckles of water landed on his skin and seemed to rouse him, waking him from a trance he hadn't known he was in. He took a deep breath. Locking the car behind him, Zach walked to the edge of the low cliff. A narrow path ran unevenly through tan-coloured earth and rocks to the beach, and without a second thought he began to pick his way down it, skidding on loose scree until he reached the bottom. He made his way across the rocks to the shoreline, crouched down on one large, flat boulder and dipped his fingers into the water. It was shockingly cold. As a child he'd have been in, regardless. He'd never seemed to feel the cold, although there were pictures of him, skinny in saggy wet trunks, grinning over a bucket of shrimps with his lips quite blue.

Beneath the water the dull rocks came alive in shades of grey and brown, black and white. Some of the clots of foam floating nearby were an unhealthy yellow, but the water was glassily clear. Sometimes things were too big, Zach suddenly thought. They were too big to step back and look at them all at once. Doing so was overwhelming, frightening. You had to get up close, look at each constituent part, and tackle something of a manageable size first. Start small. Build up to the bigger picture. He put his fingers back into the water and touched a flat rock that had a bright white stripe running across its exact centre. He thought about painting it, sifting through colours in his mind to find the exact blend he would need to recreate the cold water, the immaculate stone. He wasn't sure if he still could, but it had been many, many months since he'd even felt the urge to try. Calmer, Zach stood up and dried his fingers on the seat of his jeans. His stomach rumbled hotly so he went back to the car and back to Blacknowle, where he'd passed a promising-looking pub.

The Spout Lantern was a crooked building, with walls of Portland stone beneath an undulating tiled roof. The hanging baskets outside were dry and leggy at the end of the season, with strings of brown lobelia trailing from them; the sign showed a curious-looking metal lamp with a handle on top and a long, tapering tube sticking out from one side – it looked more like a misshapen watering can than anything else. The pub sat in the centre of the village, where the buildings clustered around a tiny green and crossroads. The pub was the only amenity he could see; a faded Hovis sign painted on the wall of one cottage spoke of a long gone shop; a letterbox in the wall of another told of a vanished post office. Inside, the pub was cool and shady with that familiar, sour background smell of beer and people that was no longer masked by cigarette smoke. An elderly couple were eating fish and chips at a small table near the fireplace, even though the fireplace was empty and swept clean for the summer. Their whippet eyed Zach dolefully as he crossed to the bar and ordered half a pint and some ham sandwiches. The barman was friendly and highly vocal. He spoke too loudly in the quiet room, and made the whippet wince.

A few other people were scattered further along the room, eating lunch and talking in hushed voices. Zach suddenly felt too conspicuous to take a table by himself, so he stayed at the bar, sliding onto a stool and peeling off his jumper.

'Looks cold but it isn't, is it? Funny sort of day,' the

barman said cheerfully, passing Zach his drink and taking his money.

'You don't know how right you are,' Zach agreed. The barman smiled curiously. He spoke with a Home-Counties accent at odds with his rustic appearance – a battered flannel shirt and canvas trousers that were frayed and thready around the pockets and hems. He looked about fifty, and had curls of grey hair reaching down to his collar, growing in a ring around a bald pate.

'So what brings you to Blacknowle? Holiday? Looking for a second home?'

'No, no. Nothing like that. I'm actually . . . doing some research.' He felt suddenly uneasy about saying so, as if once this was known he would have to act differently. Act as if he knew what he was doing. 'Into an artist who used to live near here,' he pressed on. In the mirror behind the bar, he saw the elderly couple by the fire pause when they heard this, a gradual slowing of movement, then a halt. They stopped fiddling with the food on their plates, stopped chewing. Exchanged a look between them that Zach couldn't read, but that made the back of his neck prickle. The barman had cast a glance in their direction too, but he quickly looked back at Zach and smiled.

'Charles Aubrey, I'll bet.'

'Yes – you've heard of him,' Zach said. The barman shrugged amiably.

'Of course. Bit of a claim to fame, he is. Local celeb. He used to come in here all the time, back before the war. Not that I was here then, but I've been told; and there's a photo of him over there – sitting outside this very establishment with pint in hand.'

Zach put down his drink and crossed to the far wall, where the framed photograph was hanging in a foxed mount speckled with dead thrips. The picture had been enlarged and was grainy as a result. It was a photo Zach had seen before, reprinted in an old biography of the man. He felt a peculiar frisson to think that he was standing in the same pub that Charles Aubrey had visited. Zach studied the picture closely. The light of an evening sun lit Aubrey's face from the side. He was a tall man, lean and angular. He was sitting on a wooden bench with his long legs crossed, one hand cupped over the upper knee, the other holding a glass of beer. He was squinting against the light, his face turned partly away from it, which threw his bony nose into relief; his high cheekbones and broad brow. His jaw was hard and square. Thick, dark hair, the light gathering in its kinks and waves. It wasn't a classically handsome face, but it was striking. His eyes, staring right into the camera, were steady and intense; his mood impossible to read. It was a face you had to look twice at – compelling, perhaps unsettling; as if it might be terrifying in rage, but infectious in mirth. Zach couldn't see what it was that women had seen in him, that apparently *all* women had seen in him, but even he could sense the power of the man, the strange magnetism. The picture was dated 1939 – the summer his grandparents had met the man. Later that year, war would break out. Later that year, torn apart by grief and loss, Charles Aubrey would join the Royal Hampshire Regiment, which would form part of the British Expeditionary Force that set out into mainland Europe to meet Hitler. The year after, he would be caught up in the chaos of Dunkirk, and killed; his body buried hastily in an allied cemetery, his tags brought home by comrades.

When Zach turned away, the old man was watching him with a grave expression, eyes of such a pale blue they were almost colourless. Zach smiled and gave him a nod, but the old man looked back down at his empty plate without acknowledging him, so Zach returned to the bar.

'I wonder, do you know of anybody still living in the village who might remember those days? Who might have met Charles Aubrey?' Zach said to the barman. He kept his voice low, but in the quiet of the pub it was plainly audible. The barman smiled wryly and paused. He didn't glance over at the elderly couple. He didn't need to.

'There might be some. Let me have a think.' Behind him, the couple got up. With the slightest of salutes to the publican – a raised, gnarled index finger – the man cupped one hand around his wife's elbow and steered her towards the door. The whippet followed at their heels, tail curled tightly between its legs, toenails tapping delicately. As the door swung shut, the publican cleared his throat. 'The thing is, those that do might not be that keen to talk about it. You have to understand, lots of people have come asking questions about Aubrey over the years. He caused a bit of a scandal around here, back in the day, and since he wasn't actually *from* Blacknowle, most feel no need to play up the association.'

'I understand. But, surely, you know – seventy-odd years later . . . people can't still be upset about him, can they?'

'You'd be amazed, mate,' said the publican, with a grin. 'I've lived here seventeen years now, and run this pub for eleven. The locals still call me a latecomer. They've got long memories and they can hold a grudge like you wouldn't believe. The first week we moved in my wife pipped her horn at some sheep blocking the lane. She didn't see the farmer coming up behind them. And one thing's clear – she'll *never* be forgiven for such a display of impatience.'

'People hold a grudge against Aubrey? Why?' said Zach. The other man blinked, and seemed to hesitate before answering.

'Well, if they think my wife wasn't the right sort for sounding her horn at some sheep, can you imagine what they thought of a man who only came for the summer, made his money drawing saucy pictures of young girls and lived in sin with a foreign mistress? And all this back in the thirties?'

'Yes, I suppose he must have caused a bit of a stir. But I'd hardly call his pictures saucy.'

'Well, not to us maybe. But back in the day. I mean, he never painted the plain ones, did he?' The man chuckled, and Zach felt a defensive prickle on Aubrey's behalf. 'And then there was all that other business . . .'

'Other business?'

'You must know about . . . the tragedy that happened here?'

'Oh yes, of course. But . . . that was just a tragedy, wasn't it? Not Aubrey's fault at all.'

'Well, there's some that might argue with you there. Ah – here's your lunch now.' Zach's sandwiches were brought out by a grumpy-looking girl. He smiled as he thanked her, but she could only manage a flick of her mascara-laden eyelashes in return. The publican rolled his eyes. 'My daughter, Lucy. Loves working for her old man, don't you, Lu?' Lucy didn't answer as she drifted back to the kitchen.

'So you don't think anybody will talk to me about him? What about . . . do you know of anybody who has some Aubrey pictures they might be willing to let me see?'

'Couldn't tell you, sorry.' The publican leant his knuckles on the bar, tipped his head and seemed to think hard. 'No, no idea. Worth a pretty penny these days, aren't they? I don't think folk round here would have any – if they once had they'd have sold them. Farming folk for the most part, around Blacknowle. Either that or catering for tourists, neither trade well known for making the money roll in.'

'What if . . . do you think if I offered to . . . pay for information, or rather memories, of Aubrey . . . do you think that might get me anywhere?' said Zach, and again the publican chuckled.

'Can't think of a faster way to get yourself ostracised,' he said, jovially. Zach sighed, and concentrated on his sandwiches for a while.

'I suppose you must see a lot of tourists and second-home owners down here; it must be easy to resent them. My parents brought me here on holiday once – to Blacknowle itself, and to Tyneham and Lulworth. We stayed in a cottage not three miles away. And my grandparents used to come here too, back in the 1930s. My grandma remembered meeting Aubrey. I always suspected . . . I always suspected she remembered more than just meeting him, if you catch my drift,' said Zach.

'Did she now? Well, I daresay she wouldn't be the only one! I don't resent the tourists. The more the merrier, as far as I'm concerned. It's been too quiet this summer, what with the weather being so crap. Are you staying in the area for a while, while you do your research? Got a lovely room upstairs, if you're interested. Lucy's a right thundercloud in the morning, but she does a great fry-up.'

'Thanks. I . . . hadn't really thought about it. I might go for a walk and take in the views that inspired the artist; but if nobody will talk to me and nobody has any pictures I can look at, there's not really a lot of point in me staying,' said Zach. The landlord seemed to consider this for a while, wreathed in steam rising from beneath the counter as he dried clean glasses from the dishwasher. His face shone with the moisture.

'Well, there is one place you could try,' he said, carefully.

'Oh?'

The publican pursed his lips, and seemed to consider for a second longer. Then he leant forward and spoke in a hushed tone, so conspiratorial that Zach almost laughed.

'If you just happened to take a walk along the track that heads south-east out of the village towards Southern Farm, and about half a mile along there you took the left fork, you'd come to a cottage called The Watch.'

'And . . . ?'

'And there's somebody there who might talk to you about Charles Aubrey. If you pitch yourself right.'

'And what would be the right way to pitch myself?'

'Who knows? Sometimes she'll chat, sometimes she won't. It might be worth a shot, but you didn't hear about her from me. And go carefully – she lives alone, and some people are . . . protective.'

'Protective? Of this woman?'

'Of her. Of themselves. Of the past. Last thing I need is it getting out that I've been helping a stranger ferret for information. This lady's the private kind, you know. Some of us in the village used to drop in on her, to make sure she was all right, but she's made it known over the years that she doesn't appreciate it. Wants to be left alone. What can you do? Must be a lonely life for her but if a person doesn't want help . . .' He went back to wiping glasses, and Zach smiled.

'Thanks.'

'Oh, don't thank me. It may come to nothing, just to warn you. I'll make up that bed upstairs for you, shall I? The rate's forty-five a night.'

'Take a credit card?'

'Of course.'

'I'm Zach, by the way. Zach Gilchrist.' He held out his hand, which the landlord shook with a smile.

'Pete Murray. Good luck at The Watch.'

She had been dozing again, after a lunch of hard-boiled eggs and salad leaves. Two of the hens were going into moult. They looked patchy and bedraggled, and she muttered to them when she found no eggs underneath them. *Lay, lay my girls. Let the eggs drop or be straight to the pot.* Repeated over and over, the little rhyme sounded like a spell, and soon the voice she heard was her mother's, not her own. Valentina kept coming back to her since her waking dream, since her vision, her premonition. Her mother had been gone a long time. She'd thought maybe for ever, and hadn't been sad about that – apart from the endless quiet sometimes, the stillness. But lately she'd caught her mother watching her from the citrine eyes of the ginger cat; in the coils of skin as she peeled an apple; reflected, minute and upside down, in the bloated drip of water that always hung from the kitchen tap. After the night of the storm, after the night she saw Celeste and had her premonition, she'd found the old charm on the hearthstone. Knocked out of the chimney by the wind after nigh on eighty years, a shrivelled nugget of old flesh the size of an egg; the pins gone rusty, and some of them missing. And then the dreams had started. That was how Valentina had got in; and that was a puzzle, because the charm should only keep evil spirits away. Perhaps not such a puzzle.

She would have to make a new charm, and soon. Where to get a bullock's heart, fresh, no more than a day old? Where to get a packet of new pins, clean and sharp? But each day without it the house was open to intruders. A wide open door, especially when she slept. She roused herself from her doze and caught a flash of yellow hair, reflected in the windowpane. Dull yellow hair with black, black roots; gone when she blinked.

'Good day to you, Ma,' she whispered, just to be civil. Just to stay on the safe side. She stood carefully, straightening her back with caution. The light outside was still grey, but bright enough to make her squint. There was much to do before night fell. All the animals to do, and something found to eat, and a new charm of some kind for the chimney flue. She couldn't make a proper one yet, but something to tide her over – a mermaid's purse would be a start. Down to the shore then? She hardly ever went any more, didn't trust her own feet. Didn't like to be seen. But there might be one tucked away somewhere, around the house, and she resolved to look because it was unsettling, having Valentina back. Unsettling to think that her mother might notice her looking for a mermaid's purse, and guess at her purpose. The retribution would be awful.

She turned from the window but as she did her eye was caught again. Not Valentina, not a vision. A *person*. A man. Her heart got caught in her throat. He was young, tall and lean. For a second, she hardly dared to believe it, but it could have been . . . But no. Not tall enough, too broad at the shoulder. The hair too light, too short. But of course not, of course not. She shook her head. A rambler, nothing more. Not many came past the cottage, because the track was not a footpath; he shouldn't have been there. It was private land, her land, and beyond the cottage he would find no way through. She watched him approaching. Looking at The Watch intently, slowing his pace. Curious. He would get to the bottom and then have to turn around and go back again. Would he be one of those that gazed in at her windows? Twenty years ago nobody ever walked past, but these days there were more. She didn't like the intrusion. It made her feel as though a tide of people was gathering out of sight; growing, swelling, coming to nudge up against her. But this one wasn't walking past. This one was coming to the door. He had nothing in his hands; he wore no badge, no uniform. She couldn't tell what he might want. The hairs stood up all along her arms. This was him, then. This was the one she'd seen coming. Valentina capered in the slant of light on the side of the teapot, but whether it was in warning or simple glee, she couldn't tell.

Zach listened hard at the door, trying to hear some sound of movement behind the hum of the sea and the fumbling breeze. The Watch was a long, low cottage, the upper storey built well into the eaves of the thatch. The straw was dark and uneven, sagging into deep pockets in some places; great tufts of grass and forget-me-nots grew along the ridge and around the chimney stacks. Zach knew precious little about thatch, but it was obviously badly in need of replacing. The stone walls were whitewashed, and it sat facing west at the top of a long slope that ran down into the valley, where Zach could see scattered farm buildings half a mile or so below. The track to the cottage was dry and stony but looked as though heavy rain would turn it to mud. It approached from the north, towards one end of the house, so Zach had seen that the place was only one room deep. Behind it was a yard enclosed by a high wall, and behind that a small stand of beech and oak trees left over from an earlier century. The breeze whispered through those trees, twisting the dry leaves, speaking of the coming autumn.

Zach knocked again, louder this time. If there was nobody at home, he was back to square one; and pointlessly paying for a room for the night. He turned and looked at the view, which was wide and lovely. The cliff, a short way beyond the cottage, was much higher here, dropping perhaps thirty or forty feet. Below, down the slope, he could see the lane which he had driven along earlier that day – following the crease of the valley down to where the land dipped into the sea. The footpath turned inland from the eastern side of the little car park, crossing pasture and then the track to The Watch further up towards the village. He couldn't understand why it did this, instead of simply following the cliff edge, and was leaning backwards, trying to peer around the end wall of the cottage, when the door cracked open.

The face that peered around the door was pale, lined and bright with anxiety. An elderly woman with a thick cascade of white hair, hanging loosely around her face. Cheeks limp and deeply scored, and a hump across her shoulders that forced her to turn her head slightly to look up at Zach. She took a step backwards when their eyes met, as if she'd changed her mind and would slam the door again, but froze. Hazel and green eyes watched him with such suspicion, such doubt.

'Hello . . . I'm sorry to bother you.' He paused in case she would greet him, but her mouth stayed shut. It was a wide mouth, thin lipped, but the ghost of bow shape, of a delicately pronounced upper lip, was still visible. 'Um, my name's Zach Gilchrist and I was told . . . that is, I was hoping I might be able to have a quick chat with you about something? If it's not too much trouble, if you're not busy?' There was a long pause and Zach's polite smile began to feel too heavy for his face. He struggled to keep it from drooping. The breeze went in through the door and lifted up tresses of the woman's white hair, moving it gently like seaweed underwater.

'Busy?' she said eventually, and quietly.

'Yes, if you're busy now I could . . . come back another time? Maybe?'

'Come back?' she echoed, and then Zach's smile did fade to nothing, because he feared that old age had muddled her, and she didn't understand what he was saying. He took a steadying breath and prepared to take his leave, disappointment gripping him. Then she spoke again. 'What do you want to talk about?' She spoke with a Dorset accent so strong the words seemed to buzz in his ears, and had a peculiar cadence that was somewhat hard to follow. Zach remembered what Pete Murray had said, about pitching himself right. He had no idea what might be the right way, and on instinct he chose the family connection.

'My grandmother knew Charles Aubrey – she met him while she was on her summer holidays here, back before the war. The artist, Charles Aubrey? In fact . . . I've always wondered if there's a chance he was my real grandfather. I think they might have had an affair. I was wondering if you might remember him? Or her? If you could tell me anything about him?' he said. The woman stood as still as stone, but then gradually her mouth fell open a little and Zach heard her breathe in; a long, uneven breath like a gasp in slow motion.

'Do I remember him?' she whispered, and Zach was about to answer when he saw that she wouldn't hear him if he did. Her eyes had slipped out of focus. 'Do I remember him? We were to be wed, you know,' she said, blinking and looking up with a sketchy smile.

'Really? You were?' Zach said, trying to square this with what he knew of Aubrey's life.

'Oh yes. He adored me – and I adored him. Such a love we had! Like Romeo and Juliet it was. But real. Oh, it was real,' she said, intently. Zach smiled at the light in her eyes.

'Well, that's wonderful. I'm so glad to have met some-body who remembers him fondly . . . Would you be willing to tell me a bit more about it? About him?'

'You looked a little bit like him, as you came down the track. Now I think not. I think not. I can't see how you could be his grandson. No, I can't see it. He had no other love but me . . .'

'Perhaps, but surely he . . . he had other . . . women,' Zach said haltingly, and then regretted it at once when he saw how her face fell. 'Could I come in, maybe? You can tell me more about him,' he said, hopefully. The woman seemed to consider this, and a little colour came into her cheeks.

'Other women,' she muttered, peevishly. 'Come in, then. I'll make tea. But you're not his grandson. No, you're not.' She stepped back to let him in, and Zach thought she didn't sound wholly convinced by her own words. He scrolled hastily through what he knew, trying to recall a list of Aubrey's lovers, and to guess which one this elderly lady might be.

Inside the door was a dim central hallway from which wooden stairs led up, the boards worn and cracked. Doors opened to the back and to either side, and the old woman led him through the right-hand one, to the kitchen, which was at the far southern end of the cottage and had windows looking south and west, out over the sea. The floor was laid with stone slabs, massive and worn; the walls had once been whitewashed but were now patched and flaking, and the ceiling crowded down, heavy with sinuous beams. There were no fitted units, just an array of wooden cupboards and sideboards and dressers, arranged in the best possible fit. The cooker was electric and looked fifty years old, but everything was clean and well ordered. Zach hovered awkwardly behind the woman as she filled the kettle, which was a modern, bright white plastic one, highly incongruous. Her movements were steady and even, in spite of her age and the bulge at the top of her spine. She wouldn't have been tall, even if her back had been straight, and there was little spare flesh on her bones. She wore a long cotton skirt with a blue and green paisley print, over what looked like men's leather work boots, and a long, colourless cardigan and grubby red fingerless mittens. Her white hair swayed behind her when she turned, and suddenly Zach could almost see her in her youth – see the curves her body would have had, the grace of movement. He wondered what colour that mass of hair had been.

'I've just realised, I didn't catch your name?' he said. She twitched as if she'd forgotten he was there.

'Hatcher. Miss Hatcher,' she said, with a curious bob of her head, like the ghost of a courtesy.

'I'm Zach,' he said, and she smiled quickly.

'I know that,' she replied.

'Right, of course.' She lowered her eyes and turned back to the sideboard to fetch clean mugs, and again he got the impression of something almost girlish and coy about her. As if her spirit had remained in its youth, even as the body around it withered. *Hatcher, Hatcher.* The name was familiar to him, but he couldn't place it.

When the tea was poured they crossed to the room at the north end of the house, where a sagging, threadbare sofa and chairs were arranged around a hearth black with centuries of smuts. There was a prickling, tangy smell, of ash, salt, wood, dust.

'Sit, sit,' said Miss Hatcher, her accent making the words sound like *ʒet, ʒet*.

'Thank you.' Zach chose a chair near the window. On the sill was a ginger cat, small and thin and fast asleep, a drizzle of drool hanging from its lip. Now he was inside the house, Miss Hatcher seemed eager to please, eager to speak. She sat with her knees tight together and her hands resting upon them, on the edge of her chair, like a child.

'Ask away, then, Mr Gilchrist. What did your grand-mother say about my Charles? When was it she thought she knew him?'

'Well, it would have been in 1939. She came to Black-nowle with my grandfather, on holiday, and they met Aubrey while they were out walking one day. He was sitting out somewhere, painting or drawing. Anyway, my grand-mother was very taken with him . . .'

'1939? 1939 . . . so I'd have been sixteen. Sixteen! Can you believe it?' she said with a smile, raising her eyes to the cracked ceiling. Zach did some quick mental arithmetic. So now she was eighty-seven years old. With her chin raised up he could see fine, downy hairs along her jaw.

'The weather was a bit of a let-down that year, ap-parently. My grandma always said they'd been hoping to swim in the sea, but it never felt quite warm enough . . .'

'It was grey, most days. We'd had the most shocking spell of late cold – there was snow on the ground into March, and a wind blowing through like someone left the door open on the downs . . . It was bitter, it was. Our sow died – she'd been sickly, but that cold snap finished her off. We tried to cure all the meat but our hands got so cold, rubbing that dead flesh, that we both had chilblains by the end of the day and our fingers went as red as poppies. Oh, you've never felt a stinging like it! No amount of parsnip peelings or goose grease could cure them. After that we all wanted a hot summer, even a drought. A chance to dry out and be warm, but we didn't get it. No. Sunny days were a rare blessing that year. Even if it was dry, late on, it stayed overcast. The sun seemed a sad and sorry thing.'

'Both of you? Who did you live with then?'

'Aged sixteen? My mother of course! What do you take me for?'

'Sorry – I didn't mean . . . Do carry on. What was Aubrey like?' Zach asked, amazed to hear Miss Hatcher speak in such detail, as though that summer had been two or three years ago, rather than seventy-one.

'What was he like? I can't begin to explain it. He was like the first warm day of spring. To me he was better than anything. He meant more than anything.' A delighted smile fell from her face, and the shadow of loss crept in to replace it. 'That was the third summer they came. My Charles and his little girls. I'd first met them two years before, when I was hardly more than a child myself. He drew me all the time, you know. He loved drawing me . . .'

'Yes, my grandmother had a painting Aubrey had done of her, too . . .'

'A painting? He *painted* her? A proper painting?' Miss Hatcher interrupted him with a troubled frown.

'Yes . . . it's in a gallery in London now. It's quite a famous one. It's called *The Walker* – you can see my grandma at a distance, walking along the top of the cliff on a sunny day.' Zach fell silent and watched the old woman's face. There was a desperate look in her eyes, and they were bright, and her lips moved slightly, shaped by silent words.

'He painted her?' she whispered, and sounded so desolate that Zach made no reply. There was a bloated pause. 'But . . . from a distance, you say?'

'Yes – the figure is only a couple of inches high, in the picture.'

'And no sketches of her? No sketches done from up close?'

'No. Not that I've ever seen.' Miss Hatcher seemed to relax, and breathe more easily.

'Well, then – she could have been just anyone he'd happened to meet. He was always very interested in people, very easy to talk to. Perhaps I do remember your grandparents, now . . . perhaps I do. Did your grandfather have black hair? Very black – black as ink?'

'Yes! Yes he did!' Zach smiled, delighted.

They were all together – Charles and Celeste and the two little girls, and this new couple, a pair of strangers she'd never seen before. Holidaymakers – there were always some. She came along the lane because it had rained in the night and the fields were muddy — the red, clay mud of the peninsula where The Watch stood; the white, gluey mud of the chalk hills to the west. The strange woman wore loose slacks of a lovely fawn twill, and a fine white blouse tucked into them; and even though her hand was looped through the man's arm, it was obvious how rapt she was, leaning towards Charles as if she couldn't help herself. Pulled like the tide. Her own skirt was torn at the hem, and her sleeves picked by brambles. Sea salt from the breeze had made her hair a wild mess like a crop of bladderwrack, clinging to her skull, and as she approached she tucked it behind her ears, ashamed. She didn't want to speak to them, to the strangers. She hung back, skirted around them, wished she could hear what they were saying. The stranger spoke and Charles laughed, and she felt hot and angry about it. He looked her way, then — the stranger. The light caught on his hair, or rather, it didn't. It vanished into it — she'd never seen hair so black before. Blacker than pitch, blacker than a crow's wing, with no hint of green or blue like the sullen fire of those feathers. He caught her eye but then looked away again, back to Aubrey and Celeste. Dismissing her, like she was nothing. Again, that heat, that anger. But then Delphine saw her, came over to her waving with the fingers of one hand, wanting to go off together. So she never found out how long they stayed together, talking; her Charles and this strange woman who offered herself to him with every tiny move she made.

'So you suppose she broke her wedding vows, do you?' Miss Hatcher said. Zach shrugged.

'Well, they were engaged but not actually married at the time of the visit. It would have been wrong of her even so, of course, to betray my grandfather. But these things happen, don't they? Life is never black and white.'

'They happen, they happen,' Miss Hatcher repeated, but Zach couldn't tell if she was agreeing with him or not. Her expression was sad, and Zach tried to move the conversation on.

'Perhaps she didn't. Perhaps she just remembered him fondly, and that was as far as it went. I know I don't really look like him . . . plus he's meant to have had this animal magnetism. I sure as hell don't have it.' He smiled. Miss Hatcher flicked her eyes over him appraisingly.

'No, you don't,' she said. Zach felt slightly crushed.

'I do . . . paint, though. So perhaps my artistic side . . .'

'Are you a good painter?' Outside, the sun came out and lit her face suddenly, falling into the hollows under her eyes, in her cheeks. Her face was a delicate heart shape, her eyes wide-set, the chin a soft point, now all but lost in pouched skin. Zach felt the sudden shock of recognition, a physical jolt.

'I know your face,' he blurted out, inadvertently. The old woman looked at him, and the trace of a smile warmed her expression.

'Perhaps you should do,' she said.

'Dimity Hatcher? *Mitzy?*' he said, astonished. 'I can't believe it! When you said he drew you all the time, I didn't realise . . .' He shook his head, stunned. That she was alive. That he had found her, and that it seemed nobody else ever had. Now she was smiling, delighted; she tipped her chin up, made some effort to straighten her shoulders. But the sun dipped back behind clouds, and it was gone. That ghost of remembered beauty. She was a bent old woman again, colourless, self-consciously smoothing the length of her hair against her chest like a girl.

'Glad to know I'm not so very changed, after all of it,' she said.

'Yes,' Zach said, as convincingly as he could. There was a pause; his mind was racing. 'I've got a picture of you hanging in my gallery at home! I look at it every day, and now here we are, face to face. It's . . . amazing!' He couldn't keep from smiling.

'What picture is it?'

'It's called *Mitzy Picking*. It's of you from behind, but you're almost looking over your shoulder. Not quite, but almost, and you're putting something into a basket . . .'

'Oh, yes, I remember that one.' She clasped her hands together, pleased. 'Yes, of course. I never really liked it. I mean, I couldn't see the point of it, not seeing my face and all.'

She hadn't been picking at all, she'd been sorting. Delphine had been out to collect herbs and collared Dimity as she passed, asking her to check her spoils before she took them into the kitchen. She'd been on her way into the village, on an errand for Valentina. How that woman would storm and swear if she took too long, so she ran her fingers through the plants quickly, removing the dandelion leaves that Delphine had thought were lovage, picking the chickweed out of the chamomile. All morning a tenacious song had been running through her head. It came again then, a low mumble on her lips, a sign of impatience. *As I were a walking for my recreation, all down by the river I chanced for to stray; I heard a fair maid making loud lamentation, singing Jimmy will be slain in the wars I be feared . . .* She stopped suddenly, heard the faintest echo of the tune carrying on behind her. In a deep voice, a man's voice – *his* voice. Prickles like the lick of a cat's tongue went roughly down her spine, and she froze. In the silence then she heard the pencil, softly scraping the paper. A dry caress. She knew not to move, knew that would annoy him. So she carried on, her mind no longer on the job, letting grass stems stay amidst the chives, and buttercup pass for cress. And all the while she could feel him behind her, feel his eyes upon her, and as if all her senses had come alive she noticed the sun shining hotly on her hair, and the touch of a breeze on the skin of her lower back where her blouse had ridden up. A small area of skin that suddenly seemed utterly, wantonly naked. *In her hand she had posies, her cheeks were like roses . . .* she sang on, and behind her he answered the tune, and she felt it fill her heart, fill it up to bursting.

'What colour was your hair?' Zach asked suddenly. Dimity blinked, and seemed to come back from far away. 'Sorry, that must sound very rude . . .'

'Charles said it was bronze,' she said, quietly. 'He said when the light shone on it, it looked like burnished metal; like a statue of Persephone come alive.' In Zach's mind he saw all the drawings – all the many, many drawings of Mitzy, and he put this colour into the wild hair described by Aubrey's long, lavish pencil lines. *Yes.* He could picture it now, as if the colour had always been there, waiting for him to see it.

Suddenly, there was a muffled sound from upstairs. The thump of something being dropped, the smaller thump of it bouncing, just once, and the shuffling creak of a footstep. Dimity turned her eyes to the ceiling and waited, as if something else was coming. Puzzled, Zach also glanced up at the sooty rafters as if he might be able to see through them.

'What was that?' he asked. For a second, Dimity looked at him as if he hadn't spoken, then her expression changed, grew startled.

'Oh, nothing. Nothing at all. Just . . . mice,' she said, rapidly. Her fingers in their red mittens fiddled with her hair, rolling the frayed ends to and fro, twisting them. She looked away, her gaze floating aimlessly along the wall.

'Mice?' said Zach, dubiously. It had sounded like something bigger than that. The old woman considered at length before replying. She rocked her feet one way then the other – to the toes, to the heels, back again.

'Yes. Nothing to worry about. Just mice.'

'Are you sure? It sounded like somebody dropped something.'

'I'm sure. Nobody up there to go dropping anything. But maybe I'll check. So then, you'll go on for now? Finished up your tea?' she said, standing stiffly and holding out her hand for it. She looked troubled, distracted. Zach was only halfway down his cup, but he handed it to her anyway. The rim was chipped hazardously, and it tasted as though the milk had turned.

'OK, sure. It was lovely to meet you, Miss Hatcher. Thanks for the tea, and for talking to me.' She was herding him to the door, bustling around him, eyes down.

'Yes, yes,' she said, vaguely. She pulled the door open and that warm, fresh breeze washed in, and all the sounds of the sea with it. Zach stepped out obediently. The front step was worn into a bowl and water had gathered there; moss in all the pocks and crevices of the stone.

'Could I come back and see you again, do you think?' he asked. She began to shake her head automatically. 'I would be so grateful . . . I could bring some of the pictures Aubrey drew of you, if you like? Not the original ones, of course, but prints of them . . . in books. You could tell me what it was like as he drew them . . . what you were doing that day. Or something,' he tried. She seemed to consider this, toying with the ends of her hair again. Then she nodded.

'Mind and bring me a heart.'

'A what? Sorry?'

'A bullock's heart no more than a day old – I need one. And some pins. New pins,' she said.

'A bull's heart? What, a real one? Why on earth . . .'

'A *bullock's*, and no more than a day old – mind you

check.' She was closing the door on him impatiently, her thoughts already elsewhere.

'Well, all right. I'll—' The door shut firmly, and Zach was left talking to its bleached wood. 'I'll be sure to check,' he finished.

He turned his back to the door and looked up at the sky, bright whites and shades of grey. Dimity Hatcher. Alive and well and living in Blacknowle – still, after all the many, many years since Aubrey did his drawings of her. Zach could hardly believe it. That she was here, and that nobody else had ever been to see her. He thought quickly, sifting through all the books on Aubrey he'd ever read. Most focused on his life in London, his upbringing in Sussex, his bohemian morals, his relationship with Celeste. A few spoke about Blacknowle, and Dimity Hatcher, but only in terms of the depiction and significance of both in his work. No, he was sure. None of the biographers had ever spoken directly to Dimity about the man. He smiled to himself, and wondered what on earth she would do with a bullock's heart and a packet of pins.

He turned towards the sea instead of back along the track to the village, and walked a hundred yards or so to the edge of the cliff. He went as close as he dared, since the grassy lip curled away out of sight, and he worried he might be standing on nothing but a thin slice of turf, suspended precariously above the drop below. Low waves skirled in over slabs of rock that tumbled steeply from halfway down the cliff to the water. He could see no way down, and the rocks looked dangerous – sharp and half hidden by the churning sea. Not a good spot for a swim. In the lull between waves was a whispering sound; a sigh as the water receded. He looked to the east and then understood why the footpath went inland – the trees he had seen behind The Watch marked the edge of a steep gully, a ravine, slicing into the land. It cut inland for around seventy metres, and at its apex was a tiny shingle beach, empty but for driftwood and other detritus. There could be no way down to it – the walls were sheer. Large white gulls perched on it, resting their wings; some asleep on one leg with their heads tucked away. The Watch was cut off on two sides by the sea, and sat solitary on its own small peninsula.

For a while Zach stood there and gazed far out at the flat water, and thought about Elise. What was it that made children love the seaside so? And made adults feel more alive? Perhaps it was the far, distant horizon, putting troubles into perspective, or the way the light seemed to shine up from the ground as well as down from the sky. They had taken Elise to the beach many times, he and Ali – on holidays in Italy and Spain. Back when they were a pair; when their names fitted snugly together, tripping off the tongue. *Zach and Ali*. But Elise seemed to like the British coast more – seemed to long for rock pools rather than hot sun, seaweed rather than fine white sand. One time she watched, patient and rapt, as Zach poured water from a bucket over some limpets, at regular intervals, for five minutes or more, until they were tricked into thinking that the tide was coming in and began to slide into life. She gasped when they did, hadn't believed they were alive until then; too still, holding on too tightly – part of the rock most likely. They couldn't pull one free, however – as soon as they were touched the limpets clamped themselves tight to the rock again. Elise tried indignantly, digging with her small pink fingernails until Zach told her to stop, that she would scare them. Then she ran her fingers over them gently instead, and said sorry; apologising to a scattering of limpets for frightening them.

Turning, Zach walked back past the cottage and was level with the front door when movement down in the valley to his left caught his eye. He paused and looked down the slope to the farm at the bottom. Four or five barns and sheds of various sizes were arranged around two concrete yards, a large one and a smaller second one. The farmhouse was square and painted white, and sat a short distance further up the valley towards the village, facing The Watch. Its front door was set at the exact centre of four sash windows, with an identical row of windows on the floor above. The movement that he'd seen came from a small jeep, which had come into the yard from one of the fields. The driver got out to close the gate, and Zach noticed with some surprise that it was a woman. Short and slight, an unlikely build for a farmer. She strode quickly to the yard gate and as the wind dropped he heard the flat metal clang as it slammed shut, carried up to him a fraction of a second after he saw it connect. She turned briskly and he saw a crop of dark, curly hair, cut to shoulder length, held back by a bright green scarf. As she was about to get back into the jeep something made her pause. She looked up at The Watch abruptly and Zach, who hadn't been moving, still felt himself freeze. Caught out, watching a stranger, uninvited. He almost turned away, guiltily, but the way she had also frozen stopped him. There they stood, half a mile apart, staring at one another, and Zach was sure he could sense her surprise. Surprised to see somebody up at the cottage perhaps. They stood that way for a heartbeat, two, then she got back into the jeep and slammed the door. The sound of the engine was lost to the wind, but as she pulled away towards the house he saw the pale flash of her face through the window, turning to look at him again.

Zach spent the rest of the afternoon walking along the cliff path in a westerly direction, thinking hard. He needed to go back to his notes, start to restructure the book. It could take on a different format, a different focus. It could be all about the last years of the artist's life – about his years in Blacknowle. Aubrey had died at what most considered to have been the height of his artistic prowess; the pictures he produced in Blacknowle, and the commissioned portraits he completed in his London studio during those years, formed the bulk of the best of his work. Everybody already knew about his upbringing, his education, his early career, his string of mistresses. But nobody had found Dimity Hatcher before. He thought quickly, totting up. Off the top of his head he could think of twenty-five drawings of the adolescent girl, made during the thirties. And she appeared in three large oil canvases as well – in one as a Berber maiden, surrounded by desert; in another by some ruins in a deeply forested scene, looking fey and Puckish; and in another as herself, walking along the beach with a basket on her hip full of some dark stuff that Zach had always wondered about. Now he could ask her, he thought with a rush of excitement. In spite of her great age, Dimity's memories of that time seemed startlingly sharp. Perhaps – no, he was sure – she would remember who Dennis had been. That amorphous young man, whose expression had eluded the artist so.

When Zach arrived back at the Spout Lantern, Pete Murray showed him to his room, ducking his head to avoid the low beams along the upstairs corridor. The room was at the far end of the building, away from the bar. It had a small double bed draped in a patchwork quilt, and a nautical theme – model boats on a shelf with a dried-up starfish; the walls pale blue; seahorses printed on the curtains. An hour or so later Zach ate a plate of fish pie at a table facing the bar, surrounded by the low buzz of a moderate crowd of locals. He got some nods and smiles, but nobody tried to talk to him, no doubt taking him for a holidaymaker, transient, just passing through and not worth the bother.

People wandered in and out with their dogs, sinking a

quick pint as part of their evening walk, and Zach amused himself watching the animals circle and sniff while their owners did the same. He felt heavy with lassitude, the after-effect of fresh air and exercise. His muscles lengthened and relaxed, his glass of beer made his head light, and he didn't feel in the least bit conspicuous, or unwelcome. Not until the door rattled open again and a woman strode in, small and wiry, her figure in tight-fitting jeans lost beneath the baggy swathes of a huge tartan shirt. Her legs disappeared into slouchy leather boots, the toes white with dust. Dark curls of hair held back by a peacock-green scarf, its edges frayed and grubby. He recognised her from the jeep at the farm in an instant, and for some reason her sudden appearance gave him a jolt, as if once again he'd been caught out doing something he shouldn't.

She moved with the same speed and purpose as he had witnessed in the yard, and only slowed when she reached the bar and was greeted by several people. She smiled and shook hands with a few people, which Zach found strange and refreshing – to see a woman shake hands rather than offer kisses, like the women he knew in the art world would have done.

'The usual?' Pete greeted her, and though the landlord smiled Zach noticed he looked slightly uncomfortable, al-most nervous. The woman smiled at him and Zach caught her expression in the mirror behind the bar – the raised eyebrows, the slightly mocking tilt of her lips.

'As usual,' she said. Zach found himself straining his ears to pick up her voice. Pete put a shot of whisky in front of her, which she knocked back as he pulled her a pint of dark ale. Zach saw her watching the landlord carefully; saw him flick his eyes up at her. As he put the pint down in front of her he tilted his head to one side and seemed about to speak, but the woman held up her hand. 'Don't bother, Pete.

Seriously. I've had a crap day and I've just come in for this one, OK?'

'OK, OK. Don't bite my head off! I didn't say a word.'

'You didn't have to,' she muttered, picking up her pint and lowering her head to sip without spilling. As she did, she raised her eyes and caught Zach's gaze in the mirror. He flinched and looked away. When he looked up again she was still watching him, and again he looked away. He looked down at his hands; he looked at a circular drip of beer on the table; he looked at his phone, which had no signal, not even one bar. Then he looked up because she was standing right in front of his table.

'You were up at The Watch today,' she said, without preamble.

'You recognise me?' he said, trying not to sound pleased.

'Not difficult. You stand out like a sore thumb in those clothes.' Her voice was textured, slightly hoarse; the words spoken in the same quick, abrupt manner in which she moved. Zach looked down at his dark jeans, his leather shoes, and wondered what it was that made them so conspicuous. 'Got lost, had you? Looking for the coast path?'

'No, I . . .' He hesitated, wondering if he should own up to what he'd been doing. 'I was visiting somebody.'

'What do you want with her?' the woman demanded.

'Is . . . that any of your business?' Zach said, carefully. The woman tipped her chin up a little, as if squaring up to him. Zach almost smiled at her fearless belligerence, and then felt a tug of recognition. He paused, trying to place the feeling. 'I'm Zach Gilchrist,' he said, holding out his hand. 'Have we met somewhere before?' She eyed his hand suspiciously, and paused before shaking it with a single jerk.

'Hannah Brock. And no, we haven't met before. I'm Miss Hatcher's nearest neighbour and I look out for her. Make sure she's not . . . bothered by anybody.'

'Why should people bother her?' Zach asked, wondering how much Hannah knew of Dimity Hatcher's claim to fame.

'Why indeed?' she asked, raising one eyebrow. She had dark eyes to match her hair, a narrow face tanned from the summer sun. It was hard to tell her age because an outdoor life had put fine lines at the corners of her eyes and mouth, and yet she exuded a vitality that was almost unnerving. The hand that had clasped his briefly had been hard, dry, and tiny. Zach hazarded a guess at late thirties.

'I don't think I bothered her. She seemed quite happy. She made me tea,' he said, smiling mischievously.

'Tea?' Hannah echoed, sceptically.

'Tea,' Zach repeated. She studied him for a while, and he sensed a little of her hostility give way to curiosity.

'Well,' she said, eventually. 'You are honoured.'

'I am?'

'It took me near enough six months to get a cup of tea out of her, and that was even after I . . . Well, never mind. So, what did you want to see her about?'

'You're her next-door neighbour. Which makes this . . . what? Extreme curtain-twitching?' said Zach. She gazed at him steadily for a moment, and then had the good grace to smile briefly.

'Miss Hatcher is a . . . special case. I wonder if you know how special?'

'I wonder if you do?' Zach retorted.

'Well, this is getting us nowhere.' Hannah sighed. 'I just wanted to let you know that I'm looking out for her. And I won't put up with her being . . . harassed. OK by you?' She turned on her heel and started to cross towards a group of people at the far end of the bar.

'She invited me back again. She even set me an errand,' Zach called after her. Hannah glanced back over her shoulder at him and now her frown was puzzled, not hostile. With an impatient roll of her eyes, she turned her back, and Zach chuckled.

When the tall young man had gone Dimity stood for a long time at the foot of the stairs, listening. Now there was silence from above, apart from all the normal sounds of The Watch. The scuffles of mice in the thatch; the wind in the chimney breast; water dripping onto metal somewhere, striking with a musical note. But there had been a sound; they had both heard it. The first one in a long time, and her heart had leapt at it. Hesitant, bewildered, she began to climb the stairs. In the hallway mirror behind her, Valentina waved a finger, wagged her chin mockingly. Dimity ignored her, but when she got to the top step her heart was thumping painfully. The small landing was gloomy and smelled damp, where the rain was finally coming in through the thatch and soaking the ceiling plaster. A bloom of concentric, tea-coloured rings marked the spot. To the left was her bedroom, the door open, a window over the sea letting in a bluish light. To the right a closed door. She stood still again, and listened. She felt herself watched from above; reflected in the clustered eyes of incurious spiders. Slowly, she crossed to the closed door, pressed a cautious hand to the wood. A nervous song hummed in her throat, unbidden. *In her hand she had posies, her cheeks were like roses . . .*

'Are you there?' she said, but it came out a croak, and the words sounded all wrong to her own ears. The spiders watched and there was no reply, no sound at all. She waited a little longer, uncertain. The silence behind the door was like a cold, dark well, and the sadness rising from it threat-ened to consume her. She fought it, pushed it back. Let herself believe again. The ginger cat appeared behind her from her bedroom and wound itself around her shins, and in its loud purr she heard Valentina chuckling.

Valentina Hatcher: a woman who said her ancestors were Romany gypsies, and had travelled the length and breadth of Europe curing ills and casting fortunes. Odd then that she should choose to make her hair yellow, but then, it wasn't a glossy gypsy brunette when left natural. It was a sad-looking mousey brown. That smell was one of the first things Dimity remembered – the piercing reek of household bleach, filling the whole house. She did it in a tin tub of water on the kitchen table, with rags all around to mop up spills. Dimity hovering in the doorway to watch, fascinated, but trying to keep out of sight because if her mother caught her, opened one screwed-up eye and saw her, she would be made to help.

'Hand me that towel – no, the other one! Get it off my neck!' Barking like a terrier. Dimity standing on a chair, wobbling, mopping the thick, vicious stuff from her mother's skin. She hated it, and cried if she got any on her fingers, even before it started to burn.

When it was done it did look magnificent, for a while. Like a mermaid's hair, as bright as gold coins. Valentina sat outside to dry it, with her face tipped to the sky and the breeze running by. Skirt rucked up across her sturdy knees so the sun could warm her legs while she smoked a cigarette.

'Tha'll pull ships onto the rocks sitting there like that, Val Hatcher,' said Marty Coulson one time, walking down the track with his bandy legs and his tweed cap right down to his ears. Dimity didn't like the way he grinned. Marty Coulson always grinned when he came to The Watch. Yet when Dimity saw him in the village he looked the other way as if he couldn't see her. No grinning then.

'You're early,' said Val, sounding annoyed. Marty stopped by the front door and gave a lopsided shrug. Stubbing out her cigarette Val got to her feet, brushed the grass from her backside. 'Mitzy – go on into the village. Buy a cake for tea from Mrs Boyle.' She fixed Marty Coulson with a flat, unfriendly eye until he reached into his pocket, found a shilling and gave it to Dimity. She was always happy to run an errand into Blacknowle. To get away from The Watch, even for a while, and see people other than her mother.

Almost as soon as she was big enough to walk she had been sent out alone; certainly by the age of five or six. On simple missions to buy tea or deliver something mysterious, wrapped up in paper. A charm, or a spell. A new-made besom to build into a door lintel, for luck; shrivelled bits of rabbit pelt to be rubbed on warts and then buried, to remove them. People didn't like to see her at their door, didn't want it known that they had bought something from Valentina. They took what she brought them and ushered her quickly away, casting their eyes up and down the street. But they couldn't help themselves. If they needed luck, or a baby, or to get rid of a baby; if they needed a miracle, or a catastrophe, then they tried Valentina as well as prayer. *Belt and braces*, Valentina sneered, when they'd been and gone from the cottage or, as was more usual, had dropped a written request through the door and fled. *I hope the sweat makes their backsides itch when they simper at the vicar come Sunday*. Dimity learnt all the routes around the lanes, paths and fields by trial and error. She learnt where everybody lived, and all of their names; who might give her a halfpenny for her trouble, and who would slam the door on her.

While she was still small, Valentina went with her on more specialised missions, foraging, picking and finding. Which stream for watercress, good for strength and digestive tonics; never to pick it from a stream that ran through livestock pasture, since the plants picked up their parasites, and would pass them on. How to tell wild parsnip from water hemlock, the latter to be dug up with gloves on, the roots grated carefully and rolled into sticky balls with suet and treacle, to make rat bait that sold all year round. Bucket loads when someone had a plague of them. Like Mr Brock, at Southern Farm one time. He bought two buckets full – almost their whole supply. Dimity carried one and Valentina the other, sliding down the hill from The Watch with the handles cutting into their skin and the pails bumping their shins. *Got a problem, have you?* Valentina asked the man when they got to the yard. He beckoned them over, a queasy look on his face. Lifted up one end of a tin trough to show them a swathe of bobbing brown bodies that squirmed from the light. *Had a lamb gnawed to the bone before I found it t'other night.* Dimity's skin had crawled like it was covered in ants. The farm terrier was in a frenzy, chasing and snapping at them. Christopher Brock, the farmer's son, killed one with a cudgel as they scattered the pellets around the yard. Dimity heard the crack of its bones.

They kept chickens in the backyard, and a pig, but sometimes Valentina wanted gulls' eggs, or ducks'. There was kindling wood to find, furze roots to be dug up and dried. These made the best fuel for the stove, burning with a clean, hot flame. They hunted for mushrooms and crab apples; or a rabbit, taken from someone else's snare. Dimity hated stealing them. Her fingers shook and she often cut herself on the sharp wire. The wires were usually covered in blood already, and she wondered if it would get into her veins, if it would make her part rabbit. Valentina cuffed her around the ear for being careless, stuffed the rabbit into a canvas bag and stomped onwards. Dimity hoped that it was the time together that her mother relished, on these outings; the pleasure of teaching and passing on knowledge. But as soon as Dimity knew all that her mother could teach her, she was sent on these missions alone. It seemed that she had been trained up simply to take over.

From a young age, she knew how to tell when her mother

wanted something brought straight back, or when she just wanted Dimity out of the way. When it was the latter she roved far and wide, wandering around caught up in thoughts and stories. To the west, along the coast from The Watch, was a long, deep beach, mostly stones but with sand revealed at low tide. She spent hours on that beach, staring into rock pools. Ostensibly to catch a few shrimps for soup, to pick mussels, or Irish moss – Valentina used its purplish fronds to make jellies and set-milk puddings. Everywhere Dimity went, she had a cloth bag or a basket with her; somewhere she could stow the things she found.

One day the sharp edge of a rock pulled a hole through the rope sole of her shoe. She set the shoe to sail on the surface of a pool, watching it bob and wobble. Seeing how many shells she could load onto it until it started to sink. Then she heard voices above her and she looked up as the first pebble hit the rock pool, sending up a splash that was cold on her cheek. Children from the village, up on the cliff. Mostly boys but the Crane sisters too, with their eerie, identical faces all excited and smiling. A stick followed the pebble, catching her arm. She scrambled up and was away over the rocks to the foot of the cliff in moments, to where she knew she could not be seen from above. She heard them calling out names, laughing and chanting; saw a few more missiles strike near where she had last been seen. She moved away along the beach, still in the shelter of the cliff. *DIMity!* She heard them shout. *Dim, dim, she's oh so dim!*

Dimity knew many other paths up from the beach; she didn't need to use the main one where they might wait, if they were bored enough. She realised as she reached the finer gravel that she'd left her shoes behind. One on the rock, one in the pool with a cargo of shells. She would have to go back for them later; and she did, once Valentina had snapped at her for losing them, and given her a stinging slap that Dimity thought disproportionate. But she'd forgotten how close to the shore she'd been when she'd taken them off, and the rising tide had swept them away. She scanned the surface of the sea for long minutes, in case she would see them floating nearby. They would not be replaced, she guessed, at least not for a while, even though her mother had found the money for a new lipstick and stockings that week. And she was right, and lucky that the weather set fair and dry. But she picked up a gorse thorn in her left heel. It refused to come out and she limped for a week, until Valentina pinned her down, heated the spot with steam from the kettle and squeezed, ignoring Dimity's howls, until the thorn rode out on a jet of yellow filth.

School was a kind of slow torture. It was a forty-minute walk to the draughty buildings in the next village, and there she sat at the back and tried to pay attention when all the while she was glanced at and whispered about, and notes were flung at her with crude drawings and insults scrawled on them. Even the poorest children, even the ones whose fathers were always drunk or beat their mothers or had lost their jobs and slept all day under the hedgerows, like Danny Shaw's did; even they looked down on Dimity Hatcher. When the teacher caught them at it she told them off, and ostensibly encouraged Dimity during lessons, but Dimity always saw the look on her face, pinched and faintly disgusted; as if teaching her was above and beyond the call of duty, and almost more than she could bear.

At home time Dimity was always torn between wanting to get away quickly, and not wanting to walk with the others behind her, back along the lane to Blacknowle. Mocking her all the way, throwing names, throwing things, laughing. Sometimes she hid until they had all set off, then she walked alone at the back, careful to keep one curve in the road between them. She wasn't scared of them, exactly, more tired. Every bit as unwilling to interact with them as they were with her. *Don't touch that! Dimity's touched it! It's got her fleas now!* Every insult, every name they hurled was like a dart that would strike, and stay stuck in her skin, hard to brush off. She would try not to feel as she walked behind them, careful never to let them see her cry. They were like a pack of hounds in that way, driven wild by any sign of weakness. She heard their chatter, drifting back to her on the breeze; heard their games and their jokes and wondered what it might be like to be a part of it all, just for one day; just for a short while. Just to see how different it would feel.

Sometimes Wilf walked with her. Wilf Coulson, a skinny runt of a lad, born late to the grinning Marty Coulson and his beleaguered wife Lana who, at forty-four years of age and the mother of eight, had thought her travails were over when Wilf was conceived. He had a permanently runny nose, and a crusted left nostril. Dimity offered him rosemary oil on a handkerchief to clear it but he always shook his head, said his mother told him not to take things from her.

'Why not? Your dad comes to see us, sometimes. So your ma can't mind us so much,' she said one time. Wilf shrugged his skinny shoulders.

'She don't like it though. Ma says we're not to talk about you, even.'

'That's stupid. And it's perfectly safe. I made it myself, from our bushes in the backyard.'

'Don't go calling my ma stupid. It's got something to do with you not having a dad, I think,' said Wilf. It was November, the fields all sludgy and ploughed. They slipped and skidded along a track that cut between great loops in the lane, the pale grey mud caking their shoes, making them walk wide-legged, inelegantly. The sky was the same colour as the mud, that day.

'I have got a dad only he's lost at sea,' said Dimity. This

was what Valentina had told her, when she'd asked enough times to be wary of the woman lashing out. She'd been sitting on the front step, gazing out at the horizon. Smoking, squinting. *Will you give it a bloody rest? He's gone, that's all you need to know! Lost at sea, for all I care.*

'Was he a sailor then?' said Wilf.

'I don't know. I suppose so. Or a fisherman maybe. So he's only lost; he'll come back one day and then he'll pick up Maggie and Mary Crane by their collars and shake them like a pair of rats!' For the rest of the day she sang 'Bobby Shaftoe' in her head, humming it softly. *Bobby Shaftoe's gone to sea . . .* It was some years before she realised that lost at sea meant dead; meant not coming back.

One stormy day, while the wind tore the water into high, angry waves, she stood and watched them hammer ashore, picturing all the drowned sailors and fishermen, from the beginning of time, swirling down into the depths like autumn leaves in an eddying breeze. Their bones ground up, turned into sand. The coast where she lived was a treacherous one, and wrecks abounded. The year before, she'd gone on the bus with Wilf and his brothers to see the carcass of the *Madeleine Tristan*, a three-masted schooner that had blown into Chesil cove. It sat lopsidedly on the beach, surrounded by tourists and locals alike. Dimity and Wilf, along with all the other children, climbed the loose rigging to peer onto the deck and play at pirates. It was the best playground they'd ever had, and they went back again and again until rats took it over, infesting it with their bustling bodies and whip-like tails. Just along the beach from the *Madeleine Tristan* sat the massive, flaking iron boilers of another ship, the *Preveza*. Wrecks upon wrecks; layers of lost ships, lost lives.

Realising that her father would never knock at the door of The Watch, take her side or shake the Crane twins like rats, made Dimity sad for a long time. And when Ma Coulson found out that her boys had taken Dimity Hatcher along with them to the wreck of the *Madeleine Tristan*, she stood by with her arms folded while Marty took his belt to each one of their backsides. From her hiding place in the black-currant bushes, Dimity heard the crack of leather on skin and heard the lads whimper and yelp. She chewed on her lip until it bled, but didn't leave until the last beating had been given.

When Dimity was twelve, Valentina said she wasn't going to go to school any more; that it was a waste of time and she was needed at home. Dimity was surprised to find that she missed it. She even missed the other children, who she mostly hated. Missed seeing their new pencils and clothes, missed hearing their stories. Missed walking back with Wilf. She didn't feel she was missing any learning though. What use was maths and knowing where Africa was? What use was being shown how to bake a pie by a horse-faced woman whose bosoms rested on the waistband of her skirt, when she'd been baking them since she was old enough to stand on a stool and reach the worktop? The things Valentina taught her were more important. All the other children were staying on till they were fourteen at the least. That was the law, but nobody said anything when Dimity left. Dimity thought the headmaster might come knocking at The Watch and demand she go back; but he didn't. She looked out for him for a few days, but not very many.

It was Dimity who first found the way down from the bluff by The Watch to the narrow beach below. In fact, she cleared the path. One day, with her heart thumping, making her knees shaky; one day when she'd been sent out of the house and told to keep herself busy. That meant for hours. She inched carefully over the edge, fingers knotted into the wiry grass, feeling with her toes for a rock she thought would take her weight and not slip or tilt. If it came loose and she lost her footing, nothing would stop her until she hit the jumbled shore below. The soles of her shoes slid a little on a layer of grit, but then they gripped. The rock didn't move. From there she could see a long, narrow zigzagging way, going first to her right, then left to the bottom. Some of the gaps between safe-looking stones were huge, and she had to stretch her leg right out, or jump, which was terrifying. To voluntarily leave off all handholds, abandon all safety. But she did it, she found a way down, and then spent hours building better steps with rocks small enough for her to move; swivelling them until they stopped rocking, until she could trust them. The sun was bright and the breeze gentle, a gorgeous May day. Halfway up the cliff was a kittiwake nest, the parents out at sea, hunting, and in the nest one fat fluffy chick. It eyed her with dumb acceptance, bobbing its ungainly head. She knew not to touch it, even though she wanted to. But she wriggled down close to the rocks a short way away and lay still, so still, watching the parent birds come and go with their ink-dipped wings and their throats full of fishy mush for their baby. The other way round than it was for her, she noticed. It was usually her who brought food to Valentina.

She stayed by the nest for a long time, until the mother bird came to roost and the sun was setting. Drowsing in swathes of golden light, tucked out of the breeze. Her skin had that sticky, prickling feeling of being covered in salt; she was heavy with fatigue, but enjoying the company of the birds as they whistled and muttered to each other. She liked the way their wet beaks and feet glistened when they came in from the water, and how they never stayed away long before coming back to check on the chick; preening it, nudging it towards a better place in the cramped nest.

She wondered how long it would be before Valentina checked on her. Surely not much longer. It had been about two o'clock, after lunch, when her mother had glanced up at the kitchen clock and told her to make herself scarce. It must have been nearly eight by now, with the sun so low and buttery. Valentina must have been wondering where her daughter was. None of their visitors ever stayed so long – a couple of hours at most. She decided to wait and see, while the kittiwake's eyelids sank lower and lower; but once the sun had gone she was chilly, and the rocks began to dig into her, and she didn't dare try to navigate the top half of her new path in the dark. So she got up as quietly as she could, which still made the mother gull squawk, and made her way up with the help of hands and feet. *I'm home!* she called, rushing in through the door. Happy even to be scolded, just to know she'd been missed. But The Watch was in darkness and Valentina fast asleep in an armchair, her robe gaping open around one boneless leg. Lipstick smeared around her mouth, an empty bottle beside her.

Later, when she had fed herself a supper of stale bread and bacon and her mother was still snoring in her chair, Dimity crept out of The Watch and went to the Coulson's house. Shrouded by the darkness, she lingered in the blackcurrant bushes for a while, breathing in their cat's piss smell, peeping in at the windows from a safe distance. When she saw Wilf she waved, and gestured for him to come out, but he didn't seem to see her. One by one, all of the lights in Wilf's house went out, and the night clung close to Dimity, cold and lonely as a winter sky.

3

In the dark and quiet of the Spout Lantern, Zach sat alone in the bar, lit only by the ghostly glow of his laptop. Pete Murray had kindly given him the password to his wireless broadband, and the bar was the best place to pick up a signal. It was one o'clock in the morning, and Ali was supposed to have called by now so that he could tell Elise a bedtime story. As the minutes ticked by he got more and more nervous, that same odd stage fright as when they'd first brought her home from the hospital, and he'd felt as though all eyes were on him, waiting for him to mess up. Without a book to help, his mind suddenly emptied of stories. He'd read all her favourites enough times, over the years; he'd thought that they would be ingrained in his memory. But perhaps he'd been reading them in a haze of boredom, the words going from eyes to mouth without passing through brain. Back when he thought things would always be that way, when it never occurred to him that everything could change, overnight, and he would be powerless to stop it. Seven minutes passed. He took a short, angry breath and held it, suddenly bone weary. Head in hands, he thought about Dimity Hatcher. About the improbability of him being the first Aubrey fan to find her; and he'd done it without even trying. It had to be the new angle his book had been waiting for.

The ring tone when it came seemed impossibly loud in the deep quiet. Zach fumbled to accept the call, and in a heartbeat Ali appeared, her hair held back in a neat ponytail, wearing tight jeans and a fitted white shirt. Looking elegant, looking lovely. There was still sunshine over there, coming in through a nearby window and covering her in gold. It looked like a different world. In a small corner of the screen Zach could see himself – a pale wraith lit by computer light, with bags under his eyes and holes at the neck of his T-shirt. He might have laughed, if he hadn't felt so wretched.

'Zach, how are you? You look . . . where the hell are you?' Ali said, accepting a cup of something that steamed from a hand that came briefly into shot. So Lowell was right there in the room with her, waiting on her. Listening. No privacy with his wife any more, not even on a phone call. *Ex-wife*.

'I'm in Dorset, in a pub. It's one in the morning, and it's been a long day. How are you? How's it going over there?'

'Oh, great. We're really starting to settle in. Elise . . . she loves it here. Why are you in Dorset? In a pub? In the dark?'

'I'm in the dark because . . . I couldn't find the light switch. Don't laugh. And everyone else has gone to bed. I'm in a pub because I needed somewhere to stay, and I'm in Dorset because I've come down here to finish my book.'

'What book?' She frowned, only half paying attention, blowing the steam from her drink and sipping it carefully. He shouldn't expect her to care any more, and yet it always hurt to be reminded that she didn't.

'Never mind. It's not important.'

'The Aubrey book, you mean? You're finally going to finish it? That's great, Zach. And about time!' She smiled. He nodded, and tried to look resolute. The task still reared up in front of him like a vertical cliff face, Dimity Hatcher or no Dimity Hatcher. 'So you're in Blacknowle? You're going to do some digging about your granddad as well?'

'I don't know . . . maybe. Probably not.' Zach shook his head. What he wanted to find, what he needed to find, was too amorphous, too fragile, to explain. 'So, where's Elise? Is she ready for her story?'

'Zach — I'm really sorry. We were out all day today and she was just shattered. She went to bed an hour ago. I only just remembered to call now and let you know. I'm sorry.'

Zach felt all his nerves dissolve into a wash of disappointment.

'And so it begins,' he said, a tightness in his chest making his voice sound strained.

'Hey — it's not like that. She was wiped out — what was I supposed to do?'

'Text me and tell me to get online an hour earlier?'

'Yes, well, I didn't think of it. I said I was sorry. I didn't get to tell her a story either you know. She was out before she hit the pillow.'

'Yes, but you get to put her to bed and kiss her goodnight and be with her all day. Don't you?' he said, not caring how childish he sounded.

'Look, I'm tired too. I don't want to argue.' Her shoulders were braced against the chair back behind her. She flicked her eyes away from the screen, a look of appeal, of exasperation. To Lowell, of course, the hidden listener. Zach was at least grateful that he wasn't watching the screen, so he couldn't see how shabby Zach looked. He sighed.

'Fine. Tomorrow night then. For the story, not the argument.'

'Tomorrow night she has a sleepover . . . Sunday night?'

'OK. Same time. Please—' He wasn't sure what he'd been about to ask. Or beg. That weariness again. He shut his eyes and rubbed the lids with his thumb and fingers until red blooms spangled across his vision.

'Sunday night. I promise,' Ali said, nodding emphatically, as if to reassure a child.

'Goodnight, Ali.' He cut the call before she could

respond, but it was a pathetic gesture and gave him no satisfaction. He switched off the computer and stumbled up to his room in darkness.

Ali had always been in control, right from the very beginning. Zach could see it now, in a way he hadn't at the time, blinded by love, and by wishful thinking. When he proposed, she took forty-eight hours to decide. He'd waited in a state of almost unbearable anticipation, knowing that she must say yes, because he loved her so much – because they loved each other – but at the same time plagued by the underlying notion that she might say no. When she finally accepted, he was too happy to reflect on this long hiatus; but now he saw that she really had been in two minds; that she really had needed all that time to weigh up the pros and cons, and decide he was worth the risk. He had vowed to reward this trust of hers, this gamble. He had vowed to make her happy, to be the perfect husband and father, but once Elise was born there were a thousand tiny comments, a thousand fleeting frowns to let him know he was falling short. *Give her to me*, he heard again and again, when he couldn't get Elise to sleep, or get her arms into her cardigan sleeves, or stop her crying. *Give her to me*, in a tone of stifled exasperation.

It was around that time that they began to talk about moving out of London; about moving to the West Country to see if Zach could make a better go of a gallery there. For a year they both resolutely pitched this plan as a step forwards, as an expansion of their lives, not as a step away, a contraction, a last chance. Only once or twice, as they were shown around disappointingly small apartments, did he catch her looking at him with something like contempt in her eyes – gone when she blinked but shocking enough to chill him. Bath didn't suit Ali. She missed her law firm in London, and their social life there, and when Zach's falling income meant she had to return to work to support the three of them, she found the work stultifying and dull. Zach suspected that Ali made up her mind a long time before she finally decided to leave him. He suspected that she made the decision calmly, rationally, and chose her moment with as much care as she had chosen to marry him in the first place.

First thing in the morning he took the car into Swanage, one of two small towns nearby that he guessed would have a butcher. It was a bright morning; the sun was warm but the light seemed paler than even a week ago as the turning season stretched it thinner, sapping its strength away. The dusty gorse bushes lining the road were more grey than green; all spines and shrivelled yellow flowers. Swanage nestled around its sandy beach and harbour, the streets still busy with late holidaymakers; but without any children, now that the schools had gone back, all the bright little shops seemed somehow bereft. Zach found a popular butcher's shop, the stock of meat in the chiller disappearing rapidly and leaving only its bloody tang to hang in the air.

'How old are your hearts?' he asked, when he got to the front of the queue.

'Oh, everything's perfectly fresh, sir,' said the young man behind the counter.

'No, I mean – I'm sure it is. But I need a . . .' He paused, feeling foolish. 'I need a bullock's heart no more than a day old.'

'Right,' the butcher said with a smile, and if he thought to ask why, he thought better of it. 'Well, all the hearts we have are from bullocks, generally, so no need to worry about that. As for less than a day old . . . well, these came in to us yesterday morning, so they'll have been slaughtered the day before, probably. So more like thirty-six hours rather than less than twenty-four. But, really – they're perfectly fresh. I don't see how you'd tell the difference. Have a sniff if you like.' He picked one up in his gloved hand and hefted it a couple of times before holding it out to Zach.

'No, thanks, I'll take your word for it,' Zach said, recoiling. The heart nestled perfectly in the palm of the butcher's hand. He was suddenly sure that Dimity Hatcher didn't want it for culinary purposes, and if it wasn't food then it was . . . what? Entrails. He swallowed.

'Do you ever get any in less than a day old?' he asked, aware that he was beginning to sound weird. But the young man smiled affably. Perhaps he was used to even odder requests.

'Well . . . let me think. Tuesday's probably your best bet. I can keep one back for you, if you like? If you come in first thing it'll still be less than a day old.'

'Tuesday? That's longer than I wanted to wait.' Zach eyed the heart still sitting in the butcher's hand. 'I'll take that one. Like you say, I'm sure it'll be fine even if it's a bit over the time limit.' The butcher wrapped it up with the hint of a smile on his lips. Zach decided that the damage was done, and to go all out with the weirdness. 'Is there a haberdashery near here? Somewhere I can buy pins?'

He found the shop, thanks to the butcher's directions, and after being briefly bewildered by the range of pins a person could buy, he picked plain, old-fashioned ones. All steel, no plastic heads, no fancy sizes. As he came out of the sewing shop he saw a small stationer on the opposite side of the street, and he paused. He was reluctant to attempt to paint or draw anything, in case it turned out every bit as flat and disappointing as his last efforts. He felt a kind of dread, in case that hadn't been a blip, or a lack of inspiration at the time. In case he really had spent whatever talent he'd once possessed. It was over a year now, since he'd tried. He went in just to see what they had, and came out with two large sketch pads, some chalks, some inks, pencils, a tin of water colours with a mixing tray in the lid and a couple of brushes, one fine and one as thick as the tip of his little finger. He hadn't meant to spend so much, but being in possession of such fundamental tools felt like seeing old friends. Like remaking a childhood acquaintance. He drove back to Blacknowle with the underlying excitement of having a present to unwrap, waiting for when he arrived.

But the first present wasn't for him, it was for Dimity Hatcher. He parked at the pub and walked down to her cottage, not trusting his car to make it along the rutted, stony track. As he reached The Watch he looked down the hill to Southern Farm, eyes searching for a dark-haired figure, moving quickly, precisely. Strange that the way she walked had already embedded itself so firmly into his memory. But there was no sign of life, other than a scattering of beige sheep in the big field behind the house, so he knocked loudly on the door of The Watch.

When Dimity Hatcher opened the door she peeped out through the crack just as she had previously, and every bit as suspiciously, as though they'd never met before. Zach's heart sank. Her hair was loose again, hanging down around her face. A loose blue dress, almost like a kaftan, and those same fingerless red mittens.

'It's Zach, Miss Hatcher. I came to see you before, remember? You asked me to come back and bring you some things . . . and maybe to talk about Charles Aubrey a bit more?'

'Of course I remember. It was yesterday,' she said, after a pause.

'Oh, great. Yes, of course.' Zach smiled.

'Did you bring it? What I asked for?' she said. Zach

fumbled in his bag for the well-wrapped heart, and held it out to her.

'I wrapped it in newspaper, to keep it cool until I got here.'

'Good, good. Can't have it gone bad,' she said, almost to herself, and then murmured under her breath as she unwrapped it, wordless sounds that might have been a tune. As soon as the heart was unwrapped she sniffed it. Not a quick, cautious sniff like Zach would have given it, but a long, deep inhale. The sniff of a connoisseur, like an expert would sniff wine. Zach fidgeted a little, uneasy in his deception. Dimity poked the heart with her index finger and watched the flesh return slowly, refilling the dimple she'd made. Then she stuffed the paper bundle back into Zach's hands with a shake of her head. No irritation, just something like disappointment. 'No more than a day old,' she said, and shut the door.

Speechless, Zach knocked on the door again, but Dimity clearly had no intention of opening it. Cursing, he went to the window and put his face up to it with his hands on either side to block out the light. He was well aware that this was unlikely to aid his case.

'Miss Hatcher? Dimity? I brought the pins you asked for, and I can get you a . . . newer heart, on Tuesday the butcher said. I'll bring it to you then, shall I? Would you like the pins now, though? Miss Hatcher?' He peered into the gloom within and was sure he saw movement. As a last-ditch attempt, he pulled the *Burlington Magazine* out of his bag, opened it to a drawing of Dimity and Delphine together and held it up to the glass. 'I was going to ask you about this picture, Dimity. If you remembered when it was drawn, and what game you were playing? And what Aubrey's daughter Delphine was like?' He thought of the drawing of Delphine, hanging in his gallery, and all the long hours he'd spent gazing at it. Again came that frisson, that sense of the unreal, that here was someone who had seen his idol made flesh. Had touched her skin, held her hand. But there was no sound from within, no further movement. Zach dropped his hands and stepped back from the window, defeated. In the glass he was a black reflection, an outline, and behind him the sea and the sky were shining.

He walked past the cottage and down to the clifftop, where he sat cross-legged and squinted out at the ocean. The breeze moving over the sea made the surface smooth and then puckered; alternately matt and then incandescent with light. There were great swells on it, seeming to rise up from beneath the surface; long trails which might have been the ghostly wakes of boats that had moved out of sight, or the telltale sign of a current, pulling away from the land, all unseen. Imagining its strength, the inescapable pull of all that water, gave Zach a shiver. Faintly, just behind his eyes, came the urge to try to paint the dazzling scene in front of him, but then a flash of something pale and moving caught his eye. Hannah Brock had appeared on the beach below him. He couldn't see how she'd got down there, since she certainly hadn't come past The Watch and there didn't seem to be any other way into the little cove below. But there she was, and as he watched she stripped off her jeans and shirt and picked her way to the water's edge in a faded red bikini. Her hair, free of the green scarf this time, flew about in the wind, and she was soon up to her ankles in the water. Zach saw her fingers extend, spread wide, and then clench into fists. It must be cold. He smiled slightly. Hannah propped her fists on her narrow hips and stared out to sea, just as he had done a moment before. Such a long, flat horizon always drew the eye; it was irresistible. Zach hunkered down as low as he could, and shuffled as far back from the edge as possible whilst still being able to see her. To be caught looking again would be the death of it, he warned himself seriously. No coming back from that. The thought caught him off guard – the death of what?

Eventually, Hannah turned to her right and moved along to the edge of the cove. Her skin was pale, but not the ghastly white Zach knew was hiding under his own clothes. Her spare frame looked pared down, with nothing superfluous. Flat breasts and thin arms, only a narrowing at the waist to stop her being boyish. But at the same time she seemed as far from frail as was possible. Every inch of her looked poised and vital. Poised for a fight, perhaps. He remembered the challenge in her eyes when she'd spoken to him in the pub. *What do you want with her?* She climbed up onto the rocks at the far edge of the beach, and walked along them where they jutted out into the sea. When she got to what looked like the edge, she in fact kept going for another fifty feet or so, wading through lapping water up to her knees. Zach watched, fascinated. There must be a shelf under the water, a rock flat enough and wide enough to walk along even if the water meant you couldn't see your footing clearly. She paused at the end for a second, tensed, and dived in with one clean movement.

She didn't come up for a long time. Zach had a horrible vision of concealed rocks, and an undertow, but of course she must know the beach, and the water, far better than he. She surfaced a long way east of where she'd gone in, virtually opposite Zach as he perched on the cliff. She raked her hair back from her face, trod water for a moment and then with a splash was gone again. For fifteen minutes or so she swam, over the water and under it, sculling idly on her back, and Zach stopped worrying about her spotting him since it seemed she wasn't going to. When she climbed out her shoulders were high and tense, and he could see she was cold in the breeze. He wanted to go down to the beach and meet her, just then. With her hair streaming water and a drip hanging from her chin, and goose bumps all over her body. She would taste of salt. She dressed quickly, pulling her clothes over her wet skin with careless ferocity, and then she vanished from view, too close to the cliff for him to see where she went.

He was down by the cliff edge a long time. Dimity could see him from the kitchen window, and she returned to check every few minutes. Technically, it was her land; technically, he was trespassing on it. Valentina wouldn't have had it – she'd have been out in a flash to chase him off with her violent eyes and that voice of hers that could carry half a mile if she wanted it to. She hesitated at the window for a while, wondering if she should have asked him in after all, wondering if she still should. But she had been so hoping to make the hearth charm today, so hoping to stop any more unwanted visitors getting in. And maybe to get rid of one who'd already come back, and let herself in. She peered out at him again. That fleeting first resemblance he'd borne to Charles had gone completely. This man's hands and head were still instead of moving, glancing, switching fast like Charles's had. He had none of the fire, none of the energy. The young man on the cliffs looked more like someone walking in their sleep, and she was half afraid he might fall forwards, and tumble over the edge.

In her head was a simple tune, circling itself again and again. A tune from childhood, beating a rhythm she couldn't shake off. *A sailor went to sea sea sea, to see what he could see see see, and all that he could see see see, was the bottom of the deep blue sea sea sea . . .* At first she thought it was the drip of the kitchen tap that had conjured up the ghost of this song; the steady plink of water onto the chipped porcelain. She stood in the kitchen and shut her eyes, and at once the smell of the place grew stronger – a stale smell of bread-crumbs and milk, the tang of burning on the hob, the sickly smell of a century of greasy food remains, hiding in cup-boards and in the cracks in the floor. A flash of Valentina's perfume, the violet water she dabbed behind her ears when a guest was due to arrive. If she opened her eyes she might see the woman, Dimity thought. Catch her standing close to her daughter, smiling. *Mitzy, my girl, you've a fortune waiting to be made.* Tucking Dimity's bronze hair behind her shoulders for her, woozy and affectionate with wine on her breath and her eyes half closed.

Dimity kept her eyes shut, pressed her teeth tight to-gether so the violet smell wouldn't get on her tongue. The tune hummed itself in her throat, more of a chant than a song. *See see see, sea sea sea*, the beat bouncing, irresistible. It was the sound of hands clapping, of skin striking skin, taut across the palms of young hands. That picture he had held up to the windowpane. She'd only caught a glimpse of it, small, from a distance, but she knew it at once. The first time she met him, the first time he sketched her – sketched her before she even knew he was there, before she'd ever set eyes on him. Made her into a figure on a page; took her inside him and then recreated her, possessed her. That was how she felt, when she saw the drawing afterwards. Pos-sessed.

The house was called Littlecombe. It stood in an over-grown garden at the far eastern edge of Blacknowle, along a driveway that jutted out towards the sea. Like an echo of The Watch, like its mirror but not quite – Littlecombe was closer to the village and still a part of it, just about. Not as cut off, but still separate. From it you could walk out across pasture to the cliffs, just as you could from The Watch, and then join the path west towards Tyneham. At the back of the house a small stream cut a miniature ravine into the earth, which descended to the sea as a constant splatter of water down the cliff face, muddy and brown after heavy rain. It was one of the best places to pick cress and catch crayfish, and since the house had stood empty for three years, Dimity felt free to do so.

Before that, an old man called Fitch had lived there all his life, as far as anybody knew. Fitch seemed to have no other name. He creaked and crawled his way to the Spout Lantern every night but Sunday, coughing between puffs on a thin, unfiltered cigarette. The smoke had carved deep, stained creases into his face, and his right hand was fixed in a claw shape – index finger and thumb set a fraction apart, always ready to grip the next fag. When he didn't turn up at the pub one Saturday night, the people of Blacknowle knew what it meant. They went along to Littlecombe with a stretcher all ready, and found him in his chair, stiff and cold, with a bedraggled dog-end still hanging from his lip. Dimity could have told them he was dead, but she wasn't allowed into the pub, and people tended not to talk to her if they could help it, so, partly out of nerves and partly out of spite, she'd not told anyone what she knew. That when she had gone to fish that morning, in the stream behind the house, the black windows had screamed out at her and there was a gaping emptiness that made her skin crawl, where once she would have felt the presence of a living thing within the walls. His death was like a strange scent in the air, or the sudden ceasing of a noise you hadn't realised you could hear.

And so it had stayed for three years, empty, passed on to an estranged cousin who showed no sign of wanting to do anything with it. A few slates slipped from the roof and smashed into the flowerbeds, beheading the rampant dandelions there. Thistles grew up to brush the ground floor window sills, and in winter a water pipe burst, painting a sparkling swathe of ice all down one wall. It was a square brick box of a house, three rooms up and three rooms down. Victorian, functional, not charmless but certainly not pretty. Then one morning Dimity was halfway across one of Southern Farm's fields to it when she stopped. A thin trail of smoke rose straight up from the chimney into the crystalline air. It was early summer, the mornings still cool. She suddenly felt like a spotlight was on her, and braced her feet apart, ready to turn and flee. She hadn't heard anything about new owners in the village gossip, which she eavesdropped by loitering near the shop or the bus stop. New owners might not like her in the stream. Might see her harvesting as thieving. They might have a dog, and let it chase her, like Wilf Coulson's mother did when she went up to the door one time, dry-mouthed at her own audacity, to see if he could come out to play.

But just as she was about to retreat she saw somebody watching her. And it wasn't a scowling man or an angry woman with a dog, it was a little girl. Younger than Dimity, maybe eleven or twelve, medium height, narrow, square at the shoulders. Feet buckled into tan leather shoes, white socks pulled up to her knees and her body wrapped in a canary-yellow cardigan. She stood at the rickety gate to the little garden in front of Littlecombe, and they considered each other for a minute. Then the girl came out and walked towards her. When she got up close Dimity saw she had brown eyes, very frank, and a lot of rebellious hair escaping from the glossy brown plaits at either side of her head. Dimity's pulse raced as she waited to discover how she would be spoken to, but after a long pause the girl smiled, and held out her hand.

'I'm Delphine Madeleine Anne Aubrey, but you can just call me Delphine. How do you do?' Her hand was smooth and cool, the nails scrubbed clean. Dimity had been out since dawn, checking the snares, mucking out the chicken coop and picking greens, and her own nails were stained and had earth underneath them. Earth and worse. She shook Delphine's hand cautiously.

'Mitzy,' she managed to say.

'Pleased to meet you, Mitzy. Do you live on the farm?' Delphine asked, pointing past her and down the hill to Southern Farm. Dimity shook her head. 'Where do you live, then? We're living here for the summer. My sister too, but you'll never see her out this early. She's a lazy stay-a-bed.'

'For the summer?' said Dimity, puzzled. She was bowled over by the girl, by her calm, friendly introduction. *Strangers*, she thought. Strangers from far, far away who didn't know to hate the Hatchers yet. She'd never heard of people who only lived somewhere for the summer – like the swallows, like the swifts. She wondered where they wintered, but thought it might be rude to ask.

'Your accent's really funny! In a good way – I mean, I like it. I'm twelve by the way. How old are you?' Delphine asked.

'Fourteen.'

'Gosh, lucky you! I can't wait to be fourteen – when I'm fourteen Mummy says I can have my ears pierced, even though Daddy says that's still too young and we should concentrate on being children and not want to grow up so quickly. But that's stupid, don't you think? You can hardly do *anything* when you're a child.'

'Yes,' Dimity agreed, cautiously, still unsure how to behave in the face of such overt friendliness. Delphine folded her arms and seemed to consider her new acquaintance carefully.

'What are you going to put in your basket? There's nothing in it, and there's not much point carrying an empty basket if you don't plan to put something in it,' she said.

So Dimity led her around behind the house, from which

the sound of pots and pans and movement was emanating, as well as the smell of fresh bread, and showed her the stream and the watercress beds, and which rocks to lift to find the crayfish hiding underneath. At first Delphine didn't want to get her shoes muddy or her hands wet, snatching her fingers back from the water and wiping them hurriedly on the skirt of her pinafore, but she grew bolder as time passed. She squealed and scrambled backwards when Dimity held up a big crayfish, which waved its claws angrily at the world. Dimity tried to reassure her that it was quite safe, but Delphine wouldn't come near again until she had thrown it further downstream. She stared after it regretfully.

'It's all those legs! They're disgusting! Ugh! I don't know how you can bear to eat them!' Delphine said.

'It's no different to eating crab or prawns,' Dimity told her. 'My mother wanted some for later. She's making soup for dinner.'

'Oh, no! Will you get in trouble for letting that one go?'

'I don't always find them – there aren't that many. I'll just tell her there weren't any today.' Dimity shrugged, a show of carelessness that she didn't feel. The snares had been empty too. She would have to find something else, or hope that a visitor came and brought them some bacon or a rabbit; or there would be nothing in the soup except barley and greens. Even at the thought of such poor fare, her stomach rumbled loudly. Delphine glanced at her and laughed.

'Haven't you had breakfast? Come on – let's go in and have something.'

But Dimity wouldn't go inside; she could hardly bring herself to pass the little gate into the garden, it felt so alien. Delphine accepted this with a quizzical tilt of her head, and didn't press her for an explanation. She darted into the house and came out with two thick slices of bread, smothered in honey. Dimity devoured her slice in seconds, and they sat on the damp grass in the morning sunshine, licking their sticky fingers. Delphine polished the mud from her shoes with a dock leaf, and glanced out at the glittering spread of the sea.

'Did you know that the sea is only blue because it reflects the colour of the sky? So it's not really blue at all?' she said. And Dimity nodded. It stood to reason, though she had never really thought about it before. She pictured it on a stormy day, as grey and chalky white as the clouds. 'The Mediterranean is a different colour altogether, so I suppose the sky must be a different blue. Which seems odd, since it's the same sun and all. But it must be different air, or something. Or do you think it depends what's under the water too? I mean, what's on the bottom?' she asked. Dimity thought about it for a moment. She had never heard of the Mediterranean, and was careful not to reveal this to her new friend.

'Doubt it,' she said at last. 'A short way out it's too deep to see down to the bottom, isn't it?'

'The bottom of the deep blue sea sea sea,' said Delphine. 'You've got hay in your hair,' she added, reaching out and picking the stalk from Dimity's head. Then she clambered to her feet. 'Come on – stand up. Let's do the clapping song.' So she taught Dimity the song about the bottom of the deep blue sea, and Dimity, who'd never done clapping before, kept getting it wrong. She concentrated hard, trying to keep up as Delphine's hands moved faster and faster, and decided that it wasn't as much fun as Delphine seemed to think it was. But she persevered, to please the strange, talkative girl, and as she did she felt the prickling weight of being watched. At first she thought it was just her imagination, just the fear of always being the first one to miss a clap and get it wrong, but after twenty minutes or so a man emerged from the house carrying a large, flat book.

He was tall and thin, dressed in close-fitting grey trousers and the oddest shirt Dimity had ever seen a man wear — long and loose, and open at the neck to show a sliver of the hairy, tanned skin of his chest. It was almost like the smocks the dairymaids wore for milking, but cut from coarser fabric, some kind of heavy linen. His hair was a deep reddish brown, thick and wavy. It was parted in the middle of his scalp and grew down over his ears to brush his collar at the back. Dimity stopped clapping at once, took several steps backwards and lowered her gaze defensively. She expected to be shouted at, told to go. She was so used to it that when she glanced up at him, her eyes were full of venom. The man recoiled slightly, and then smiled.

'Who's this, Delphine?'

'This is Mitzy. She lives . . . nearby. This is my father,' Delphine said, grabbing Dimity's hand and pulling her closer to the man. He held out his hand to her. A grown-up had never, ever done that before. Bewildered, Mitzy took it; felt him grip her hand firmly. His hand was large and rough, the skin dry and speckled with paint. Ridged knuckles and short, blunt nails. He held on to her fingers a second longer than she could stand, and she pulled them away, flicking another glance up at his face as she did so. The sun was shining in his eyes, turning them the rich, lustrous brown of newly shelled conkers.

'Charles Aubrey,' he said; his voice rumbled slightly, smooth and deep.

'Are you going out sketching?' Delphine asked. He shook his head.

'I have been, already. I drew the two of you, playing your game. Do you want to see?' And although it was Delphine who said *yes* and leaned over the book in his hands, it seemed to Dimity that he had really been speaking to her. The drawing was light, fluid; the background sketched in roughly – just hints of the land and the sky. The girls' feet and legs disappeared into long grasses described with swift, ragged pencil lines. But their faces and hands, their eyes, were alive. Delphine smiled widely, obviously pleased.

'I think it's excellent, Daddy,' she said, in a serious, grown-up tone of voice.

'And you, Mitzy? Do you like it?' he asked, turning the drawing right around so she could see it clearly.

It felt strange, and maybe even wrong. Dimity couldn't tell. The air seemed to fill her lungs too quickly, and she couldn't breathe all the way out. She didn't trust herself to speak; had no idea what the right thing to say would be. Clearly Delphine saw nothing improper about it, but then, she was his daughter. He had captured the shape of Dimity's body, underneath her clothes; caught the sun shining on the line of her jaw and cheek beneath the translucent veil of her hair. To have caught them so clearly he must have looked very hard. Looked harder than anybody had ever looked at her – she who was used to being invisible to the people of Blacknowle. She felt desperately exposed. Colour flooded her cheeks and with no warning there was a tickle at the top of her nose, and her eyes filled with tears.

'Oh, don't be upset! It's OK, Mitzy . . . really. Daddy – you should have asked her first!' said Delphine. Unable to stand it, Dimity turned quickly and walked away down the hill, towards The Watch. She tried to think what Valentina would say about a strange man drawing pictures of her, even if it wasn't her fault, and as clear as day the woman's sneer curled across her mind's eye. 'Do come again, Mitzy! He's sorry!' Delphine called after her. Then the man spoke as well.

'Ask your parents if they'll let you sit for me!'

Dimity ignored them both, and got home in time to see the door opened, and a visitor ushered inside. She didn't see who it was, and therefore didn't know how long he would stay, so she went around the back and sat in the sty with the old sow, Molly, putting up with the stink for the animal's warmth and amiable company. She wondered what *sitting* for Delphine's father would involve. She thought hard, and could come up with no answer that didn't make her uneasy. She scrubbed angrily at her eyes, where her few brief tears had made the skin itchy and stiff, and felt an unexpected pang of sorrow at the thought of not going back, and not seeing Delphine again.

The gates to Southern Farm had once been white, but most of the paint had flaked off to show the grey, ageing wood underneath. They sagged on their hinges, drooping into the long grass that had grown up around them. It was a blustery day and the wind was cooler than before; Zach thrust his hands into his pockets as he walked into the yard. A sign at the top of the lane had said there were eggs for sale, and though he didn't actually need any eggs it seemed as good a reason as any to pay an uninvited visit. Zach wanted to see the stand-offish Hannah Brock again, feeling an interest in her that went beyond the fact that she knew Dimity Hatcher. The yard was quiet and deserted. He thought about knocking at the door of the farmhouse itself, but it looked very shut, and unwelcoming. Farm buildings sat either side of the concrete yard, and Zach walked to the nearest one, a low structure with crumbling stone walls and a corrugated tin roof. From the darkness within came a shuffling of straw as he approached, and he was greeted by the pebble-eyed stares of six light brown sheep, puffing curiously at him through their noses. The stink of them was sweet and pungent.

The next barn was much bigger, and housed a large stack of hay bales and an ancient piece of farm machinery with vicious-looking spikes and wheels and moving parts. It was rusty and festooned with cobwebs. The wind moaned through a hole in the roof, and beneath that bright patch of watching sky, nettles and chickweed were growing in a patch of mouldy straw. Behind the sound of the wind was a silence that Zach suddenly found unnerving. Even the far-off cry of a sheep couldn't change the fact that the place felt dead, forgotten, like the relic of something been and gone.

'I help you?' A man's voice behind him made Zach jump.

'Jesus! You scared the hell out of me!' he said. He smiled, but the man standing behind him didn't return the expression. He examined Zach with a steady, measuring gaze that put him on his guard.

'This is private,' said the man, with a wave of his hand to indicate the barn. He was medium height, shorter than Zach but stockier, with burly shoulders. His face was drawn, the cheeks a little hollow, but Zach still thought the man might be slightly younger than he was, maybe in his early thirties. Black eyes watched from beneath a fringe of straight black hair. His skin was dark, dark enough that Zach would have guessed him to be foreign, perhaps Mediterranean, even if he hadn't spoken with such a thick, guttural accent.

'Yes, I know – sorry. I didn't mean to . . . I was looking for the eggs. The eggs for sale?' said Zach, struggling to regain his composure in the face of such open suspicion. The man studied him a moment longer, then nodded and turned to walk away. Zach supposed he was meant to follow.

They crossed the ridged concrete yard to a low building, stone built with a wooden stable door that was black with age and bitumen paint. Inside, the cobbled floor had been scrubbed and a shop counter had been improvised at one end – a trestle table with a metal strong box and a thick ledger upon it. There was also a large cardboard tray for eggs, in which five were sitting. The man eyed the tray with a look of irritation.

'There are more. Not picked yet. How many?' he said.

'Six, please,' said Zach. The dark-eyed man gazed at him with a neutral expression, and Zach fought the urge to smile. 'Five is fine, actually,' he relented, but the man shrugged.

'I get it. Wait.' He left Zach alone in the small room, which Zach guessed had once been a stable. As the sun leapt momentarily out from behind a cloud, the whitewashed walls shone brightly. There were little pictures hanging all around, the biggest no more than twelve inches wide and eight high. A mixture of landscapes and sheep portraits, done in chalks on different coloured papers. Modest prices had been stickered onto their simple pine frames – sixty pounds for the biggest one, a flat-backed sheep standing in silhouette on a near horizon, against a sky aglow with a pink dawn. They were good, all of them. A local artist, Zach assumed. He couldn't help thinking they'd have more luck in a small gallery in Swanage than here, in a farm shop that had five eggs for sale and no customers other than him.

He stood and looked at them, and wondered who the dark-haired man might be. Hannah Brock's husband? Her boyfriend? Or just somebody who worked at the farm? The latter seemed unlikely – the farm hardly looked as though it would support one person, let alone an employee as well. That only left husband or boyfriend, though, and he found he didn't like either idea. There were footsteps behind him and he turned, expecting to see the man return, but it was Hannah Brock who came into the stable. She pulled up short when she saw him, and he smiled as casually as he could.

'Good morning,' he said. 'We meet again.'

'Yes, fancy that,' she said, drily. She crossed to stand behind the table and flipped open the ledger, gazing down at it with a distracted frown. 'Can I help you with something?'

'No, no. Your . . . that is . . . the man who was here . . .'

'Ilir?'

'Yes, Ilir. He's just fetching me some eggs. Well, one extra egg, to be exact.' He gestured at the five already in the tray.

'Eggs?' She glanced up at him with half a smile. 'Aren't you staying at the pub?'

'Yes. They're for . . . They're for Dimity.' He smiled at her, and watched her reaction carefully.

'Mitzy has half a dozen hens of her own out the back. All of them good layers, as far as I know.'

'Yes. Well.' Zach shrugged. Hannah eyed him and seemed in no rush to speak, and Zach found the silence hard to bear. 'Mitzy. So, you know who she is, then?' he said.

'And I'm guessing from your barely contained curiosity that you do, too,' Hannah replied.

'I'm an expert on Charles Aubrey. Well, when I say an expert . . . what I mean is, I know a lot about him. About his work and his life . . .'

'You don't know anything compared to what Mitzy knows,' Hannah said quietly, with a shake of her head. She seemed to regret her words at once, and scowled.

'Exactly. I mean, it's incredible that nobody has come to interview her before. The stories she must have about him . . . the insights into all the drawings—'

'Interview her?' Hannah interrupted. 'What do you mean, interview her? Interview her for what?'

'I'm . . . well, I'm writing a book about him. About Charles Aubrey.' Hannah raised an eyebrow sceptically. 'It's coming out to coincide with the National Portrait Gallery's retrospective, next summer,' he said, with a touch of defiance.

'And you've told Mitzy that, and she's happy to help you?'

'I may not have mentioned the book, actually. I said I was

interested in Aubrey, and she seemed really keen to talk about him . . .' He trailed off under Hannah's ferocious glare.

'Going back up there soon, are you? So am I. And if you've not told her about the book, then I will. Clear? It changes everything, and you know it.'

'Of course I'll tell her. I meant to. Look, you seem to have got the wrong impression of me. I'm not some kind of . . .' He waved his hand in the air, searching for the word.

'Snoop?' Hannah supplied for him. She folded her arms; an aggressive pose undermined by another blaze of sunshine, pouring through the window and setting her dark curls alight with shades of deep red. She waited for his reply.

'Right. I'm not a snoop, or some predator out to trick her. I'm a genuine Aubrey fan. I just want to get some kind of new insight into his life and work . . .'

'Well, maybe that insight isn't yours to get. Mitzy's memories are her own. There's no reason she should have to share them with you, after what she suffered . . .'

'What she suffered? What do you mean?'

'She—' Hannah broke off, seemed to change her mind about what she was about to say. 'Look, she loved him, OK? She's still grieving for him . . .'

'After seventy-odd years?'

'Yes, after seventy odd years! If she's spoken to you about him already I'm sure you noticed how . . . fresh the memories of her time with him are. She's very easy to upset.'

'I'm not trying to upset her, and of course her memories are her own. But if she's happy to share them with me, then I don't see that I'm doing anything wrong. And Aubrey is a public figure. He's one of our greatest modern artists – his work is in public galleries all over the country . . . people have a right to know . . .'

'No, they don't. They don't have a right to know *every-thing*. I hate that idea,' Hannah muttered.

'Why do you care so much? I'll tell her I'm working on a book about him, I promise. And if she's still happy to talk to me, then that should be fine by you as well, shouldn't it?' he said.

Hannah seemed to consider this. She flipped the ledger closed again, having not written anything new in it. Behind Zach, Ilir returned with a plastic bucket full of eggs. He made up a box of the five on the desk and one from the bucket.

'Still warm,' he said, closing his hand briefly around the egg.

'Thank you,' said Zach.

'One seventy-five,' Ilir told him. Zach looked up in surprise, and Hannah bridled.

'They're organic and free range. Not certified organic, but that's just a question of bloody paperwork . . . I'm working on it. But they are organic,' she said.

'I'm sure they'll be delicious,' said Zach, wondering what he would do with them. Give them to Pete to use in the pub kitchen, he supposed. 'I like the sheep pictures,' he said, as he turned to go. 'Local artist?'

'Very local. Want to buy one?' she said, laconically.

'You did them? They're really good. Maybe next time.' He shrugged apologetically, and wished he did have sixty pounds to spend on one of them. 'I paint as well. And draw. Well, I used to. I have a gallery now, in Bath. It's shut at the moment though. Because I'm . . . here.' He looked back at the pair of them. Ilir was hovering near Hannah, putting the fresh eggs one by one into the tray. Hannah was watching Zach with that resolute silence of hers. 'Well, I should probably get going,' said Zach. 'I can see you're busy. OK. Bye. Thanks for the eggs. Bye.' He turned to go, and as he did a smile flickered over Hannah's face, quick like the sunshine that day.

On Tuesday he was at the butcher's first thing, before it was even open. He bought the brand new heart, and went straight down to The Watch, not thinking that Dimity might not be up yet until he'd banged on the door and it was too late. When she opened it he held the heart out to her.

'The butcher told me this bullock was slaughtered yesterday afternoon. It couldn't be any fresher unless I'd gone to the abattoir and caught it as it dropped out,' he said, with a smile. Dimity took the heart and unwrapped it, and held it in her hand. Zach noticed with a faint shudder that it smeared blood on her mittens, and that a dark clot was oozing from one of the vessels hanging from it. He caught the nauseating tang of iron in his nostrils, and tried not to inhale too deeply. Dimity performed the same tests on this heart as she had the first, then flashed Zach a small, pleased smile. With a flurry of long hair and skirts, she turned and vanished into the house, leaving the door open behind her.

Zach peered through into the hallway. 'Miss Hatcher?'

'The pins?' Her voice drifted through from the kitchen. Zach stepped inside and shut the door behind him.

'Right here,' he said, handing them to her. She was sitting at the small table in the kitchen, and took the box of pins from Zach without another word. She seemed entirely focused on the heart and what she planned to do with it, and Zach sank quietly into the chair opposite her, fascinated. With a single deft movement, the old woman slit the heart open down one side with a paring knife, the blade of which looked wicked sharp. She wiped away the clots of blood inside it with her fingertips, and then opened the box of pins, covering it with rusty fingerprints. Under each of her nails was a dark red crescent. Humming softly, she pierced the wall of the heart from the inside with a pin, pushing until its head was flush to the meat. Mesmerised, Zach watched and didn't dare to ask. Snatches of the song she sang were audible, and decipherable, but most of it was a wordless mumble of her buzzing *s* sounds and drawled vowels. Zach leaned closer, struggling to hear.

'Bless this house, and keep it whole . . . bless this house . . . keep thatch, keep stone . . .'

She finished when she ran out of pins. Taking a needle and thread from the pocket of her apron, she quickly stitched up the cut she'd made, patting the heart back into shape as best she could between its new armour of pins. It looked like a horrific, surrealist rendering of a hedgehog; almost the kind of thing Zach might have created during his college years at Goldsmith's, when he'd fought his every natural urge to draw and paint, to produce figurative art. He'd wanted to shock, to be avant-garde.

'What's it for?' he asked, tentatively. Dimity looked up, startled, and had clearly forgotten he was there. She chewed on the inside of her mouth for a second, then leaned towards him.

'Keeps the nasties out,' she whispered, and looked past him as though something had caught her eye. Zach glanced over his shoulder. In the hall mirror, his reflection glanced back at him.

'The nasties?'

'The ones you don't want.' She stood up, then paused and looked down at him. 'Good long arms,' she murmured. 'Come on and help with it.'

Obediently, Zach rose and followed her into the sitting room. Under Dimity's direction, he ducked into the inglenook fireplace and stood up cautiously, noting as he did that the morning had taken a strange turn. His shoulders brushed the sooty stone either side, and when he looked up a shower of smuts sifted into his eyes. Cursing, he rubbed at them, only to find that his fingers were gritty too. The sharp stink of ash filled his nostrils, and up above his head the sky was a small, dazzling square. *How did I come to be in a chimney?* he wondered, with a bemused smile for the dark space around him.

'Feel up above your head – as far as you can. There's a nail there for it. Can you find it?' Dimity called from the sitting room. Looking down, Zach could see her feet in their ugly leather boots, shuffling anxiously to and fro. He reached up and felt about with his fingers, loosening more soot that pattered down into his hair. He tried to shake it off and kept searching until his fingers brushed against the sharp spike of a rusty nail.

'I've got it!'

'Take this then – take it.' Her arm reached into the flue and handed him the heart pin-cushion, hanging it from his finger with a loop in the thread that she'd stitched it with. 'Hang it on the nail but as you do you have to sing part of the song.'

'What song?' Zach asked, carefully lifting the heart so that it wouldn't touch him. The flue narrowed at his head height, though, and it brushed against his cheek. A cold touch of metal that left a thin scratch. He shuddered. 'What song?' he repeated, rattled.

'Bless this house, keep it whole . . .' The line was sung in a quavering voice, thin and high.

'Bless this house,' Zach echoed, tunelessly. He hung the thing on the nail and a sudden updraught carried his words away like smoke. A rush of air that whispered angrily in his ears. He got out of the inglenook as fast as he could, and stood there brushing pointlessly at his hair and clothes with filthy hands. When he looked up at Dimity, her hands were clasped in front of her mouth, the fingers meshed tightly together, and her eyes were bright. With a quiet, joyous sound she threw her arms around Zach, who could only stand in silent amazement.

When she let go and stepped away she seemed embarrassed, and looked down at her stained fingers as they fiddled with a loose thread on her apron. It didn't seem to bother her that her hands were covered in blood. As if she was used to it. Zach rubbed his own filthy palms together again.

'Could I use your bathroom to get cleaned up a bit?' he said. Dimity nodded, still without looking at him, and pointed out to the hallway.

'Through the door to the back,' she said, quietly. Zach went out past the stairs and pulled open the door, which was swollen and stiff. He had a sudden idea of the wooden skeleton of the house being bloated with damp and brittle with age. Experimentally, he gouged his thumbnail into one of the thick beams wriggling through the wall. It was as hard as iron.

Through the door was a tiny utility area, the back door of the cottage and the door to the bathroom. The ceiling was close enough to brush Zach's hair, sloping away from the back wall of the house. The temperature dropped noticeably, and Zach realised that the bathroom had just been tacked on hastily – a flimsy lean-to, no doubt thrown together to replace an old garden privy. He peered out through the glass in the outer door. The backyard was shaded and bare of plants. Just trampled, mossy earth and cracked paving slabs slimed with green algae. A variety of old sheds and outbuildings stood here and there, with their doors shut tight, secretive. One of them was indeed a chicken coop, where six brown hens were pecking and preening. Beyond the yard the trees that marked the edge of the ravine heaved their branches in the wind. Zach scrubbed his hands as best he could in the tiny bathroom basin, and tried to forget the way the updraught in the chimney had sounded, for a second, like a voice.

Dimity was making tea, humming contentedly as she set out cups and saucers. No chipped mugs this time, Zach noted. He had come up in the world. She ushered him through to sit in the living room, as pleased and adamant as a child playing house. In the end, the cup she passed him had no handle, but she obviously hadn't noticed so he didn't mention it. A smile hovered around her mouth, waxing and waning as hidden thoughts came and went. Now seemed to be as good a time as any for a confession, Zach thought.

'Miss Hatcher—'

'Oh, do call me Dimity. I can't be doing with all the Miss Hatcher this and Miss Hatcher that!' she said, gaily.

'Dimity,' he said. 'I, uh, I met your neighbour, Hannah Brock. She seems nice.'

'Nice, yes. Hannah's a good girl. A good neighbour. I've known her since she was a baby, you know. That family . . . that family have always been good folk. Keep themselves to themselves, mind. Been at Southern Farm a full century, the Brocks have, as far as I know. How frightened she is of losing it! Poor girl. Always working so hard, and getting nothing back for it. Almost like a curse on the place but that can't be right. No, I can't think who'd have done that . . .' She trailed off, staring into the distance and seeming to consider who might have set a curse on the farm.

'I think I met her . . . husband too. I went down to buy some eggs yesterday. A dark-haired man?'

'Her husband? Oh, no. Couldn't have been. Her husband's dead. Dead and gone to the bottom of the sea.' She shook her head sadly. 'So many of them down there. My own father, too.'

'He drowned? She's a widow?' Zach asked.

'A widow, yes. These past seven years or so. Drowned, gone, lost at sea. I never liked him, mind you. He was too clever for his own good. Thought he was, anyway. No understanding of the land. But honest and of good heart for all that, I suppose.' She looked around the room quickly, as if expecting the man's vengeful ghost to have heard her malign him. Zach tried to shape Hannah into the role of widow in his head. It was a poor fit. Widows were old and tearful, or else brassy and rich.

'I was married, you know. We got a divorce. Well, in truth, she left me. Ali. I have a daughter, called Elise. She's six now. Would you like to see a picture?' Dimity gave a vague nod, looking puzzled, so Zach persevered and handed her the picture from his wallet. Elise grinning, holding a cloud of candy floss bigger than her head. She'd been so excited she couldn't keep a straight face. Then afterwards the sugar gave her a headache and she was vile to everyone, and ruined the day. But in the picture her eyes were bright and her hair was shiny, and she radiated the simple joy of being in possession of something wonderful to eat.

'Is she happy, your little girl? Is her mother kind to her?' asked Dimity, and Zach was shocked to see that her face had fallen into lines of sadness, and her voice had grown hoarse.

'Yes, Ali's always been great with her. She adores Elise.'

'And you?'

'I adore her too. She's a very adorable girl. I try to be a good dad, but I suppose that's something that time will tell.'

'Why did your wife leave you?'

'She fell out of love with me. I guess that happened first; and then, after that she could suddenly see all the many ways in which I was lacking.'

'You don't seem that bad to me.'

'Ali has . . . high standards, I suppose. Now she's met

somebody who matches up to them better than I ever could.' Zach smiled briefly. 'It's funny – you know what people say about first impressions? I think that's what our problem was. Mine and Ali's. We met at an exhibition of twentieth-century drawings – an exhibition that I had curated. I was able to tell her at great length what made each piece so great; what made the artists so great. I suppose I came across as deeply insightful, passionate . . . high-minded, successful and going places. I think it was all downhill from there, as far as Ali was concerned.'

Dimity seemed to consider this for a while.

'People's hearts . . . other people's hearts seem to fill with love and empty again, like the tide filling the bay. I've never understood it. Mine has never changed. It filled, and it stayed full. Stays full even now . . . even now,' she said, fiercely.

'Well, mine did too, for a long time after she left. It felt like the world was ending.' Zach smiled sadly. 'Suddenly there didn't seem a lot of point to anything I did, or was trying to do. You know?'

'Yes. Yes I do.' Dimity nodded, intently. Zach shrugged.

'But gradually, it's . . . faded, I suppose. There's only so long you can spend wishing things were different. Wishing you were different. Then you have to move on.'

'And have you now?'

'Moved on? I'm not sure. I'm trying to, but it's easier said than done, I suppose. But that's kind of why I'm here . . . in Blacknowle. I've been meaning to tell you, actually – I'm writing a book, about Charles Aubrey.' Dimity looked up when he said this, her eyes widening fearfully. 'I don't . . . I won't put anything in it that you don't want me to, I promise. I just want to write the truth about him . . .'

'The truth? The truth? What do you mean?' Dimity

struggled out of her chair and stood in front of him, shifting her weight. She suddenly looked very afraid.

'No – please. Look. I don't want to intrude on your memories of him. Really. And even if we talk and you tell me things you remember, but you don't want me to write them down, or record them, I won't, I promise,' he said, intently.

'What's the use of it then? What do you want from me?' she said. Zach considered his answer carefully.

'I just . . . I just want to *know* him. Nobody really seems to know him. Only the public figure, the things everybody saw. But you *knew* him, Dimity. Knew and loved him. Even if I don't write down anything specific that you tell me, you can still help me to get to know him. Please. You can tell me about the Charles you knew.' In the pause after he spoke, Dimity twisted the ends of her hair, and then sat down again.

'I knew him better than anybody,' she said at last.

'Yes,' Zach said, relieved.

'Can I see that picture? The one you held up to the window before?' She coloured up as though she'd been in the wrong on that occasion, ignoring him while he behaved so rudely outside. Zach grinned.

'I'm sorry about that. I was so keen to speak to you I forgot my manners. Here it is. It belongs to a collector who lives up in Newcastle, but he loaned it to a gallery for this exhibition.' He dug out the magazine and passed it to her. She stared at it intently, ran her fingers over the glossy paper, and sighed slightly.

'Delphine,' she whispered.

'You remember her?' Zach asked, intently, and Dimity shot him a withering glance. 'Right, sorry.'

'She was such a lovely girl. She was my first friend. First proper friend, that is. They were such townies, when they first arrived! Not used to getting her shoes muddy. But she changed. She wanted to be a bit like me, I suppose – a bit wild. She wanted to learn how to cook and how to gather from the hedgerows. And I suppose I wanted to be more like her – she was so friendly, so easy to talk to. So much loved by her family. And she knew so much! I thought her the wisest person I knew. Even later, when she went off to boarding school, and she got more interested in fashion and boys, and going to the flicks . . . she was still my good friend. She wrote to me sometimes, during the winters when they weren't here. Told me all about this teacher or that boy, or this row she'd had with some other girl . . . I did miss her, afterwards. I did miss her.'

'Afterwards? Do you know what happened to Delphine? She sort of vanishes from the public eye – not that she was ever really in it. Aubrey was very protective of his family. But after he was killed in the war, no mention is ever made of her again in any of the books . . .' Zach paused at the look on Dimity's face. Her eyes were focused on things he couldn't see, and her mouth made tiny movements, as though there were words inside not strong enough to come out. She looked for a moment as though she could see terrible, terrible things.

'Dimity? Do you know what happened to her?' Zach pressed gently.

'Delphine . . . she . . . No,' she said at last. 'No, I don't know.' Her voice was unsteady, but when she blinked and looked back at the magazine a tiny smile lit her face once more. Zach had the strongest feeling that she was lying.

'May I?' He took the magazine from her and flicked forward a few pages, to the first picture of Dennis that had surfaced for sale, about six years ago. 'What about this one? The date would suggest that the drawing was done here in Blacknowle. Did you ever know this man, Dennis? Do you remember him at all?' He passed the magazine back to the old woman. She took it, but reluctantly, and barely glanced at the picture. Two spots of colour appeared in her cheeks, and a mottling started to rise, staining her neck. A blush of guilt, or anger, or shame . . . Zach couldn't tell. She took a quick, shallow breath, and then another.

'No,' she said again, sharply, holding the magazine away from her as if she couldn't bear to look. Her breathing stayed high and fast in her chest, clearly audible, and her fingers shook slightly as she flicked back to the picture of her and Delphine. 'No, I never knew him.'

Careful not to put her off talking at all, Zach let her return to the earlier picture without asking any more questions about Dennis, or the fate of Delphine. He realised he was every bit as keen to know about Delphine, the girl he had spent so long trying to know from her portrait, as he was about her father, but he saw that it would have to wait, and be tackled gently. For now he was happy to sit and listen as Dimity talked about the first time she met the Aubrey family, and the house they took for the summer in 1937, and how she was careful to keep her acquaintance with them hidden from her mother for as long as she could.

'You think your mother would have disapproved of them? I know that some people in the village thought the set-up was far too liberal . . .' he said, and then wished he hadn't. Dimity scowled at the interruption, and sat silent for some moments as she seemed to digest his words, which were obviously wrong in some way. In the end she ignored the question, and carried on with her tale.

The second time she met them was four days later. She'd been torn between her desire to go back and see Delphine again, and her uncertainty – one that bordered on fear. Fear of not understanding them, not behaving the right way, of what Valentina might say if she ever found out about the drawing; that sketch that had seemed to capture a little bit of her soul, trapping it for ever on the paper. At fourteen, Dimity's body was no longer that of a child. She had breasts, still growing, that felt bruised all the time. Valentina pinched them sometimes, grinning, amused by them for some reason, and the unusual pain made Dimity feel sick in the pit of her stomach. Her hips had spread – so quickly that rose-coloured marks appeared in the skin, and then faded to leave faint silvery stripes. She walked with a sway that slowed her rapid gait, so that some heads that had once turned away when she went into the village now turned towards her instead. In some ways, Dimity found that worse. She was not ready to be looked at the way their visitors sometimes looked at her mother, when they arrived at The Watch with their hair slicked down and their boots pulled on hastily, not laced properly. Soon to be kicked off again.

She made her way to the wide beach that lay along the coast, west from Blacknowle; taking the long route inland because a group of boys were hanging about on the cliff path. They still threw things and called names, but they made other suggestions now too. They grabbed at her, tried to pull up her skirt or blouse; unbuttoned their trousers and came swaggering over with the floppy lengths of their penises waggling to and fro, or sometimes poking up, stiff as an accusatory finger. She was still taller than most of them; could hit just as hard and run as fast. But the time would come when that would change, she guessed, and on instinct she avoided them more than ever before. Wilf Coulson was with them that time. He saw her from a distance, but he didn't wave or call out, or alert the others. He was still as thin as a lath, still a boy, still plagued by his sinuses. When he saw her he stuffed his skinny hands into his pockets and turned his back; deliberately didn't look or draw attention to her as she quickly widened her route and dipped out of sight behind a fold in the land. She would give him something for this loyalty, when she saw him next. She was always mixing up new treatments for his nose, or things to help him grow, but what he wanted more often than not was a kiss.

It was low tide – the full moon had just passed, towing the water far out from the shore to reveal a narrow arch of dark brown sand. With a bucket looped on one arm, Dimity made her way along the water's edge, barefoot, setting her feet down as carefully and gently as she could so as not to startle her prey. It was a still day, warm and bright. Through the shallow water her feet were luminous white; and the sand, carved into hard ridges by the water, felt good on her soles. There was no sound but the wheeling cries of gulls overhead, and the gentle slosh of her stealthy steps; the water was sparkling. Where the sun warmed the sand it smelled glassy and clean. The holes she was looking for were no more than an inch or so across. If they felt the vibration of her approach the razor clams, with a contemptuous squirt of water, dug themselves deeper into the sand, out of reach. In her right hand Dimity carried an old, thin-bladed carving knife, bent into a crook at its tip. When she spotted a hole she placed her feet either side of it, softly, softly; crouched down and with a quick stab and twist, pulled the clam from the sand before it could escape. The creatures hung disconsolately out of their shells, bubbling and reaching, trying to find something to cling onto, to pull themselves to safety. She had ten in her bucket already when she heard people coming, and knew that the harvest was ruined.

Four figures – two large, two smaller – walking towards her from the opposite end of the beach. The children were squealing, running in criss-cross patterns around their parents. Feet thumping into the hard sand, splashing the water high onto their dresses. Dimity could feel the vibrations through her own feet as they got nearer, and when she looked down, a few telltale puffs of sand and water marked the retreat of the clams. With a flash of annoyance she looked up again, and then remembered that Delphine had said she had a sister. She realised who they were. Irritation became confusion, and caused her cheeks to flare. There was no way she could turn away, nowhere to hide. In that instant Delphine recognised her, and ran ahead of the others to meet her. Half happy, half awkward, Dimity raised her hand in greeting.

'Hi, Mitzy! I thought it was you. How are you? What are you doing?' the girl said breathlessly, splashing to a stop in front of her. The hem of her dress was soaked six inches above her knees with water. The dress was light blue with yellow flowers and a neat, scalloped collar; and the cardigan she wore over it had pretty pearl buttons. Dimity noticed them enviously, and was relieved that there was a good excuse, this time, for her being barefooted.

'I was catching razor clams. Only . . . they live in the sand, and if they hear you coming they run and hide, so I won't catch any more,' she said, proffering the bucket where her ten clams lay helpless.

'You think they heard you? Oh, no!' Delphine covered her mouth with one hand in realisation. 'It was us, wasn't it? Last time I made you throw away your crayfish, and now we've scared the clams!' She seemed to think for a moment, chewing her lip in consternation.

'It's no bother,' said Dimity, embarrassed by her concern. 'I've got a good few—'

'You'll have to come to lunch. It's the only answer – and the best one! Let me just ask!'

'Oh, I can't—' But Delphine had turned back to her approaching family, and called out to them.

'Mitzy can come for lunch, can't she? We've scared off all the clams by being noisy!'

Her sister was the first one to reach them. Smaller than Delphine by several years, more lightly built, and darker. Darker skin, dark brown hair and matching eyebrows that gave her face a serious cast. Her expression was one of natural suspicion. She had intent black eyes that moved swiftly over Dimity, assessing with an assuredness beyond her years.

'*You're* the one Daddy drew,' she said. 'Delphine said you'd never done a clapping song before. How come? What do they do at your school, then?'

'I've seen other girls do it, I just never . . .' Dimity shrugged. The girl she assumed was Élodie kinked her eyebrows into a contemptuous shape.

'Couldn't you learn it? It's *easy*,' she said.

'Élodie, do be quiet,' said Delphine, giving her sister a censorious nudge. By now the girls' parents had reached them, and Dimity, thinking to avoid embarrassment, looked at the woman instead of the man. She caught her breath in an audible gasp. The girls' mother was the most beautiful woman she had ever seen in her life. More beautiful than the woman in the Ovaltine poster taped up in the shop window. More beautiful than the postcard of Lupe Velez that had once been passed around the village boys – Dimity had caught a glimpse of it during its brief sojourn in Wilf's pocket. 'This is our mother, Celeste,' Delphine said, smiling, clearly pleased by Dimity's reaction.

Celeste had an oval face with a delicate lower jaw, full lips in a perfect bow and black hair hanging down, thick and straight, around her shoulders. Her skin was a pale golden brown, flawless, but what were most arresting of all were her eyes. In spite of her dark colouring, and the dense, sooty lashes around them, her eyes were a pale blue-green, huge and clear. They were almond-shaped, and seemed to shine from her face with their own unearthly light, brighter even than the summer sky above her. Dimity stared.

'It's very nice to meet you, Mitzy. I have never heard the name Mitzy before. Is it a local name?' Celeste's voice was deep and accented – not an accent that Dimity had heard before, or could place.

'Dimity. Short for Dimity,' she managed to say, still terrified and fascinated by the woman.

'*Dimity*? That's a silly name!' said Élodie, clearly nonplussed that somebody else should be the centre of attention.

'Élodie! You will mind your manners,' said Charles Aubrey, the first time he'd spoken. The little girl scowled resentfully, and Dimity felt gratified.

'I liked Charles's picture of you and my Delphine. So pretty, playing together like that. You are most welcome to come and eat lunch with us. I hope you will? To make up for him not asking your permission,' said Celeste. She shot Aubrey a mildly chastening look, but he merely smiled.

'If I'd asked, the moment would have been lost,' he said.

'There are worse things, my love. Well, then. Let us walk on and leave this young girl to her hunt. You know the way to the house, of course? Come at midday and eat with us. I insist.' She looped her hand through Charles's arm and they walked on, before Dimity could collect herself sufficiently to speak. Valentina might have a visitor, she thought desperately, or one of the moods that made her drink herself to sleep in the afternoon. She might get away without being questioned, if she was lucky.

'See you later, Mitzy.' Delphine waved. Élodie turned up her nose and moved away, stepping delicately now, as though to show superiority through decorum. Too late, Dimity realised that the front of her blouse was wet and sandy from the clam picking, and was sticking to her midriff. Too late she remembered that she hadn't brushed her hair that morning. She raked her fingers through it in agitation, and stared after the figures moving along the beach. Celeste had slim arms and a tiny waist above broad hips; she moved like deep water – smoothly, gracefully. Her beauty caused a pang of some unidentifiable emotion in Dimity, and as she stood there, admiring her and fiddling with her own ragged appearance, the artist man looked back at her. A long, deliberate look over his shoulder, much more than a glance; too far away by then for her to guess at his expression.

Dimity lingered on the beach for a while. There was no point carrying on, since all the clams would have gone deep, but she didn't want to follow the family either. She went further up the beach, hitched her skirt higher and sat down where the sand was dry enough. With a hand to shield her eyes from the glare, she watched Delphine and her family until they were tiny, and she could just make them out as they turned and began to climb up to the path. The artist put his hand in the small of Celeste's back to guide her, then reached out for Élodie's hand, and held on to it as they picked their way over the rocks. This was a new kind of father. Kind and strong, not like Wilf Coulson's dad, and lots of the other dads in the village, who were often sour and glowering. This was how her own father might have been. She tried to imagine what it would have been like to be Élodie's age and have a man like Charles Aubrey reach out to take your hand when the ground got rough.

As noon approached, no visitors arrived at The Watch. Dimity combed her hair as best she could – it was almost impossible without washing the salt out of it first. She put on a clean blouse and tried to keep out of her mother's way. Valentina was in the kitchen with a pair of newly skinned rabbits, scraping the underside of the skins with vicious strokes of the knife, ready for curing. Her face was red and sweaty, tendrils of damp hair falling into her eyes. When immersed in a task like this, she worked with a frightening intensity and a dull, angry light in her eyes. It was a bad time to bother her, to be seen, or dare to ask anything. Dimity happened to peek around the door jamb just as Valentina paused, straightening up to stretch her back and push her hair behind her ears. The room stank of dead meat, and Valentina's flat glare caught her.

'You'd better have done what I asked you, and not have been mooning about all morning. You'd better have finished digging those spuds out or I swear, I'll skin you next of all,' she said, biting the words.

'I have, Ma. It's all done.' Without a word, Valentina went back to her scraping, and Dimity thought about taking her leave, or perhaps making up some errand. In the end she just slipped away, since Valentina was caught up in thoughts that had nothing to do with her.

The front door of Littlecombe was wide open, and as Dimity approached she saw that the back door, opposite it along the hall, was open too. Air surged through the house, creating a moving tunnel that seemed to draw her on when she hesitated on the threshold. She still wasn't sure that the invitation to lunch was real. There were voices from the kitchen, and laughter, and when she knocked Celeste's lovely face appeared around the doorway, smiling.

'Come in, come in!' she said. She was drying her hands on a cloth, and the wind picked up her hair and floated it in front of her eyes. With a chuckle she brushed it away. 'I love to feel the air moving like this, right through the building. You English always have such stuffy houses! I hate that.'

Not sure if she was being reprimanded, Dimity followed Celeste into the kitchen, where the table was set for five and a bottle of wine was already open. Dimity had never had wine before – not poured from a bottle, into a glass. Wine was what her mother drank when a visitor had brought some with him – and that was rare. She far preferred the cider they made from the apples of the gnarled tree beside the cottage. Popping open their skins because there was so much juice inside them. Dimity fought the wasps for them every day from August through to September, brushing away their drunken belligerence as they staggered from fruit to bubbling fruit.

She thought about The Watch, with its heavy thatch, thick walls and small windows. This was a different place indeed. Light poured in through wide sash windows, and the walls had fresh white paint on them, not yellowed with age or dirt. The floor was laid with red clay tiles; the lower portion of the walls clad in wainscoting painted a soft green colour. It was the first time Dimity had ever been inside somebody else's house. She knew their back doors well; their front steps; their rooflines from a distance. But never before had she been invited inside.

Élodie had decided to play the hostess. She made Dimity sit down, and complimented her on her blouse, and fussed around her and brought her a glass of water, all with only the merest hint of disdain. Delphine had an apron tied neatly over her sundress, and was standing on a small stool at the stove, stirring something that steamed and smelt good. She turned and smiled at Dimity.

'Come and taste this – I made it! It's pea and ham.'

'My budding cook. So good, you are,' said Celeste, putting her arm around Delphine's hips and squeezing her.

Dimity obediently sipped some soup from a spoon. She thought it would be much improved by adding fresh bay, and by having used the water in which the ham was boiled as a base. But she smiled, and agreed that it was good.

'I can cook too, you know,' Élodie interjected. 'I made cheese biscuits the other day. Daddy said they were the best ones he'd ever tasted.'

'Yes, yes. They were excellent. I am lucky to have such talented daughters,' Celeste said, soothingly. She stroked Élodie's black hair back from her forehead and planted a kiss on it. 'Now, stop showing off and fetch the bowls for the soup.' She said it lightly, but Élodie scowled as she did as she was told. Dimity sipped her water, perching on the edge of her chair with the alert, uneasy feeling that she should be doing something to help. But when she tried she was pushed back into the chair by Celeste's long, elegant hands.

'Be still. You are the guest here! All you have to do is eat and enjoy,' she said, in her heavy accent. Dimity longed to ask her where she was from. It might be as far away as Cornwall, or even Scotland.

Charles came in from outside just as the soup was put on the table. He was windswept, his cheeks pink and the bridge of his nose scorched to match. Hair in disarray. He put down the canvas bag he was carrying and slipped into a seat with a distracted air. A glance passed between Celeste and Delphine, which Dimity couldn't read. When he looked up at them it was, for a second, as if he didn't know them. There was a pause. He blinked, and then he smiled.

'What a bevy of beauties,' he murmured. 'What more could any man wish to come back to?' His daughters smiled, but Celeste watched him carefully for another second, her expression intent.

'What more indeed?' she said quietly, then picked up the

ladle and started to serve the soup. Aubrey's eyes lit upon Dimity.

'Ah! Mitzy. So good of you to join us. I hope your parents didn't mind sparing you for a couple of hours?' Dimity shook her head, wondering if she should mention that she only had a mother.

'My father was lost at sea,' she blurted out, and was then horribly embarrassed to see Celeste's expression cloud with dismay.

'You poor child! What tragedy for one so young! You must miss him terribly, and your poor mother too,' she said, leaning forward and gripping Dimity's arm, staring at her fiercely with those glorious eyes. Dimity had hardly expected such a reaction. *Lost at sea, for all I care.* She nodded mutely, and said nothing of Valentina's anger whenever she mentioned him. 'How does your mother cope? Oh, it must be hard, living in a backwater like this, just a woman alone with a child to support. No wonder we see you always looking so—' She cut herself off. 'Well. Tell us instead about your mother. What is she called?'

'Valentina,' Dimity said, woodenly.

She could think of nothing she wanted to speak about less, and nothing else to say about her mother. But there was a long, significant silence, and she felt her throat go dry with nerves, felt herself teetering on the brink of failure. 'She's a gypsy, her people were, originally. From far, far away. She makes medicines and charms from herbs and all sorts, and she teaches me how. The people in the village, they pretend not to believe her, but they all come sooner or later, to buy something, or ask something. My mother is very special,' she said, and even though none of it was lies she still felt the deceit hanging heavy around her, like thick clouds; thought at the same time how wonderful it would be if the real Valentina matched this portrayal.

'A hedge witch,' said Charles, staring at her. She was acutely aware of the sun from the window shining on her face, making it impossible to hide. 'Fascinating . . . I've never met a real one. I must go and introduce myself.'

'Oh, no! Don't!' Dimity gasped, before she could stop herself.

'Why on earth not?' he said, with a smile. Dimity couldn't think of anything she could reply with, so she sat and stared miserably at her soup, and jumped when his hand settled on her forearm, the fingers thick and strong. They squeezed, and a shiver ran through her. 'Don't worry, Mitzy,' he said, softly. 'I don't shock easily.'

'What do you mean, Daddy?' said Élodie. She spoke quickly, keenly, and looked a little crestfallen when Charles ignored her.

After the soup Celeste fetched a round pastry pie from the oven, cutting it open to reveal spiced minced lamb and whole almonds. The pastry was sweet, thin and crispy, and Dimity had never eaten anything as delicious, and when she said so Celeste laughed.

'You and your people are the masters of herbs, maybe, but my people are the masters of spices. This is a *pastilla*. In here you can taste cinnamon, ground coriander seed, nutmeg and ginger. It is very Moroccan. Very typical of my country,' she said, proudly. She cut another slice and held out her hand for Dimity's plate.

'Where is Morr . . . Mocc . . . your country?' she asked, and jumped when Élodie snorted with laughter, almost choking on her mouthful.

'That will teach you, hmm?' said Charles, mildly.

'Don't you know where Morocco is? We've been three times! It's amazing,' said Élodie. Celeste smiled fondly at the child.

'It is good to be proud of your heritage, Élodie,' she said.

'Morocco is in North Africa. It is a country where the desert blooms. The most beautiful place. My mother is of the Berber people, from the mountains of the High Atlas where the air is so clear you can see right up into heaven. My father is French. An administrator for the colonial government in Fez.'

'Are all Berber women as beautiful as you?' said Dimity, meekly, trying desperately to hold on to all the foreign names as they began to slip at once from her head. Celeste laughed, and Charles joined in, and Delphine smiled around a mouthful of pie.

'Such a sweet girl,' Celeste said, warmly. 'It is a long time since I was paid a compliment so sincere.' She flashed a challenging look at Charles, then held out her hand for his plate. As she did so Dimity noticed there was no wedding ring on her finger, or on his. She swallowed, and said nothing, trying to picture those mountains Celeste had mentioned, where the people shone their beauty back up at the sky.

After lunch Delphine was excused the washing-up because she'd helped to cook, and she interrupted Dimity's stuttering thanks to pull her friend outside. Dimity took a deep breath once they were out in the garden. However fascinating the house had been, and the food, and the people and the feeling of being a guest, they had been bewildering too, and she felt as though some vast pressure was released once the clouds were high above her head again. Delphine showed her the vegetable patch, where a few stunted radishes and lettuces were growing.

'Look! More droppings! The rabbits keep eating everything I grow!' she lamented. Dimity nodded, crouching alongside her to examine the evidence.

'You need wire to keep them out,' she said. 'Or some snares to catch them.'

'Oh, poor bunnies! I don't want to hurt them . . . Why don't you want Daddy to go and say hello to your mother?' she asked, curiously. Dimity picked up a couple of the telltale rabbit pellets, rolled them around in her palm and didn't know how to answer. 'It's OK,' Delphine said at last. 'You don't have to say.' She stood up and put her hands on her hips. 'Come on. We'll find a crayfish to make up for the one you lost, and the scaredy-cat clams that got away!'

Delphine was brave enough to touch the crayfish this time, letting a droplet of water from the tip of her finger wash over one of its black eyes as it flexed its legs and curled its tail protectively. But she still couldn't bear for Dimity to keep it, since it had waved its feelers at her just *so*, and she decided to name it Lawrence. Bemused, Dimity returned the creature to the stream, and instead showed Delphine how to tell watercress from marsh marigold, since there was so much of it growing nearby and the rabbits had so decimated her crop of salad leaves. The skinny girl was an apt pupil, and as the days passed the lessons ranged further from Littlecombe, along the cliffs and inland to the woods, always skirting the village and steering clear of The Watch. Soon Delphine, with Mitzy to guide her, was adding wild fennel, fat-hen, marjoram, horseradish roots and lime blossoms to Celeste's kitchen supplies, the latter of which caused Celeste to exclaim with delight, holding the flowers up to her nose and breathing deeply. *Ah! Tilleul!* She sighed appreciatively, putting the kettle on to boil.

One morning, Dimity arrived to find Élodie on the front lawn, standing with her arms rigid at her sides and her face frozen in fear because a huge bumblebee, with a dusting of yellow pollen on its jet-black fur, was buzzing around her legs. Delphine was standing nearby with her arms folded.

'Dumbledore won't hurt you, Élodie. He's got no stinger. It's only the honeybees that might,' Dimity said.

'That's what I said, but she doesn't believe me,' said Delphine, patiently. 'What did you call it?'

'Dumbledore. That's how they're called, isn't it?' Dimity shrugged.

'Not in London, or in Sussex. Tell us some other Dorset names for things.' They all turned to watch as the bee gave up on Élodie, rose into the air and let the bass rumble of its flight carry it away. With a small cry of relief, Élodie flew into her sister's arms and hugged her tightly. 'There you go, Élodie. Safe now,' said Delphine, patting her shoulders. Then they passed a contented hour as Dimity named as many things around them as she could, and the two younger girls leapt delightedly upon those they'd never heard before. *Want-heave* for mole hill; *palmer* for caterpillar; *emmet butt* for ant hill; *vuʒʒen* for gorse; *scrump* for apple; *tiddy* for potato.

They called in at Southern Farm one day, and Dimity shyly introduced Delphine to the farmer's wife, Mrs Brock, who was friendlier than most and sometimes gave her lemonade or a slice of bread, if she wasn't too busy. The Brocks were both in their fifties and had steel hair, lined faces. After a lifetime of farming their hands were creased and brown, the nails thick and stained, hard as animal horn. They had two grown-up children: a daughter who had married and moved away; and a son called Christopher who worked on the farm with his father. The one who clubbed the rats, and was never without a terrier at his heels. A tall, silent young man with a thatch of ruddy hair and soft, steadfast eyes. Christopher came into the kitchen while Delphine was telling Mrs Brock all about her Moroccan mother and her famous father. Dimity had been marvelling at her boldness, the way she hid nothing about herself, and when she looked at Christopher she read a kind of muted marvel on his face too – or perhaps it was just curiosity. As if here was a puzzle he might have to solve at some point.

Often, as she approached or played near Littlecombe, Dimity was aware of being watched. Sometimes she caught sight of a far-off figure standing on the cliffs while she and Delphine were on the beach; or a shadow at a window in the house if they were in the garden. Once, by the stream, with her sleeves pushed up and her skirt rolled around its waist-band to raise it – not foraging for once but playing with Élodie, trying to keep the younger girl occupied because Celeste had a migraine – Dimity looked up and saw him leaning on the door jamb, smoking and watching her with his eyes half shut against the sunshine. So intent, so lost in thought that he showed no sign of having noticed he'd been spotted. Dimity coloured and looked away quickly, and saw that Delphine had noticed him too. Delphine tipped her head to one side and considered her friend for a moment.

'He wants to draw you again. I heard him telling Mummy so, but she says he can't if you don't want him to, and definitely not without asking your mother first. He says you're a *true rustic*. I heard him,' she said, in a low tone.

'What's that mean?' Dimity asked. Delphine shrugged.

'I don't know. But Daddy only draws nice things, so it can't mean anything bad.'

'I don't see what's so special about *her*,' Élodie complained to her sister. 'I don't see why Daddy should want to draw her at all.'

'Don't be so mean, Élodie. I think Mitzy's very pretty. Mummy was angry because he's meant to be working on a big painting – he's meant to be painting the portrait of some famous poet in time for it to go on the front of his new book of poems. But there isn't much time left and all Daddy wants to do is draw your picture instead,' Delphine said to Dimity. Élodie sulked and Delphine swirled a stick to and fro in the water, and there was a long pause in which Dimity digested all this information.

'Do you really think I'm pretty?' she asked at length.

'Of course. I love your hair. It's like a lion's mane!' said Delphine, and Dimity smiled.

'You are too,' she said, gallantly.

'When I grow up, I shall be as beautiful as Mummy,' said Élodie.

'Nobody is as beautiful as Mummy,' Delphine pointed out, patiently.

'Well, I will be. She told me so herself.'

'Well, aren't you the lucky one, then? Eh, Smelly Élodie?' Delphine sank her fingers into her sister's ribs, and they squealed and squirmed for a moment before collapsing, giggling helplessly, onto the grassy bank.

While the two sisters tussled, Dimity cast a quick glance back at the house, where the girls' father still stood, lean and watchful, thinking and puffing out mouthfuls of blue smoke. After a while she found she didn't mind his eyes on her as much as she had at first. His face was inscrutable, a pattern of planes and angles she couldn't read. *He only draws nice things*. She felt herself stand a little straighter, felt her face relax, the blush recede from her cheeks. *Nice* and *pretty*, two words she'd never heard used to describe herself, now used within seconds of each other. She hoped that both were true, and that all the other words hurled at her before now had been the wrong ones. The thought made the blood seem to tingle in her veins, made her suddenly want to smile, when really there was no reason to. Not with her feet going numb in the stream, and Valentina's knife of a tongue to go home to later.

'Maybe I don't mind so much. If he wants to draw my

picture again,' she said at last. Delphine smiled encouragingly.

'You really don't mind?'

'No. He's a very good and famous artist, isn't he? That's what you told me. So I suppose I . . . I should be honoured.'

'I'll tell him. He'll be very happy.'

'You should feel *humbled* that he wants to draw you,' Élodie corrected her. But Delphine merely rolled her eyes, so Dimity ignored the remark.

Two days later, the thing that Dimity had been most dreading occurred. She was upstairs in her bedroom, getting changed for breakfast after feeding the pig and the chickens, collecting the eggs and emptying the chamber pots down the privy. Her bedroom had a small window facing north, over the approach along the lane, and as she arranged her hair into a twist at the back of her head, stabbing it with pins to hold it, she saw Charles Aubrey approaching the cottage. He had on his close-fitting dark trousers and a blue shirt with a waistcoat done up against the early morning cool. With her heart hammering, Dimity put her face up to the window glass and craned her neck to watch as he came right up to the door. What had Valentina been wearing? She tried desperately to think; hoping she wasn't still in her robe, the diaphanous green one that swirled dangerously and let the outline of her body show through, with all its shadows and patterns. She debated whether she should run down herself, get to the door first and make some excuse to send him away. The kitchen table was strewn with dead frogs. She pictured it, and shut her eyes in horror. Dead frogs with their soft bellies slit open and their guts scooped out into a bowl; bodies cast aside with filmed, sightless eyes and webbed feet dangling. Valentina had two charms to make: one to break a curse, one to keep a new baby safe. The pink and grey entrails would be packed into glass jars and sealed up with wax; sprigs of rosemary wound around the tops as if the herb could hide the death inside.

Too late. Dimity heard him knock, heard her mother at the door almost at once, and then their voices rising muffled through the floor. His a deep rumble, soft like the hum of a breeze, Valentina's low and hard, challenging. Dimity inched to her bedroom door and cracked it open as softly as she could, just in time to hear the front door close, and two sets of footsteps move into the sitting room. With that door shut, there was no way she could hear what they were saying. The Watch had walls of solid stone, walls that had absorbed centuries of words, and kept hold of them. Five minutes or so later, she heard him leave. She waited as long as she could force herself to and then went downstairs, wearing her trepidation like a garland.

Valentina was sitting at the kitchen table, smoking a cigarette with one hand and picking up odd fragments of entrails with the other, flinging them into the bowl.

'So,' she said, heavily. 'That's where you've been running off to, when you should have been helping me. Tarting yourself around with posh incomers.' Dimity knew better than to try to defend herself. It only made Valentina more angry, more vicious. Cautiously, she pulled out the chair opposite her mother and sank into it. Valentina was wearing the green robe, but at least there was an old apron tied over it, smeared with blood and stains. Dirty, but opaque. Her rough yellow hair was tied back with a piece of twine, and her eyelids were still smudged with last night's green eye shadow. 'There was I, thinking you were out finding us useful things. Wondering what was taking you so long on every errand. Now I know!' Her voice rose to a bark.

'I was, Ma! I swear it – only Delphine's been helping me

– she's learning all the plants and helping me . . . that's Mr Aubrey's daughter . . .'

'Oh, I know all about her, about all of them. He's been telling me all about it, though I never asked to be told. Peering into every corner, curious as a cat. I had to shut the sitting room door because I couldn't stand his roving eyes no more! He had no business coming here, and you had no business telling him he could.'

'I didn't, Ma. I swear I never did!'

'Oh, you'll swear to anything, won't you? I see that now. I won't know from one minute to the next if you're telling me the truth from now on, will I? Shut up!' she snapped, when Dimity tried to speak. They sat in silence for a minute, and Dimity looked at her hands and heard her pulse thump in her ears while Valentina took long, aggressive pulls on her cigarette. Then, like a snake she struck, reaching forwards and grabbing Dimity by the wrist. She pulled her arm onto the table top, the soft underside uppermost; held her glowing cigarette an inch from the skin.

'No, Ma! Don't do it! I'm sorry – I said I was!' Dimity cried. 'Please! Don't!'

'What else have you not told me? What have you been doing up there with them?' Valentina asked, with her eyes screwed up suspiciously and her breasts swaying behind the apron as Dimity fought to pull her arm away. Her grip was like iron. 'Stop pulling at me or I'll cut your bloody arm clean off!' Valentina snapped. Dimity went still, her body slack with fear even as her heart rose up in her chest, perilously high. She didn't think her mother would go that far, but she couldn't swear to it. Sweat broke out across her brow, chilly and slick. A glowing ember came loose from the cigarette and landed on her skin, where it sank in and smoked. At once a blister began to form, a white bubble at the centre of a bright red ring. Still Dimity did not flinch, too frightened to move even though the pain of it was shocking. Tears blurred her eyes and she had to swallow several times before she could speak.

'It was just as I said, Ma,' she said, frantically. 'I was playing with the little girl, and teaching her the plants. That was all.' Valentina glared at her a moment longer, then released her.

'Playing? You're not a baby any more, Mitzy. There's no time for playing. Well then,' she said, putting the cigarette back between her lips. 'Some good may come of your lies after all. He wants to draw you. Reckons he's an artist. So I told him he'd have to pay for the privilege.' The thought seemed to raise her spirits, and after a while she got up and put her arms above her head to stretch; then she wandered off towards the stairs, ruffling her fingers through Dimity's hair as she passed. 'Finish those charms while I'm resting,' she said. Only once she had left the room did Dimity dare to blow the ash from her arm. Her chest was so tight it was hard to draw the breath to do so. She turned the blister to the light, saw the way the surface shone. She waited, careful not to disturb her mother with the sound of her crying. Then she got up and went to find witch-hazel ointment to smear onto the burn.

'So how did your mother react when Aubrey came to ask if he could draw you? I suppose that's the kind of thing that not everybody would be keen on. Especially with you only being, what, fourteen, was it?' The young man opposite was talking, asking more questions. He had a way of leaning forwards and steepling his fingers between his knees that put her on edge. Overeager. But his face was kind, only ever kind. Her left arm was itching, and she rubbed her thumb along it, pressing the pad into her slack flesh until she found the scar standing proud of the skin. A small, smooth bobble of hardened tissue the exact size and shape of the blister it replaced. She'd kept knocking the scab off inadvertently, kept losing the plasters Delphine stuck over it. *I was frying liver and the fat spat*. Underneath the scab the wound was deep and angry. The silence in the room was profound, and suddenly she sensed more ears than the young man's waiting for her to answer him.

'Oh,' she began, then had to pause, clear her throat. 'She was pleased, of course. She was quite a cultural woman, my mother. And free-spirited. She didn't hold with all the whispers about Charles and his family, passing round the village. She was happy to have such a famous artist draw her daughter.'

'I see. She sounds like a very liberal woman . . .'

'Well, when you're something of an outcast yourself, you're drawn to others in the same boat. That's how it was with her.'

'Yes, I see. Tell me, did Charles ever give you any of his drawings of you? Or of anything? As a present, or to say thank you for posing for him?'

'Posing for him? Oh no, I hardly ever posed. He didn't want drawings like that, not normally. He was always just watching and waiting, and when everything seemed right to him, he would start. Sometimes I wasn't even aware of it. Sometimes I was. He would ask me to stop, sometimes.' *Mitzy, don't move. Stay exactly as you are.*

Once when she had been stretching, standing up to look at the sunset after hours of shelling peas. She had been thinking of going home, and how much she didn't want to. After being at Littlecombe, with all the company and the laughter and the clean smells, The Watch seemed dark and damp and unwelcoming. Her own home. *Don't move, Mitzy*. So she'd stood for over half an hour with her arms on her head, crossed over her hair, the blood running out of them until at first they tingled, then went numb, and by the end felt like they were made of stone, and no longer belonged to her. But she didn't move a muscle until his pencil went quiet. This always marked the end – for a while his hand kept moving, making sweeping gestures over the page, but the pencil no longer touched – it simply moved, like a third eye, inspecting. Then at last his hand stopped too, and he frowned, and it was done; and Dimity felt that cold, tumbling feeling inside each time – the feeling of something wonderful ceasing, and the longing for it to resume. She'd had no inkling then, of what was to come. She hadn't seen the darkness gathering; hadn't been prepared for the violence that lay in wait.

4

Zach sat in front of his laptop, surrounded by notes and papers and catalogues, and suddenly realised, almost twenty-four hours later, how neatly Dimity Hatcher had sidestepped his question about Aubrey ever giving her pictures as presents. He was intrigued by her reaction to the picture of Dennis he'd shown her – the way she'd blushed and seemed reluctant to look too long. He opened two magazines and the recent Christie's catalogue to the pages of the Dennis pictures, and set them side by side. He was sitting at a dark, sticky table in the snug of the Spout Lantern, and he'd had two pints of bitter with lunch, which had been a mistake. His head now felt warm and slightly slow. Outside, the sun was a smear of gold over the dusty window glass. He'd been hoping that the alcohol would ease his thoughts; let him make abstract leaps through the stodge of all his notes and come up with a new plan, a plan of brilliant clarity. Instead, his thoughts kept returning to his dad, and his grandpa; and the way the silences between them had sometimes seemed to grow to fill the whole room, the whole house. Grow so heavy and tangible that Zach would squirm and twist and find it impossible to sit still; until finally he would be sent to his room, or into the garden. He remembered the way his grandpa would criticise all the time, and find fault, and how crestfallen his dad would look with each remark. A bit of car maintenance gone awry; the incorrect decanting of wine; a critical school report for Zach. Zach couldn't count the number of times he caught his mum glaring blackly at his father. *Why don't you ever stand up to him?* Then his father would be the one to twist and fidget in discomfort.

'Pete's sent me over because your long face is putting off the punters.' Hannah Brock was standing by his table with a pint in her hand and a nonchalant air. Surprised, Zach sat up straighter, and was momentarily lost for words. Hannah took a swig from her pint and gestured at the piles of paper and files surrounding him. 'What is all this? Your book?' She tapped the nearest catalogue with her fingertips, and Zach noticed a bold stripe of dirt under each of her nails.

'One day it will be. Maybe. If I can ever get my head around it all.'

'Mind if I sit down?'

'Not at all.'

'There are plenty of books about Charles Aubrey already, aren't there? Can't you just copy one of them?' She gave a wolfish sort of grin.

'Oh, I've done all that. When I started this thing years ago, I read them all, then all his letters, then I went to all the places where he'd been – born, grew up, educated, lived, worked et cetera, et cetera. And after I did all that I realised that my book . . . my book, which was going to be all new and essential and visceral . . .'

'Was exactly the same as all the other books?'

'Precisely.'

'So what's brought you here now, to finish it?' she asked.

'It seemed to be the best place,' he said. He looked at her, curiously. 'You're very interested all of a sudden, for some-body who didn't even want to give me the time of day before.' Hannah smiled and drank again. She was already halfway down her pint.

'Well, I've decided you can't be all bad. Dimity's a pretty good judge of these things, and you've managed to talk your way in there. Perhaps I was a little . . .'

'Hostile and rude?' He smiled.

'Suspicious, before. But, you know, a lot of people come and go from here. People on holiday, people with weekend homes, or summer homes. People with Aubrey fixations.' She flicked her eyes at Zach. 'It's hard on the people who live here. You invest time and energy getting to know people, welcoming them, then off they go again. After a while, you stop bothering.'

'Dimity told me that your family had lived here for generations.'

'That's right. My great-grandparents bought the farm at the turn of the last century,' said Hannah. 'So, what else did she tell you about me?' Zach hesitated before answering.

'That . . . you lost your husband, some time ago.' He glanced up but her face was calm, unruffled. 'And that you're working really, really hard to keep the farm going.'

'Well, that's true enough, God only knows.'

'But not today?' He smiled again, as she drained her glass.

'Well, some days the sheep are all out eating grass without a care in the world, the to-do list is as long as your arm and the coffers are full of cobwebs, and there really is nothing else you can do but get pissed at lunchtime.' She stood up and nodded at his pint, barely a third empty. 'Another?'

While she was at the bar, Zach stared at the pictures of Dennis again, and wondered at her change in demeanour. Possibly it was as innocent a reversal as she'd explained – he hoped so. Dennis. Three young men, all similar, all sweet, all with an air of goodness and innocence that was childlike, as though the artist had been keen to prove that here was a person who had never had a base thought in all their life. Never bullied anyone, or taken advantage of another person's weakness. Never acted selfishly or deceitfully in pursuit of lust or envy or financial gain. But he just could not get away from the notion that there was something wrong with them. Each face was minutely, subtly different; either physically or emotionally. As if they were three different young men, not the same one. Either three different young men, drawn by Aubrey and all called Dennis; or else the same young man drawn three times, by somebody other than Aubrey. Neither option made much sense. He ran his hands through his hair in confusion and wondered if he was cracking up. Nobody else seemed to have any doubts about their authenticity.

Zach checked the information in the front of the Christie's brochure. The sale was in eight days' time, viewing had been two days ago. He knew a member of the fine art team at the auction house – Paul Gibbons, who'd been at Goldsmiths with him. Another artist who had sidestepped from trying to make a living selling his own art to making a living selling other peoples'. Zach had already tried to discover the identity of the vendor of the recent Aubrey pictures from Paul, and been told in no uncertain terms that strict anonymity was a condition of sale. Now he wrote Paul a quick email to ask if there was some way he could get in touch with any of the people who'd bought one of the portraits of Dennis. It was a long shot, he knew, but there was a chance that seeing the work in the flesh might provide some extra insight.

'Who's that?' said Hannah, looking at the catalogue as she sat back down and passed Zach another pint, even though he'd refused her offer. 'Drink up,' she said.

'Therein lies the mystery,' Zach said, and took several gulps from his glass. Suddenly, getting drunk at lunchtime with this hard, vibrant woman, who smelled of sheep but swam in a red bikini, seemed like as good a plan as any. 'Dennis. No other name, no reference to him in any of Aubrey's letters or in any of the books about him.'

'Is that a big deal?'

'Most definitely. Aubrey was faddy, obsessive; he fell in love with something – a place or a person, or an idea – and he painted and drew that thing or person exhaustively, until he'd got everything from it he could, creatively. Then he . . .'

'Dumped them?'

'Moved on. Artistically speaking. And during that time of immersion he wrote about them in letters, and sometimes in his workbook. Letters to friends, or other artists, or his agent. Listen to this one he wrote about Dimity – I must show her this, actually. I think she'd be pleased. Listen.' He scrabbled around in his notes for a moment, until he found the page he was looking for, marked with a pink paper tag. 'This is a letter to one of his patrons, Sir Henry Ides. *I have met the most wonderful child here in Dorset. She seems to have been raised half wild, and has never left this village in all her young life. Her whole sphere of reference is the village and the coast within a five mile radius of the cottage where she grew up. She is untouched, in every sense, and this innocence radiates from her like light. A rare bird indeed, and quite the loveliest thing I have ever seen. She draws the eye the way a splendid view will, or a lance of sunshine breaking through clouds. I enclose a sketch. I plan a large canvas with this girl to embody the essence of nature, or English folk at their very core.*' Zach looked up, and Hannah raised an eyebrow.

'I don't think you should show that to Dimity.'

'Why not?'

'It'll upset her. She has her own memories and . . . ideas about what passed between her and Charles. I don't think it would sit well to hear herself described so objectively.'

'But . . . he says she's the loveliest thing he's ever seen.'

'That's not the same as being in love with her, though, is it?'

'You don't think he was?'

'I don't know. How should I know? Maybe he was. I'm just saying that that's not what he's saying in this letter, is it? I wouldn't show it to her, but it's up to you,' she said.

'I think it shows love. But perhaps not *that* kind of love . . . She ignited his . . . his creative zeal. She was his muse, for a while. A long while. But this Dennis . . . he never mentions him. And when I showed Dimity one of these pictures of him, she said she'd never seen him before, and didn't know who he was. It just strikes me as . . . very odd.'

'Aubrey was only here two or three months of the year, you know. This young man could be someone he met during any one of the remaining ten months, somewhere other than here . . .' She trailed off as Zach shook his head.

'Look at the dates. July 1937; then February and August 1939. We know Aubrey was here in July 1937, in London in February 1939, and here and in Morocco in August 1939. So, did this Dennis travel with him? From Blacknowle, or from London? Surely if Aubrey knew him well enough to take him on holiday, there'd be mention of him somewhere? But that's not the only weird thing. These three pictures all came from an anonymous collection in Dorset. All from the same seller. But I don't think . . . I don't think they're by Charles Aubrey. There's something just not quite right about them.' He slid them towards Hannah but she barely glanced at them. A tiny frown had appeared between her brows. She pushed the catalogues away from her.

'Does it really matter?' she said.

'Does it matter?' Zach echoed, louder than he'd intended. He realised he was definitely quite drunk. 'Of course it does,' he said, more quietly. 'Wouldn't Dimity know? Shouldn't she know who this Dennis is, if these drawings were done by Aubrey here in Blacknowle? She says she spent as much time as she could with him and his family . . .'

'But that doesn't mean she was there *all* the time, or that she knew *everything* he was doing. She was just a kid, remember?'

'Yes, but . . .'

'And if you don't think Charles Aubrey drew these, who do you think did? You think they're forgeries?' she asked, lightly.

'They could be. And yet . . . and yet, the shading, the draughtsmanship . . .' He trailed off, bewildered. Hannah seemed to think hard, and tapped her fingernails on the page of one of the catalogues for a moment; a rapid little staccato that, just for a second, betrayed some kind of agitation. Then she stopped, and curled the hand into a loose fist when Zach spoke again. 'I think,' he said, still lost in thought, 'I think these pictures were here, in Blacknowle, before they were sold. And I think there could be more of them.'

'That's a big theory. You mean Dimity, I take it? You think Mitzy Hatcher is a skilled enough artist to forge Aubrey works so that they could pass as genuine?'

'Well, maybe not. Aubrey must have given her the pictures, then . . . or perhaps she took them for herself. That would explain why she's so cagey about certain things . . .'

'Come on, Zach. Mitzy? Little old Mitzy with the dowager's hump? Does she really live like someone with a hidden stash of priceless artworks?'

'Well, no, not at all. But if she really needed the money, she might have started to sell a few of them . . . she'd be reluctant to, of course. She would want to keep anything with connections to him.'

'And she just nips out and takes them up to London from time to time, and makes thousands?'

'Well . . .' Zach struggled. 'When you put it like that, it doesn't sound too probable. But she could phone the auction house and get them to send a courier for them, or something.'

'It doesn't sound probable because it's wholly improbable. She doesn't even have a phone, Zach. And there are loads of big houses tucked away around here – any one of them would be far more likely to have an art collection like that. What makes you even think they're in Blacknowle?'

'It was . . . kind of just a hunch.'

'Or wishful thinking, perhaps?'

'Maybe,' said Zach, deflated.

'You know what I think?' she said.

'What?'

'I think you should stop chewing it over for now and drink more of the Spout Lantern's finest.' She raised her glass to salute him before downing the last of her own. Zach smiled woozily at her.

'Just what is a spout lantern, anyway?' he said. Hannah turned in her seat and pointed up at a rusty metal object on a high shelf, amidst green glass floats and old fishing nets, and he recognised it as the kind of distorted watering can that was on the pub's sign.

'Smuggler's lamp,' she explained. 'There's a little oil lamp in the main body of it, but the light is only visible if you're standing directly in front of the spout. A single beam of light, great for signalling and guiding a boat ashore . . .'

'I see, like a laser beam, eighteenth-century style.'

'Precisely. So, tell me something about the wider world. I don't get out much,' Hannah said, with a smile.

They talked for a while about the gallery and about Elise, and touched lightly on the subject of missing spouses, although Hannah would not be drawn to talk about her husband other than to give his name as Toby. She paused after she said it, as if that single word had the power to rob her of speech. Zach wondered if his body had been recovered, or if he was lost at sea, washed away like so many before him. He had a sudden idea that chilled him. That when Hannah swam, she was looking for him. He remembered the way she had dived, again and again, swimming as much below the surface as above it. He sensed that she was determined enough, resolute enough for this. Strong enough to keep searching, years later, for something she'd lost beneath the waves.

'Do you swim in winter? In the sea, I mean?' he asked.

'Talk about your non-sequitur. Yes. I swim all year round. It's good for you, clears out all the junk.' She looked at him curiously. 'In case you're picturing it, I have a wetsuit for the winter months.' Her tone was wry.

'No! No, I wasn't picturing it. I . . . Good idea though – a wetsuit. Must be freezing otherwise.'

'It'd make your bollocks jump right back up inside your body,' she said, dolefully, then grinned. 'Luckily, I don't have to worry about that.' They laughed, rather drunkenly.

'Hannah, have you ever seen anyone else at Dimity's place? I've heard these odd noises, coming from upstairs,' said Zach. She stopped laughing at once, as suddenly as hitting a brick wall. She stared into her glass for a moment, and Zach retraced his verbal steps, trying to work out what he'd said wrong.

'No. No, as far as I know, nobody else ever goes there,' Hannah said. There was an uneasy pause, then she stood up unsteadily. 'I should really be getting back. Things to do, you know. Down on the farm.'

'What can you do after all that beer? Stay and finish your pint at least. We don't have to talk about . . .' But he trailed off as Hannah turned to go. She looked back, and her delicate features were serious now, and steady. Her eyes looked sharp, not drunk at all, and Zach felt like a fool.

'Come down to the farm, if you want to, another day. I'll show you around. If you're interested, that is.' She shrugged one shoulder and walked away, leaving Zach with the beer she'd been drinking and her empty seat, and a sudden, unexpected sense of loss at her absence. Pete appeared and gathered up the empty glasses.

'You look a bit green around the gills.' He shook his head incredulously. 'It's a foolish man that tries to out-drink Hannah Brock. What did you say to her to make her march off like that? Usually once she's had two pints she's here till closing time.'

'I don't know. I really don't,' said Zach, mystified.

Something had hold of Dimity's throat, gripping tightly, and for once it wasn't Valentina. In the night she'd dreamt of the moment Charles Aubrey and his family left, at the end of that first summer. She'd known that they would leave, Delphine had told her so, yet she hadn't prepared herself for it. She'd been daydreaming about going with them to the harvest home, when there was a huge fête on the village green after the church service; a band and bunting and songs and games. Apple pies that smelled divine. Wilf Coulson had fetched one for her the year before, bringing it to where she was hiding behind a tent, enveloped in the heady, exciting smell of canvas – a once a year smell of something different, something fun. Dimity had always longed to be able to walk around the fête like everyone else; buy a hop garland and play all the games – skittles, splat the rat, the coconut shy – rather than watching from a hidden place.

Valentina never went to the harvest home; never wanted to go. She curled her lip, sneered at the idea. *I've no need to watch them play merry-go-bloody-rounds, like they're all so good and wholesome.* Every year she made Dimity spend some time circulating with a tray hanging around her neck, selling posies and charms and tonics. Valentina's famous gypsy beauty balm, guaranteed to halt the signs of ageing – a sticky mix of lard and cold cream, scented with elderflowers and infused with red dock root for its regenerative properties; or her Romany balm, an arcane brew of the fat from a pig's kidney, horse hoof clippings, house leek and elder bark; known to cure any kind of skin complaint, boil or bruise. The village kids all followed her, calling her names and throwing nuggets of dung, knowing that she couldn't chase or fight back, not with the heavy tray swinging in front of her. But the Aubreys weren't afraid of the people of Blacknowle, even if people did whisper that Celeste was his mistress, not his wife; even if they did put their noses up slightly and pretend to disapprove. People still accepted them, and were polite to them. They couldn't help themselves. Charles was too charming, and Celeste too beautiful; and their daughters were so safe and happy that they didn't even notice it when the publican's wife's lips pinched up the way they did.

Dimity was plucking two pigeons when she heard the news she so didn't want to hear. She pulled out the feathers a pinch at a time, her fingers moving slowly so she wouldn't finish before Charles had done his drawing. She was facing him, sitting cross-legged with the dead birds in her lap. She'd tied her hair back, but she knew there were still tiny feathers caught up in it. She could see one, hovering at the edge of her vision, up above her eyebrows. A tiny grey feather that trembled in the still air. When she looked up at it she could snatch a look at Charles too. The intensity of his gaze frightened her at first. He sometimes looked so stern that she expected to be scolded. But gradually she realised that he wasn't even aware of her gaze. She let her eyes linger on his face, fascinated. A deep crease marked the bridge of his nose, and as the sun sank west that nose threw a dark, pointed shadow onto his cheek. The cheek had a slight hollow below the ridge of bone around his eye, making a steep line to his jaw, which was long and angular. Studying it like this, she came to know his face every bit as well, perhaps even better, than she knew her own; than she knew Delphine's, or Valentina's. There were few times when it was acceptable, or possible, to examine someone for such a length of time.

That day she fell into a kind of trance, because the sun came around to the side of them, creeping slowly, silently, until it lit Charles's right eye and made the iris flare with bright browns and golden tones. Like a jewel of some kind, or a precious metal. Behind him the sea was a silvery blur, and the short turf she was sitting on was soft and springy; the sky was a vast dome of chalky blue studded with gulls like the daisies on a lawn. Dimity's fingers went still, stopped plucking, because she didn't want the world to turn any more, or time to move on from that exact moment. Warm and still, with Charles's topaz eyes fixed upon her, and Delphine digging her little vegetable patch behind her, and Celeste cooking with Élodie – something that she could just about smell on the air, drifting towards them. Something savoury and delicious, something she would be asked to share.

But she wasn't, in the end. She was given a piece to take home, with her two shillings for Valentina – her sitter's fee from Charles. Celeste came out with the pie wrapped up in tough brown paper, wearing one of her long dresses again, a pale cream colour with long, swinging sleeves, belted in at the waist with a plaited cord. She smiled her wide, lovely smile at Dimity, then ruined everything.

'Time for you to go home now, Mitzy.' She walked around behind Charles, let her hand rub his shoulder, and stay to rest there. Dimity blinked.

'Am . . . am I not to stay for supper then?' she asked. Charles put up a hand to rub his eyes, as if he too were waking from a dream. How perfect it had been, Dimity thought sadly. How perfect.

'Well, we leave for London tomorrow, so I think tonight we shall be just family, the four of us. On our last night.' Celeste's smiled faded as chagrin bloomed across Dimity's face.

'You're leaving . . . tomorrow?' she said. *Just family*. 'But I don't want you to,' she said, the words coming out louder and wilder than she'd intended. She took a deep breath, and it hurt her chest.

'Well, we must. The girls must go back to school soon. Delphine! Come and say goodbye to Mitzy!' Celeste called to her eldest daughter, who stood up, wiped her hands on the seat of her slacks and came over to them. Stiffly, Dimity struggled to her feet. She was breathing quickly, and for the first time in weeks, she didn't know how to behave with them. She couldn't look up; kept her eyes fixed on the grass and saw that it was peppered with rabbit pellets.

'Can't she stay for dinner? It is the last night, after all,' said Delphine, squinting up at her mother.

'Because it is the last night, I'm afraid not. Say goodbye now.' Charles handed her the coins, and brushed his knuckles lightly against her shoulder.

'Thank you, Mitzy,' he said, smiling softly. Celeste pressed the packet of pie into her hands, and Dimity felt the warmth of it through the paper. She felt like throwing it back at her. Throwing the money at Charles, throwing a curse at Delphine. Something was building up inside her, gathering strength. She didn't know what it was, except that she didn't trust it, so even as Delphine was talking she turned on her heel and fled.

Dimity stayed out very late, sitting in the thick hedgerow

that enclosed the track to The Watch as the blackbirds' resonant song gradually petered out, and the sun buried itself behind the swell of the land. An invisible fist had clenched itself around her throat, and there was a stone in her gut. A stone of dread, at the thought of waking up the next morning and knowing that they were gone. She hadn't even asked if they would be back the next year; hadn't dared to ask, in case the answer was no. Having them there, having their company, even petulant Élodie, had made everything else more bearable. She cried for a long time, because being left behind felt a little like being laughed at in the schoolroom; like having stones thrown; like waiting in the dark for someone to notice her. A little like all of those things, but worse. Eventually she got up, walked down to the front door and let herself in. She had the pie and the plucked pigeons to placate Valentina, not to mention the shillings; and the scolding she got was a routine one. Valentina even took her by the shoulders afterwards, fingers digging in, and ran narrowed eyes over her daughter.

'You've feathers in your hair, little dicky bird,' she said, patting Dimity's cheek in what was as close as she ever came to a display of affection. Somehow, this only made things worse, and Dimity went off to find a comb with tears hot and blurry in her eyes once more.

Zach woke up the morning after his boozy lunch to thoughts of Hannah; of her quick, impulsive face and the way it had closed off when he'd asked about the noises upstairs at The Watch. He drank two cups of coffee in quick succession and decided to take her up on the offer of a tour of the farm. On a whim, he picked up his bag of art supplies on his way out. However pleased he'd been to buy them, he'd remained reluctant, as yet, to use them. It had rained hard in the night, hard enough to wake him with the sound of it fretting at the windowpane. Zach's shoes were soon filthy, as he walked inland for a while instead of heading directly towards Southern Farm. The cool breeze felt good on his face and in his lungs, clearing his head and making his limbs feel lighter.

He climbed a steep hill to the copse at its summit. There he turned, and was welcomed by a wide, sweeping view of the coast as it rolled for miles in either direction. A blurred patchwork of green and yellow and grey, sharply delineated by the contrasting colour of the sea. Below him, Blacknowle was toy houses; The Watch a white speck; Southern Farm invisible behind a dip in the land. He perched on the leathery trunk of a fallen beech and took out his sketch pad. *Just draw a line. Just start.* Drawing had once emptied his mind for him, cleared out all the things clamouring for his attention and let him see a clear way ahead. Reassured by his own talent, in this thing that he was able to do. At Goldsmiths, his tutors had always urged him to draw and paint more; to be true to his abilities, rather than rebelling against them. At the time, he'd been too caught up in appearances to heed their advice.

Zach drew a line; the horizon. He stopped. How could he have got it wrong? The horizon was a line – a straight one; bright with light, immobile. The line he had drawn was straight, gentle. And yet it was wrong. He stared at it, trying to work out why, and eventually decided that he had put it too high up the page. The picture would be unbalanced – there should be an even split between land and water and sky; a pleasing trio, layered one after the other with satis-fying natural rhythm, and by putting the horizon where he had, he'd cramped the sky, robbed it of all sense of space and volume. With one single pencil line, he had ruined the drawing. Shutting his sketchbook in disgust, Zach set off for Southern Farm.

Hannah was in one of the fields near the lane, climbing out of her jeep and opening up the tailgate. A small flock of cappuccino-coloured sheep puttered at her heels, clearly eager for whatever she was bringing them. They all had thin, ridged horns curling back from their heads, which clattered together as they crowded in. Zach waved, and with a high sweep of her arm Hannah beckoned him in, so he climbed the gate and went over to her, dodging piles of fresh sheep shit. She was lifting slices of hay out of the jeep and strewing it into wire mangers. On the back seat of the jeep, a grey and white border collie was watching the flock, ears pricked and eyes alight.

'Good morning. Is now a good time for that tour you promised me?' he said, as he reached her.

'Sure. Just let me get this lot fed, and I'm all yours.' Hannah gave him a quick, appraising glance that made him feel slightly conspicuous; an odd, long-absent flutter of nerves. Then she grinned at him.

'How was your head this morning?' she asked.

'Rotten, thanks to you,' he said.

'Not my fault. How could I have forced you to drink if you didn't want to? I'm just a tiny little woman,' she said, archly.

'Somehow I doubt you've ever had much trouble getting people to do what you want them to.'

'Well, depends on the person. And on what I want them to do,' she said, shrugging slightly.

There was a pause as she went back to the jeep for more hay.

'I thought sheep only needed hay in the winter?' said Zach.

'Then, too. But there's not much grass left for them at this time of year, and these ladies will be lambing soon, so they need plenty of sustenance.' There was hay in Hannah's hair, and all over her jumper. Tight grey jeans, smudged with grime.

'I thought lambs came in spring.'

'They usually do, unless you give the ewes hormones to shift their cycle. But these girls are Portlands. An old rare breed – they can lamb pretty much whenever you like. That way you can get organic lamb ready for spring, when people bizarrely expect to see brand new lambs out gambolling in fields full of buttercups and also to have six-month-old lamb ready for their Easter roast at the same time,' she said. Zach helped her right one of the mangers, which had got knocked over onto its side. It left mud and sheep manure on his hands.

'Yuck,' he said absently, holding his fingers splayed in front of him and trying to think where he could wipe them. Hannah glanced at him and grinned.

'You're a real man of the land, aren't you?' she said. 'Bet you don't notice when your hands are covered in paint.'

'Paint doesn't come out of a sheep's arse,' Zach pointed out.

'Oh, it's only half-digested grass. There are far worse chemicals in paint. Here, use this.' She handed him a twist of hay from the back of the jeep, and he wiped his hands on it gratefully. 'Come on, hop in. I'll rush you to some hot water and soap.' They climbed into the car and she knocked it into gear, pulling away with a slither and spin of mud from the wheels. 'So it begins. Season of mud and cold water,' she muttered. 'I hate winter.'

'It's still only September.'

'I know. But it's all downhill from here.'

'So the farm's organic, is it?' said Zach.

'It is. It will be, if I can ever get through the testing and certification process.'

'Long-winded?'

'Unbelievable. Everything has to be organic and proven and tested – from the veterinary treatment they get, to the hay, to the way I treat the hides after slaughter. It costs hundreds and hundreds of pounds every year to keep it up – just to be a member of the right organisations, and have the right checks done at the right times. But come the spring there should be lamb in the chiller, ready to send out; fully tanned sheepskins ready to sell; and a website where you can actually order things, rather than just look at nice pictures of Portland sheep.' She paused, hopping out of the jeep to shut a gate behind them. They crossed a chalk track, the smooth surface of it sliding like glue after the rain. 'Either that or I'll have gone bust and be living in a caravan in a lay-by somewhere,' she said, with forced jollity.

'So why bother with the whole organic thing? Why not just grow a load of sheep as cheaply as you can?'

'Because it doesn't work. That's what my father did, all his life. But however cheaply I can raise a sheep, the price I'd have to sell it at would be too low to make a living. I haven't got enough land to raise a huge flock. And I haven't got enough help to run things on such a scale. The only chance to keep the place running is to specialise. Do something different, get a name for excellence in one particular thing.'

'Organic Portland lamb?'

'Exactly. And not just spring lamb, old season lamb – and the mutton is excellent too. Very lean, full of flavour. And the fleeces from the shearlings are softer than a baby's bum. But . . .' She tipped her head to one side, and in spite of the airy way she spoke, there was anxiety around her eyes.

'But?'

'I have to survive the winter, until this first crop of lambs are old enough to slaughter. And I have to get the bloody organic certificate in place, like yesterday.'

'So you're right at the beginning of this whole venture, really.'

'Either the beginning or the end, depending on how optimistic I happen to be feeling that day,' she said, with a quick smile. 'Toby and I tried to work the old flock – we tried for five years to scrape by with it. I sold the last of them the year he died. Then it took me a while to work out what the hell I was doing.'

'But you've figured it out now, by the sounds of it.'

'Well, Ilir came along. Not much use having a man about the place when there was no livestock and nothing to do but watch the place crumble. He kind of gave me the boot up the behind that I needed.'

'Yes. Important for a man to be useful,' Zach said quietly, feeling a flare of pointless hostility towards the blameless Ilir.

The jeep bounced and slithered up the track onto the concrete yard, and this time Zach was quick enough to get out to open and close the gate before Hannah could. She roared the engine to a halt outside the farmhouse and opened the front door for him with a heave of her shoulder and a kick to the bottom edge of it.

'The cloakroom's the first door on the right. And if you say one word about my housekeeping I'll knock you down, just see if I don't,' she said. The inside of the farmhouse was filthy. Not just untidy, not just in need of hoovering. Properly filthy. Zach picked his way over mounds of discarded rags, bits of rope and bailer twine, wisps of straw, empty milk bottles and odd implements he couldn't guess at the function of. There was a plastic dog bed that had been chewed into a strange, stippled sculpture; the blanket inside grey with accumulated hair. A log pile against one wall had shed a wide halo of sawdust and bark and dead woodlice all over the floor, and when Zach looked up in horror, the high ceiling was strung about with blackened cobwebs like some kind of macabre bunting. The basin in the cloakroom had the cracked, half-dissolved remains of several bars of soap slumped around the taps, but the water was hot and he managed to scrape some soap from the heap with his fingernails. He washed his hands quickly then glanced along the corridor to the next room.

The kitchen – every bit as ripe with sheep and dog as the inside of the jeep had been. A tabby cat was asleep on the range cooker; every surface was covered in plates, pans and packaging. A bottle of milk had been left out by the kettle, and a housefly was feasting on the yellow crust around its lip. A vast oak refectory table was piled high with accounts, printouts, ledgers and old newspapers. Zach looked at the dirty crockery for a while, and only moments later realised what he was looking for, and what he was indeed seeing: pairs of things. Two wine glasses with purple stains at the bottom, two coffee mugs, two plates with the bones of what might have been pork chops on them. Evidence that Ilir shared the house with Hannah. There was a sudden bang and the sound of footsteps coming down the stairs at the far end of the room. Zach's pulse gave a lurch and he turned on his heel, dodging back along the corridor as fast as he could, and out onto the yard.

Hannah was looking at something on the bonnet of the jeep, and the way she jumped reminded Zach of himself, seconds earlier. She'd been looking through his sketchbook, and now she closed it with a defiant expression and a tilt of her chin, as if refusing to be embarrassed at being caught out.

'Find everything you needed?' she said. Zach folded his arms and smiled, glancing at his sketchbook on the bonnet.

'Yes thanks. Lovely house.'

'Thanks. I grew up in that house.'

'You must have an incredible immune system,' he said, and struggled to keep a straight face.

'Careful, now. I did warn you.' Hannah balled her fists for a second, but her expression was amused. She gestured at his sketchbook. 'I didn't mean to pry. I just didn't want you to leave your bag behind in the jeep. And, you know . . . the curiosity of a fellow artist and all that . . . But don't worry – I don't really feel like I've seen into your soul,' she said. He thought of the only drawing he'd done so far – his failed attempt earlier that morning.

'I was trying to draw the view from the top of the hill,' he admitted.

'And that's as far as you got?'

'I think I may have . . . lost my mojo,' he said. She looked at him shrewdly, eyes screwed up against a sudden flare of sunshine.

'Is that so?' she murmured, not unkindly. Zach held his ground, but could think of no succinct way to elaborate. 'Well, I always think it helps to remember why you're drawing the thing you're drawing. Why did you climb the hill and try to draw the view, for example?'

'Um . . . I don't really know. Because it was beautiful?'

'But was it? Did you decide to draw it because it was beautiful, or because you thought it ought to be? Because you thought it was the sort of thing you should want to draw?'

'I'm not sure.'

'Stop to ask yourself next time. You might not get the answer you thought you would.'

'I'm not sure I know what I want to draw any more.'

'Then perhaps try to think about why as well. Or in other words, who. Think about who you're drawing it for. That might help,' she suggested.

'Why did you run out on me the other day?' he asked,

surprising himself. Hannah handed Zach's sketchbook back to him with a cautious smile.

'I didn't run out.'

'Come on. Yes, you did. It was when I asked about there being anybody else at The Watch.'

'No, no, I just had to get on, that was all. Really. There's nobody else at The Watch. I know that much for a fact.'

'Have you been upstairs there?'

'Hey – I thought you wanted a tour of the farm, not to quiz me about my neighbours?' She started to turn away but Zach put out his hand and caught her arm. He dropped it again at once, startled by the thinness of the limb beneath the fabric of her shirt. The warmth of it.

'Please,' he said. 'I was so sure I'd heard somebody moving around up there.'

Hannah seemed to consider carefully before answering.

'I've been upstairs. And there's nobody else living there,' she said. 'Now, do you want the tour or don't you?' She eyed him sternly for a moment, arching her brows, but somehow even her fiercest expressions brought a smile to his lips.

The winter months were a blur of aching fingers and numb, stiffened toes. Dimity had heavy boots, the leather of which was rigid with age and the damage done by winter weather. They were too big for her – they'd been left at The Watch by a visitor, one who had exited swiftly by the back door as the sound of his wife's fist on the front door reverberated through the cottage. He never came back for them, so now the boots were Dimity's. But her socks had worn through at toe and heel, and her repairs rarely lasted longer than a few days. She could feel the gritty innards of the boots through these holes when she walked; they caused blisters to form, then calluses. When she met Wilf Coulson in Barton's hay loft, she would sink down into the loose hay and pull the boots off, rubbing her toes with her hands, massaging heat and movement back into them as best she could.

'I'll do that, if you want. My hands are warmer,' Wilf offered one time, when rain was falling outside in straight rods of chilly grey. Barton kept his cattle in the barn when the weather was as wet as it had been. His fields drained badly, and were churned to an impassable quagmire otherwise. The heat from the cows rose up to infuse the hay loft, along with the sweet, shitty stink of them. Half sunk in the hay, it was possible to feel warm at a time when it seemed like the sun would stay weak and wan for ever.

'It tickles when you do it,' said Dimity, snatching her feet away from his bony hands. She and Wilf were fifteen by then, and he seemed to grow even while she watched him. He was still thin but his shoulders were wider, sharply angular; his face was longer, more serious, heavier across the brows. When he spoke his voice wavered between a soft tenor and a hoarse, ragged squeak.

'Let me try,' he insisted. He took her feet firmly, and she was embarrassed by the dampness of her stringy socks, and the unwashed smell coming from them – imprinted there by the boots' previous owner. Wilf clamped her chilly toes between the palms of his hands and for a blissful moment she felt the heat of him flood into them. She shut her eyes for a second, listening to the rain hammering on the tin roof, and beneath that the shifting and breathing of the cows. She and Wilf were out of sight, out of earshot. Untouchable.

When she opened her eyes again Wilf was looking at her that way. It was appearing more and more frequently, this look of his – intent and serious, mouth a little open. At once vulnerable and threatening, somehow, and in his lap the strain of trouser fabric across the bulge at his crotch. Dimity scowled and snatched her foot away again.

'And what'd your mother say, if she caught you up here with me, then?' she demanded. Wilf frowned and looked down through the barn doors, as if he half expected Ma Coulson to appear on the boggy, rutted mud of the threshold, amidst puddles the colour of tea and pocked by the rain, with her face every bit as grim.

'She'd box my ears and no mistake. No matter that I'm half a head taller than her already,' he said, sullenly. 'She gets crosser every week that passes, my ma.'

'And mine. Last week she belted me one for leaving shit on the eggs when I brought them into the house – never mind that there was hail coming down outside fit to smash them all before I could wipe them.'

'Shame they can't be friends. Or at least meet up and box each other's ears instead of ours.'

'Who do you think would win?' Dimity asked, rolling onto her side and smiling.

'My ma's not afraid to use a stick, if she has to. You should've seen the state of our Brian's behind when she caught him stealing from her purse!'

'Valentina would use whatever she could set her hands on,' Dimity said, falling serious, no longer liking the image of the two women fighting. 'I do think she would kill a person, if they caught her at the wrong moment.' Wilf laughed and threw a handful of hay at her, which Dimity swatted aside crossly. 'I mean it! She would as well.'

'If she laid a hand on you, I would have words with her. No – I would!' Now it was Wilf's turn to insist, when Dimity laughed.

'You would not, for she does lay hands on me, regular as the tide, as you well know. But I don't blame you for it, Wilf Coulson. If I could steer a course right around her, good and wide, I would. When I'm old enough, I will.' She rolled onto her back and held a stalk of hay up in front of her eyes, knotting it as carefully as she could without breaking it.

'Would you marry, then, Mitzy? To be away from her? You could soon enough. If you wanted to. Then you'd never have to go back there again, if you didn't want.' Wilf's voice was so laden with casual curiosity that it shook with the strain.

'Marry? Maybe.' Dimity pulled the knot tighter with a sudden jerk; snapped the stem and threw it to one side. Suddenly, the future rolled out in front of her like a long, unsettling thunderclap. A future that seemed to suffocate her. Her stomach twisted beneath her ribs, and she realised she was afraid. Horribly afraid. She swallowed, determined not to let it show. 'Depends if I meet anybody worthy of marrying, I suppose, don't it?' she said, lightly. There was a long pause. Wilf fiddled with the waistband of his trousers, and his shirt beneath his jumper, which had come untucked.

'I'd marry you,' he muttered. Words pitched so low that the sound of the rain almost swallowed them.

'What?'

'I said, I'd marry you. If you wanted to. Ma'd come around once she got to know you. Once you weren't living down at The Watch no more.'

'Shut up, Wilf – don't talk like an idiot,' said Dimity, to hide her confusion. Better to laugh, better not to take it seriously, in case it proved to be mockery of some kind. A trick, which she did not think Wilf would play, but still could not be sure. Her heart was banging so loudly she was glad of the roaring overhead to hide it.

'I wasn't. I wasn't talking like an idiot,' Wilf mumbled, still examining his clothes, his hands, then gazing across the barn as if the far flint wall, smeared with manure, held some vast and crucial wisdom. Neither of them spoke for some time, and neither could have guessed the other's thoughts.

Eventually the warmth and the steady racket lulled Dimity into a doze, and when she woke a while later, Wilf's head was on her shoulder, one hand resting lightly on her stomach. His eyes were shut but she could sense, somehow, that he was not asleep.

That winter was long, with late snows driving in on bitter north winds, killing off the first green shoots that had dared to show themselves. Dimity's chilblains got so bad that she could hardly stand it; she was forced to sit, shuddering in disgust, with her feet in a basin of piss to cure them. She had a stabbing pain in her ears where the frigid air had seeped into them. There were hardly any visitors, except the two men that Valentina called her bread and butter, and so fewer gifts of food or coins; no sitter's fees earned by Dimity, and far less for her to find, out foraging. They ate the eggs fried in old dripping that tasted bitter and burnt from re-use, on slices of bread that Valentina made herself – she had a rare skill with dough. Dimity thought it was the anger with which she kneaded it. They were both tired, and their skin grew sallow and chapped. Dimity came home from delivering cold remedies to the people of Blacknowle with her lips cracked by the wind, and her fingers curled into reddened claws.

In those deadened days Valentina kept to her bed, vague and listless. There was a knock at the door late one evening, but she wouldn't come down. Dimity peeped out around the door in the end, because the man wouldn't stop knocking. She didn't recognise him. His face was dark, pitted and lined, with ragged black stubble all over his cheeks. His eyes were watery and grey.

'What about you? You'll do. I was told this was the place to come,' he said, in a hoarse, reedy voice, when Dimity told him Valentina wasn't available for guests. She stared at him in shock, frozen.

'No, sir. Not tonight,' she said, softly. But he gave the door a shove, caught her around the waist and pushed against her with all his strength, pinning her with the doorframe biting into her back. He dropped one hand down, ground it hard between her legs.

'Not tonight, she says? Filthy teasing harlot . . . Come on, the apple never falls far from the tree,' he rasped into her face, and Dimity cried out in fear and surprise. His breath reeked of fish and beer.

'Ma!' she shouted out in panic. '*Ma!*' And against all odds Valentina appeared on the stairs, her face clogged with sleep but such a fire of rage in her eyes that the man put Dimity down and was already backing away when she fell on him, raining blows and hurling curses that would shock a sailor. The stranger scurried away up the track, muttering furiously all the way.

Afterwards they lay down together, in Valentina's bed. Dimity wasn't usually allowed into her room, with its veiled lamps and pink candlewick bedspread, but that night they lay down and Valentina wrapped herself around her daughter, lying close like two spoons. She didn't stroke her hair, or sing, or speak. But when she saw that Dimity's hands were shaking, she clasped one in her own hand, tightly, and didn't relax her grip even when she fell asleep. The skin of her palm was tough and smooth, like leather. Dimity stayed awake for hours, her heart still bumping from the shock of the man's rough touch, and from the alien unfamiliarity of Valentina's embrace. She welcomed it, though, enjoying the warmth that grew between their two bodies, the feeling of safety married so uneasily with the knowledge that it all might end at any second. Which it did, come morning. Valentina woke her abruptly, with a slap on the thigh. *Get out of my bed, you useless lump. Go and make breakfast.*

Then, on a glorious day in mid-April, spring blew in off

the sea on a warm breeze as sweet as the taste of ripe strawberries. Such a blessed relief that Dimity laughed, out loud and all alone, standing on the cliff path on the way back from Lulworth with a bag full of sprats and a bottle of cider vinegar in which to cook them. The sea shimmered with life and the land looked up at it, like some great animal befuddled by the cold, slowly coming out of deep sleep. Dimity thought she could hear the sap rising, fizzing up into the trees and the grass like a massive inward breath, held, poised for the flourish of summer. Sap rose in the men of Blacknowle and its surrounding farms too, and sent them to knock on the door of The Watch, so that suddenly the residents of that cottage were surrounded by abundance. But it wasn't the food or the warmth that Dimity yearned for the most. Even the welcome touch of the sunshine couldn't fill the space in the world that the Aubreys had left when they departed. Dimity longed for the summer because she longed for them to come back. She longed for their bright chatter and their affection, the way their love for each other spread out around them, and the way she had been allowed to step into that world, and be part of it. She longed to see them, so that she wouldn't be invisible any more.

5

Dimity blinked, and hummed a little in her throat, and Zach roused himself from reverie. The silence had grown so long as she'd studied the picture that his attention had wandered, and he'd let himself notice the isolated grains of sand on the floor, glinting in a shaft of sunlight; the gentle sound of the sea coming down the chimney with a faint, tunnelling echo to it; a huge, thin spider sitting as still as an etching between the beams above his head, surrounded by the tiny, speckled cloud of her young. In the old woman's hand was a piece of paper, a colour printout Zach had made, borrowing Pete Murray's computer, of a large oil canvas of Mitzy standing amidst mossy ruins, so highly textured by the dappled light that she seemed a part of the forest, a part of the land, like some mythical creature merging with the hues and foliage around her. There was a gargoyle above her head, distorted and ill-defined, but it seemed to have her face; an echo in stone of the same lovely girl standing beneath it. Dimity's mouth moved again and this time words almost formed, so Zach cleared his throat.

'Dimity? Are you all right?'

'He did so many sketches, up at that chapel. That's St Gabriel's chapel, the haunted one. He couldn't decide what was best, how I should stand. For three weeks we walked to and fro, to and fro. We trod the path up the hill deeper than it ever had been, I reckon. One day I got so tired, standing still for so long, and with my belly rumbling as I'd had no time for breakfast – he wanted the early morning light, he said – that my head started spinning and everything wobbled in my ears and the light went dark, and before I knew what was what I was on the ground and he was cradling my head, my Charles, like I was a precious thing . . .'

'You fainted?'

'Dead away. I reckon he was half annoyed at me for moving for a moment, till he realised I'd swooned!' She laughed a little, rocking back in her chair, clasping her hands together and raising them up. The paper flapped like a solitary wing. Zach smiled, and fingered the notebook across his knees.

'That was in 1938, is that right? The year before he went off to the war.'

'Yes. That year . . . I think that was my happiest time . . .' Her words faded to a whisper, then to nothing. Her eyes shone for a moment, frozen and still. She dropped the printout of the painting and her fingers went to the ends of her long plait, stroking, rolling. 'Charles was happy too. I remember it. I begged him not to go, the year after that . . . I wanted us to always be that happy . . .'

'It must have been hard . . . with such a recent death in the family, and under such tragic circumstances. So much upheaval,' said Zach. For a moment Dimity didn't answer, and there was a pause, but instead of her gaze falling into the past, Zach saw rapid thoughts flying across her face. Her mouth fell open slightly, thin lips parting, and she held the tip of her tongue between her front teeth. Keeping it still, until the right words were ready.

'It was a . . . terrible time. For Charles. For all of us. He was going to leave them, you see. Leave her to be with me. And then when it happened, he felt very guilty, you see.'

'But nobody blamed him for what happened, surely?'

'Yes, some did. Some did. Because he was an older man, and me still so young. Young in my body, perhaps, but I had an old soul. I always thought that – even when I was a child, I never felt like one. I think we only stay children if people let us, and nobody let me. There was talk, you see – about sin begetting sin. *As ye sow, so shall ye reap.* I heard Mrs Lamb up at the pub say that to him one night, as he was walking past. As though by loving me, he was causing bad things to happen. Bringing punishment on himself. But he was never wed to Celeste, you know. He broke no vows to her, by loving me.'

'I never thought Charles Aubrey would be bothered about what people said about him. He never seemed to mind much the rest of the time. About society, and convention, I mean.' At this Dimity frowned, and looked down at her fingertips, the split wisps of her hair. Zach saw her draw in a long breath, as if to steady herself.

'No. He was a free man, truly. Guided only by his heart.'

'And yet . . . I've always been bewildered by his decision to go off to the war,' said Zach. 'He was an ideological pacifist, after all, and he still had responsibilities. People who needed him – like you, and Delphine . . . Do you know why he went? Did he ever explain it to you?'

Dimity seemed unsure how to answer him, and though it seemed for a while that she would, in the end the silence stretched and her face grew anxious, suffused with all the mute desperation of a child at the front of the class who has been told they may not sit until the equation is solved.

'He went off to war because . . .' Tears gleamed in the corners of her eyes. Shocked, Zach stayed silent. 'I don't know why! I've never known. I'd have done anything to keep him here with me, anything he asked. And everything I did, I did for him. *Everything.* Even . . . even . . .' She shook her head. 'But he was in London when he went, when he joined the army. He went from London, not from here, so I didn't get a chance to stop him. And . . . I never told her!'

'Never told who, Dimity?'

'Delphine! I never told her that . . . that it wasn't her fault!'

'That what wasn't her fault? Dimity, I don't understand . . . it was Delphine's fault that he went to war?'

'No! No, it was . . .' She broke off, tears making the words thick and unintelligible. Zach reached over to her and took her hands.

'Dimity, I'm sorry, I . . . I didn't mean to upset you, really. Please, forgive me.' He squeezed her hands to distract her, but she kept her face turned to the floor, with tears running down the creases in her skin to gather along her jaw. She rocked herself a little, back and forth, and made a quiet keening sound, a sound of such profound sadness that Zach could hardly stand it. 'Please don't cry, Dimity. Please don't. I'm sorry. Listen, I don't understand what you're telling me about Delphine, and about the war. Can you explain it to me?' Gradually, Dimity's sobbing eased, and she fell still.

'No,' she croaked then. 'No more talking. I . . . can't. I can't talk about him dying. And I can't talk about . . . about Delphine.' She turned her face to him, and it was raw with emotion. Not just grief, he suddenly saw. He blinked, startled. There was far more there than simple sorrow. It looked for all the world like guilt. 'Please go now. I can't talk any more.'

'All right, I'll go. And we won't talk about the war any more. I promise,' said Zach, even though he knew then, he was *sure*, that Dimity knew far more about what had happened that last summer of Charles Aubrey's life than she was prepared to tell him. 'I'll go, if you're sure you'll be all right? Next time I won't ask you anything. I'll answer *your* questions instead, how about that? You can ask me anything you like about me or my family, and I'll do my best to answer. Deal?' Wiping at her face, Dimity looked up at him, bewildered but growing calmer. In the end she nodded, and Zach squeezed her hands again before he left, bending to put a kiss on her damp cheek.

Outside, the day was blowy and carried the dusty perfume of gorse flowers. Zach took a deep breath and let it out slowly, only then realising how tense he had been, how much Dimity's tears had worried him. He rubbed one hand over his face and shook his head. He had to tread more carefully, be more sensitive; not go blundering in with his questions when it was her life and loss he was asking about, not just some figure from history he had never even met, even if that figure's blood was running in his veins. He wondered whether he might safely raise the subject of Dennis again – who the young man was, and where the collection that his portraits had come from might be. Zach glanced at his watch, and was surprised by how late it was. He had a date with Hannah, and set off towards the beach below Southern Farm to meet her.

Hannah was already on the shore when Zach got there, standing barefoot in the shallows with the hems of her jeans rolled up. She turned and smiled as he approached, folding her arms for warmth.

'I was going to swim, but I can't decide if I fancy it or not. But now you're here you can keep me company,' she said.

'Oh, I don't know. It's not that warm today, is it?'

'That only makes the sea seem warmer. Trust me.'

'I haven't got a towel.'

'Diddums.' She gave him a look, appraising and expectant, and Zach had the sudden feeling that he was being tested.

'All right then. I've been up at The Watch for the past few hours. I could do with washing that place off my skin.'

'Oh? What happened?'

'Nothing specific. It's just . . . there seem to be so many pent-up memories there. And not all of them that happy.' He thought of the way sorrow sometimes seemed to sit, stony and cold, in every corner. 'Talking to Dimity can be a bit intense.'

'Yes. I suppose it can,' Hannah agreed.

They turned and walked side by side along the shoreline for a while.

'So how are you finding our little corner of Dorset? Not missing the bright lights of Bath?' Hannah asked, flicking stray curls of her hair out of her face where the breeze was playing with it.

'I like it. It's kind of restful, being surrounded by land-scape, rather than people.'

'Oh? I had you down as more of a culture vulture than that.' She glanced across at him briefly, and he smiled.

'I am. But as soon as I left London I was stepping back from that way of life, I suppose. London feels like it's . . . in my past, now. I studied there; I got married there. I wouldn't want to live there again. Not after everything that's happened since. Do you ever feel that? Not wanting to go back to significant places?'

'Not really. All my significant places are here.'

'I suppose that is a bit different. And you never wanted to leave at all – leave where you grew up and try something completely different, somewhere else?'

'No.' She paused. 'I know that might not be very fashion-able; might not seem very adventurous. But some of us are born with strong roots. And wherever you go, you're still you, after all. Nobody ever really starts a *new life*, or anything like that. You take the old one with you. How can you not?'

'And yet I find myself constantly trying. To start over.'

'And has it ever worked? Have you ever found yourself to be any different?'

'No, I suppose not.' He smiled ruefully. 'Perhaps you're just more content with who you are than the rest of us.'

'Or just more resigned to it,' she said, also smiling.

'Still, your roots must be pretty strong, if you didn't even think of leaving when . . . when you lost your husband. When you lost Toby.'

Hannah was silent for a while after he said this, and she turned her head to gaze out to sea.

'Toby wasn't from Blacknowle. He blew into my life for eight great years . . . and then he blew out again. The farm, and the house, were the only things that kept me anchored when he died. If I'd left then . . . I'd have lost myself as well,' she said. They had reached the far corner of the beach, and Hannah stopped. She took a deep breath and then pulled her shirt over her head in one clean movement. Zach looked away, tactfully, but not before he'd noticed a scattering of pale freckles descending the bony line between her breasts. 'So, are you swimming fully clothed, or what?' She turned to face him in her bikini, hands on hips. Zach felt curiously voyeuristic – strange for it to be acceptable for him to see her like this, outside, when it would be invasive to look at her in her underwear, indoors. He pulled off his top and dropped his jeans. Hannah let a measuring gaze rise from his white feet to the spread of his shoulders; so bold and overt that he almost blushed. 'Last one in's a rotten egg.' She smiled fleetingly, turned, and made her way nimbly across the pebbles to the water. Three strides took her knee-deep, then she lunged forwards, dipped her head beneath the swell of a wave and started swimming.

Zach followed her, cursing under his breath when he felt the cold grip of the sea around his ankles. It seemed to bite, but then Hannah surfaced nearby, skin shining and hair smoothed back, as slick as a seal's, and the sight of her urged him on. He took a huge breath and dived in, feeling every muscle contract as the water closed over him. He surfaced with a gasp.

'*Jesus wept!* It's freezing!' But even as he spoke the water seemed less shocking, more bearable. He stopped flailing and swam in a small circle till he caught sight of Hannah.

'There, that wasn't so bad, was it?' she said. It had been a long time since he'd swum in a British sea, so very different from a warm holiday sea where the water was as clear as a swimming pool, the bottom sandy and featureless. No possible threats, nothing unseen. He put his feet down gingerly, felt rocks and the leathery touch of seaweed, imagined crabs and spiked urchins, things with stinging tentacles. He snatched his feet back up, peering down, but could only see his own legs as a blurry paleness, no more detailed than that. 'Swim out a bit more. It gets sandy. Do you see where the water's breaking over there? Avoid that if you can. Some sharp rocks under there. Come on.' Hannah floated on her back, issuing this steady stream of instructions, and Zach took a breath, ducked under the surface and kicked hard towards her.

They swam side by side for a while, away from the shore, and the rhythm of it was calming, meditative. Hannah dipped beneath the surface every few strokes, and Zach watched the cloud of her hair, following her down into the heavy water. He swam on, and at one point she surfaced too close to him, with salt in her eyes, blinding her. They collided, and Hannah twisted onto her back, the hard length of her torso touching his as it passed, skin sliding; a lithe and fleeting caress. 'Won't Ilir swim with you?' said Zach.

'No, he's a big wimp. Scared of the currents.'

'There are currents?'

'Too late to worry about that now! Just stick with me – you'll be fine. The tide hasn't turned yet. The chances of you being sucked out to sea are really . . . not that high.' Hannah smiled, and Zach decided that she was joking. 'Here. Watch out – we can climb onto the jetty. Great spot for diving off, sunbathing, and making tourists think you can walk on water.' She scrambled carefully upwards, to stand as Zach had seen her before, on a spar of flat rock about a foot beneath the water, jutting out into the bay. 'Even at low tide, the far end of this jetty stays covered, and the water off the end is deep enough for a small boat,' she said. 'A couple of hundred years ago, smugglers used it all the time.'

'What did they smuggle?'

'Oh, anything. Wine, brandy, tobacco. Spices. Cloth. Anything easy to carry that they knew they could shift once they got it here. Why do you think Dimity's cottage is called The Watch?'

'I see.' Zach searched with his toes for footholds in the rock, feeling the bite of barnacle shells as he climbed.

They sat side by side on the edge of the rock platform, and the breeze felt colder where it dried them. The sea flickered reflections in their eyes, under their chins.

'So, is that what you're doing here in Blacknowle, really? Trying to start over again?' said Hannah. She pulled her knees up to her chest and wrapped her arms around them.

'Not exactly. I mean, I have Elise now. I wish I had her in my everyday life, like before. I wish she wasn't thousands of miles away, but I'm her dad, and I wouldn't want to be anybody else. And she is in my everyday life, in a way. I think about her all the time. I suppose I came here because . . . I needed to know more *about* who I am. And my family has been connected to this place for generations.'

'Has it?' said Hannah. Zach smiled at her dubious expression.

'Yes. There's a strong possibility that Charles Aubrey was my grandfather, you see.' Hannah blinked, and a tiny frown appeared between her eyebrows.

'Your grandfather?' she echoed.

'My grandma always claimed to be one of Aubrey's women. They came here on holiday in 1939, and met Aubrey here. He even put her in a painting. And you know what they say about Charles Aubrey – that he was one of those men who patted the head of every child he passed in the street, just in case it was his.'

'Charles Aubrey's grandson.' Hannah shook her head slightly, then tipped back her chin and laughed.

'What's so funny?'

'Oh, nothing. Just the way things work out sometimes,' she said, offering no further explanation. She thought for a while, resting her chin on her crossed arms. Goose pimples spread up along her narrow thighs. 'Do you still love Ali?' she asked, eventually.

'No. I love . . . the memory of her. I love the way things were, in the beginning. Do you still love Toby?'

'Of course.' She shrugged. 'But it's different now.' She pressed her lips together and turned her head to look at him. 'Very different.' She shook her head. 'God, I'm so used to avoiding any mention of him in front of Ilir that I even find it hard to say his name!'

'Right,' said Zach, heavily. 'Does it make him uncomfortable, then?'

'Yes, but not in the way you're thinking.'

'What way am I thinking?'

'Ilir always says – his people say – that it's not right to

speak of the dead. That you shouldn't. It's like some rigid social code where he's from.'

'His people?' said Zach. Hannah paused, as though unsure whether to go on.

'Ilir is Roma,' she said.

'You mean he's a gypsy?'

'If you like,' she said, neutrally. 'They don't have a great name in this country.'

'Where is he from? I've been trying to place his accent,' said Zach. Hannah narrowed her amber eyes, and again seemed oddly reluctant to answer.

'Kosovo,' she said, shortly. 'Ilir was a childhood friend of Toby's. Well, not really childhood, I guess. Teenage. They met in Mitrovica when Toby's father was in business over there, before the war started. When the boys were about thirteen, I think. Twelve or thirteen. He came over to help me when he heard Toby had died.'

'And never left?'

'As you see. Not yet, anyway. Ironic, really – the one person in my life who could share memories of Toby with me, and he refuses to.' She gazed away towards the farm for a while, and Zach thought he could see the bond between them, like strands in the air mirroring the currents in the water beneath them. It gave him a sinking feeling.

'Shall we swim? It's too cold out here,' he said.

'I told you the water was warmer than it looked, didn't I?' said Hannah, standing up. 'Let's dive.'

'Is it deep enough here?'

'Such a worrier!' She looked down, and gave him a smile. Zach stood up next to her, a full head and shoulders taller so that she had to tilt her head. She studied him for a moment, in that appraising way he was getting used to. 'Come back to the house afterwards, if you want,' she said, watching him steadily.

'What for?' Zach asked. Hannah shrugged one shoulder, and dived.

Dimity saw them sitting side by side on the rock jetty like they'd known each other for years. She watched from the kitchen window, and felt something tickling in her stomach. Something that made her clasp her hands there, to hold it; made her shift from foot to foot and turn from time to time, to pace the floor. What were they saying? She wondered about this. The boy had so many questions, all the time, and when she answered them it only made more come. He was insatiable, like that. A hole into which all her stories could pour, and never be filled up. *Here's a robber coming through, coming through, coming through*, she sang softly, watching them still. She'd started making a charm for Hannah. Pushing pins through small corks, and working them gradually, painstakingly through the neck of a glass bottle. Something to keep her safe, to put on her hearth or over her door. In case there really was a curse on her, or on the farm — that had been her initial thought. Now she thought: to close her mouth as well. To not let this curious boy pull words from her like he pulled them from Dimity. *Here's a robber coming through, my fair lady*. Hannah knew things, bad things. Secrets she must never tell. Because in the end, Dimity could not do everything herself; she had to ask for help sometimes. Young hands and arms, full of the strength that age had stolen.

When she saw him walk along the beach with the girl she was happy at first. They seemed to match, in spite of the difference in height, and the colour of their souls. Hannah's had always been red, but the young man's was more blue and green and grey. Shifting, not quite knowing what to be. But soon after she felt happy, she felt anxious, then afraid. *He stole away my wedding ring, wedding ring, wedding ring* . . . For a second, she almost wished Valentina would come back again. Somebody to hear her thoughts, even if help was beyond her. Valentina had never been a helper; could never muster sympathy. Her heart was a thing of wood and stone, hard minerals. Dimity thought about what she had said to Zach, earlier, when suddenly words and feelings had built up an unbearable pressure inside her. What she had said, and had mercifully not said, even though for a moment the truth had hovered on her lips. The truth could be divided, and given in halves, or smaller fractions. The way saying the sky is not green is not the same as saying that the sky is blue. True, but not the same.

Dimity rubbed the ring finger of her left hand; rubbed it at its base, and thought she felt a callus; hard skin in a ridge between finger and palm. *She stole away my wedding ring, my fair lady*. Dimity hummed the tune, mumbled the words, did not notice that *he* had become *she*. She watched Hannah stand, and dive back into the sea; watched the young man do the same. He was a follower, that one. Not sure where he was going, and happy to take direction as a result. If she was careful, she could lead him where she wanted, and where he thought he wanted. But she must be careful. *Have a care, Mitzy. Don't make things harder on yourself*. Valentina's words, from long ago. Loaded with scorn and menace. Better not to talk to him at all, however much she liked the words in her mouth: Charles, and love, and devotion. Other words ran alongside them, refusing to stay silent. Celeste. Élodie. Delphine. *Whore*. Better not to talk at all, then, but it made her sad to imagine Zach never coming again. To think of him outside, knocking, bringing pictures of her that sang like joyful songs in her head when she saw them again. Windows to a time she loved, a time she lived; windows so clear and crystalline bright. *But have a care, have a care*. The pair of them swam out of sight beneath the cliff and she turned from the window, went up the stairs without thought and stood outside the door to the right. The closed door. She put her hand to the wood the way she'd done so many times before.

Then came the rush of hope, of fear. She thought she heard something move, inside. Several times now, since Zach Gilchrist had started to visit. Since the hearth charm had fallen down, and left the house wide open for a while. Holding her breath, she put her ear to the door, pressing her head close to it, spreading the old flesh of her cheek. Her hand rose up, went to the doorknob and closed around it. She could open it, and go in. She thought she knew what she would see but she wasn't sure, not completely *sure*. And she wasn't sure she wanted to see. There were knots in the wooden door, and a face within them. She thought it was Valentina's but it could have been Hannah's; wide eyes, open mouth. Saying *Dimity, what have you done? What have you done?* The things Hannah knew; the things she saw that night. Hannah's heart had been beating so hard that Dimity had heard it clearly, clattering against her ribs, and she'd been shocked to see such fear, such horror, twisting the girl's face and making her body shake. Swallowing, Dimity uncurled her hand from the doorknob, and stepped back.

At the farmhouse, Hannah disappeared into what might have been a laundry room – there were heaps of clothes and cloth, spewing from several baskets around the floor; ranks of empty soap boxes. She came out with a lurid beach towel, striped and multicoloured; Zach took it and rubbed it over his hair. The rest of him had dried on the walk up the valley from the beach, but his boxers were sodden and cold, clinging and clammy against his skin. He fidgeted with them surreptitiously beneath his jeans, but Hannah saw, and smiled.

'Got a problem down there?' she said.

'Bit of sand, bit of seaweed. Nothing I can't handle.'

'Coffee?'

'Is it safe to drink?'

'Yes, I think so.' Hannah eyed him, haughtily. 'The boiling water kills the germs.' She went through to the kitchen, stepping deftly, automatically, around the piles of debris in the hallway. The piles had clearly been there a long time. The grey collie, which had appeared at the edge of the yard and followed them in, slunk into its bed and watched them wistfully as they passed.

'Seriously, though . . . the yard is so tidy . . .' Zach looked around the kitchen and raised his hands at the chaos. 'How do you ever find anything in here?'

'The yard's important, that's why it's tidy. And I find that the stuff I need rises to the surface in here, eventually.' She cast her eyes around the room, and as if really seeing it for once. The corners of her mouth twitched, and turned down. 'My mum was very house-proud. She'd be horrified, if she saw this. Especially her kitchen. It used to be the kind of kitchen where you'd come in from school and there'd be a tray of fresh scones cooling on the table.' Zach said nothing. 'But . . . Toby was messy. I was appalled, when he first took me back to his room at college. In himself he was clean, tidy – a bit too tidy, almost. But his room looked like a bomb had gone off. It smelt of mouldy bread and old socks. I had to throw the window open and lean out for air; grip of passion or no grip of passion. When he died . . . when he died it seemed a fitting homage, of a kind. The mess. Like I could let him have it his way, since he'd gone and left me.' She shrugged, sadly. 'But to be honest, once it gets past a certain point, cleaning ceases to be an option. You don't even see the mess any more.'

'I could help you, if you like? I mean, if you wanted to have a clear out, one day.'

'One day?' She shook her head. 'It'd take a month.'

'Well,' said Zach, then couldn't think what to add. Hannah picked up two mugs and ostentatiously washed one under the hot tap. She gave Zach an arch look, and he tried not to notice that there was no washing-up liquid, and that the sponge she used to wash it was stained and bedraggled. But Hannah paused and looked at it, discarded it and used her fingers to finish the job.

'Stop it,' she said.

'Stop what?'

'Stop watching me, stop making me notice. I haven't got time to sort it.'

'Sorry. I didn't mean to.' Hannah put the mugs down by the kettle and spread her hands on the worktop for a moment, leaning her weight onto them, arms rigid and straight. Her bikini had imprinted a wet echo of itself through her shirt and trousers, and the rat-tail ends of her hair were hung with droplets of water like beads. The kettle began to make a quiet groaning sound, and she flicked it off again with a quick, decisive movement.

'Come on,' she said, abruptly, reaching out a hand to him. 'Let's get out of these wet things.'

She took him upstairs to a large bedroom that faced the sea. The afternoon light poured in through two huge sash windows, warming the scattered corpses of flies on the sill. If there had once been curtains, there weren't any more. The bed had a high brass headboard; the duvet was crumpled, half on the floor. Cracks zigzagged like lightning through the pale blue paint on the walls. Hannah shut the door behind Zach and turned to face him as she pulled off her shirt and the wet, red bikini top. She fixed him with a challenging expression, the pale ghost of her swimsuit diffuse against the summer tan on her skin, outlining her small breasts, making her nipples stand out darkly. Zach stepped forwards, put his hands around her waist and ran them up along her spine to the hard lines where her shoulder blades pressed through the skin. He kissed her, and tasted salt. The sea was on her lips, on her chin and cheeks. Cold drops of it fell from her hair onto his arms when he wrapped them around her; and he felt her body tense up, pushing herself closer to him. Desire stormed through him, choking and irresistible, made his arms tighten until the breath was squeezed from her, and her mouth grew softer. When he opened his eyes her look was no longer measuring but calm and urgent. It was an expression Zach could read at once; one he recognised, finally, and without doubt. He didn't loosen his grip for a second. He straightened up, lifting her so that her feet came off the floor. He turned towards the bed, and they fell together. The feel of her arms wrapped around him, the movement of her body, its taste, its smell, were all-consuming; made the world and everything in it vanish. For a while there was only the two of them, tangled together, and nothing else mattered.

When Zach woke up he was sprawled across Hannah's mattress like a starfish. The sheets smelt faintly of sheep. Every limb felt warm and heavy, but his mind was clear. He looked up and saw her standing in front of the window, still naked, chewing at the skin of one thumb. He took the opportunity to study her, knowing that he only could when she wasn't aware of it. Her big toes turned up slightly at the ends, no paint on the nails. There was a tiny, dark tattoo of a seahorse on her right hip, just where the bone showed its shape. Her buttocks sank slightly down, creasing the skin into a single, neat fold. He could count her ribs, which were scattered with freckles. Her hair was dry now, a wild, knotty-looking thatch. Wide eyes, focused far out to sea.

Again he had the strangest feeling that he knew her, had seen her before. There was something naggingly familiar in everything, even the way she stood, lost in thought, and Zach wondered if this was some deeper level of recognition than the physical, than the mundane arrangement of features on a face. Something instinctive, needful. He felt something crack inside him then; a small rupture and a bruising sensation, at once new and familiar. He greeted it with mixed feelings – a dismayed sort of welcome.

'Hello,' he murmured. Hannah stopped chewing, looked over at him.

'Back in the land of the living?' she said.

'How long was I asleep?'

'Oh, only about half an hour. I wouldn't call it sleep, though. Coma is more like it.'

'Sorry. You took me by surprise, a bit. Come here.' For a second she ignored the command, but then she crossed to the bed and sat down cross-legged, entirely unselfconsciously. 'Aren't you worried about people seeing in?' he said, smiling.

'There's nobody out there to see in. And the curtains caught fire, once.' She sniffed, turned to look at the window. 'The wind blew them into a candle. So I took them down and never got around to replacing them. It helps me get up in the mornings, anyway. The light coming in.' Zach tried not to think about Hannah's room, candlelit; about such a romantic gesture, and who it might have been for. He put out his hand and ran it along her arm, caught her wrist and pulled her towards him. She resisted at first, frowning, but then relented and lay down next to him, curled towards him, not touching.

'Hannah, what about Ilir?' he asked, tentatively.

'What about him?'

'You don't think he'd mind? Us sleeping together?'

'No, he wouldn't mind. It's none of his business, really.'

'You mean you and he aren't . . . you know. A couple?'

'Well, I'd hardly be shagging you in broad daylight if we were, would I?'

'I really don't know,' said Zach, with complete honesty.

'No, Ilir is not my . . . lover. He never has been. As far as he's concerned, I'm family. He's a friend and . . . a colleague, in a way.' She looked at him frankly, and behind the lightness of her tone was something more serious. 'There's nobody else.'

'Thank God,' said Zach, relieved. 'I would have hated to have to fight him. He looks . . . tough.'

'No, I don't think that will be necessary.' Hannah chuckled.

'It . . . feels right, to me. This. Being with you, I mean. I feel like I've known you for a long time. Do you know what I mean?' he said.

'I don't know.' Hannah turned her face to the ceiling, unblinking. 'Let's not rush things, Zach.'

'No, of course not. I only meant . . . that I was glad. Glad to have met you,' he said. She turned to face him again and grinned.

'I'm glad to have met you too, Zach. You have a very nice arse.'

'One of many fine attributes, I assure you,' he said, linking his hands behind his head and leaning back with conspicuous satisfaction. Hannah jabbed him sharply in the ribs with one finger. 'Ouch! What was that for?' he said, laughing.

'Just pricking that ego, before it gets too swollen.' She smiled. Zach grabbed her hands before she could strike again, pulled her close and kissed her.

'I've bruised you,' he said, putting his fingertips to her collarbone, where a pinkish mark was blooming.

'I'll live.'

He laced the fingers of his left hand into those of her right, and pulled her hand to his mouth to kiss her knuckles. He ran his thumb over her palm and along her thumb, and felt a hard ridge in the flesh.

'What's this?' He held her hand further away, so he could focus his eyes. A thick, straight scar ran diagonally right across the pad of her thumb. Silvery white, and raised. 'How did you get this? Looks like it was deep,' he said.

'It was . . .' Hannah paused, frowning slightly. She withdrew her hand and cradled it in front of her face. 'It was the night Toby died. I shut it in the car door. Hard. Nearly split my thumb in half. But I didn't even notice I'd done it until the next day, when somebody pointed it out to me. It was numb. Like the rest of me, I suppose.'

'Jesus. You poor thing.'

'Me?' She shook her head. 'I wasn't the one drowning.'

'Hannah, I'm sorry. I didn't mean to—'

'No, no, it's OK, Zach. I actually want to talk about him. I know that sounds weird, probably too weird for you. But it's been ages since I have. I guess you don't want to hear about him. About that night.' She turned a steady gaze on him, her eyes dark and diffuse, hidden from the light.

'Tell me,' he said. Hannah took a slow breath in.

A night of thumping wind and solid rain. A night when the sky spat out crystals of ice to cut into your eyes and lips, and the air was sucked out of your lungs before you could speak or breathe. A night so black that any light dazzled you rather than guided you. Weather that found every leak in your roof and seam in your clothes; every loose tile and weak spot, every chink. Toby was a volunteer lifeboat crewman, though he'd grown up in Kensal Rise. Living out a boyhood fantasy of taming the bucking waves and coming like a guardian angel to people waiting for the sea to claim them. And live it out he did, for three years once he'd completed the training. He loved it – loved helping, loved the adrenalin, loved to be so needed. So that night, his last night, he gave her a grin from the bedroom door as he went out, and Hannah got dressed and followed him. Followed her feet down to the shore where the water was boiling angrily around the rocks; because that grin of his had been too excited, too pleased, and she believed in a watching fate that took pleasure in punishing those who went too lightly into danger.

She could see nothing from where she stood. The boat in trouble, a luxury yacht on its way back from St Ives, was five miles out from the coast and further west, beyond Lulworth. She took the jeep, drove with reckless haste to that cove, slammed her hand in the door and felt nothing. She could see no more from the high path above Lulworth Cove, but still she waited with the weather blaring all around her and her ears throbbing with it, feeling the spray scorch her face until she was numb all over, with fear or with cold she couldn't tell. Eventually, so chilled she thought her heart might stop, she drove back to the farmhouse and waited in the kitchen. Waited for the news she knew was coming. The night stretched on and a knot of dread appeared inside her, hard and heavy. She picked up the phone but the gale had brought the lines down. Her mobile had no signal. But still she started grieving before she was even told what had happened, because she already knew she'd lost him. A stray line from the yacht had whipped out in the darkness, caught him around the head with stunning force. He was over and into the rolling black waves before anybody could act. And then gone. Swallowed by the ten-metre crests and the sucking depths of the troughs; water like flint, closing over him implacably.

'The couple on the yacht were rescued, cold and scared but none the worse for it. But Toby was gone. That's what Gareth, his closest friend on the boat told me. He was just gone.'

'Did they ever find him?'

'Yes.' She swallowed. 'A week or so later, about twelve miles down the coast. What was left of him, anyway.'

'He must have been brave, to go out there and do that,' said Zach. Hannah sighed and moved a bit closer to him.

'No, he wasn't. Bravery is facing down your fears. Toby wasn't frightened to begin with. I'm not sure if that makes him a hero or a bloody idiot. Possibly both.' She let her head roll forwards until their foreheads touched. 'It feels good, talking about him. After so long not talking about him. I can't remember when I last said his name out loud until you came here.'

'I'm not sure what to do with that,' said Zach, entirely truthfully. Hannah smiled briefly, and shrugged.

'You don't need to do anything with it. It wasn't meant to be a gift, or a burden. I just wanted to know what it would feel like. Saying it all out loud.'

'I'm glad you told me.'

'Really?'

'Really. If it helps . . . if it makes you feel better.'

'Well, I'm not sure if better is the word . . . lighter, maybe. Thank you.' They lay in silence for a while and then Hannah kissed him, opening her mouth gently, inviting him back in. Zach gathered her up in his arms, pulled her on top of him, held their bodies close together.

Ducking through the pub's doorway on his way back from Southern Farm, his mind busy with thoughts of Hannah and new memories of the taste and scent of her, Zach bumped into an old man who was coming out.

'Excuse me, sorry,' he said, putting out his hands to right the man, who staggered a little before catching his balance. The man made a sort of rumbling grunt in his throat, which Zach took as an acceptance of his apology, and he was about to pass him by when something stopped him – when their eyes met, a peculiar expression flooded the old man's face. Zach paused. The man was thin and frail-looking, his face one of deep contours – in his cheeks, around his eyes and mouth and chin. A face of shadows and hiding places. His eyes swam with moisture and the end of his nose was purplish with a spread of broken thread veins. The look he gave Zach was one of recognition, and distrust that bordered on hostility. 'We haven't met,' said Zach, hurriedly, as the man tried to move away. He held out his hand. 'I'm Zach Gilchrist. I'm staying here at the pub for a while, and doing some research into the life of Charles Aubrey . . .' The old man didn't shake his hand, and he didn't introduce himself. Zach's smile faded. 'I'd be very interested in talking to anybody who was living in the village at the time . . . in the late 1930s that is . . .'

'I know who you are. What you want. I've seen you,' the man said at last, in a voice every bit as thick with the Dorset burr as Dimity's. 'Thought you'd have been gone again by now,' he added, in a faintly accusatory tone. There was something familiar about him, and suddenly Zach remembered – the old man who'd been having lunch with his wife on his first day in Blacknowle. The one who'd got up and left when he started to ask about Aubrey.

'Have you lived here a long time, sir?' he asked. The old man blinked, and nodded.

'All my life. I'm from this place, I've a right to be here.'

'And I haven't?'

'What good are you doing?'

'What good? Well . . . the book I plan to write would

really put Blacknowle on the map. I mean to show just how crucial to his life and work Aubrey's time here was . . .'

'And what good will that do?' the man pressed.

'Well, it . . . it can't do any harm, I wouldn't have thought.'

'You think that because you don't *know*, that's all. You don't know.' The old man sniffed, and took a faded green handkerchief from his pocket to blow his nose.

'Well, I'm starting to know . . . I mean, I'm trying to learn. Please believe me when I say that I'm here with the best of intentions. As a scholar of the artist. I've no wish to offend anybody.' He paused, and thought for a second. 'Your name's not Dennis by any chance, is it?' The old man hesitated, as if considering whether to answer, then shook his head.

'Never known a Dennis. Not round here,' he said, and in spite of himself there was a spark of curiosity in his voice. 'What's this Dennis got to do with anything?'

'Well, I'd be happy to sit down and discuss my research with you, if you'd be willing to talk to me about your time here in the thirties . . .' Zach smiled. The old man hesitated, sucking in his lower lip. 'I've had several very useful talks with Dimity Hatcher already,' said Zach, hoping to persuade the old man, but her name had the opposite effect. His face settled into fixed lines, hardened with resolve.

'I've nothing to say to you about Dimity Hatcher!' he snapped, and he suddenly sounded hurt, almost frightened. Zach blinked.

'Well, all right. It's Aubrey I'm really interested in, after all . . .' But as he said this, he realised that it was no longer true. His curiosity about Dimity's life had grown since he first met her, and continued to grow each time they spoke, each time there were things she would not talk about, or was confused about. Or was lying about. 'Might I at least know your name?' he said. Again, the old man paused and considered before answering.

'Wilfred Coulson,' he said.

'Well, Mr Coulson, you know where I am if you change your mind. I really would be so grateful for any help you could give me, even if the memories might not seem relevant to you. Anecdotes, anything. Dimity's already told me about her love affair with Charles Aubrey . . .' Zach said, out on a limb, hoping for a reaction and getting one.

'Love affair? No.' Wilf Coulson's eyes blazed into life. 'That was not love.'

'Oh? But . . . Dimity very much seems to think otherwise . . .'

'What she thinks and what is what don't always match up,' the old man muttered.

'What do you think was between them, if you don't think it was love?' Zach asked, but Wilf Coulson only frowned, looking past Zach into the dark interior of the pub, and a sudden wave of sadness engulfed his face. 'That was not love,' he repeated, then he turned and walked unsteadily away from the building, leaving Zach to puzzle over this adamant declaration.

It was early in the evening but Zach's stomach was growling, so he ordered his dinner and sat down in what was becoming his regular spot, on an upholstered bench beneath a west-facing window, looking into the heart of the village. He was waiting for his computer to boot up when a bark of male laughter filled the room and a group of four men sauntered in. Zach didn't pay them any attention until Pete Murray put both sets of his knuckles on the bar and braced his arms resolutely.

'Gareth, you know I'm not going to serve you, so why bother coming in?' he said.

'What? You're telling me I'm still barred? That was

bloody months ago!' said a skinny man with a gaunt, ageless face and glittering eyes. He could have been twenty, or forty; his expression was one of deep distrust, and disaffection. Behind him was a huge bulk of a man, tall and bearded, and wearing a faded lilac sweatshirt that looked oddly endearing on his huge frame. Sitting as close as he was, Zach could see the haze of grime on the garment. The quartet all carried the faint smell of unwashed clothes and fish.

'Barred is barred, until I say you're not barred.'

'Well, are you going to say it or what?' The thin man leaned menacingly towards the bar. Beside him, the huge lilac man loomed, his brows pulled so low they almost covered his eyes.

'You're barred,' said Pete Murray, and Zach admired the steady tone of his voice. 'Go somewhere else.'

Conversations around the bar fell silent as the four men stayed where they were for a hung moment. Then the thin man thrust his hands into his pockets and turned away, knots writhing at the sharp corners of his jaw.

'What the fuck are you looking at?' he snapped at a pair of middle-aged women as he passed their table, and they exchanged a startled expression above their white wine spritzers.

'Sorry about that, ladies. How about another, on the house?' said the publican, once the four men had left.

'Who were those guys?' Zach asked, as Pete brought over his food a short while later. The landlord sighed.

'They're pretty harmless really. Well, I *think* they are. Fatty and skinny are James and Gareth Horne. They're brothers, fishermen, both of them. I don't know the other two – just mates of theirs, I suppose. But the Horne bothers – well, every village has its tearaways, doesn't it? When they were kids it was graffiti, sniffing glue, getting drunk and smashing up the telephone box. Once they started going out to work on the boats they calmed down a bit, but then there were rumours of more serious drugs, and back in the spring I caught Gareth dealing to some youngsters out the back here. They cleared off and got rid of it before the police caught up with them, but they're barred for life as far as I'm concerned.'

'They sound lovely.'

'Give them a wide berth, that'd be my advice,' said Pete.

When Zach finally managed to log in to his email, he found a message from Paul Gibbons at the auction house in London, which he opened eagerly. After a brief preamble, Paul wrote that the buyer of one of the previous Dennis pictures, a Mrs Annie Langton, happened to be an old family friend and would be happy to meet him and let him look at the picture; he gave her contact details. Zach checked his watch. It was still only seven in the evening, not too late to call somebody. As usual, his mobile phone had no signal, so he fed coins into the pub's payphone, and rang Annie Langton straight away. She sounded elderly but bright, and very well-to-do, and he arranged to visit her on the following Thursday. She lived in Surrey, and Zach used the postcode she'd given him to pull up some online directions. It would take him a good two and a half hours to drive it, and he silently wished that it would be worth it. There was something to be found, he knew. He could feel it in his gut; an ill-defined but unmistakeable sense of something amiss, like entering a familiar room and finding the furniture moved. He prayed that whatever it was, he would find it in Annie Langton's picture of Dennis.

6

Dimity stood and stared. There was a car parked outside Littlecombe; a flawless deep blue with flowing black arches sweeping over the front wheels and a bright metal grille gleaming at the front. A wholly different thing to the battered, muddy old machines that usually went rattling through Blacknowle, or the wide, ungainly buses that ran east and west along the top road, belching clouds of black smoke behind them. This car looked like it belonged in a fairy story, or one of the movies Wilf went to see occasionally, on visits to his uncle in Wareham; returning with stories of vastly wealthy men and graceful women in silk gowns living in a world so clean and lovely that nobody ever cursed or got ill. Dimity peered through the window. The seats were of deep brown leather, with neat rows of stitching. She longed to run her hands over them, put her nose up close and inhale the scent of them. There were some sprigs of cow parsley caught under the left corner of the front bumper, and Dimity bent to remove them, wiping away the smears of green juice with her fingertips. In the curving, mirrored metal, her reflection stared back at her, warped and misshapen. A flash of hazel eyes and knotted bronze hair; a smudged face and a scab on her lip made by one of Valentina's fingernails, which had caught her as she'd dodged a blow.

'Quite a beauty, isn't she?' said a voice close at hand. Dimity knew it at once, and she caught her breath. Charles. She whirled around and stepped away from the car.

'I wasn't doing nothing! Only looking!' she gasped. Charles smiled and held out his hands.

'It's all right, Mitzy! You can look. If you like, I'll take you for a drive sometime.' He stepped forwards and pressed a brief kiss onto her cheek. 'You look well. It's nice to see you again.' He said it calmly, as though he didn't know that their reunion was the one thing she'd dreamed of for ten long months. Charles looked past her at the car, his expression one of guilt and rapture. Dimity couldn't speak. His kiss was burning into her skin, and she put up her hand in case she might be able to feel the wound. 'I shouldn't covet this car so. It's only a machine. But then, can't a machine, can't something man-made, also be a thing of beauty?' He spoke almost to himself, running his fingers along the roof of the car with a rapt expression.

'It's the most beautiful car I ever saw,' Dimity managed to say, breathlessly. Charles smiled, glancing at her appraisingly.

'You like it, eh? It's brand new. A friend of mine got his up to sixty miles an hour! Sixty! It's an Austin Ten – the new Cambridge model. Twenty-one brake horse power; four-cylinder, side-valve engine . . .' He trailed off, reading the utter incomprehension in her face. 'Never mind. I'm glad you like it. I wasn't even sure I needed a car. It was Celeste's idea really, but now that I have it I can't remember how I managed without. It seems so outmoded and restrictive to rely on trains and taxis. With a car, the world is your oyster. You can go anywhere, at any time.' He paused and looked over at her, but Dimity could think of nothing else to say about it. She could see that he expected her to, and felt desperation making her throat clog up and heat build at the top of her nose. 'Well, I'll take you for a drive soon, I promise. Go on into the house – Delphine's been dying to see you.'

She did as she was told, however reluctant her feet were to move away from Charles and the heavenly blue car. Inside the house, voices were raised. Dimity knocked, but could tell that she hadn't been heard. She edged cautiously into the kitchen just in time to see Élodie, so much taller than she had been, stamp her foot on the floor, fists clenched at the ends of rigid arms. Her black hair was cut into a shoulder-length bob that swung around her jaw as she yelled.

'I'm eight years old and I will wear what I like!' she said, her voice piercing and loud. Celeste turned from the sink and put her hands on her hips.

'You are eight years old and you will do as you're told. *Laisse moi tranquille!* That is your best dress and those are your best shoes. We are in Dorset, by the sea. Take them off and find something more suitable to wear.' Celeste's blue eyes were even more arresting than Dimity remembered. In anger, they seemed to glow.

'I *hate* all my clothes! They're so *ugly*!'

'*C'est ton problème.* Go and get changed.'

'I will *not*!' Élodie screamed. Celeste fixed her with a look that would have made the blood run cold in Dimity's veins had it been directed at her, even accustomed as she was to Valentina's sudden assaults. Slowly, Élodie's hands went limp, and her mouth opened a little, and a scorching blush flooded her face. She turned to run from the room and bumped straight into Dimity. 'Oh, great! *You're* here again. How simply *marvellous*!' she said, pushing past her.

'*Merde.* That child, she will fight me all the way!' Celeste sighed, pushing a hand through her heavy hair. 'She is too much like me. Stubborn as a mule, and just as bad-tempered. Mitzy! Come and say hello.' She held her arms wide and Dimity stepped into a quick, surprising embrace. Delphine got up from the table, grinning. 'How are you? You've grown! Even prettier than you were,' said Celeste, holding her at arm's length. How could that be? Dimity thought of the long, biting winter; the chilblains on her toes, the way the wind chapped her cheeks and how long she and Valentina had gone without a decent, filling meal. Delphine was hovering excitedly next to her mother, and as soon as Celeste released Dimity, she stepped in to hug her too. Dimity felt a rush of happiness, and something like relief; so powerful she thought for a second she might cry. Their affection was like a language she hardly knew, like occasional words emerging clearly from a confusing babble of sound.

She quickly rubbed at her eyes with her fingertips, and Delphine, seeing how moved she was, laughed with delight.

'It's so nice to see you! We have *so* much to catch up on . . .' she said.

'Have you eaten, Mitzy?' asked Celeste.

'Yes, thank you.'

'But I bet you could eat more, right?' said Delphine, taking Dimity's arm and looping it through her own. Dimity shuffled her feet and didn't like to answer, when in truth the kitchen smelled wonderful, as usual. Celeste smiled.

'Don't be polite, Mitzy. Say if you would like some,' she said.

'Yes, please. I would.' Celeste cut two thick slices of yellow cake and wrapped them in a napkin.

'I'll have some too – now I've finally stopped feeling sick from the journey. Daddy drives the new car so fast we get thrown about in the back seat like pinballs! We drove into the hedge at one point – there was a tractor coming the other way around a corner. You should have heard Élodie scream!'

'I saw you had cow parsley stuck under the metal at the front,' Dimity said, and Celeste smiled.

'So Charles introduced you to his new baby before he even let you come in and say hello? This is no surprise. I'm afraid he loves that thing more than he loves any of us,' she said.

'Not really, he doesn't. Not more than us,' Delphine said, nudging Dimity's shoulder when she took these words seriously.

'No. Like a child with a new toy. The thrill of it will start to fade before long,' said Celeste.

'Come on – let's go down to the beach! I've been dying to go paddling. I thought about it all the time at school. They make us wear these awful itchy socks, even when it's sunny.' Delphine towed Dimity towards the door.

'Ask Élodie to go with you,' Celeste called after them.

'Oh, all right,' Delphine sighed, leaning around the banister to shout up the stairs. '*Hell-odee!*'

As they left the house and crossed the garden, Dimity turned to look for Charles. The car sat gleaming on the driveway, but there was no sign of its owner anywhere. Reluctantly, she looked away.

They spent that afternoon and the next catching up on all that they had seen and done in the intervening ten months since Delphine and her family had left Dorset. They roamed the fields and hedgerows picking herbs and spotting fledgling birds; keeping Élodie appeased with long loops of daisy chains around her neck, and twisted garlands of poppies for her hair. They sat on the beach, at the high-tide line where a boundary of cuttlefish bones and dry, weightless fish eggs split the sand from the pebbles, watching Élodie do cartwheels and scoring her out of ten for each one, until she was breathless and red in the face, tired and dizzy enough to settle to some quiet task like drawing in the sand, collecting sea glass, or popping the blisters on a sheaf of bladderwrack. Delphine was particularly interested in hearing about Wilf

Coulson, even though Dimity was deliberately vague on the subject of him.

'So, is he your boyfriend?' she asked, in hushed tones. She glanced up at her little sister, who was a silhouette against the sparkling sea, trailing a stick across the sand in ever increasing circles.

'No! He's not that!' said Dimity.

'But you've let him kiss you, you said?'

'Yes, I have. Not very often, just once in a while. When he's been kind to me. Really he is just a friend, but you know what boys are like.'

'Do you think you'll marry him?'

Dimity laughed easily, and for a while tried to pretend she had many offers, many alternatives. Plenty of time to wait. 'I doubt it. He's a bit skinny, and his mother hates my guts and no mistake. I don't think he'd even dare tell his pa he goes about with me sometimes. Though I may tell him myself one day – he comes down to see my ma often enough.' As soon as she spoke, Dimity regretted the words.

'Why does he do that?'

'Oh, you know. To buy remedies and the like. To hear his fortune,' she invented hastily, the lie making her face flush.

'I know who I'm going to marry,' said Delphine, lying back with her hands clasped behind her head. 'I'm going to marry Tyrone Power.'

'Is that a boy at your school?' Dimity asked, and Delphine laughed.

'Don't be daft! There are no boys at my school. Tyrone Power! Haven't you seen *Lloyd's of London*? Oh, he is just divine . . . the most divine man who ever lived.'

'Is he a movie star, then? However will you meet him?'

'I don't know. I don't care. But I will – and I will marry him or die alone,' Delphine declared with quiet certainty.

They paused to reflect on this, listening to the scratching sounds of Élodie's spiralling, the constant susurration of the restless water. 'Mitzy? What's it like? Kissing a boy?' Delphine asked at length. Dimity considered this for some time.

'I don't know really. I thought it was disgusting at first, like having a dog push its wet nose into your face. But after a while it's OK, I suppose. I mean it's nice.'

'How nice? As nice as having somebody brush your hair for you?'

'I don't know,' said Dimity, at a loss. 'Nobody's ever brushed my hair but me.'

'I can plait with five strands, you know, not just three,' said Élodie, who was passing near the older girls.

'It's true, she can. Élodie's very good at hair-dos,' said Delphine.

'I'll do yours for you later,' said Élodie. She paused, apparently as surprised as Dimity by this sudden show of generosity. 'If you want.' She shrugged.

'I'd like that. Thank you,' said Dimity. Élodie glanced up at her and smiled. A flash of her small, white teeth, as pretty and rare as wood anemones.

Later that week, Charles took Dimity out in the car, just as he'd promised to. The Austin Ten tore out of the driveway away from Littlecombe at such a speed that Dimity grabbed the door handle with one hand and the edge of the seat with the other. The inside of the car was ripe with the smell of oil and warm leather, a heady smell so thick she could almost taste it. The seat itself was hot enough to radiate through her skirt, heating the backs of her legs until sweat began to prickle there.

'And you've really never been in a car before?' Charles

asked, winding down his window and gesturing for her to do the same.

'Only the bus, once or twice, and sometimes a tractor trailer to go potato picking, or cobbing before the harvest,' she said, suddenly apprehensive. Charles laughed.

'A tractor trailer? I really don't think that counts. Well, hang on tight. We'll go up to the Wareham road so I can really open her up.'

Dimity could hardly hear him above the thunder of air through the open windows and the roar of the engine on top of that. As they swerved along the lane between rows of Blacknowle's cottages, she saw Wilf and some of the village lads lingering by the shop. She put her chin up haughtily as the car sped past, and was pleased to see them watch, agog, as the sunshine glanced from the blue paintwork, and the wind caught at tendrils of her hair. Wilf raised his fingers, surreptitiously, but though Dimity caught his eye for a second, she deliberately looked away.

'Friends of yours?' Charles asked.

'Not as such, no,' Dimity said. Charles treated them to several loud blasts of the horn and then glanced at her, merrily, and Dimity laughed – could not help herself; it bubbled up inside her like something boiling over, mixing with her nerves and bursting out, irrepressibly.

At the top road Charles turned left towards Dorchester, and with a lurch of the gears they were away, gaining speed until Dimity thought they couldn't get any faster. The sides of the road were a rich green blur, the landscape seemed turned to liquid, flowing by. Only the sky and the far pale sea were unchanged and Dimity gazed out at them as they roared along, swerving out around a sluggish bus and other, slower cars. The air through the window was warm but still cooling compared to the heat of the day, and she put her hands up to her hair, twisting it into a knot and holding it so that the back of her neck would dry. From the corner of her eye she saw Charles look at her, keenly, dividing his attention between her and the road.

'Mitzy, don't move,' he said, but the words were almost lost in the din.

'Beg pardon?' she shouted back.

'Never mind. Nowhere to stop just here, anyway. Will you do that for me later – twist your hair up like that? Exactly like that? Can you remember how you did it?' he said.

'Of course I can.'

'Good girl.' Valentina appeared in Dimity's mind, and she chewed her lip as she thought about her, and how to phrase what she felt she must. Word of the Aubreys' return had carried to The Watch on the grubby tide of its visitors, like the driftwood and trash that swept along on the channel currents. Dimity could not keep it a secret.

'My mother will say . . .' she began, but Charles cut her off with a wave of his hand.

'Don't worry. There'll be money to keep Valentina Hatcher on our side,' he said, and Dimity relaxed, relieved not to have to ask.

When they got to Dorchester they made a quick circuit of the town before taking the same road back in an easterly direction, every bit as rapidly as before. Dimity held her fingers in the streaming wind, playing with the feel of it, letting it force her hand back on her wrist, then holding it steady, flat; then letting it flex her fingers into a fist.

'I understand it now,' she said, almost to herself.

'What do you understand?' Charles asked, leaning closer to hear her better.

'How a bird flies. And why they do love it so,' she said, never taking her eyes from her hand as it cut through the rushing air. She could feel the artist watching her, and she let him, not challenging his gaze by returning it. She stared at her hand as it flew, her fingertips glowing in the sunlight; she breathed in the fiery smell of the car and felt the rumble of the world going by, and to her it seemed a wholly new place, a place of a scale and wonder that she hadn't known before. A place where she might fly.

Charles had in mind a painting of the soul of English folklore. He told them this over lunch one day, as Dimity filled her mouth with chunks of cheese and pickles, piled onto slices of tough bread that Delphine had made herself. It was chewy, but she had put fresh rosemary into the dough, like Dimity had suggested, so the flavour was as delicious as the aroma.

'I painted a gypsy wedding in France. It was one of the best things I have done,' the artist said, without pride or modesty. 'Somehow you could taste the earthiness, the connection between those people and the land they lived on. Their gaze – I mean their inner gaze – was on the here, the now. They could feel their roots reaching down into the ground, and back through the years, even though some of them had no idea who their fathers had been, or their fathers' fathers. Never looking too far ahead, never looking too far afield. That is the key to happiness. Realising where you are, and what you have right now, and being grateful for it.'

He paused to take another mouthful of bread. Celeste took a steady breath, and smiled slightly when he looked up. Dimity got the impression that she might have heard the speech before. When she looked at his daughters, they both wore glazed, faraway expressions. Either they had heard it before as well, or they weren't bothering to listen. The speech was all for her, she realised. 'Take Dimity here,' he said, and her own name made her jump. 'She has been born and raised here. This is her land and these are her people, and I'm sure she would never think to leave. Would never assume the grass was greener elsewhere. Would you, Mitzy?' His eyes were on her and their gaze was steady, compelling. Dimity started to nod her head, then realised he wanted a negative reply, so shook it instead. Charles tapped a finger on the tabletop to show his approval, and Dimity smiled. But Celeste gave her an appraising look.

'It is easy to see things as they appear to be, and to make guesses, and form opinions. Who is to say that they are correct? Who is to say the happiness of the gypsies wasn't in your own mind, and then in your hand as you painted them?' she said to Charles, with a challenging tilt of her chin.

'It was real. I only painted what was there, in front of me . . .' Charles was adamant, but Celeste interrupted him.

'What you *saw* in front of you. What you *thought* you saw. Always, there are questions of . . .' She waved her hand, searching for the right word. 'Perception.' Charles and Celeste locked eyes, and Mitzy saw something pass between them, something she couldn't decipher. A muscle twitched in the corner of Charles's jaw, and there was a tense, angry look on Celeste's face.

'Don't start that again,' he said, with stony calm. 'I told you it was nothing. You're imagining things.' The silence at the table grew strained, and when Celeste spoke again her voice was far harder than her words.

'I was merely entering the discussion, *mon cher*. Why not *ask* Dimity, instead of *telling* her how she feels about it? Well, Mitzy? Do you want to always live here? Or do you think it might be better to try living somewhere else? Do you have strong roots, roots that keep you tied to this place?'

Dimity thought again of the long winter – swathes of sea

mist rolling in like clouds sunk low, so that the whole world contracted to the sullen earth in front of her feet; a fine layer of ice on the slurry pit by Barton's farm, which broke when she stumbled onto it, splashing her boots with foul black water; grounded fishermen cutting the reeds for thatch instead, working in rows, their arms swinging to and fro, the swish and crunch of their scythes loud in the deep quiet. Days when the whole world seemed ended and dead, and Dimity made her way to and from The Watch with her canvas coat pulled tight around her, the hems of her dungarees soaking wet and her old felt hat dripping from its brim; hearing the wheeze and whistle of swans in flight above her head, invisible in the murk. How she longed to fly away with them, longed to fight her way free of the stifling cold and the way each day started and ended the same. There were roots indeed, holding her tightly. As tightly as the scrubby pine trees that grew along the coast road, leaning their trunks and all their branches away from the sea and its battering winds. Roots she had no hope of breaking, any more than those trees had, however much they leaned, however much they strained. Roots she had never thought of trying to break, until Charles Aubrey and his family had arrived, and given her an idea of what the world was like beyond Blacknowle, beyond Dorset. Her desire to see it was growing by the day; throbbing like a bad tooth and just as hard to ignore.

She realised that Charles and Celeste were both waiting for her reply, and she found a way to answer that was honest, but ambiguous.

'My roots are here, and very deep,' she said, and at this Charles nodded again, satisfied, and cast a glance at Celeste, but Celeste watched Dimity a while longer, as if reading the vast unspoken truth behind the words. If indeed she saw it, though, she said nothing; she held out her hand for Élodie's empty plate, which the child handed to her without a word.

'Where shall we go then, Mitzy? Where is most rich with the folklore of this place? We'll go somewhere and I'll draw you surrounded by the old magic,' said Charles. Dimity felt pride swelling her up, to be consulted, to be the expert. Then she realised she had no idea where to suggest, and wasn't really sure what he meant by the old magic. She thought rapidly.

'St Gabriel's chapel,' she said, abruptly. It was a ruin in a copse on a hill, said to be haunted. The village boys held vigils in it, daring one another to spend a night there alone, with no camp fire, no torch. Huddled in amongst the damp green stones, hearing all kinds of fell voices in the shifting wind.

'Is it far?'

'Not far. An hour to walk it, I suppose,' she said.

'We'll go this afternoon. I'd like to see the place, get a feel for it.' His face had come alive with a kind of inner fervour, an intense enthusiasm. 'Will your mother spare you?'

'If there were coins for her, she'd spare me for ever,' Dimity murmured, then felt stupid for saying so. She remembered the idealised description of Valentina she'd given them last summer, and remembered that only Charles had met her – only he knew that it had been half-truths at best. 'That is . . . I mean . . .' she floundered, but Celeste put out her hand, and patted Dimity's.

'Only a fool would take coins in exchange for something priceless.' She smiled, but then she looked at Charles and the smile faded a little. 'You said you would take the girls to Dorchester this afternoon. To buy new sandals.'

'It's not urgent, is it? Tomorrow we'll go, girls,' he said to them, with a nod.

'That's what you said yesterday,' Delphine protested gently. 'My toes are touching the ground over the front of mine.'

'Tomorrow, I promise. The light is perfect today. Softer than it has been.' He seemed to talk almost to himself, turning his gaze to the table top. Feeling some scrutiny, Dimity looked at Celeste and found the woman watching her with a strange expression. When their eyes met Celeste smiled, and went back to collecting up the plates, but not quickly enough for Dimity to mistake what she'd seen. Celeste had looked worried. Almost afraid.

For three weeks the weather set fair, with a warm sun and soft breezes. Charles drove them all west to Golden Cap, the highest cliff along the Dorset coast. They climbed up through woods and fields, lugging heavy baskets packed with food, with sweat blooming through their clothes, to burst out onto the summit into fresher air and an endless view that took their breath away.

'I can see France!' said Élodie, shading her eyes with her hands.

'No you can't, you dope,' said Delphine with a chuckle.

'What's that then?' her sister demanded, pointing. Delphine squinted into the distance. 'A cloud,' she declared.

'No clouds today. I have decided it,' said Celeste, spreading out a striped blanket and unpacking the picnic.

'Ha! Then it must be France,' said Élodie, triumphant.

'*Vive la France*. Come and eat your lunch.' Celeste smiled. 'Dimity, come. Sit. Ham sandwich, or egg?'

When the picnic was finished Charles lay back, tipped his hat forward over his face and slept. Celeste gave up swatting at the flies and wasps that had come to feast on the leftovers and lay back as well, resting her head on Charles's stomach and shutting her eyes. 'Oh, how I love the sun,' she murmured. The five of them whiled away the afternoon there, the three girls watching the drowsy bees sway from flower to flower amidst the furze and heather; spotting ships far out to sea; waving and hallooing the other walkers and holidaymakers who appeared on the Cap. Elderly couples with dogs; young men and women with their fingers entwined; families with sturdy children, flushed from the climb. As they nodded and smiled, Dimity realised that they didn't know. These strangers didn't know that she was not an Aubrey, but a Hatcher; there was nothing to betray the fact that she was not one of the family. And so, for a while, she *was* one of them, she belonged with them, and this made her happier than she had ever known. She could not keep from smiling, and had to turn her face away from Delphine at one point because the feeling got so strong it prickled her nose, and threatened to turn into tears.

As the shadows lengthened at last, they packed up the hampers and made their way down from the summit. They drove the short distance to Charmouth and spent an hour or so hunting in vain for fossils, before taking tea and scones at a little café beside the rocky shore. Dimity's skin felt dry and stretched from a day in the sunshine, and she could tell from the quiet way they spoke that the Aubreys were feeling the same pleasant weariness that she was. Celeste didn't even scold when Élodie piled so much cream and jam onto her scone that she couldn't fit it into her mouth, and dropped a huge blob of it down her blouse. As if startled that there was no remark about this, Élodie pointed it out.

'Mummy, I've spoiled my blouse,' she said, mumbling around the hefty mouthful.

'That was stupid, hmm?' said Celeste, not breaking off her distant gaze, which was fixed on a high, floating gull. Delphine and Dimity exchanged a glance and laughed, and proceeded to pile their own scones every bit as high as

Élodie's. Dimity's stomach churned slightly, unused to such rich food, but it was too good to pass up.

'Mummy, can I go for a swim?' said Élodie, after a contented silence.

'I suppose so. If one of the big girls goes with you,' said Celeste.

'Don't look at me – you know I don't like swimming when it's rocky, not sandy,' said Delphine.

'Mitzy, will you? Please, please, pretty please?' Élodie begged.

'I can't, Élodie. I'm sorry.'

'Of course you can! Why can't you?'

'Well, because . . .' Dimity fidgeted, embarrassed. 'I can't swim.'

'Of course you can swim! Everybody can swim,' said Élodie, shaking her head stubbornly.

'I can't,' said Dimity.

'Is this true?' said Charles, who had not spoken for half an hour or more. Dimity nodded, hanging her head.

'You've lived your whole life by the sea, and never learned to swim?' He was incredulous.

'There's never been any call for me to swim,' said Dimity.

'But there may be, some day, and when that time comes it could well be too late to learn. No, it will not do,' said Charles, with a shake of his head.

By the end of the week, he had taught her. Dimity had no swimsuit, so she swam in her shorts and vest, splashing in small circles around him while he held her afloat with one hand underneath her, pressing into her midriff. At first she thought she would never manage it. It seemed impossible, and she spluttered and panicked, swallowing seawater that burned her throat, until she gradually stopped feeling as though the water was trying to kill her. She stopped fighting it and learnt to relax, to lengthen her body out and let the water lap her chin, to push through it with her arms and legs, to breathe normally. Delphine swam around them, calling out encouragement and scolding Élodie for laughing. Then, finally, she mastered it. It was late in the day, and the sun was low and yellow, dazzling like fire on the surface of the water. The pressure of Charles's hand got lighter and lighter, and then vanished altogether, and Dimity did not sink. She felt vulnerable without his touch, frightened without his support, but she swam, scooping with hands and legs and making slow but steady progress alongshore for some thirty feet before she put her feet down. She turned back to Charles with a smile of pure delight, and he was laughing too.

'Excellent, Mitzy! Well done! Like a proper mermaid,' he called. His hair was wet and dark, plastered to his head, and the skin of his chest shone with water, catching the rich sunlight so that he seemed to glow. Dimity stared; the sight of him was glorious, almost painful, but she couldn't look away.

'Hurray!' shouted Delphine, clapping her hands. 'You did it!'

'Can we go in for tea now?' said Élodie.

Dimity walked with them up to Littlecombe, weary but elated. Her hair hung in salty strings down her back and there was sand underneath her fingernails, but she had never felt as wonderful. There were already five places set at the table. Five, not four, and no question of whether or not Dimity would stay. Celeste had cooked a spiced chicken dish with rice and steamed courgettes from the garden, and they sat down to eat in a storm of chatter about the swimming lessons and Dimity's first proper swim. She and Delphine were allowed a little white wine to drink, diluted with water, and it made them giggle, and turned their cheeks pink, and later in the evening made their heads droop into their hands at the table.

By ten o'clock it was fully dark outside, and velvety moths fluttered in through the window to flirt with the lights. Élodie had curled up against Celeste's side, within the protective circle of her arm, and was already fast asleep.

'Right. Bed, for you three,' said Celeste. 'Charles and I can clear up the dinner things.'

'But it's early,' Delphine protested, but without conviction. She stifled a yawn, and Celeste smiled.

'I rest my case,' she said. 'Go on. Up.' Élodie mumbled in protest as Celeste stood and picked her up off the bench.

'I should go, then,' said Dimity. She got up reluctantly, and realised how little she wanted to return to her own home.

'It's pitch black and you haven't a torch. Sleep here tonight – your mother can't mind,' said Celeste. They all knew by then that Valentina minded little, so long as she was paid.

'You mean . . . I can stay?' said Dimity.

'Of course. It's late. You can sleep with Delphine. Go on, child. You are half asleep on your feet as it is! Better to stay than to stumble over a cliff in the dark.' Celeste smiled and ushered them upstairs. With a mixture of happiness and trepidation at what Valentina would say come morning, Dimity obeyed.

With the lights off and the blankets making a tent above their heads, Delphine and Dimity lay side by side for a while, chattering and giggling as quietly as they could. But Delphine soon succumbed to sleep. Behind the soft sound of her breathing, Dimity listened to Charles and Celeste downstairs; to the sound of crockery being washed and put away, and a conversation carried on in hushed tones. From time to time Charles's laughter rumbled up through the floor, warm and rich. Dimity shut her eyes, but even though she was bone weary, sleep did not come for a long time. She was distracted by feelings that seemed too big to keep in, feelings she could hardly give a name to, she was that unused to them. She dropped her hand to her stomach, to where, all week, Charles had pressed his own hand to keep her afloat in the water. That touch seemed the embodiment of everything she was feeling, everything that was perfect about that summer. It was security; it was protection. It was acceptance, and inclusion, and love. Before long she thought she could feel his hand there instead of her own, and she smiled into the darkness as sleep stole over her.

The following week, Charles took the car and went up to London. *Preliminaries for a commission*, Celeste told Dimity, when she asked, and Dimity had no idea what that meant. She tried not to let her disappointment at his departure show. Without him, and without the car, they were more tied to Blacknowle than they had been, but on Friday Celeste took them on the bus to Swanage, to go shopping. At first, Dimity was less than enthusiastic about the trip. Shopping, as far as she knew, meant picking up fish and potatoes for dinner, maybe a cake or some biscuits if a visitor had been particularly generous. It meant comparing the prices of what was on offer, making a few coins stretch as far as they possibly would, and then returning home to be told she had chosen badly. Shopping, as far as Celeste and her daughters were concerned, was a very different thing.

They drifted from shop to shop, trying on shoes and hats and sunglasses. They bought ice creams and sticks of rock, and then fish and chips wrapped in newspaper for lunch, hot and greasy and sublime. Élodie got a new blouse, pale blue with a printed pattern of little pink cherries; Delphine got a new book, and a jaunty sailor's cap. Celeste bought herself a beautiful red scarf, bright scarlet, and tied it around her hair.

'How do I look?' she asked, smiling.

'Like a film star,' said Élodie, whose lips were drenched in mint and sugar from the rock. Dimity was more than happy to watch them make their purchases, but suddenly Celeste seemed to notice her empty hands, and she looked uncomfortable, almost angry.

'Mitzy. How thoughtless I am. Come, child. You shall have something new,' she said.

'Oh, no. I don't need anything, truly,' said Dimity. She had a shilling in her pocket, that was all. Nothing like enough to buy a blouse, or a book, or a scarf.

'I insist. None of my girls shall go home with nothing, today! It will be a present, from me. Come. Come and choose something. What would you like?'

It felt very strange, at first. Dimity had never had a present from her own mother, not in fifteen years; it wasn't even her birthday, or Christmas. It was peculiar to be invited to spend someone else's money, on something just for her, and she had no idea what to choose. Élodie and Delphine made suggestions, holding up blouses and handkerchiefs and bracelets of beads. In the end, bewildered and in need of something she could hide easily from Valentina, Dimity chose a tub of hand cream, heavily scented with rose oil. Celeste nodded in approval as she paid for it.

'A lovely thing, Dimity. And very grown-up,' she said. Dimity smiled and thanked her repeatedly until she was told to stop. They rode back on the bus in time for tea, and Dimity watched Celeste covertly, as the Moroccan woman chatted to her daughters, thinking how beautiful she was, and how kind, and how she had called Dimity one of *her girls*. She realised with new clarity just how different life could have been if she'd been born to a mother more like Celeste, and less like Valentina Hatcher.

Days later, when Charles was back from London, Dimity walked to Littlecombe through the village with her head held high; past the scattered men with their glasses of beer, sitting along wooden benches outside the pub. She ignored their hisses, cocked a scathing eyebrow at them and approached the house boldly along the driveway. Raised voices stopped her. Celeste's first, so she thought it was probably Élodie being shouted at, but then Charles's voice joined in. The sound made her uneasy. She walked nearer, slowly, tucking herself close to the side of the house, in the shelter of the porch, to hear their words better.

'Celeste, calm down, for God's sake!' said Charles, and anger pulled the words tight.

'I will not! Must this happen every time you go to London? *Every* time, Charles? If it is so then tell me now, for I will not sit here in the middle of nowhere while you do that. I won't!'

'How many times must I say it? I drew her. Nothing more.'

'Oh, so reasonable, you sound! Then why do I not believe you? Why do I think you are lying? Who is she, this pale-headed creature? The daughter of your patron? Some whore you found, to replace the whore you found in *Maroc*?'

'Enough! I have done nothing wrong and I will not be spoken to this way! It will not do, Celeste!'

'You *promised* me!'

'And I kept my word!'

'The word of a man. Long years have taught women what such a thing is worth.'

'I am not any man, Celeste. I am *your* man.'

'Mine when you are here, but when you are not?'

'What do you suggest? That I never leave your side? That I consult with you on my every movement, my every action?'

'If your action is to fuck this girl, then yes, I do suggest this!'

'I told you, she was not my lover! That is Constance Mory, the wife of a man I met at the gallery. She has an unusual bone structure . . . I wanted to draw her, that was all. Please, you must not pounce every time I draw a female face. It does not mean betrayal.'

'Not always, perhaps. But I have only my experience to learn from,' said Celeste, hoarsely.

'What's past is past, *chérie*. I've drawn Mitzy Hatcher dozens of times, and you don't suspect anything there, do you?'

'Oh, Mitzy is a child! Even you would not stoop so low. But that is how you love a woman, Charles. This much I know. That is how you love a woman – you draw her face.' Dimity's heart gave a squeeze, and something hot surged into her blood. It rushed to the tips of her fingers, and made them shake. *That is how you love a woman – you draw her face.* She could not count the number of times Charles Aubrey had drawn her face. Many, many times. Her pulse made her muscles twitch, and she shifted her feet as quietly as she could.

'I love only you, Celeste. My heart is full of it,' said Charles.

'But my face is not in your drawings any more. Not for many months.' Celeste sounded sad as she said this. 'You are so accustomed to me that you do not even see me any more. That is the truth. So you leave me here by myself, bored and forgotten about, while you go off and have your fun. This place feels like exile when you go, Charles! Don't you see that?'

'You're not alone, Celeste. You have the girls . . . and I thought you hated London in the summertime?'

'I hate being left behind more, Charles! I hate waiting while you see other women, while you draw other women . . .'

'I told you, it's—' Charles broke off at a loud crunching sound, and Dimity looked down in horror, at the crushed fragment of clay pot beneath her shoe. She had no chance to run, or hide, so she dithered, hung her head. 'Mitzy!' Charles's face appeared around the side of the porch. 'Is everything all right?' Dimity nodded dumbly, her cheeks blazing red. 'Delphine and Élodie are down by the stream,' he said. She nodded again, and turned away quickly, not to find the girls, but to flee.

Late in August the sea mist came in like a wave grown massive, swelling over the cliffs and rolling almost half a mile inland. The droplets of water were almost visible, almost big enough to fall as rain, but not quite. It was rare in summer but not unheard of, and for the first two days, Élodie and Delphine loved it. They threw blankets around their shoulders and played at highwaymen, or murder in the dark; *murder in the mist*, as it was renamed. The three of them ran around the garden and the spread of pasture along the cliffs, looming up behind each other suddenly, squealing with delighted fear. Élodie asked Dimity for ghost stories, and listened wide-eyed to her tale of a whole army of drowned Viking warriors, who left Wareham to attack the Saxons in Exeter, only for their ships to be wrecked by a storm in Swanage Bay. *Every year for nigh on a thousand years, they've roamed the beach and cliffs on the anniversary of their deaths, coughing up water and weed, looking for their horses and their sunken treasure, and for people to slice open with their swords!* Élodie was entranced, and gripped

Dimity's skirt with tight little fists, her mouth hanging open in fascinated horror. The moisture made their hair hang limp, and words fell from their lips like pebbles, carrying no distance at all. The mist was like a cloak itself, turning the world mysterious and hidden, but by the third day all these things were telling.

Élodie's temper grew sullen, and Delphine's quiet and preoccupied. The two girls spent more and more time inside with the wireless radio chattering to them; Delphine on the couch reading a novel or *Lady's Companion* magazine, Élodie drawing at the table, frowning in concentration and angrily discarding one failed sketch after another. When Dimity knocked at the door, Celeste ushered her in as if relieved to see her, her expression tense and impatient, as though she was being made to wait too long for something important.

'How long will it last, this . . . *brouillard*? How do you say it?' she asked.

'The fog?'

'Yes. The fog. I am not sure how you people stand it, without running mad. It's like death, don't you think? Like being dead.' Her voice was hushed, intense.

'It shouldn't be much longer, Mrs Aubrey. It ought not to have stayed this long already. Only in winter, normally, would it linger for a week.' Celeste smiled briefly.

'Mrs Aubrey? Oh child, you know I am not that. I am Celeste, that is all.' She waved a hand in agitation. 'And still he goes out to paint! What does he hope to paint? White upon white?' she muttered. She crossed to the window and stood looking out with her arms folded. 'It is so dull,' she said, to nobody in particular.

The air inside the house was stale and overused, and Dimity thought it small wonder that the girls looked groggy and tired. She thought about trying to persuade them to come out for some air, but then Celeste went to the table and reached up to a high shelf above it, fetching down an atlas. 'Come, Dimity, let me tell you about somewhere more alive. Had you heard of Morocco, before you met me?' she said.

'No, I had not,' Dimity confessed. She did not mind saying such things to Celeste. The woman had no scorn in her, made no judgements about Dimity's education. She peered down at the complex drawing on the page. It made no sense to her at all. She searched for the familiar mouse-like shape of Britain, which she remembered from school; only once she'd found it could she gather where in the world this country of Celeste's birth might lie. She looked sideways at the woman. It seemed unreal to her, that a person might come from so far away, and to Blacknowle.

'How did you meet Mr Aubrey?' Dimity asked.

'He came to Morocco. To Fez, where I grew up and was living with my family. It was magnificent once, a thriving place full of learning and trade. Now it is much declined, though the French have built better roads. But Charles loved it all the more for that, I think. The decay. The decline. The way the buildings are fading and . . . blurring into each other. He saw me one day in the market, as I went to the old town bazaar to order a new mattress. Does that not show how fate works? How powerful it is? That the very morning Charles should be sitting drawing outside the mattress-maker's shop, a workman should accidentally spill paint all over my mother's bed? Hmm? It was destined. He came to Morocco to find himself, and instead he found me.'

'Yes,' said Dimity. Was it destiny, then, that there should be watercress growing behind Littlecombe, and that Dimity should go there to pick it, and that a great man like Charles Aubrey should choose to rent this very house, and come here, of all the places in the world? Here, to where Dimity was. To where she had always been, waiting. With a shiver, she hung the words *fate* and *destiny* onto this, her own life, her own meeting with him. They seemed to fit, and this startled her.

Celeste sighed and ran her fingers over the map of Morocco with its vast empty spaces of desert and the twin ridges of mountains curving through it in the south. Here she tapped her nail.

'Toubkal,' she said. 'The tallest mountain. My mother grew up in its shadow, in the shelter it gave. Her village was built into the rocks at its feet, where the wind through the pine trees was like it breathing. There is no better way to always know your way home than to live beside a mountain, she says. It has been too long since I went back to her; back to Fez. How I should love to see them again!' Celeste put her hand flat on the page, and shut her eyes for a second, as though feeling the heartbeat of her home through the paper. Dimity wondered if she would feel this pull for home if she ever travelled away from Blacknowle. If she would come to love it, once she was far from it; as though distance might give it a shine, a glow it wholly lacked now. The thought that she might never travel away from Blacknowle sat inside her and took something from her, a little bit every day, like a parasite. 'It has been too long. When I think of it, of how beautiful it is, it seems strange to me that we choose to be here.' Celeste glanced around at the kitchen's four walls. 'In Blacknowle,' she said, her voice laden with *ennui*. Dimity felt a sudden nudge of disquiet, a little warning bell in the back of her mind.

Just then, the door opened and Charles appeared with a swirl of mist. Droplets of moisture hung from his hair and his clothes, but he was smiling.

'Ladies. How are we all?' he said, cheerily.

'Bored and bad-tempered,' said Delphine, and though she said it lightly, Dimity heard a warning for him in the words.

Charles glanced from his daughter to Celeste, and registered her flat expression.

'Well, perhaps this will help.' He held aloft a white envelope. 'I ran into the postman in the village. A letter for us from France.'

'Oh! We are not quite forgotten, then?' cried Celeste, snatching it from him.

'Who's it from? What does it say?' demanded Élodie, as her mother tore open the envelope.

'Hush, child, and let me read.' Celeste frowned at the paper, standing by the window for better light. 'It is from Paul and Emilia . . . they are in Paris,' she said, eyes rapidly scanning the page. 'They have taken a large apartment on the Seine, and they invite us to go and visit with them!' She looked at Charles, her face lighting up; Dimity felt all the air dribble out of her lungs.

'Paris!' Élodie gasped in excitement.

'It is only two weeks until school starts . . .' Charles pointed out, taking the letter from Celeste.

'Oh, do let's go, though. It'll be so much fun,' said Delphine, taking her father's hand and squeezing it. Dimity stared at her in horror.

'But . . . the mist will clear soon, I know it . . .' she said. Nobody seemed to hear her.

'Well?' Celeste said to Charles, holding her clasped hands up to her mouth, her eyes wide and avid. He smiled at her, and shrugged a shoulder.

'Paris it is, then,' he said. The girls whooped with delight, and Celeste threw her arms around Charles's neck, kissing him. Dimity stood rooted to the spot, reeling with shock. She felt like she was drowning and nobody could see. She knew instinctively that this time she would not be included.

'But . . .' she said again, the word lost beneath the racket of their excitement.

He'd been hoping she might come to the pub to find him, but she hadn't. He went into Wareham first, to the small supermarket there, and then down to the farm, where he parked on the concrete yard by the house. There was no answer to his knock on Hannah's door, so Zach carried on down to the beach.

Hannah was standing far out at the end of the submerged rock spur with her arms folded, her jeans rolled up to the knee and a loose blue shirt belling out behind her, catching the wind like a sail. The breeze was strong, whipping the surface of the sea into a thousand tiny crests, spinning salt into the air. Zach called out to her, but with the wind in her ears she didn't hear him. He put down the carrier bags he was holding and sat on a rock to take off his shoes and socks, watching her all the while. He wanted to draw the resolute line of her spine, the way she was almost lost against the seascape, a single figure surrounded by agitated water that seemed to lie in wait – for her to stumble, for her to miss her footing. She looked at once immoveable and in grave peril. He thought about who this drawing would be for, and knew at once that it would be purely for himself; to preserve the simple joy of seeing her. The very same reason that Aubrey drew his women, Zach thought, though he smiled to think how Hannah might react to being called 'his woman'. He took a few tentative steps onto the rock shelf, finding it hard to trust the path when he could not see it. He spread his arms out in case he tripped; felt the wind rush around his fingers.

'Hannah!' he called again, but either she still couldn't hear or was so lost in thought that she didn't. Zach waded close behind her, cursing as he stubbed his toe on a small, hidden step. Still she gazed out to sea, and for a second Zach stopped, and did the same. He wondered if it was still Toby that she was looking for, that she was waiting for. Everything in her stance said she would wait as long as she had to, and Zach wanted to grab her, spin her around to face him and break off the vigil. A flash of light caught his eye. There was a small boat, a very typical fishing boat, making slow progress east to west about a hundred and fifty metres offshore. Zach had barely even noticed it, but now he saw that its progress was particularly slow, and that a figure on board appeared to be studying the shore every bit as intently as Hannah was studying the sea. The flash of light came again – the sun catching fleetingly on glass. Binoculars?

'I think that fisherman fancies you,' he said, close to Hannah's ear. She jumped and spun around to him with a gasp, then slapped him across one cheek, not hard but not entirely playfully either.

'Damn it, Zach! Don't sneak up on me like that!'

'I did call out to you – several times.'

'Well, obviously I didn't hear you,' she said, her face softening.

'Sorry,' said Zach. He ran his fingers down her forearm, and took her hand.

Hannah looked away again, following the small boat that was finally motoring out of sight around the coast. Had she been watching the boat, then, and not waiting for Toby at all? Zach squinted at it, and saw a flash of pale purple as somebody moved across the deck. The colour was familiar, but he couldn't quite place it.

'Do you know that boat? The people on it, I mean?' he asked. Hannah looked away from it quickly, flicked her eyes up at him.

'No,' she said, curtly. 'Not at all.' She pulled her hand away from his, ostensibly to push her hair out of her face and tuck it behind her ear.

'I've brought a picnic. Bought a barbecue and everything. Are you hungry?'

'Starving,' she said, with a smile. Zach held out his arm,

and was glad when she looped hers through it as they walked back towards the beach.

They set up the little foil barbecue he'd bought on some flat rocks up the beach, beyond the high-tide line of shells and cuttlefish bones. It gave off the faint reek of paraffin as Zach lit it, and Hannah shook her head.

'Shame on me,' she said.

'What for?'

'I could have built us a proper cook fire. There's even a grate and long handled tools up in one of the barns.'

'Well, I'll tend to this one, you build a campfire over there. For later.'

'Later?'

'This little thing won't keep us warm once the sun goes down,' said Zach.

'All right. Give me the wine – I'll put it in the cooler.' Hannah smiled and held out a hand for the bottle, then took it down to the shore and buried it up to its neck in the fine grit by the waterline. She stayed to wander near the water, gathering driftwood for fuel. The evening grew mild and the wind dropped, so that small waves curled against the shingle with a sound like quiet voices. The sky was pale lemon, a kind light that softened everything. Zach waited for the flames in the tray to die down and then started to cook the prawns and chicken legs he'd brought. They ate them hot, as soon as they were ready, burning their fingers and their lips. Lemon juice and chicken fat shone on their chins, and they drank the wine from paper cups.

Driftwood gave the bonfire flames a pale green colour, almost invisible while the sun was still up, but unearthly and lovely as the sky began to darken overhead. Zach stared at sparks as they spun upwards and vanished into the air. With the wine in his blood and his stomach full, the world suddenly seemed very serene, as though time had slowed;

or as though there, in Blacknowle, the rest of the world mattered less than it once had. The firelight got caught up in Hannah's hair, and made her lovelier than ever; not so much softening her hard edges as gilding them. She stared into the fire with her chin on her knees, and Zach thought he could see something of his own tranquillity in her as well.

'I've never done this before,' he said.

'What's that?' She turned her face to him, laid her head down. Behind her a tiny, bright sliver of moon rose.

'Had a barbecue on the beach – a romantic barbecue on a beach. It's the sort of thing I've always meant to do, but never actually got around to.'

'Shouldn't the things on your bucket list be slightly more radical? Like sky-diving, or learning to play the bassoon?'

'This is better than learning to play the bassoon.'

'How do you know?' She grinned at him, then moved back to sit beside him, leaning on the smooth side of a huge boulder. 'So your wife isn't an outdoors type of girl, then?'

'Ex-wife. And no – definitely not. She did have some wellies, I think, but they were for getting from door to door without slipping on wet pavements. They never saw mud.'

'And have your wellies seen mud before?'

'I . . . I don't even own any wellies. Please don't dump me,' said Zach, smiling. Hannah chuckled.

'I'd kind of guessed as much.'

'I think I could get the hang of it though. Country living and all the rest of it. I mean, it's beautiful here, isn't it? It has to be good for the soul.'

'Well, come back on a rainy day in January, and see if you still feel the same way.'

'Maybe I'll still be here in January,' said Zach. For a long time, Hannah said nothing to this, but then she took a deep breath, and exhaled a single word.

'Maybe.' She picked up a limpet shell and turned it over in

her fingers. 'We used to come and have dinner on the beach all the time.'

'Who – you and Toby?'

'The whole family. Mum and Dad, even my grandmother sometimes, when I was still just a girl.'

'Did she live with you then?'

'Yes, she did. She was like you – a city girl by birth. But she married into the family, and fell in love with life down here; with the coast. But it was a quiet kind of love. I think she was one of those people who find the sea melancholy. She died when I was still a grotty teenager, so I never got the chance to ask her about it.'

'There's so much I've never asked my grandparents. Important things as well. Grandpa's dead now, so that's him off the hook.'

'Of course – the neglectful grandpa, embittered by rumours of Charles Aubrey's unstoppable trouser snake,' said Hannah.

'You don't buy it at all, do you?'

'That you're one of Charles Aubrey's bastard grandchildren?' She arched an eyebrow, mockingly, making Zach smile. 'Who knows?' Hannah flung the shell away from her and leaned back into the welcoming circle of his arm. Zach kissed the top of her head, noticing the spring of her curls against his skin; the scents of the sea and of sheep's wool in her hair. They caused him an almost painful stab of tenderness.

They stayed on the beach until it was fully dark, talking about the small things that made up their lives, and the big things that came along to scatter everything else into chaos. Hannah was halfway through describing the various problems she'd encountered with her flock since buying them, from an attack of scab to a ram that wouldn't tup, when she cut herself off.

'Sorry. I must be boring you to death.'

'No, keep talking. I want to know everything,' said Zach.

'What do you mean?' She leaned away from him slightly so she could see his face.

'I mean, I want to know everything about you.' He smiled.

'Nobody ever knows everything about a person, Zach,' she said, solemnly.

'No. I guess life would be pretty boring if they did. It'd be the death of mystery, after all.'

'And you do love a mystery, don't you?'

'Doesn't everybody?'

'Yet you're determined to uncover the truth, as you put it, about Aubrey's time here. About Dimity's time with him. Won't that kill the mystery?'

'It might, I suppose,' he said, puzzled that she should mention it. 'But that's different. And I wasn't talking about Charles Aubrey. I was talking about *you*, Hannah, and—' He broke off and suddenly looked at his watch. 'Oh, bollocks!' He rose clumsily to his feet.

'What?'

'It's Saturday. I was meant to Skype Elise at eleven!'

'Well, it's quarter to now. You'll never make it back to the pub in time.' Hannah stood up and brushed her hands on the seat of her jeans.

'I have to try. I'll have to run. I'm sorry, Hannah . . .'

'Don't be. I'll come with you,' she said, simply, turning to kick the fire into embers.

'Really?'

'Unless you don't want me to?'

'No, of course I do. Thanks.'

The pub was virtually empty, and while Zach turned on his laptop Hannah sauntered over to the bar to greet Pete Murray, who'd been chatting to a solitary drinker perched on a stool. They'd missed last orders, but Pete still poured Hannah two fingers of vodka and put it down in front of her.

'Listen, Hannah,' Zach heard the barman say, 'about your tab . . . I've really got to ask you to settle up.' Hannah took a swig of the vodka.

'I will soon, I promise,' she said.

'You said that two weeks ago. I mean, I've been patient, but the bill's gone over three hundred now . . .'

'I just need a few more days. I've got money coming in, I promise. And as soon as it does, I'll be in to settle up. I give you my word. Just a few more days.'

'Well, all right – as long as it won't be any longer than that. You're not the only one with a business to run, you know.'

'Thanks, Pete. You're a diamond.' She smiled at him, and tipped her glass in salute before draining it.

Hannah waited at a tactful distance as Zach, slightly self-conscious at first, told Elise everything he'd been doing, and heard about everything she'd been doing – including her first taste of pumpkin pie. Then he told her a bedtime story, even though it wasn't quite bedtime, that involved several silly voices and sound effects. He knew he was drawing attention to himself from the handful of people in the pub, but Elise was giggling uncontrollably, and he decided that as long as she found it funny then he didn't care how mad he sounded. Afterwards, he smiled sheepishly as Hannah came and sat with him.

'Sorry about that,' he said.

'Don't be. She sounds sweet. Not that I'm much of an expert on children.'

'Me neither, believe me. My learning curve has been as steep as hers these past six years.'

'Well, I should be getting back. Got a horribly early start

tomorrow – the lovely people from the organic certification body are coming to do an audit at the crack of dawn.'

'Oh,' said Zach, disappointed. 'That sounds important.'

'Big day.' She nodded. 'Want to show me your room first?' she said. Zach paused, and glanced at Pete Murray, who was wiping a very dry glass behind the corner of the bar nearest to their table. The barman had a blank look on his face, all his attention on what he was hearing.

'Step this way,' said Zach. He led her along the corridor to the stairs, then looked back over his shoulder. 'Well, that's torn it. I get the feeling that once Pete knows something around here, everybody knows it.'

'So what?'

'Well, I don't know. I kind of got the impression you didn't like other people knowing your business.'

'What does anybody really know? I'm not worried about their opinion of me, if that's what you mean. You're a reasonably good-looking bloke. Clean. Youngish. Why should I try to hide the fact that I've pulled you?' she said. Zach shrugged, pleased.

'Well, when you put it like that . . .' He opened the door to his small room, wincing at the stuffy air that smelt of sleep and the lime air freshener on top of the wardrobe. Hannah shut the door behind them.

'Cosy,' she said, sitting down on the patchwork bedspread with a bounce.

'So, *you've* pulled *me*, have you?' said Zach. Hannah hooked her fingers through his belt and pulled him onto the bed.

'Now, don't go pretending to anyone that it was the other way around. Not even to yourself.'

'I wouldn't dare.' They made love almost without foreplay, hurried and intent. It was all over with breathless urgency; Hannah locked her ankles behind his back, arching her whole body away from him. Black spots danced in the corners of Zach's eyes, and while he waited to catch his breath, Hannah extricated herself from his heavy limbs and pulled her jeans back on.

'I really do have to go.' She pulled her hair back into a ponytail.

'Not yet. Stay for a while. Stay the night.'

'I really can't, Zach. I do have to be on the ball – and on the premises – first thing tomorrow.'

'Wham, bam, thank you, ma'am.' Zach put his hands through his hair and grinned at her.

'You're welcome.' Hannah glanced at him, then leant over, kissed his mouth.

'See you later. And thanks – this was just what I needed.' She smiled mischievously and left him there with his shirt still on, tangled threads where two of the buttons had been.

'Without so much as a by your leave,' he murmured to himself, wondering briefly if this was what *he'd* needed, and deciding it was pretty close.

The following afternoon Zach set off to visit Dimity, wondering if she would consent to sit for him. He wanted to try to capture the ghost of youthful beauty that haunted her lines and wrinkles, and the way her eyes looked into other worlds, other times. But then, her reaction to seeing his work when she was used to seeing Aubrey's might snuff out the fragile new spark of creativity he was so carefully nurturing. Zach's eyes drifted down the hill to where the houses of Blacknowle petered out, ending with an unattractive, sixties-built terrace. A flash of colour behind the fence of the nearest cottage caught his eye, and this time he recognised it at once. Lilac. Zach saw the head and shoulders of a large man above the fence, tall and thickset, with a fat neck and barrel chest. He had long brown hair tied back off his face, and an unkempt beard to mask his double chin. James Horne, one of the brothers who had such a bad reputation in Blacknowle. He was talking to somebody concealed by the fence, and it was clearly a serious conversation. The man's face was like thunder, and he jabbed his finger on some words, to emphasise them. And yet his voice didn't carry at all. Zach had stumbled upon a hushed argument.

He knew he shouldn't watch, in case James Horne looked up and noticed him. It was a bad time for him to interrupt. He sped up as much as possible to get past, and tried to look as though he hadn't noticed anything but the tarmac up ahead. James Horne was big, and he didn't look friendly. Just then, the argument ended and the man with the lilac sweatshirt turned to watch the person hidden by the fence move away. Zach kept looking straight ahead as he walked past the house towards the track to The Watch. At a safe distance he glanced back over his shoulder, and was startled to see Hannah stalking away in the opposite direction with her fists clenched angrily at her sides.

Zach doubled back and jogged slightly to catch up with her.

'Hannah, wait!' She spun around and Zach was shocked by the expression on her face. She looked furious, and frightened. When she saw him she blinked, and though her mouth twitched, she couldn't seem to smile.

'Zach! What are you doing here?'

'I was just going down to visit Dimity. Are you all right? What was all that about?'

'Yes, I'm fine. I was just . . . Are you going back to the pub?'

'No. To Dimity's, like I said . . . But I can come back with you, if you—'

'Good. Let's walk.'

'All right, then. That was James Horne, wasn't it?'

'What was?'

'That man you were talking to. That was James Horne.'

'Getting to know all the locals, I see,' she muttered, striding along rapidly at his side.

'He was in the pub the other night, giving Pete a bit of stick. Well his brother was, anyway. And I thought I saw him on that fishing boat you were watching the other day, off the end of the jetty,' said Zach. Hannah scowled, but didn't look at him.

'You might have done. He is a fisherman, after all.'

'It looked like you were arguing, just then.' Zach had to walk quickly to keep up with Hannah's implacable pace. She ignored his statement. 'Hannah, wait.' He caught her arm, and pulled her to a stop. 'Are you sure you're all right? He wasn't . . . threatening you, was he? Do you owe him money or something?'

'No, I bloody don't! And I'd hardly go knocking on his door if I did, would I?'

'All right! Sorry.'

'Just . . . forget about it, Zach. It's nothing.' She started walking again.

'Clearly not nothing . . .' Zach said, but fell silent at the look she shot him. 'All right, fine. I was just trying to help, that's all.'

'You can help me by buying me a pint and not worrying about James Horne.'

'OK! How did the organic audit thing go this morning?' Finally, Hannah slowed her pace. They were nearly at the Spout Lantern, and she paused to look down towards the sea, and her farm. There was colour high in her cheeks, and her nostrils flared slightly as she caught her breath. For a second she seemed lost in thought, but then she smiled; a smile of genuine delight.

'It went well,' she said, and they went inside.

Over a glass of beer she told him all about the inspection, but he found himself only half listening, some of the time; distracted by her connection to James Horne and why she might refuse to talk about it; speculating about what they could have been arguing about. He pictured the way she had stood at the end of the jetty while Horne's boat – and he was sure it had been his – had swung slowly across the bay. The flash of light he'd seen, as though someone on board had binoculars. As if she had been marking that spot, demonstrating the end of the submerged platform. These thoughts worried him, but he couldn't shake them. They caused a deep, ugly unease to settle inside him, increasing all the while.

It wasn't until later in the afternoon that Zach made his postponed visit to The Watch. As he'd promised, Zach didn't ask Dimity anything about the Aubreys. They talked instead about his own past, his career and his family, and inevitably the subject of his lineage came up. Dimity's voice turned guarded, almost surreptitious when she asked about his grandmother.

'That summer your gran was here, that was 1939, yes? Well, that was the summer Charles and I were finally together, you see. So don't you think I'd have known if there was another woman as well?' She picked at a loose thread on her mitten with her thumb and forefinger.

'Yes, you're probably right,' said Zach, thinking that a man like Charles Aubrey could easily charm a woman into believing she was his only one.

'What was your granddad like? Was he a strong man?'

'Yes, I suppose he was.'

'Strong enough to keep a woman at his side?'

Zach pictured his grandpa, who would sit for hours after

Sunday lunch with the newspaper across his knees, and wouldn't let anybody else look at it until he'd solved the crossword, even though his eyes were shut and his chin dropping down. He tried to remember seeing tenderness, affection, pass between him and his wife, but the more he thought back, the more he realised how rarely they were even together in the same room. When he was in the sitting room, she was in the kitchen. When he was in the garden, she went into her dressing room to look at her Aubrey picture. At dinner they sat at opposite ends of a seven-foot table. Surely it couldn't always have been like that? Surely it had taken sixty years of marriage for such a distance to grow between them?

'Tell me this,' said Dimity, interrupting his thoughts. 'If your granddad really did think she had an affair with my Charles, why on earth did he go ahead and marry her?'

'Well, because she was pregnant, I suppose. That's why they had to bring the wedding forward.'

'So he must have thought the baby was his.'

'At first, yes. I suppose he must. Unless he was just being . . . honourable.'

'Was he that kind? The chivalrous type? I've known few enough men that are. Not really.'

'No, I suppose that doesn't seem quite right . . . but he might have done it to, you know, take the moral high ground.'

'To punish her, you mean?' said Dimity.

'Well, not exactly . . .'

'But that's what it would have been. If he knew, and she knew he knew. What better way to remind her of it every day of her life, and to make her suffer for it, than to marry her?'

'Well, it backfired on him, if that was his plan. She made

no secret of how pleased she was about the connection. About the scandalous rumours.'

'Well, that was Charles, you see. If she . . .' Dimity paused, and pain splintered her expression, robbing her of words for a second. 'If she loved him, she'd have been proud, never ashamed.' She hung her head for a second, and rubbed the thumb of one hand over the opposite palm. 'So . . . perhaps she did. Perhaps she did love him, after all.'

'But I'm sure . . .' Zach took one of Dimity's restless hands, and squeezed it. 'I'm sure that didn't mean he loved you any less. Even if she loved him . . . it could have been unrequited. He may well have thought nothing of her,' he said, feeling an odd pull of loyalties to speak that way about a grandmother he loved.

Zach was struck by the idea that Aubrey was the kind of man women were proud of. He thought back and tried to identify a time when Ali had been proud of him – proud to be his woman, his wife – but what came instantly to mind were her expressions of disappointment. That slow exhalation through her nose as she listened to his explanation of some mishap, some missed opportunity; the wrinkle between her brows that she was often wearing when he caught her studying him. With a slight shock he realised he'd seen the exact same expressions on his mother's face, before she'd left. While his grandfather had been criticising his father for something trivial; while the three of them had roamed the footpaths of Blacknowle, years ago, and his dad had searched in vain for answers. Was it in the blood, then? Would men like Aubrey always make men like the Gilchrists seem the poor alternative? Zach was troubled by this idea – that he would inevitably disappoint the women in his life, including Hannah.

'Haven't you brought any pictures with you this time?'

said Dimity, as Zach stood up to leave. 'Pictures of me?' There was a hungry light in her eyes.

'Yes, but I didn't think you wanted to talk about that this time?'

'Oh, I always want to see the pictures. It's like having him here in the room again.' Zach rummaged in his bag and withdrew the latest set of printouts he'd made. Several drawings and one large oil canvas of a crowd of figures, kicking up dust with their feet. There were blue and red mountains behind them, and the ground was orange-brown, the sky above a vast, clear swathe of green and white and turquoise. The people were wrapped in loose robes, some of the women veiled as well, with only their eyes left naked. In one corner was a woman with her hair piled up loosely on her head and many strings of beads swinging around her neck. She was standing, calm and nonchalant, her face turned towards the viewer. She wore no veil, and her eyes were heavily kohled, cat-like. She was wearing a cerulean kaftan, which billowed in a hot breeze that the viewer could almost feel; the fabric clinging to the shape of her thighs and hips. It was not the Mitzy Zach knew from the early sketches, nor the Mitzy standing in front of him now. It was a fairy-tale version of her, a vision; a desert princess with her face standing out from the crowd like a single flower in a field of grass. The painting was called *Berber Market*, and it had set the record for an Aubrey painting when it sold in New York eight years ago. It was easy to see why. The painting was like a window into another world.

Zach handed the picture to Dimity. She took it with a small cry, lifted it up to her face and inhaled, as though she might be able to smell the desert air.

'Morocco!' she said, with a beatific smile.

'Yes,' said Zach. 'I have more drawings of you from there as well, if you'd like to see them . . . Haven't you got copies of these? In books, or as prints, I mean? Copies you can look at?' Dimity shook her head.

'It didn't seem proper, to gaze at myself like that. Vanity, I suppose it seemed. And never the same as seeing the real thing of course, and knowing that your hands were touching where his touched before . . . I haven't seen this since it was painted. And even then I never saw it finished.'

'Really? Why not?'

'Charles . . .' A shadow dulled her delight. 'Charles went up to London to finish it, once my part was done. He had . . . other business there.' She studied the image of herself closely and smiled again. 'That was the first time, you know,' she said, conspiratorially.

'Oh?'

'The first time we . . . were together. As man and wife, I mean. As we should have been. The first time we realised how much in love we were . . . I've never been back there. To *Maroc*. Some memories are too precious to risk, do you see? I want it to always be as it is now, in my head.'

'I understand, yes.' Zach was surprised to hear her use the French pronunciation: *Maroc*. 'How long were you over there with him?'

'Four weeks. The best four weeks of my life,' she said.

Dimity shut her eyes and in front of them was a light so bright that everything glowed red. That was her first impression of the desert, the first thing she remembered. That and the smell, the way the air tasted. Nothing like the air in Dorset; different in the way it touched the back of her throat, and the inside of her nose; in the way it filled her lungs and ran through her hair. She felt heat scorch her skin, even as she sat at her own kitchen table with its sticky linoleum top pressing into the heels of her hands. She tried to find the right words. Words that could somehow convey all the things she'd seen and felt and tasted; bring them back to life. She took a slow breath in, and Valentina's voice echoed angrily down the stairs, *Morocco? Where the bloody hell is that, then?* In a flash she saw Valentina's eyes, bloodshot and bewildered, trying to work out how much such a trip was worth. *And how in God's name has this come about?* Was it her mother, she wondered, who cursed the trip? Was it Valentina's envy and spite that made the best four weeks of her life also the worst?

7

Dimity waited. She waited for Charles Aubrey and his family to come back, and waiting made the winter longer than ever. Dimity spent it alone. Wilf spent more and more time working with his father and brothers, and only rarely came to meet her. When he did he was warm and eager, as ever; but Dimity was distracted, only half present, and he often went away frustrated. Dimity roamed the cliffs, the hedgerows and the beach. She picked baskets full of smooth, white field mushrooms and sold them door to door for a few pennies. She loitered in the village, missing the company of other people more than ever before, and seeming to notice more than ever how peoples' eyes brushed over her, cold and dismissive. Nobody noticed her the way Charles did.

They came later than usual, not until the beginning of July. In the last two weeks of June Dimity checked at Littlecombe four times a day, and carried around a weight of dread and worry in her stomach that made it hard for her to eat, or to think. Valentina swore at her. Gave her a shove that cracked her head against the wall one day when she let the potatoes boil dry; shook her; made her drink a tonic of oak bark to improve her appetite, because her collarbones were standing proud above her ribs and her cheeks had lost their fullness and bloom.

'You looked younger than your years till this winter, Mitzy. Better by far to keep that than to lose it. No man'll want you if you're old before your time.' Valentina scowled as she pressed the cup of bitter tonic to her daughter's reluctant lips. 'Marty Coulson's been asking after you lately.

What do you say to that?' she said, curtly, and had the good grace to look away when the implication of this hit home, and her daughter's eyes widened with horror. Dimity made a choking noise in her throat, and could not speak. Valentina said abruptly: 'We all must pay our way in this world, Mitzy. You weren't born with that face for nothing, and if that artist of yours don't show this year . . . Well, you'll have to find some other way to make it pay, won't you?'

It was warm and bright, the morning they finally came. Dimity was sitting on a field gate to the west of Littlecombe when she spotted the chalky sheep wash billowing above the lane – the rising cloud of dust that told of an approach. When the blue car pulled up she went so boneless with relief that she slithered forwards from the gate and knelt on the dusty ground in front of it. She was crippled by joy, unsurprised to feel tears running down her cheeks. She wiped them away with gritty hands as she made her way down towards the house. She saw Élodie and Delphine run off, together with another girl she didn't know, through the garden gate and down towards the path to the beach. Élodie had grown much taller, and Delphine's hair was much longer. Their appearances spoke of the wealth of life they had seen and experienced since their last visit, whilst Dimity had remained the same, static. She watched their slender figures vanish, and walked up to the open kitchen door with her blood crowding her head so that she could hardly hear a thing.

At that moment Celeste stepped out, saw her and stopped. The Moroccan woman pressed her lips together and for a moment Dimity thought she saw irritation flash across her face, before a sort of resignation, and then a smile.

'Mitzy. And before the kettle has even boiled,' she said,

taking Dimity by her upper arms and kissing her on both cheeks. 'How are you? How is your mother?'

'You're so late,' Dimity mumbled in response, and Celeste shot her a quizzical look.

'Well, we did think about not coming this year. We thought about taking a house in Italy instead, or perhaps Scotland. But the girls wanted the beach, and Charles has been working very hard, and left it too late to organise anything else, so . . . here we are.' She did not invite Dimity in, did not offer her tea. 'We probably won't stay the whole summer. It depends on the weather.' Just then, Charles appeared from the car with a bag in each hand, and Dimity whirled around to face him.

'Mitzy! How are you, dear girl? Come to see Delphine already, have you?' He bustled past her, pausing to brush her cheek with a fleeting kiss as he carried on up the stairs with the luggage. Dimity shut her eyes and pressed her hand to the place on her face where his lips had touched. The kiss sent a bolt of sheer pleasure to the pit of her stomach. When she opened her eyes, Celeste was watching her carefully, and something measuring, something vaguely like suspicion, crossed her face. Dimity blushed, and though she tried to think of something to say, her mouth and her head remained empty.

'Well,' Celeste said, eventually. 'The girls have gone straight down to the beach. Delphine has a friend to stay this first week. Why don't you run down and see them?'

Dimity did as she was bid, but it was obvious at once that things wouldn't be the same, not with Delphine's friend to make their trio a foursome. The girl's name was Mary. She had pale blonde hair set in a very grown-up wave and blue eyes that sparkled with amusement as they took in Dimity's ragged clothes and bare feet. Mary looked at her in the same way as the other youngsters in the village, and in spite of

Delphine's warm greeting, Dimity felt at once that she was not wanted. Mary had on a blouse of soft raspberry silk, which fluttered in the breeze. Mary had jewellery that sparkled, and a touch of paint on her lips.

'Hello, Mitzy!' Élodie called, as she cartwheeled around them on the sand. 'Look at Mary's bracelet – isn't it just the prettiest thing?' Smiling haughtily, Mary held out her wrist, and Dimity agreed that it was a pretty bracelet. She caught Delphine's eye, and saw her friend's cheeks colouring, saw her fidget uncomfortably. In front of Mary, Delphine did not want to be the kind of girl who picked from hedgerows or learnt the Dorset names for things. In front of Mary, she wanted to be the kind of girl who might marry a film star. Inventing some errand, Dimity backed away, and as she turned she heard the blonde girl say, in a supercilious tone:

'Oh dear, do you think I frightened her? Do you think she's ever seen a charm bracelet before?'

'Don't be unkind,' Delphine chided her, but without much heat.

'Daddy said she's never left this village in her whole life. Can you imagine how *boring* that must be?' said Élodie.

'Élodie, stop showing off,' Delphine snapped at her sister. Dimity fled, and heard no more.

The girls gave each other a wide berth that week, and though Dimity burned with impatience, and longed to visit Littlecombe, she felt too cowed and angry after Celeste's cool welcome and without Delphine to visit. But she spotted the three girls on the beach and in the village, and more than once down at Southern Farm, flirting with Christopher Brock, the farmer's son. Mary twirled her hair in her fingertips and postured and simpered at him like an idiot, but it was Delphine who seemed to be able to flummox him with a word, or a glance. Whenever she spoke to him he hung his head, smiling shyly, and once Dimity was close enough to see the blush infusing his cheeks. Delphine's friend laughed like a jay when she saw, and tried not to show how much she minded, but Dimity smiled secretly to see her swallow her pride over it.

When eight days had passed, Dimity began to consider visiting again, since Mary ought to have left. She was in the privy one afternoon, surrounded by the sweet, pungent stink of the pit and the buzzing of insects, tearing up squares of newspaper to hang on the hook and arranging branches of elder to discourage the flies, when she heard Valentina shout through the back door. She had been dreaming about the indoor plumbing at Littlecombe, with the cistern high up on the wall and a brass chain to flush it by, and soft rolls of toilet paper. No rough wooden seat or festering slurry underneath. No checking under the lid for the fat, brown spiders that hid there to startle the unwary. Valentina shouted again.

'What, Ma?' Dimity called, letting the privy door slam shut behind her as she crossed the cluttered backyard. To her surprise, Élodie and Delphine appeared around the side of the cottage, looking around curiously. Dimity stopped in her tracks. 'What are you doing here?' she said, horrified. The girls stopped; Delphine smiled uncertainly.

'We came to find you . . .' she said. 'I . . . we . . . hadn't seen you for a while. Up at the house, I mean. I thought you might go foraging with me again?' Dimity was puzzled by this since they both knew why she had not visited – it had turned out that Dimity was a fall-back friend, a friend to be had when no better alternative was around. She felt a flare of resentment towards Delphine.

'I'm too busy. I'm not on a summer holiday, you know – I must help my mother and do my work, same as I ever did.'

'Yes, of course. But—'

'I suppose it's a bit boring for you, now Mary's gone,' she said.

'Oh, yes. It really is,' said Élodie. Dimity looked at the youngest girl, with her pretty, petulant face. But there was no rancour in it, no sneer. It was a simple statement of fact, laden with misunderstanding. Delphine blushed and looked stricken.

'I didn't mean to throw you over! Honestly not. It was just a bit difficult with Mary here – I had to entertain her, you see. I was the hostess, and she rather wanted us all to herself. You do understand don't you?' she said. Dimity felt her heart soften, but she wasn't quite ready to forgive her. 'It was only a week,' Delphine went on. 'She's gone off home now, and we have the whole rest of the summer.'

Dimity considered this apology, and wasn't sure how to respond. It was one of the first she had ever had, from anybody. Élodie sighed and put her hands in her pockets, swinging her hips side to side impatiently.

'Can't we go inside for tea?' she asked. 'Will your mother have made any? She seemed in rather a bad mood.'

'That's just how she is,' Dimity told her, shortly. Sometime during the past two years the pretence of Valentina being a warm and caring mother had evaporated. She didn't bother to explain how absurd an idea it was that she could invite them in, have them sit down inside The Watch to a tea that Valentina had prepared. It was pure fiction.

'Is that your loo?' said Delphine, after the silence had begun to stretch. Delphine sounded cheerful and curious, and Dimity felt a wave of heat rise through her. The heat of humiliation, and anger.

'Yes, it is.' Her voice was half choked. *It stinks in the summer and it's freezing in the winter, and there are spiders, and flies, and the newsprint leaves ink on your skin when you wipe, and there is no neat flush and splash of clean water to whisk away your foul doings – they sit there beneath you in a heap, steaming, for you and all who come after you to see. This is the bloody privy. This is my bloody life. This is no summer holiday.* But she did not say any of that.

'Oh, I didn't mean . . .' Delphine's cheeks turned pink again; she looked around with a vague smile and seemed at a loss. 'Well,' she said at last. 'Obviously you're very busy today. Perhaps we could go tomorrow? Foraging, I mean?'

'You don't need me to do that with you any more. You know your plants well enough.'

'Yes, but it's far more fun when all three of us go.'

'*I* don't think it's more fun,' Élodie pointed out.

'Yes, you do.' Delphine nudged her sister and frowned at her. Élodie rolled her eyes slightly.

'Oh, do come with us, Mitzy,' she said, obediently. 'Really. We should love to have you.'

'Perhaps. If I can get away,' said Dimity.

'I'll wait for you up at the house, then, shall I? Come on, Élodie.' The sisters walked away across the yard.

By morning Dimity's anger had melted away, and she was glad to escape from Valentina to visit the Aubreys. She and Delphine were awkward with each other for a minute longer, and then, with smiles, everything was all right again. They swam in the sea, though it was colder than usual, and foraged, and walked into the village to buy liquorice allsorts from the shop. It was during that week that two things began to make Dimity uneasy. Firstly, she saw Charles and Celeste talking to the tourist couple in the village. Saw them talking, and saw the way the strange woman wore her regard for Charles like a bright red ribbon, for the whole world to see. And secondly, she realised that Charles had seen her several times that summer, but had not yet asked to draw her once. Valentina had asked about the money, but Dimity longed for more than that. She longed for his concentrated attention, for the feeling she got when he studied her, when he sketched her. She felt more real, more alive at those times than at any other, and the thought that he might not want to, for any reason, made panic scramble in her gut. Yet somehow she knew she could not ask. She should not ask.

So each time she was in the same room as Charles Aubrey, Dimity followed him with her eyes, and put herself in his way, and tried to stand prettily. She scuffed her fingers through her hair to make it huge and wild, bit her lips and pinched her cheeks the way Valentina did before a guest arrived. And though Charles did not seem to notice, she found Celeste watching her more than once, with that same measuring look, and she was forced to turn away hastily for fear of giving herself away. But more often than not, Charles had gone out, by himself, before Dimity even arrived at Littlecombe. In desperation, she roused herself before dawn one day, and was outside on the driveway, waiting to catch him as he left the house. In the dewy grass she waited, with damp chilly toes and her heart beating only for him. He came out, dressed to paint, before the sun was an inch above the horizon, and Dimity stepped out in front of him, smiling.

'Mitzy!' There was a smile in his hushed voice, a joyous note, and happiness roared in her ears. 'Dear girl. Are you all right?'

'I am,' she said, nodding breathlessly.

'Well, well. They're not even awake yet, in the house. Fast asleep, the lot of them. I'd give Delphine another good hour before you knock, if I were you. She told me you were taking her foraging again soon, is that right?' Dimity could only nod, tongue-tied. 'Splendid. Well, have fun, won't you. À bientôt.' He carried on along the driveway, lighting up a cigarette; taking long, languid strides.

Behind her, she heard the latch click and the door creak softly as it opened, and she turned to see Celeste coming along the path. She was still in her nightgown, with her long, dark hair hanging over an emerald-green shawl that was wrapped around her shoulders. No make-up on her face, just the kiss of the early morning light to make her as beautiful and terrible as any fairy queen. Her face was set and sad, but her loveliness made Dimity's heart wither a little, hopelessly. Dimity took a step backwards, and Celeste raised her hands to reassure her.

'Wait, please, Mitzy. I would like to speak to you,' she said, in a soft voice.

'I was just . . .' Dimity didn't finish the sentence. It did not matter what excuse she gave. Celeste could see right through her.

'Dimity listen to me . . . I know how you are feeling, believe me, I do. When his attention is on you, it feels as though the sun is shining, does it not? And when that attention moves on . . . well, it feels as though the sun has gone out. Cold and dark. For two years he drew and painted me just as he did you. And I fell in love with him, and never fell out of love. And I believe he still loves me, and still wants to be with me, and he loves our girls very much. We are a family, Dimity; that is a sacred thing. Do you hear what I am telling you? He has moved on from you – in his art, in his mind. You must move on from him too, because you cannot get it back, once it has gone. I mean only to be kind, in telling you this. Your life . . . your life lies with another, not with Charles. Do you understand?' Celeste held the shawl tightly around her shoulders, and Dimity saw goose pimples rising along her forearms. She said nothing in reply, and Celeste shook her head slightly. 'You're still so young, Mitzy, still just a child . . .'

'I am not a child!' said Dimity, looking down at her feet

as her blood raced and she rejected every word the Moroccan woman was saying.

'Then let me speak to you as a woman, and listen to me as a woman, and hear the truth in what I say. Life and love are like this. There are times when they will break your heart and kill the spirit of you, kill it right inside you.' She bunched her hand into a fist and held it tight against her chest. 'But these times do pass, and you will be whole again. But only once you look at the truth in the face, and see it for what it is. You must forget what you cannot have. I know you don't want to hear any of this, but you must. Come back later and be with my girls – with my Delphine, who loves you. But go now, if you want to. I am sorry for you, Mitzy. Truly. You were not prepared for any of this, I see that now.' Celeste turned, letting her gaze linger on Dimity for a moment longer, stern and sad.

But Dimity could not go back to see Delphine; not that day, or the day after. She could not, in case what Celeste said was true, and Charles would never want to draw her again. She felt a peculiar teetering sensation when she considered it, as though she was on the cliff top on a windy day, and the turf by her toes had started to crumble. They could slip away, she suddenly saw. Slip away out of her life as easily as they had slipped into it, and leave her with no hope of rescue. They were like a bright light, shining, which cast shadows over everything else, and Charles was the brightest of all.

On the third day, she was taking in the washing when her eyes fell on a blouse of Valentina's. It was one of her favourites, one she often wore when meeting a new guest for the first time. It was made of a slightly diaphanous, pale blue cheesecloth that was gathered into smocking at the waist and sleeves, and was fitted over the bust. It had a wide, low neckline with a frill to it, and only one of the wooden buttons was missing from the front. When Valentina wore it, she had to wrestle her bosoms into the bodice, where they perched precariously and jiggled when she moved. Dimity rolled the blouse up carefully and tucked it inside the waistband of her skirt. It would not do to be caught borrowing it; she couldn't even guess what the consequences of that might be. Before leaving the house she combed her hair savagely, eyes watering as each knot was pulled through, then piled it all up on top of her head and secured it with pins, so that a few stray tresses fell to brush her neck. Safely behind a hedge away from The Watch, Dimity put on Valentina's blouse. She was smaller than her mother, her waist narrower and her bust less voluminous, but the blouse fitted nicely. She had no mirror to check her appearance, but when she looked down at her own chest in the wide neckline, she knew she was no longer looking at the body of a child.

Dimity seated herself in a patch of clover flowers near the cliff path, with a basket of beans to pod, and set to work. It was a guess, but she had often seen Charles walk that way, and before long she saw his long striding figure approaching. Her heart careened wildly behind her ribs, and she sat up straight, pushing her shoulders back and tweaking the blouse so that it sat wide across them, exposing the straight line of her collarbones, the soft curve downwards where her arms began. The sun was warm on her skin. She tried to keep her expression relaxed, but it was hard not to narrow her eyes in the bright sunshine. In the end she had to blink, and lower her brows; squint a little. She pursed her lips at the onslaught, fretting because she couldn't look up again without giving away her plan to be found, caught unawares. The breeze stirred the wisps of hair against her neck and made her shudder. And then she heard the words she had longed to hear for almost a year, and she shut her eyes in bliss.

'Mitzy, don't move. Stay exactly as you are,' said Charles. So she didn't move, even though inside she was smiling and had a tremulous feeling, like she might laugh. *Mitzy, don't move.*

It was a rapid drawing, one of open-ended lines and suggested space; sparse, hazy. But somehow the glow of the sunlight was captured, and even in Dimity's scowl the ghost of her delight was hiding, right there on the page. Charles finished it without a flourish, just that slow ceasing of movement through his hand, his pencil; a frown of his own and a quick, hard exhalation of air through the nose. Then he looked up and smiled, and flipped the sketchbook around to show to her. And what she saw made her catch her breath, and made a rosy blush spread up from her neck. As she had hoped, the drawing was indeed of a woman, not a child, but she was unprepared for how lovely that young woman would be, with her smooth, sunlit skin and her face full of her own private thoughts. Dimity looked up at Charles in amazement.

There was a mirror at The Watch, in the hallway; an ancient one with silvery glass and the mottled spots of age all over it. It was four inches across, and in it Dimity knew her own face of old. Filling the round glass, somewhat shapeless and dim. Like some slave in the belly of a ship, peering out through a porthole. She knew the whites of her own eyes well. Here in this drawing was a different creature entirely. He hadn't drawn her with blood under her nails, hunched to avoid being noticed, a child who hid along hedgerows. He had seen past all that, and drawn what had been hiding underneath. She gaped at it, at him. As if puzzled by her reaction, Charles took the drawing back.

'You don't approve?' he said, studying it with a frown.

But then, as if he also realised what had changed, his mouth thinned into a thoughtful line, and curled up at one side. 'The poor ugly duckling, who was bitten and pushed and laughed at,' he said, softly. He smiled. Dimity didn't understand. She heard only the words *ugly*, *poor*; she felt crushed. 'Oh, no, no! My dear Mitzy! What I meant was . . . the story then goes on to say: "It does not matter that one has been born in the hen yard as long as one has lain in a swan's egg . . ." That's what I meant, Mitzy. That the new swan turned out to be the most beautiful of them all.'

'Will you teach me that story?' she said, breathlessly.

'Oh, it's just a silly children's story. Élodie will read it to you – it's one of her favourites.' Charles waved a hand dismissively. 'Come on. This sketch is a good start, but only a start.'

'A start for what, Mr Aubrey?' Dimity asked, as he stood up, gathered his bag and his folding stool, and strode away towards the stream.

'My next piece, of course. I know exactly what I want to do now. You have inspired me, Mitzy!' Dimity hurried after him, tugging her blouse higher over her shoulders; bewildered, alight, joyful.

She spent the following afternoon on the beach with Élodie and Delphine, and as Élodie hopped in and out of the waves, squealing at the chilly water, she told Dimity snatches of the story of the ugly duckling, and it made Dimity smile all the way through to think that this was how Charles thought of her.

'Everybody knows that story, Mitzy,' Élodie pointed out, patiently, studying the bubbling waves that foamed around her angular knees. Delphine was swimming slowly to and fro just offshore, and she laughed, and winked at Dimity, who had rolled up her trousers and was wading around the rocks in the shallows, dropping mussels and edible weed into a bucket.

'And now I know it too, Élodie. Thanks to you,' Dimity said, happiness making her generous.

'Why do you ask about it now?' the youngest girl asked.

'Oh, no reason. I heard it mentioned, that was all,' Dimity lied easily. She was calm, and felt like she might be glowing. *That is how you love a woman, Charles – you draw her face.*

When they returned to Littlecombe late in the afternoon, they found the tea things only half laid out on the kitchen table, and Celeste sitting rigidly on the bench with a paper in her hand, which she was studying with a strained expression.

'What is it, Mummy? Are you all right?' said Delphine, going over to sit beside her.

Celeste swallowed, and frowned as she looked up as if she didn't recognise them. But then she smiled a little, and put the paper down on the table. It was Charles's latest sketch of Dimity. Dimity's heart gave one loud, exaggerated beat, like a bell sounding.

'Yes, dearest. I'm fine. I was just tidying up before tea when I found this drawing your father has done. Look at our Dimity, look how lovely she is!' Celeste exclaimed, and though the words were generous, they sounded brittle.

'Gosh – look, Mitzy! You do look very pretty,' said Delphine.

'So he is planning another piece with you in it? Did he say so?' Celeste asked.

'He said something like that, I think,' Dimity said, and though she felt bashful about saying it a part of her wanted to shout it out – that Celeste had been wrong and Charles did still want to draw her; that he had not moved on and lost interest in her. Celeste took a deep breath and got up from the bench.

'Strange, this turnaround. I had thought it would be that tourist woman next, with her milksop English skin.'

'What tourist woman, Mummy?' said Élodie, opening a packet of biscuits and tipping them out onto a plate. Celeste put her hand to her forehead for a moment, then ran it down to cover her mouth. There were furrows in her brow. 'Mummy?'

'Nothing, Élodie. It doesn't matter.' Celeste put her hands on her hips and surveyed the three of them. 'Well! What a gaggle of messy creatures! You've been swimming I see, so you will be hungry. *Alors* – go and get changed and I will finish the tea. *Allez, allez!*' She herded them from the room, her cheeriness keeping those same sharp edges as before, and Dimity noticed that she kept her eyes askance, and would not look her in the face.

Dimity tried to keep the pale blue blouse, but Valentina flew into such a storm when Dimity suggested that it might have blown away that she had to pretend to find it in one of the trees behind the backyard. She got no thanks for returning it, just a scowl and an admonition to peg things more securely.

'You've no idea how many meals this blouse has fed you, over the years,' she said. With a pang, Dimity handed it over. She had far more to thank the garment for. It had brought Charles back to her; brought her back from the cliff edge. For the next few days she ran her errands with a springing step, swinging her basket and singing to herself. In the village one afternoon, she saw Charles sitting outside the pub with the tourist man, the one whose hair was blacker than tar. They were drinking dark ale and talking, and Dimity, giving the pub its usual wide berth, wondered what kind of things men talked about. She wondered if he would tell the man about her – about his muse, and the picture he was planning.

As she walked past the postbox across the village green, a hand on her arm startled her out of her thoughts. Celeste's elegant fingers were clasped tightly around her wrist. The Moroccan woman was hunkered down behind the pillar box as though playing hide and seek, her lovely face dangerous with anxiety and temper. Instinctively, Dimity recoiled from her.

'Mitzy, wait. Do you see that man – the one Charles is talking to?' Celeste whispered. She pulled on Dimity's arm so that they could talk closely without Celeste having to leave her hiding place.

'Yes, Celeste. Yes, I see him,' said Dimity, nervously.

'That's the milksop's husband. Have you seen her, too? You know who I mean?'

'Yes.' The large-chested woman who looked like a bitch in heat in spite of her prim outfits, she thought.

'Have you ever seen her with Charles? Just the two of them, I mean. Maybe out for a walk, or talking . . . Have you seen them?'

'No, I don't think so . . .'

'You don't think so, or you have not?' Celeste pressed. Her fingernails were cutting into Dimity's skin, but just like with Valentina, suddenly Dimity didn't dare pull away.

'I haven't. I haven't seen them together, I'm sure,' she said. Celeste stared at the two men for a second longer, then fixed her eyes on Dimity. Her grip vanished as suddenly as it had appeared.

'Good. That's good. If you do see them together, you must tell me,' said Celeste. Dimity's mouth was dry at the strangeness of the encounter, and she was about to refuse when the look in Celeste's eyes stopped her. There was something like panic, underneath her anger. Something hunted, and frantic. Dimity nodded hurriedly. 'Good girl. Good girl, Mitzy.' Celeste turned, and was about to walk away when she paused, and added: 'Say nothing of this to the girls. I beg of you.'

The next time she was at Littlecombe, with her hair piled up again in the hope of meeting Charles, Dimity was disappointed to find him out. Since it was a grey day, she agreed to stay indoors and teach Delphine and Élodie how to make strawberry jam. Delphine saw her searching the room as she entered, since the car was parked outside, and gave her a mildly censorious look.

'Daddy's gone out. Were you supposed to sit for him today?' she asked, carefully.

'Oh, no,' Dimity said, hurriedly. 'I was just hoping for . . . My mother was asking, you see. About the . . . extra money.' She lowered her voice to tell this lie, and was ashamed to see sympathy replace consternation on her friend's face.

'Yes, of course. How silly of me to forget,' Delphine murmured. 'Perhaps you can have one or two jars of jam instead, once we've made it. Would that help?'

'Yes, thank you.' They smiled at one another, and set about hulling the vibrant red fruit. Delphine asked about Wilf, and Dimity answered at mischievous length, even though in truth she had scarcely thought of him, let alone met with him, since the Aubreys' return. Soon the kitchen was rich with the scent of strawberries, and when Celeste came downstairs she took a deep breath, and smiled. She looked tired, and there were stern lines at the corners of her mouth that Dimity couldn't recall seeing there before.

'What a glorious perfume, girls!' she said. 'Something to remind us it is summer, in spite of the dark weather.' It had indeed been a bleak sort of summer until then, but Dimity had hardly cared to notice. 'Well, sunshine or no sunshine, I must have some air. I'll be in the garden, if you need me.'

Two hours later, when the jam was potted up and Élodie was up to her elbows in soap suds at the sink, scrubbing the pans, Dimity walked carefully to the back door with a brimming cup of tea for Celeste. Through the crack by the jamb she saw a flash of blue, and she paused, recognising Charles's peculiar linen tunic, the one dotted and smeared with fingerprints in paint. His voice was soft and measured, as if by speaking too robustly he might damage Celeste, inflict a wound.

'But it's impossible right now, Celeste, you know that . . . I've just started a new piece. I need Mitzy to pose for it, and we need the money . . .'

'You can work over there just as well, I know you can. Think how much work you did the first time you went!'

'Well, I had you to inspire me then,' said Charles. Through the narrow gap, Dimity saw the white gleam of his smile.

'And do you not have me to inspire you now?'

'That's not what I meant.'

'We can leave the children with your parents. I'm sure they would look after them, if you explained to them . . .'

'You know they wouldn't. You know how my mother feels, about our . . . situation.'

'But if you told her . . . if you explained that we need to go away. That *I* need to go away. And we need to be *together*, Charles. *Mon cher*. Together like man and wife, like it was in the beginning. To remember the light and the love and the life between us, when right now all has grown dim . . .'

'Delphine and Élodie are the greatest expressions of that love, Celeste, why leave them behind? They love it there, you know they do . . .'

'Or we could leave them with Mitzy! She is a sensible girl. How old is she now? Sixteen? She could look after them, I know she could. She could come and stay here in the house . . .' Hope flared in Celeste's voice.

'It's out of the question.' The words were flat, adamant. 'That mother of hers would surely involve herself in some way, and really Dimity is still only a child herself.' *No*, thought Dimity, holding her breath, poised on tiptoes. *I am a swan.* He did not want to go away with Celeste. He wanted to stay in Blacknowle, with her. Joy flared up like fire.

'Please, Charles. I feel like something is dying inside me. I just can't stay here any more. And I feel something dying between us too . . . this distance between us, always growing. I need to go *home*. I need to be where I belong. And I need to be with you, like it was on our honeymoon, like it was when we first met and we were the centre of the whole universe. Just you and me, and nobody else . . . No suspicion, no betrayal.' She reached out, grasping Charles's hand so tightly that her fingers went white. There was a long, hung moment.

'If you'd met Dimity's mother . . . there would be no question of you wanting to leave our children with her . . .'

'But Dimity can stay here with them – we can pay her well for it! That at least always pleases the mother, no?'

'Pay her well for that, and pay for us to travel again, and all the while earn nothing, for without Mitzy I cannot keep working . . .'

'*Mon dieu!*' Celeste spat in sudden rage. 'There was a time when there were more things under the sun for you to paint than Mitzy Hatcher!'

'All right, Celeste, calm down—'

'I will not! Always we go where you say, always we live our lives around you, and your work. I gave up *everything* to be with you, Charles, and I ask very little of you, and yet this one thing you could grant me, to make me happy . . . Must I fight and beg, always?' She shook her head in disbelief, and then her eyes blazed. 'It is that woman, isn't it? It's her that keeps you here!'

'What woman? What are you talking about?'

'The one staying at the pub. The tourist woman with the fiancé she barely looks at . . . the one who has to touch herself each time she sees you . . . Don't pretend you don't know!'

'But . . . I hardly know the woman! I've met her only twice! You're imagining things, Celeste—'

'I am not! And I tell you now, Charles Aubrey, either we go to Morocco and away from this damp and dreary place, or I will go alone with the girls and you will see us no more!'

There was a long, uneasy silence, and Dimity didn't dare to breathe.

'All right,' Charles said at last, and Dimity went cold. 'We'll all go,' he said.

'What? No . . .' Celeste protested. 'Just *us*, Charles. We need some time alone . . .'

'Well, that's not possible. So we'll all go.' Dimity couldn't hold herself still any longer. She crossed the rest of the hallway in steps as loud as she could make them without spilling the tea, to announce her arrival, and smiled frantic-ally as she stepped out into the light.

'Here, Celeste. I fetched your tea,' she said, fighting to keep her voice from shaking.

'Mitzy! How about it – a trip to Morocco! All five of us. Celeste can visit her family, and I can paint you as a harem girl, or perhaps a Berber princess . . . It'll be like nowhere you've ever seen, trust me. You'll love it. What do you say?' Charles stood with his hands on his hips, squinting at her with a kind of desperate fixation, as if he could feel Celeste's baleful eyes upon him, and didn't dare to look.

'You . . . want me to go to Morocco with you? Truly?' Dimity breathed, glancing from him to Celeste and back. 'I . . . I should love to go . . .' she said. 'You'll take me with you? You promise?'

'Of course. You'd be a great help to us on the journey, I'm sure. You can help look after the girls, and give Celeste and me some time to rest and be together.' Charles set his smile bravely, and finally found the courage to look across at Celeste. She was watching him, her mouth open in shock, but she did not speak.

'Oh, thank you! Thank you so much!' said Dimity, scarcely able to believe it was true. Her smile stretched from ear to ear, her face ached from it. They would go, but this time she would stay with them, with him. She would leave Blacknowle, and travel further than she had ever thought it possible to travel. She did not care if Celeste did not want her there. She cared only that Charles did; and in that moment she loved him completely.

'There now,' Charles said, awkwardly. 'Go on inside and tell the girls. And is there any tea for me, in that pot?'

'I'll fetch you some.' Dimity stepped back into the strawberry-scented house, and just before she moved out of earshot, she heard Celeste say, in a voice made frigid with rage:

'Charles. How could you?'

There was straw prickling Zach's back and the sharp smell of livestock in his nostrils, filtering through the thick mass of Hannah's hair. Her head was resting in the crook where his neck met his shoulder, and for a while he shut his eyes and enjoyed the discomfort of her nose and chin digging into him. Her breath was warm and growing steadily slower, returning to normal. From behind the bale of straw on which he was leaning came the sudden deep, loud bleat of a sheep; Hannah's head came up in an instant, her eyes fighting into focus.

'Is she all right?' said Zach. Hannah sat up straighter to look and Zach felt their bodies disconnect, the sudden touch of cool air on damp and delicate skin.

'Yes, I think so. Just getting a bit uncomfortable now, poor girl. I should check on her though.' She climbed off Zach and got to her feet, wrestling her trousers back over her hips and zipping them up. There was sheep shit on one of her knees. She went around the bale and crouched by the labouring ewe, whose quick breathing was flaring her nostrils and making her whole body rock. Hannah peered beneath her tail, put gentle fingers there to feel the shape of what was beginning to protrude. 'I can feel feet and nostrils.'

'Is that good?'

'Yes, that's good. Nostrils means a straightforward, head-first birth. Breech is trickier.'

'Oh, good. Well . . . I've never done that before. Had sex in a barn full of sheep, I mean,' Zach said, dressing and brushing the sharp bits of chaff from his skin. Hannah looked up with a brief smile.

'It certainly helps liven up the long hours of a lambing vigil. Chuck me that rag, would you?' She caught it deftly and wiped the muck from her hands as she sat back down on the bale beside him. Zach took her hand and meshed their fingers, pressing the pads of their thumbs together and feeling the hard scar running across hers.

The small, cappuccino-coloured ewes were dotted around all over the barn, some with tiny lambs curled sleepily beside them, others prostrate and panting like the one Hannah had just checked, others eating hay as though none of it was anything to do with them. It was three o'clock in the morning and an immaculate full moon had risen outside, casting silvery shadows over everything. Zach peered out through the door, up the hill to where the low shape of The Watch crouched against the horizon. There was a single light on in the kitchen downstairs, and he wondered if Dimity was still up, or had forgotten to turn it off.

'Don't you need to put a blob of that green paint on them? Or number them or something, so you know whose is whose?' He gestured to the sheep who already had lambs. All the ewes had large blobs of emerald green paint on their rumps.

'I'm sure the sheep know. And they'll all get their ear tags, soon enough. That green paint is tenacious stuff – you can't get it off you, once it's on. Not ideal for organic fleeces. It goes on the ram's chest, so we can see who he's tupped.'

'Is lambing always this easy?' he asked. Hannah shrugged.

'This is my first season with this flock, remember. Hopefully they'll all keep popping out easy-peasy, because I can't afford to call the vet right now.' Zach thought about this for a moment.

'What about . . . what about your pictures? I mean, no offence, but you hardly get a lot of foot traffic in that shop of yours. Couldn't you find some local gallery or gift shop to stock them? They'd sell really well, I'm sure they would.'

'I could, I suppose. I just . . . I don't know. The idea doesn't appeal to me.'

'What idea? The idea of being a talented artist and making some extra income through the sale of your work? What's not to like?'

'I don't want to be an artist. I want to be an organic shepherd.'

'The one doesn't necessarily preclude the other, does it?'

'Sort of. If the pictures sell really well I'll only have to do more of them . . . it's a slippery slope. Soon I'll be painting daisies on watering cans and running a gift shop rather than farming.' She shuddered, and Zach laughed softly.

'But you draw already. The pictures are there; I'm sure no harm would come of putting them somewhere they're more likely to sell. I could look into it, if you like?' he said. Hannah gave him a steady look.

'No, it's OK. I'll think about it,' she said. 'What about you? I bet you wanted to be an artist, right? What made you open a gallery?'

'The fact that nobody bought my art and I had a wife and child to feed. Actually, Ali fed herself, and me and Elise. She's a lawyer, a very good one.'

'Bet that did wonders for your ego.'

'It was my own stupid fault – the fact that I didn't make it. I had my chance and I blew it.' Zach smiled ruefully and shook his head at the memory. He'd been so full of himself at the time, so bloody cocksure.

It was the year he graduated from Goldsmiths, and his final show was being showered with praise from staff and class-mates alike, and from a journalist who wrote a piece in her magazine about young artists to keep an eye on. *Zach Gilchrist*, the article said, *combines a classical eye with a challenging, almost surrealist approach to subject and meaning.* It was rumoured that Simon d'Angelico, one of the most influential collectors of British contemporary art, might be coming to the exhibition to look at his pieces. A real, genuine rumour, not one that Zach had cooked up himself. All that promise, all that potential. Zach entirely lost sight of the fact that it was all just possibility and suggestion, nothing more concrete than that. That he was still just a new graduate, unproven – a maybe, that was all. He felt like he had made it already, so that when a woman called Lauren

Holt, who ran a small gallery near Vyner Street in the City and was building up a stable of new artists, came and spoke to him and asked about hanging his final piece and two others, he barely listened to her. He'd never heard of her or her gallery, and that told him everything he thought he needed to know. She had bright scarlet hair, even though she looked over fifty, and it clashed with her green eye-shadow. Zach supposed she thought it made her look avant-garde; he wrote her off as an eccentric amateur. Her gallery had only been open for six months, and for all he knew it was the kind of place that sold postcards of the art in a rotating wire rack. So he turned her down flat and thought no more about it, safe in the knowledge that big things were coming his way.

Nine months later, Lauren Holt hosted a private viewing at her gallery that caused a buzz of excitement in the press and in the art-world circles that Zach was trying desperately to gain access to. Simon d'Angelico never did come to his final show; there were no more articles mentioning Zach in any magazines or newspaper reviews. Zach paid Lauren's gallery a visit, and walked around in increasing dismay as he absorbed the quality of the pieces on display, the perfect lighting, the buzz of conversation. Startling pieces by people he *had* heard of, being discussed by people who mattered. Lauren Holt came in through a back door in the white wall, dressed all in black with her red hair shining. Zach tried to hide behind a piece of wire sculpture but she caught his eye and gave him a lopsided little smile, more wistful than gloating. Zach slunk away, too ashamed to ask her if she might still be interested in him. And that had been the closest he had ever come to having his work picked up by an influential gallery. In terms of his career as an artist, it was all downhill from there.

*

'Why didn't you ask her there and then if she'd still have you? The gallery was still quite new . . . if you'd grovelled she might have been flattered enough to agree, even if it was just one piece – that final year piece you did that she liked,' said Hannah, as they trod through the straw to another ewe who had the front legs of her lamb protruding from her back end, sheathed in a grey and shiny membrane.

'I couldn't. It was too humiliating . . .'

'You mean you were still too proud, even at that point?'

'I guess so.'

'Men!' Hannah rolled her eyes. 'You never will stop to ask for directions.'

'I was still hoping for a miracle from elsewhere, I suppose. But that was it. My big chance, and I blew it.'

'Come on, I don't buy that.' She wrapped her hands around the lamb's slippery legs and when she saw the ewe heave, pulled steadily until its whole body slithered free with a rush of fluid and a grunt from the ewe. 'Yes! Good sheep,' she said, as she cleared the mucus from the lamb's mouth and nose then swung it gently a few times until it sneezed and snuffled and shook its head weakly. She laid it in the straw beside its astonished mother and wiped her hands on the seat of her jeans. Zach grimaced. Lambing was gorier than he'd imagined it would be.

'What do you mean?'

'What's for you won't go by you, as my old granddad used to say. Talent will out. If you were meant to make it as a professional artist, you would have made it,' she said. 'It wasn't meant to be.'

'Hmm. I'm not sure if that's a better or worse thought, actually. Don't we make our own luck, our own opportunities in life?'

'So, what are you telling me – that you just haven't been trying all these years? That that's why you aren't a famous artist, and your gallery's about to close, and now you can't finish your book?'

'No, I suppose not. It's certainly . . . felt like I've been trying. Makes me tired just thinking about it, actually.'

'Well, there you are then. Don't beat yourself up about one missed chance of an exhibition.'

'So you're saying I was doomed to failure from the start?'

'Exactly. There now – doesn't that make you feel better?' She grinned at him, punching him lightly on the shoulder.

'Oh yes. Much,' he said, with a smile. Hannah sighed slightly and stepped forwards, grabbed him by his shirt and tipped up her chin to kiss him.

'Cheer up. I still fancy you, in spite of you being such a towering loser,' she said.

Zach slept until lunchtime the day after his long night in the lambing barns, and woke up ravenous. At two in the afternoon he sat down to a plate of ham, egg and chips amidst the drinkers and dog walkers sheltering from a steady, drenching downpour outside. Zach turned to stare out of the window at the rain, and saw Hannah. She was waiting at the bus stop wearing her outsized checked shirt but nothing waterproof; jeans stuffed into her wellies, an old waxed hat pulled down low over her hair. Zach sat up and reached out to knock on the glass to get her attention, but he realised that she was too far away and wouldn't hear him over the rain. He leaned back and started to wonder why on earth she would wait at a bus stop in the rain, when she could drive wherever she wanted to go. And if her jeep was out of action for some reason, he was sure she'd feel no compunction about asking him for a lift. So he frowned, and rested his chin on the back of the seat to watch her. She had her hands thrust deeply into her pockets, and her back fearfully straight. Her shoulders were high and set, and the more

Zach studied her the more he realised that she looked extremely tense, even uneasy. Before long the bus pulled up, wipers flailing, and two elderly ladies got out, wrapped up in clear plastic macs. Hannah did not get in.

About two minutes later Hannah glanced at her watch, but even as she did so a filthy white Toyota pickup swung to a halt in front of the bus stop, splashing muddy water from the gutter over Hannah's boots. She stepped forwards and leant down at the open window. Zach stared. There were two men inside the car, but he couldn't make them out. They spoke for no more than ten seconds, then Hannah reached into her back pocket and handed over a crumpled, letter-sized envelope. Through the windscreen, Zach could see the white of the envelope as the man in the passenger seat opened it, and rummaged inside with his fingertips. *Money*, thought Zach. It had to be. Hannah gave a nod and stepped back, and the pickup pulled away. With her hands back in her pockets, she watched it go, and as it pulled around the corner near the pub, Zach saw the sleeve of the man in the passenger seat, resting against the window. A scruffy, lilac sweatshirt sleeve. He saw the huge bulk of the man, and a scruffy bearded neck. James Horne. Hannah stood for a moment longer, looking down at her feet with the tension still rigid in her frame. Then she walked across the road towards the pub.

Hannah crossed straight to the bar, and held up her debit card to Pete Murray with a wide smile.

'What, all of it?' The landlord said, sounding quite surprised.

'Oh ye of little faith. I told you I only needed a few more days.'

'I know. I just . . . figured it'd be a few more.' Pete shrugged.

'Hit me with it. And I'll be in to start a new tab later this evening.' She waited, leaning on the bar and not looking around, while Pete processed her payment. Zach drew breath to call out to her, but something stopped him. Perhaps it was the way she did not turn to see if he was there, the way she kept her eyes fixed on the drip tray, tapping the brass impatiently with a beer mat. Perhaps it was the wealth of questions that mushroomed up inside his mind. He knew she wouldn't answer them, and so he didn't want to ask, but there was no way he could speak to her right then without asking why she was giving money to somebody like James Horne, and where that money had come from all of a sudden. But when she turned to leave he was on his feet and after her before he knew he was going to move. Her expression when he caught her arm told him everything he needed to know. Her eyes were set and guarded, her mouth a resolute line, and over all of it, a fragile colouring of regret. All of his questions died on his lips, and he felt something almost like fear. He suddenly saw himself losing her.

'Hannah,' he said, taking a deep breath. 'Whatever it is . . . you can trust me with it. I hope you know that.' Her eyes widened, and for a second she looked lonely, and afraid. But then the resolve returned, and she shook her head.

'Not with this, I can't. I'm sorry, Zach.'

The following day was Thursday, and Zach headed away from the coast to pick up the motorway to Surrey. It was the day of his visit to Annie Langton, the lady who'd bought one of the recently reappeared Dennis portraits. He had slept little the night before, preoccupied with thoughts of Hannah and the trouble he imagined her to be in. Perhaps she had just been desperate enough to take a cash loan from

James Horne, and the argument had been about her paying it back, which Zach had then seen her do. But somehow he couldn't quite make this version of events stick. You didn't pay off a legitimate loan at the roadside, with a wad of cash in an envelope. You didn't borrow from somebody like James Horne in the first place. Zach could not for one second imagine Hannah going to him for help. But if the money was for something else, then Zach didn't want to think about what it might be. And he could not think how she had suddenly come up with the cash to put into that envelope.

He'd been so tired and caught up in it all that the only reason he remembered his appointment with Mrs Langton was that his phone beeped to remind him. Startled, he realised that for over a week he'd barely even thought about the book he was supposed to be writing. He had copious notes, and a stack of index cards on which he had begun trying to shape chapters, cross-referencing which notes would be needed where. But suddenly there was a very real possibility that the book would never be written. The book he'd started to write was no longer the book he wanted to write. He knew it had been flawed, now he saw that it was worse than that. It was pointless.

He wanted to write about the man, not the artist. He wanted to write about Blacknowle, and the people who lived there, and how they reacted to the great man in their midst. He wanted to write about Dimity Hatcher, and about the recent works that had been sold from the secret collection in Dorset. He wanted to find out who Dennis was, and where Delphine had lived out her life, after her father died in the war. He wanted to know what Celeste did with the rest of her life. But the only person who could fill in all the blanks was Dimity, and he could hardly force her to tell him these things if she didn't want to. The stories she'd already told

him were fantastical, kept bright and fresh by her love for
Charles Aubrey. But they would not fill a book. He pictured
himself going back to the gallery, either to close it officially
and move out, or to reopen it and try to make it work. The
thought caused a wave of sickening dread to wash through
him. He pictured the wire rack full of postcards, gathering
dust while the sun bleached the colours from the ink. And
that's what would happen to him if he went back, he realised
with sudden clarity. He would gather dust, and his colours
would fade to nothing; and he would never see Hannah
again.

Annie Langton lived in a rambling, red-brick cottage on the
edges of Guildford. There were climbing roses all over
the front wall, shedding the last of their yellow petals onto
the gravel driveway. It looked quaint enough, but Zach
knew that, in that area, the cottage represented serious
money. A black and white cat wound around his ankles as
he knocked at the front door, and waited. Mrs Langton
herself, when she answered the door, was tiny and brisk,
wearing tailored cord trousers and a fawn-coloured shirt.
She had iron-grey hair cut into a smooth bob, and a hooked
nose beneath shrewd blue eyes.

'Mr Gilchrist, I presume,' she greeted him, with a
businesslike shake of the hand.

'Mrs Langton. Thanks so much for agreeing to let me see
your picture.'

'Come on in. I'll make some coffee, shall I?' She led him
through to an immaculate lounge full of over-stuffed sofas
and heavy, luxurious fabrics. 'Do sit down. Back in a jiffy.'

She strode back out of the room and Zach looked around
at the art on the walls. She had some other lovely twentieth-
century pieces, including what looked like a Henry Moore
sketch, a design for one of his sensuous bronzes. Then

another drawing caught his eye, because, even from across the spacious living room, he could see it was an Aubrey. He crossed to look closer, and smiled with delight. *Mitzy, 1939.* Zach remembered it – a glorious sketch of Mitzy, bare-shouldered and bathed in sunshine; it had come up for auction about eleven years ago, and Zach hadn't even bothered to bid. He'd known he wouldn't be able to afford it, because it was the loveliest drawing of her that existed, even though it was only loosely done. She was dressed in a low-cut peasant blouse, the tops of her breasts curving proudly, a sun-kissed moment from seventy years ago; a beautiful young girl with light dancing in her eyes. It would be a hard-hearted person who could look at that young face and not want to cup their hands around it and cover it with kisses. Her top lip protruded slightly, budding out like an invitation.

'Lovely, isn't she?' said Annie Langton, appearing behind him with a cafetière and coffee cups on a tray. She smiled proudly at the drawing. 'I paid far too much for that one. My husband John was alive then, and he nearly had a heart attack. But I had to have it. She just sings, does she not?'

'Yes, she does. I was at the auction, that day. I couldn't help myself, even though I knew it would be torture watching someone else buy it, and knowing I'd never see it again.'

'Which just goes to show we can never know anything in this life, not for certain. Milk and sugar?'

'Just milk, thank you.' The desire to tell Mrs Langton that he'd found Dimity, that she was alive and he'd got to know her, was immense, but he held his tongue. Let that revelation come in the book, if he ever finished it.

'Well, as I told John at the time, money is only money. Whereas, as I believe has been said before, a thing of beauty is a joy for ever.' She gazed across at the picture of Mitzy with such peculiar longing that Zach almost recognised the expression.

'Were you one of . . . Aubrey's women, by any chance?' he said, smiling. Annie Langton fixed him with a very stern gaze.

'Young man, I wasn't even a twinkle in my father's eye when Charles Aubrey went off to the war.'

'Of course not. I'm so sorry.'

'Never mind.' She waved a hand briskly. 'To someone as young as you, everyone over the age of fifty looks the same, I suppose.'

'I'm not that young,' said Zach.

'Just clumsy, then?' Her face remained serious, but her eyes sparkled, and Zach smiled sheepishly. With the ghost of a smile, she changed the subject. 'I understand from Paul Gibbons that you have a particular interest in the portraits of Dennis that Aubrey did? Do you know who he was, then?'

'No. I was half hoping you might be able to tell me that.'

'Ah, then the mystery prevails. No, I'm afraid I have no idea who he was. I've done a bit of research, although I don't claim to know as much about Aubrey as an expert like you. I've found no reference to him anywhere.'

'No, neither have I.'

'Oh dear – I hope you didn't come all this way to see if I knew?'

'No, no. I have something of a . . . theory about the Dennis pictures. I was hoping seeing yours in the flesh might help me clear something up.'

'Oh, yes?' She sipped her coffee, never once breaking off her piercing gaze. Zach saw that there was no point in trying to dissemble.

'It worries me a great deal that there's no mention of Dennis anywhere. I find it almost impossible to believe, given the dates the portraits were supposedly drawn. If the dates are correct, Dennis would almost certainly have had to be in Blacknowle at some point. But I have been to Blacknowle, and spoken to some of the people who lived there at that time. And still nobody has ever heard of him.'

'*Supposedly* drawn, you say? Am I to understand that you don't think the portraits are genuine?'

'I know that's . . . not something anybody wants to hear. But don't you think it's odd that these portraits, the only ones of Dennis we know of, all came up for sale in recent years? Apparently from the same vendor? And that they are all so similar, and yet not quite the same?'

'I agree. It is very odd. But you have only to see the draughtsmanship to know that they are indeed by Charles Aubrey. Perhaps he fell out with Dennis, whoever he was. Perhaps Aubrey himself expunged the young man from his life before he died. And perhaps he himself was dissatisfied with the pictures, and hid them away. Perhaps that's why they were never sold. Until now.'

'It's possible, I suppose. But I just can't quite believe it.'

'Well, let me take you to meet my Dennis. Perhaps he will help you make up your mind.'

She led him across the hallway to a large study dominated by a gleaming walnut desk. The walls were lined with bookcases, and wherever there was space, a picture had been hung. Zach caught sight of *Dennis* and was already walking towards the picture when Mrs Langton pointed it out. He knew the piece already, of course, having studied it repeatedly in the auction catalogue. He studied it again now, and felt his disappointment rising with each second that ticked past. Seeing the real piece brought him no greater clarity whatsoever. He was aware of Mrs Langton watching him closely, and decided that for the sake of appearances, he had better show more interest than he felt.

'Would you mind if I took it over to the window to look at it?' he asked.

'Of course not. Help yourself.' The picture was in a heavy wooden frame, and Zach held it tightly as he took it down from the wall. At the window, he turned it until the light shone full onto the paper. He stared at the pencil strokes, at the signature, at the young man's ambiguous expression. He stared, and wished for something to surface, but nothing did. Yet he still could not shake the feeling that the picture was not entirely what it pertained to be.

'He's no great masterpiece, I know, but a nice enough drawing, I've always thought. And he was a bargain,' said Annie Langton, when the silence had grown prolonged. 'Shall I leave you alone for a while?' she added.

'No, there's no need,' said Zach.

'You've got what you came for? Already?'

'Not as such, no. Did you ever find out who the vendor was, by any chance?'

'No, and I did ask – I was as curious as anyone as to where these new works were suddenly springing from. Usually the buyer can be told, but not this time. Strict anonymity.' She tipped her eyebrows ruefully.

'And it was in this frame when you bought it?'

'Oh, no. It wasn't framed at all when it arrived at the auction house. Just rolled up inside some grubby sheets of newspaper, if you can believe that – not the best thing for it at all. Luckily the newsprint had only transferred a little onto the back of the portrait, not the front.'

'In newspaper? So whoever sold it wasn't exactly reverent, then. Do you remember what newspaper it was?'

'*The Times*, I think, but I can't remember for sure. Nothing revelatory – dated about a month before the sale. I still have it, if you'd like to see it?'

'You kept it? Yes, please.' Inwardly, Zach prayed that the pages would be from a local newspaper, not a national one.

'Well, as far as I am concerned, things like that become part of the provenance of a piece, however inappropriate they may be.' Mrs Langton crossed to a large chest of drawers and bent to open the bottom drawer, withdrawing a slightly squashed cylinder of broadsheet. 'Here you go, though I don't think it'll help you much, I fear.'

The pages were from *The Times*. Disappointed, Zach unrolled the cylinder and scanned the date and a few of the bylines. He wasn't sure what he thought he would find, but there was a chance that, somehow, the picture's former owner might have left some clue to their identity. He turned the sheets over and examined the other side, and then something in the bottom right hand corner made him stop. There were a few colourful smudges on the paper; inky smears in a vibrant, emerald green. They looked like finger-marks, and as Zach frowned at them, trying to place where he had seen that colour recently, he saw something that made him go cold.

'Are you all right, Mr Gilchrist? You've gone rather pale.' Annie Langton's hand was on his arm, but her voice seemed to come from far away. Zach could hardly hear her above the thumping of blood in his ears, and in his hands, the news-paper began to shake uncontrollably. In the corner of the paper, right on the edge, was a thumbprint the exact same emerald green that marked the tupped ewes in Hannah's flock. A thumbprint with the sharp, diagonal line of a scar running across it; clear and unmistakeable.

8

Dimity was sick on the boat on the way to Tangiers.

'I thought your father was a fisherman?' said Élodie, standing on the deck of the steamer with the wind fluttering her hair around her and whipping the words away.

'But I'm not,' Mitzy pointed out, doubling over the railings again as her stomach heaved. By then there was nothing left to come up, and she wiped a string of spittle from her chin. 'I've never been on a boat before.'

'Can we get you something, Mitzy? A glass of water?' said Delphine.

'Ginger's best, if they have it; or mint,' she croaked, her throat ragged and sore; so dizzy she daren't let go of the railing. She looked around for Charles and saw him on a bench on the upper deck, sketching a pair of little boys who were playing with their model aeroplanes. She was half glad that he wasn't watching her being sick, and half jealous of the boys. Celeste was almost as unhappy at sea as she was, but the Moroccan woman remained in her cabin, lying down with the room darkened. A kind of quiet, private dignity in distress that Dimity wished she could emulate, but when she went indoors she only felt worse, and her head started to pound as well, the blood throbbing through her temples as though it had doubled in volume. Her only hope was to watch the horizon, and remain on the leeward side of the railings. When Delphine returned from the galley with a sprig of mint, asking if she should boil it or what, Dimity snatched it from her and chewed the leaves raw, desperately hoping that the lurching in her gut would stop. At least the mint masked the foul taste in her mouth. Élodie watched her with distaste and a trace of sympathy.

'It'll be worth it when we get there, honestly,' she said, staunchly.

After a while, exhaustion sent Dimity inside, where she lay down on a bench beneath a window to sleep. She had no idea what time it was when Delphine shook her awake, her face alight with excitement.

'Come and see,' she said, pulling at Dimity's hands until she rose, shakily, to her feet. Delphine led her back out onto the deck, where Charles, Celeste and Élodie were already at the rail. The light was dazzling, and Dimity shut her eyes instinctively. Such light, so strong through her eyelids that they glowed redder than a fire. When she could open them it was all-consuming, and she flinched. 'Look! We're here. Morocco!' Delphine said, nudging her closer to the rail. Finally able to see, Dimity gasped.

The city of Tangier rose up from the water's edge all around the arched harbour, almost too bright to look at; clustered white houses like jumbled building blocks, with palm trees and fragile-looking towers rising up from the mêlée. Here and there, a vibrant slew of pink flowers tumbled over a wall or from a balcony. Above the sparkling turquoise water, the city seemed to glow. The port thronged with boats of all shapes and sizes, from tiny fishing vessels painted every colour under the sun to huge, ponderous cargo steamers and passenger ships like the one she was aboard. On the dock, men with dark skins and hard faces were arguing and dealing, loading and unloading. Down on the quayside next to their boat, a heated exchange was carrying on between a man with skin the colour of treacle, wearing billowing green robes, and a white man in a smart linen suit. Dimity gaped at it all in amazement. The men's voices were an alien babble, every bit as incomprehensible as the scene stretching out before her. Just as Delphine had once said, the sea was a different blue to England, as was the sky; the thin towers looked strange and unearthly, too tall and thin to stand up to a storm. The air smelt of the sea but also of heat and dust; of spices she couldn't name; flowers she had never seen before. Stunned, she turned to look at Delphine and found four sets of eyes upon her, and smiles at her amazed expression.

Élodie burst out laughing.

'You should see your face, Mitzy! I told you it'd be worth it, didn't I?' she said. Dumbly, Dimity nodded. Celeste patted her hand softly, where it clasped the rail for support.

'Poor Mitzy! It must all be very disturbing for you. But breathe it in, immerse yourself, and soon you will come to love it. This is Morocco, my home. This is a place of wonders and beauty, cruelty and hardship. This is the landscape of my heart,' she said, turning back to take in the view. The sun did not seem to hurt Celeste's eyes; it shone on her black hair and brought it alive.

'Come along,' said Charles. 'Time to get off and find somewhere to eat. Once your stomachs have settled, ladies, you will be ravenous.'

'What do you think?' said Delphine, taking Dimity's hand and holding it tightly as they turned to disembark. Dimity searched for words to express how she was feeling. How the heat and the light and the colours seemed to fill her up to bursting, pouring into her soul like elation. How she could not quite believe that such a place existed.

'I think . . . I think it's . . . like a dream. I think this must be another world altogether,' she said, her throat sore and her head thumping.

'It is,' Delphine said, with a smile. 'It is another world altogether.'

*

They stayed only one night in Tangier, a night in which Dimity slept little, sniffing the strange air and the alien smells carried on it, feeling her head reel. It was giddy, dazzling; everything as alien and nonsensical as an imagined land. She woke many times in the night, feeling as though the land beneath her was hollow, insubstantial. As though none of it was solid, and the crust of it might give way and tumble her into nothingness. After a while, she realised why. The boom of the sea was gone; the way it echoed up through her feet in Blacknowle, beating like a vast heart, all of the time. Without it, she felt as airy as a sprite; like a kite with its string cut. In one dream it was her own leaden heart that had stopped, and waking was like being reborn in a new skin.

They hired a car and chauffeur for the long drive to Fez, the journey made slow by sand that had blown over the road in places. The car rocked along gently as the wind nudged it, and Dimity stared out of the window while the others slept, still stunned by how huge everything was, how wild and different. The sky was flawless, hard and unforgiving. Under the fierce sun, the land shimmered with heat; brown dust and rocks and parched-looking scrub, as far as the eye could see. In the far distance, along the road they had just travelled, Dimity thought she could see the dust plume of another vehicle, but it was hard to tell. It was late in the day and the sun was casting long shadows from even the smallest rock and shrub when at last the city appeared in front of them, sprawling low against the broad plain. At first Dimity thought it was no bigger than Wareham, but the closer they drew the more it seemed to spread. The others roused themselves, and Celeste pointed out that the compact cluster of buildings which Dimity had thought was the whole city, was in fact only the colonial buildings, where the French and other Europeans lived.

'Because we think we're too special to live with the Arabs and Berbers,' Delphine said mildly.

'Because we're prudent enough to keep a respectful distance,' Charles corrected her.

'Beyond these buildings is Fez el-Djid. The new Fez.' Celeste pointed to the city, where twinkling lamps had already been lit on the shady side of the streets.

'Is it new? I thought the city was old,' said Dimity.

'The new is only new compared to the old. The new is still many hundreds of years old, Mitzy. But the old . . . Fez el-Bali is the oldest city in Morocco not built by the Romans or other ancient peoples. Here it is, here. Look!' Celeste swept her arm across the sudden view, as the car slowed to a halt at the edge of a valley and the city poured down into the low ground beneath them; rooftops so clustered and chaotic that Dimity's eye could not trace the line of any one street for more than a few yards.

They got out of the car to see better, standing in a single line and staring out over the city. A steady breeze came in from the south, seeming even hotter than the still air, like the breath of some huge animal. Celeste breathed in deeply, and smiled.

'The wind comes in from the desert today. Can you feel the heat, Mitzy? Girls? That is a desert wind; the *arifi*, the thirsty wind. You can sense the power of it. On a day like today, the sun there would kill a man, as sure as a knife to the heart. It drinks the very life from your blood. I have felt it – the urge to lie down is strong, so strong; and then, you are no more. Worn away, just one more grain of sand in the vast ocean of the Sahara.'

'Celeste, you're scaring them,' Charles chided her, but Celeste tipped up her chin defiantly.

'Perhaps they ought to be scared. This is no gentle land we are in. It must be respected.' Dimity stood up straighter, trying to shake off the lassitude of the long journey in case she should fall asleep, and become nothing but sand. They all felt it, the fear and the soporific breeze. For a while nobody spoke, and the soft moaning wind and the buzzing flies were all they could hear.

Then, Dimity heard a man singing, though it wasn't like any kind of song she had ever heard before. A high, thin stream of words, at once fragile and deeply compelling, rich with meanings she would never understand. There was no sound of cars or traffic from the city, only the barking of dogs, the rumble of trolley wheels and now and then the braying of a mule or bleat of a goat; a low background hum of many lives, lived close together.

'Why is that man singing? What's he singing about?' Dimity asked nobody in particular. Her voice was hushed, and she was unable to take her eyes from the labyrinth below them.

'That's the *muezzin*, like a priest, calling the faithful to prayer,' said Charles.

'Like the church bells at home?'

'Yes.' Charles chuckled. 'Exactly like that.'

'I like the song better than the bells,' she said.

'But you do not know what he is singing. What words he says,' Celeste pointed out, quite seriously.

'That doesn't matter much, with a song. A song is only half words, and the other half music. I can understand the music,' she said. She glanced at Charles and found him watching her with a thoughtful expression on his face.

'Good, Mitzy,' he said. 'Very good.' At this, Dimity flushed with pleasure.

'Girls, did you know the foundations of Fez el-Bali were laid on the site of a Berber camp?'

'Yes, Mummy. You've told us before,' said Élodie. Celeste put an arm around each of her daughters and smiled.

'Well, some things are worth saying more than once. There is Berber blood in your veins. This city is in your blood.'

'Well, Mitzy? What do you think?' said Charles, and Dimity felt all their eyes upon her, waiting for her verdict or for some keen observation.

'I don't think anything,' she whispered, and saw Charles and Celeste's faces register disappointment. She swallowed, and thought hard, but her mind was reeling. 'I can't think anything. It's . . . everything,' she said. Charles smiled and patted her shoulder in a vaguely comforting way.

'There now. You must be exhausted. Come on. Back in the car and let's get to the guest house,' he said.

'Aren't we going to stay with your family, Celeste?' Dimity asked, before she thought to check her tongue. Delphine shot her a significant look, and Celeste frowned slightly.

'No,' she said, shortly.

They had to leave the car at the city walls, since the streets were too narrow to drive along, and walk the last quarter of a mile to where they would be staying. The door of the *riad* which was to be their guest house was tall and elaborately carved, but like the rest of the buildings fronting the narrow street, it appeared to be crumbling and dishevelled. Dimity felt slightly disappointed until they walked through the doors and into a tiled courtyard with a marble fountain at its centre, stone benches strewn with faded mats and cushions, and straggly roses growing up around the pillars that supported the upper floors of the house. As one, the girls gazed up in wonder. There was something sublime about coming into a building only to find the clear, pale green sky still spreading out above. One star had come out to shine; a single point of light that glistened. The floor was made of intricate blue and white mosaic, the walls part tiled, part plastered and painted, and everywhere there were tiny fragments missing and cracks and places where tiles had come loose and been lost; imperfections that only seemed to make the whole more magical.

'They do not build like this in Dorset, do they?' said Celeste, close to Dimity's ear, and she shook her head mutely.

A tray of heavily sweetened mint tea was brought out to them as they seated themselves in the courtyard, and a servant ran in and out of the door and up the stairs, carrying their luggage in from a handcart, a few pieces at a time. Dimity stared at the boy each time he passed; at his curling black hair and coffee-coloured skin. When she saw him with her small, tatty carpet bag in one of his hands, her stomach clenched peculiarly. Nobody had ever carried anything for her before, let alone a servant. Somebody she could make a request of, and have them be duty bound to obey her. She craned her neck to keep sight of him as long as she could, until he vanished around a turn in the staircase. Delphine, sitting next to her, gave her a nudge in the ribs and another significant look.

'Not bad, I agree,' she whispered. 'But not a patch on Tyrone Power.' Their hushed laughter spiralled around the courtyard, bouncing from the crumbling, blush-coloured plaster.

Dimity, Delphine and Élodie were to share a room with a low vaulted ceiling from which an iron fretwork lamp hung, casting fragmented patterns of light. It had a cool, tiled floor and flaking walls painted ochre. The beds were made up of low, hard mattresses with small bolsters as pillows and a single woven blanket folded at the foot of each. Tall windows opened onto a stone balustrade with a view to the neighbouring building in front, and down the hill over the rest of the city to the right. The sky was by then a velvety black, lit up with more stars than Dimity had ever seen before.

'It's like a different sky, isn't it?' said Delphine, coming to stand beside her while Élodie did handstands against the wall behind them, the legs of her pyjamas riding up to show her skinny shins. 'Hard to imagine the same moon and stars shining down on England.'

'There are nights in Blacknowle, in the summer, when perhaps there are this many stars. Perhaps; but the sky is never as black, and the stars never as bright,' said Dimity. 'Doesn't it get cooler, in the night-time?'

'By dawn it will be, yes, and out in the desert it gets freezing. But for a long time after the sun sets, it stays warm here in the city. The buildings trap the heat,' said Delphine. Dimity looked down at the narrow streets, and could almost see the hot air lying there, fat and supine as an overfed dog. Suddenly, she was so weary she could hardly stand, and had to lean against the balustrade for support. 'Are you all right? Have you drunk enough water?'

'I . . . I don't know.'

'You have to drink lots here, even if you don't feel thirsty. The heat makes you faint, otherwise. I'll fetch you some.'

'Get me some too, Delphine!' said Élodie, still upside down as her sister left the room.

The girls stayed up late, Élodie and Dimity listening, rapt, to Delphine's lurid tales of white slavers in Morocco capturing European men and forcing them to work until they died, building palaces and roads and whole cities. Capturing European women and forcing them to marry fat, ugly sultans; to live for ever in the harem, never allowed outside. Eventually, the two younger girls surrendered to sleep, but in spite of her weariness Dimity was awake for much longer, after the whole house had fallen quiet. She stayed at the window and clasped the warm stone of the balustrade, and breathed in deeply, trying to pick individual scents from the warm, loaded air.

There were roses, and jasmine too; the resinous smell of cypress trees, almost like the sea-battered pines of Dorset, but subtly different. On the breeze came a rich, herby smell, like sage or rosemary, as well as the stink of hot animal skins and manure; human sewage too – a privy smell, sweet and familiar, not constant but rising up now and then. There was a sharp, leathery, meaty smell she could not guess the source of; a metallic smell that was almost like blood and made her uneasy; a prickly scent of spices she half recognised from the food they had eaten and the *pastilla* Celeste often cooked at Littlecombe. And beneath all these new things was a striking absence – the missing salty breath of the sea. Thinking of Littlecombe, and Blacknowle, gave Dimity a jolt, and she noticed that it seemed to have receded far into the distance – not just in miles but in time too. As if her whole life up until that point had been a dream, one that was now fading fast from memory like all dreams do upon waking. This was a wholly new life; one where the heartbeat of the sea no longer tethered her, no longer trapped her own into keeping time with it. One where she was free and unfettered, and unfamiliar, and different. She gripped the stone tightly, and felt so happy that she wasn't sure she could stand it.

After breakfast in the morning, Celeste readied her two daughters and prepared to set off for her family's house, outside the walls of Fez El-Bali in the more spacious streets of Fez El-Djid. She combed the girls' hair and clipped it neatly back from their faces with quick, tense fingers, tweaking their cotton skirts and blouses into neater lines. Dimity looked down at her own attire – the same worn-out felt skirt she often wore at home – and smoothed it down self-consciously.

'Will I look all right, dressed as I am?' she asked, anxiously, and Celeste looked up with a frown until a look of comprehension replaced it.

'Oh, Mitzy! I am sorry but for this visit I must go with just my girls. It has been more than a year since I saw my parents . . . And after such a long time the first meeting should be just for us. Do you understand?' She came to stand in front of Dimity, put her hands on her shoulders and scrutinised her from arm's length. Dimity nodded, with a sudden lump in her throat. 'Good girl. Charles has gone for a walk but I am sure when he comes back he will want to start some sketches. We will be back . . . Well. I am not sure when. It depends . . . Anyway, we will see you later on.' She ushered the younger girls towards the door, and they each gave Dimity a smile as they passed – an apologetic one from Delphine, a heartless one from Élodie. In the doorway, Celeste looked back at her. 'You cannot wear those woollen clothes here. You will be too hot. When we come back I will find something lighter for you to wear.' She nodded to confirm the promise, and was gone.

Left alone, Dimity hugged her arms tight around herself, and fought against a wave of nerves. Transfixed by uncertainty, she didn't know whether to stay in her room or leave it. She didn't know what was right, what the rules were. She tiptoed to the top of the stairs and looked down at the courtyard, where the fountain was splashing gently and the curly-haired boy was sweeping the floor with a stiff bristled besom. Muted voices echoed up to her, their meanings lost in a blur of fluid, incomprehensible sound. She walked right the way around the terrace onto which their bedroom door opened, staring at the ornate tiles and the carvings on the wooden doors, peering down at the courtyard from every available angle, and up at the sky which was clear and blue overhead. She had never seen such a fine building, let alone been inside one, or stayed in one. Eventually she plucked up the courage to go downstairs, but when she got to the bottom she saw that the front door was shut. Making sure the coast was clear, she went over to it and tried the handle, tried to pull it open, but it wouldn't budge. Suddenly, the servant boy appeared beside her and spoke, his teeth very white in his dark face. Dimity stepped back, her shoulders hitting the door. The boy smiled, and spoke again, this time with words that had the more regular, almost familiar sound of the French she sometimes heard Charles and Celeste speak. But even though she could pick out distinct words, she was none the wiser as to their meaning. She edged away from him, then turned and fled back up the stairs.

Hours later she dozed on her low mattress, gazing up at the ceiling and drifting in and out of a dream in which she was lost in the middle of the vast dry landscape they had crossed the day before, and could feel the wind turning her to sand and blowing her away, one grain at a time. Footsteps outside and a sudden knock roused her, and Charles appeared around the door before she had a chance to answer. He had caught the sun across the bridge of his nose and along his cheekbones, and his hair was sweaty and windswept. Dimity scrambled to her feet, brushing back her hair and fighting to focus her mind. She couldn't tell if her dizziness was from standing up too fast, or from the devastating sight of him.

'Mitzy! Why are you here alone?'

'They went to Celeste's family, only I couldn't go since I'm not family,' she said, rubbing the sleep from her eyes. Charles frowned.

'Well, she shouldn't have left you here by yourself like

that; hardly seems fair. Come on. Are you hungry? I was going to eat then take a mule up to the Merenid tombs above the city. Would you like to come with me?'

'Yes,' she said at once, and then began to wonder how she would ride a mule with any modesty whilst wearing a felt skirt.

She followed Charles, almost trotting to keep up, as he strode down the dusty streets deeper into the heart of Old Fez. She dodged between thronging people, moving like slow-shifting snakes in either direction, all dressed in robes of chalky grey or fawn and brown; desert colours, as though the sand and rock and crumbling plaster all around had seeped into them. Small shops lined the street, their wares more often than not hanging on hooks outside, making the way even narrower. Vast metal plates and jars; bolts of fabric; huge bunches of dried herbs; leather goods of every description; lanterns, baskets, machine parts and unidentifiable hardware.

'We won't go too far in. There's a little place not far from here where we can eat, and a man next door who will loan us some mules for the rest of the day,' Charles called back over his shoulder. A sudden flurry of wings made Dimity look up, and a scattering of bright white pigeons rose up from a rooftop. Also watching them were two tall women on a balcony overhanging the street, their skins as black as pitch, the jewellery hanging from their necks and ears as bright as flames against their dark colours. Dimity goggled at them until she bumped into a woman walking the other way, swathed head to foot and veiled in grey, with her children hanging from her hem. The children wore silk kaftans in shades of indigo, lime green and dusky red, as fine and pretty as butterfly wings. The veiled woman muttered something angrily, and her children giggled and smiled as they passed.

They turned a corner into a steep, cobbled street, and Charles turned his head to speak. 'Watch your step, we're close to the butchers here.' Puzzled, Dimity looked down instead of up, and saw a river of bright red blood running along the middle of the alleyway, bubbling and rippling over the cobblestones. Hurriedly, she stepped to one side of it, and watched as a single white feather travelled by like a tiny boat on a grim and visceral river.

'How many animals could contain that much blood?' she said.

'Many, many. But it's bloody water, not all blood. The butchers sluice it out of their shops by the bucketful,' Charles told her. He looked at her briefly. 'I can't imagine a hunter like you being squeamish?'

'No, Mr Aubrey,' she said, shaking her head, even though her knees were aching in an odd, sickly way. She liked him calling her *a hunter*. The smell of the blood was clinging and rich. She took another cautious step back from the flow and her heel caught on something, tripping her. She looked down into the slotted eye of a goat, and recoiled. There were hundreds of eyes, all staring and still. A pile of severed goat's heads, trailing red from their necks; straight little teeth behind pulled-back lips. The old man behind this gruesome heap laughed at her, and Dimity hurried away after Charles, her stomach churning.

The place where they had lunch was not a restaurant as such, just a niche in the wall bordered by wooden shutters, where an old woman was stretching flatbreads and cooking them rapidly on an iron plate that smoked with heat. She filled them with handfuls of scrambled eggs and olives, and folded each one deftly before handing them to Charles. They sat on an ancient doorstep opposite the shop to eat, burning their lips on the hot bread and waving away a crowd of fat-bodied flies, metallic and blue, which buzzed around them. Without them even asking, a boy arrived with two glasses of tea, and Charles wiped his fingers on his trousers before taking them and handing the boy a coin in return. He seemed entirely at his ease, entirely used to the way of life that Dimity was finding so alien. She struggled not to show her amazement and to ignore the flat, curious stares she got from the Arab men as they passed. As if also suddenly noticing their attention, Charles gave her a quick smile.

'Don't wander off on your own, will you, Mitzy? It's probably quite safe, but it's so easy to get lost in the old town. I did, on my first visit here. It took me four hours to find my way out! In the end I chose one pack mule and just followed it. Luckily, it led me to one of the gates, and I found my way from there. Best if you stick close to me, I think.'

'I will, I promise,' she said. Charles took another bite and chewed meditatively for a moment.

'There's a piece coming to me. I can't quite see it yet, and I think it might be desert, not city . . . we shall see. While you're here you must see the tanning vats. They're truly amazing. Not too soon after lunch, though, I think. They have a powerful aroma,' he said with a smile. Dimity nodded. She wanted to do all of it, everything Charles suggested she do.

Their mules had raw, pinkish leather saddles which gave off a meaty smell to blend with the reek of the animals themselves. Charles negotiated at length in French with the muleteer, eventually handing over some coins with the air of a man who knows he's been robbed. Only once they were on and riding away did he wink at Dimity, and whisper that he'd got them a bargain. Dimity, who'd had no choice but to ruck her skirt up around her hips in order to sit astride her mule, was sweating under a blanket that had been provided for her to drape around her lower body for modesty's sake. She tied it behind her waist, wearing it like a giant apron, and the coarse fabric made her knees itch. Within a few hundred yards the press of the saddle into her seat bones was giving her a numbing pain, but her mule followed Charles's with quiet obedience, and she would do just the same.

They rode for an hour or more, through the powerful heat of the afternoon, ever upwards onto a rocky hill north of the city. Ahead, Dimity could see the boxy, crenellated remains of buildings which she guessed to be their destination. Sweat trickled down her spine, and she wilted in the saddle, feeling the sun singe her face. Charles was wearing a broad-brimmed hat, and she wished she had something similar. Her hair clung to her scalp and the back of her neck, and she daydreamed about diving off the quay at Tangier, and feeling the cool turquoise water close over her head. For a long time the only sound was the clatter of the mules' hooves over rocks and pebbles on the ground, the creak of the saddles and the moaning of the breeze. Then, near the summit, they began to walk through a field of goat skins, stretched and pegged out to dry beneath the roasting sun. They had been dyed bright red, bright blue, bright green, and lay around on the rocky ground like petals dropped from some vast flower. Dimity stared at each one, astonished by the colours, as her mule picked its way around them.

When at last they arrived at the foot of a tall, tumbled-down stone tomb, Charles dismounted and took a long pull from a bottle of water before handing it to Dimity.

'Oh, blast it – you've burnt your face! Haven't you got a hat?' he said. Dimity shook her head, which was aching, and did not care about her sunburn because as she drank from his bottle, her mouth was touching his. 'Never mind, you can wear mine on the way back. Come and sit in the shade for a while.' It was only once Dimity had slithered stiffly from her mule to sit with her back to the crumbling stones that she understood why Charles had undertaken the hot and uncomfortable trek. The whole of Fez was laid out below them, and beyond it the plain and the rocky hills circled all around. The sun was dipping in the west, and everything was alight with an orange glow; the city walls seemed to flame. She gasped at the spectacle of it, and Charles smiled, also turning to look.

'You can understand why these ancient kings wanted this to be their final and everlasting view, can't you?' he said, softly. Dimity nodded. Below them, lights were starting to come on down in the medina, where the shade was deepest. They sparkled like fallen stars.

'I never imagined a place like this, in all the time I was in Blacknowle. It doesn't seem fair that this should have existed all the while, yet I never knew of it.'

'There are a million more places besides, Mitzy. The more you travel, the more you will understand how vast the world truly is.'

'Will you take me to other places, then, Mr Aubrey? Will you take me with you, when you go?' In the instant after she spoke these words, she could hardly believe she'd let them sound out loud. Charles said nothing for a long time, and Dimity's heart curled in on itself, braced for a blow.

'I'll do my best for you, Mitzy. Who knows which way life will take us?' he said at last. Dimity glanced at him, as he gazed out over the city with the light of it shining in his eyes. Such an intent, faraway look; as though he was trying to stare into a future that neither of them could see. She blinked, and her heart uncurled itself. *I'll do my best for you, Mitzy*. Suddenly all the vast promise of the world resounded in those words. *For you, Mitzy*. They sat for a long time while the sky overhead grew dimmer, blushing pink against the turquoise; a few wisps of high cloud glowed silver and gold. A heavenly scent surrounded them, and Dimity looked over her shoulder to see a jasmine plant scrambling along the broken wall of the tomb, arching over them to release its perfume like a wedding bower.

Celeste and the girls were already at the *riad* when Charles and Dimity returned, parched and dusty, as true darkness began to fall. The three of them were in the courtyard; Celeste and Élodie curled together on a low couch while Delphine sat on the edge of the fountain, leaning over to watch the constant play of the water. Celeste looked up when Charles greeted her, and with a shock Dimity noticed how red and puffy her eyes were, how streaked and salty her face.

'My darling! Are you all right? What happened?' asked Charles, crossing to crouch down in front of her. His words, his posture, gave Dimity a nasty feeling. She hung back, skirted them and went to sit near Delphine, who did not look up. As she passed, she felt Celeste's eyes flicker up at her. She didn't need to see her face to know what expression would be on it. That same hard look as when they had found her sitting in the kitchen at Littlecombe, with Charles's picture of Dimity in her hand.

'I will tell you later. Where have you been? We were worried.' Celeste's voice was hoarse.

'Just up to the tombs. I told you I wanted to go and see the view . . .'

'And you took Mitzy with you? I thought we decided we would all go up to the tombs tomorrow? Delphine wanted to . . .'

'Well, we can go again. You can take the girls, anytime you want to. And of course I took Mitzy – she'd been here on her own all morning.'

'I am sure Mitzy can cope with being by herself for a little while,' said Celeste, her voice taking on a dangerous edge. Dimity didn't dare look up, and beside her Delphine's fingers, which had been stirring slow whirlpools, went still.

'It hardly seemed fair,' Charles said, carefully.

'Our daughters might like to spend a little time with you too, Charles.'

'You took our daughters to see your family. Must the whole world wait and hold its breath until you return?' Charles said, coldly. There was a loaded pause. Dimity looked up cautiously and saw the way the two of them glared at one another. Still nestled into her mother's side, Élodie looked tense and unhappy.

'Girls. Go upstairs to your room,' said Celeste. Without hesitation, all three of them obeyed.

Their voices echoed up from the courtyard, and Dimity tried not to make it obvious that she wanted to listen. As if she could tell, Élodie sang a tuneless song about a frog, over and over again, so that her parents' exact words were impossible to distinguish. From quiet to loud, from a whisper to an angry crescendo from Celeste, the argument churned on like a stormy sea. Delphine leant out over the balcony, as if to put herself as far from it all as she could. Since she couldn't hear what the fight was about, Dimity went over to join her. Delphine gave her a small, worried smile.

'They do this sometimes. But they always love each other again afterwards,' she said.

'Why are they arguing? It looked like your ma had been crying before.'

'She got upset at *grandmère et grandpère*'s house.'

'What about?'

'Well . . . her mother was so happy to see her. We had a

lovely lunch there with her. She is Berber, but of course you know that. But when her father came home, he—'

'Delphine! You don't have to tell her *everything*!' Élodie snapped, breaking off her song. In the quiet after she spoke, Charles's voice rose from below:

'You're being irrational. You always are when you've been home to your parents!'

'I have given up *everything* for you!' Celeste cried.

'But I have given you everything you wanted!' Charles countered. Quickly, Élodie resumed her singing.

'What did her father do?' Dimity asked.

'He . . . well, he's French and he's quite old. Mummy sometimes says he's from another age, and she means he's quite old-fashioned. But he won't see her or speak to her, or to us, because . . .'

'Because they're not married?'

'Yes.' The two girls looked out across the scattered city lights in silence for a while, listening as the words of Élodie's song got tired and jumbled and began to descend into nonsense. Beneath it, the other voices seemed to have stopped, and as Élodie stumbled into silence, all three of them listened, ears tuned to the least noise. None came, and after thirty seconds Delphine exhaled, her shoulders slumping. 'There. Over,' she said, with quiet relief.

'Why haven't they got married?' Dimity asked.

'God, Mitzy, you're such a nosey parker!' said Élodie, and though even Dimity agreed with her this time, she still needed to know.

'Daddy won't. He can't because—'

'Delphine! You know you're not supposed to say!' Élodie cried.

'I won't tell,' said Dimity, but Delphine bit her lip, shook her head.

'I can't say, but he has a good reason why he can't. She

doesn't mind most of the time. It's only because of the way her father treats her now. He won't . . . he won't even let her into the house. He was so angry when he came home today and saw her, but you can see it hurts him too. It was horrible. Straight away he demanded to see her hand, and when he saw that there was no ring on her finger, that was it. He said she had to leave. Poor Mummy! She loves her father very much.' Delphine spoke with a kind of gentle desperation, but Dimity hardly heard her. Her mind was racing, picking at the threads of what had been said; picturing the way Celeste had looked at her downstairs, the way Élodie had prevented her sister from telling her the whole story. She started to guess at why Charles would not marry Celeste, and the answer she came up with made joy blaze through her like the sun rising.

The following day, Celeste beckoned Dimity into her room and opened up a canvas bag on the bed. The bag was full of clothes.

'These were mine when I was growing up. I thought they might fit you. I fetched them yesterday from my parent's house . . . they will be better for you to wear while you're here.' She pulled a few items out and handed them to Dimity. Her eyes were no longer swollen, but her face still seemed heavy with sadness. Her hair, hanging straight around her face, was tangled. 'Well? Would you like to wear them or not?'

'Yes please, Celeste. Thank you,' said Dimity meekly, rolling the clothes she'd been handed into a bundle. The cottons were soft and light.

'Well, don't just stand there! Go and try them on!' Celeste snapped. For a second her eyes lit with anger, but then sadness filled them again. 'Sorry, Mitzy. I am not angry with you . . . It's not your fault that . . . you are here. I am angry with . . . men. The men in my life! The rules they design for us, to have a stick with which to beat us. Go; go on. Try the clothes. The trousers go on first, underneath the long tunic.' She waved her hand at Dimity and turned back to the canvas bag, lifting out more clothes and laying them in matching piles.

In her own room, and with Delphine's help, Dimity put on baggy trousers with a string-tie at the waist and buttoned cuffs at the ankles, a lightweight vest and a long, open tunic with swinging sleeves, which was belted around her ribs with a wide sash. It was very similar to the robes she often saw Celeste wearing in Blacknowle, but on her own body the outfit felt alien and unusual. She twirled, and watched the way the long swathe of fabric swirled out around her. It was a deep shade of violet and had embroidery around the neckline; so weightless compared to the heavy fabric of her felt skirt that she could hardly feel it. It was finer than anything she had ever worn before. She slipped her feet into her shoes, and Delphine laughed.

'Do I look silly?' said Dimity.

'You look lovely, but . . . you can't wear those heavy old shoes with it! They look daft. Here – borrow my sandals until you have some of your own. You look like a proper Moroccan lady now. Doesn't she, Élodie?' Delphine looked at her little sister, who was scowling with fury, and Dimity took that to mean that the outfit suited her well.

'She's not Moroccan, though – *we're* more Moroccan than she is! *I* want to wear a kaftan. I'm going to tell Mummy!' Élodie stamped her foot and stormed from the room.

'Oh, do grow up, Élodie!' Delphine called after her, then she looked at Dimity and they laughed. 'The boy who lives here will fall over backwards when he sees you,' said Delphine. But Dimity didn't care about him in the slightest. She looked down at the brightly coloured fabric wrapped around her body and wanted to know if Charles would like it.

Feeling nervous and proud, Dimity went downstairs with the girls to find Charles and Celeste waiting on one of the couches in the courtyard.

'Well? What do you think of our Moroccan Mitzy?' said Delphine, gently pushing her into a twirl. She ran her hands nervously over the bright fabric, fitting it to the contours of her body. Charles approved, she could tell. His eyes widened slightly at first, and then narrowed in thought, and he tipped his head to one side when he looked at her, so she knew he was almost ready to draw, or to paint. Celeste gave her a steady stare, her expression hard to read, but when Dimity crossed to sit near to her, she noticed that Celeste's body was rigid, trembling ever so slightly; her nostrils had tiny pale crescents in them, where even they were held stiff, flared, fixed.

'How old are you now, Mitzy?' she asked, quietly.

'I was sixteen over the winter, I think.'

'You think?'

'Ma never . . . Ma's never been too clear on which year I was born, but I've been able to guess it, kind of.'

'Truly a woman now, then, and old enough to wed,' said Celeste, still with that same preternatural stillness to her that was making Dimity deeply uneasy. She was relieved when Élodie, ever hungry, roused them all to go in search of lunch.

In the following weeks Charles sketched Dimity many times, as though seeing her in Moroccan costume was all he had needed to make the images in his head coalesce. He painted her in shifting watercolours, a medium he rarely used, sitting by a well beneath one of the city gates which was said to have healing powers and could cure any woman of an aching back. He sketched her in oils, drawing water from one of the ornately tiled drinking fountains in the city, or sipping from her cupped hands with the swinging sleeves of her kaftan pushed back to keep them dry. At the Merenid Tombs again, this time with Celeste and the girls as well, he drew her half hidden by the decaying stonework, with the wide vista from that vantage point laid out in front of her. And each time she posed for him, Dimity felt every stroke of the pen or the brush or the graphite, as though it were his hands not his eyes that moved over her in constant appraisal. She shivered at it, felt her skin go cold and yet burn at every imagined touch of his fingers. Twice, three times he had to ask her to open her eyes, because she had shut them unconsciously, turning all her attention inward to focus on the ecstasy of the feeling.

But Celeste did not smile, if she happened to see; she looked serious, and questioning, as though she could read Dimity, and had suspicions about what made her close her eyes like that. When Charles talked to them about the piece he was planning, a Berber market scene with one young maiden as the symbol of all that could be lovely in a barren landscape, Celeste suggested that he had two genuine Berber maidens and one Berber mistress to choose from for the picture. Dimity felt anxious for a moment, but Charles merely shrugged and said, absently: 'I see Mitzy for it. She's the perfect age.' *Perfect, perfect* . . . The word sung gladly in her ears.

'Delphine is not even two years younger, and is just as tall,' Celeste pointed out.

'But Delphine does not have Mitzy's . . .' He trailed off, uncomfortably.

'Mitzy's what?' said Celeste, in a dangerous tone of voice.

'Never mind.'

'What, Charles? Tell me. Tell me what it is that fascinates

you so, that you must put her face in every picture, and your daughters', your mistress's, in none?' Celeste leant towards him and stared intently into his eyes. Dimity was glad that Delphine and Élodie were a good way off, and would not hear. Her own cheeks blazed, and she kept her eyes down, hoping to escape Celeste's attention.

'There's nothing in it, Celeste. It is only a matter of her age, and the propriety of using one's own child to model for a celebration of nubile beauty—'

'I see. So I am not young enough, and Delphine is not beautiful enough. You are honest, even if you are not loyal,' she snapped, rising to her feet and glaring savagely at Charles. Dimity snatched a glance at her, but averted it at once when the Moroccan woman's eyes turned to alight on her. There was a dreadful pause, and then relief as Celeste stalked away without another word, and Dimity let the pleasure of hearing Charles talk of her beauty echo in her head.

For ten days they took outings together, fitting them in around Charles's spasms of creativity. Dimity noticed that Celeste chose to walk close to her daughters, rather than with her or Charles, and she was happy with that arrangement. They visited *El Attarine*, the sprawling thatched souk in the centre of the city, where anything under the sun was available to buy if you knew where to go within the cramped plethora of shops. They climbed the stairs of a house, tipping the elderly man who lived there a few coins, and walked out onto his roof to see the tanning and dyeing vats laid out below; row upon row of white clay pits, full of stinking hides and tanning solution or the wild, rainbow colours of the dyes. They saw blue and white pottery and tiles being made and painted and fired; and once, by mistake, they saw a small brown goat hung up by its back legs, kicking desperately as its throat was cut. From another vantage point they gazed upon the jade green tower of the Karaouine Mosque, and the array of mosaicked college buildings and sacred courtyards surrounding it, forbidden to infidel feet.

'What would happen if a Christian were to go inside?' asked Dimity, in awe of the beauty and grandeur of the place.

'I think it might be best not to find out,' said Charles.

'It's so beautiful and perfect . . . and yet so many of the other nice buildings in the city are being left to fall to pieces,' said Delphine. Celeste put a hand on her daughter's shoulder.

'Moroccans are a nomad people. Berbers and Arabs both. We may build homes for ourselves from stone and brick these days, but still we think of them as tents. As though they are temporary, not permanent,' she said.

'Well, there's no surer way to make a building temporary than to neglect it, I suppose,' said Charles, grinning at Celeste to show he was joking. She didn't smile back at him, and his grin faded to nothing.

At dinner that night talk turned to the end of the trip, and a return to Blacknowle before the summer was spent. Celeste fixed Charles with steady, unforgiving eyes.

'I could stay here for ever. But we are at your disposal, as ever. As I choose to be,' she said, flatly.

'Please, Celeste. Don't be that way,' said Charles, taking her hand.

'I am as I am. Feelings do not go away.' She shrugged. 'Life would be simpler sometimes if they would.' She gazed at him without rancour, but with such strength of feeling that he looked away, and said nothing for a while. Dimity sat in the heat of the night and felt herself burn, as if all her pent-up thoughts would ignite. *No*. The word scorched her silent tongue. She wanted the trip to last for ever – not a trip at all but a new life, a new reality. In this place where she could sit for Charles every day and nobody whispered or called her names; and there was no Valentina, all pinched with spite, demanding she ask for money; where food was brought to her by black-eyed young men, and she did not have to hunt for it, or find it in a drenched hedgerow; skin or pluck or cook it herself; where she could wear colours as bright as the bougainvillea flowers and the tiles on the walls and the roofs of the holy buildings, clothes that swung and floated around her like royal finery; where she lived in a house with a fountain at its heart and a hot sky instead of a ceiling. Morocco was a place of dreams, and she never wanted to wake up.

The next day, Celeste took her daughters and went again to visit her mother. Dimity tried not to let her excitement show; tried not to let them see how happy she was to be left alone with Charles. She felt elated, and dreaded that Celeste would be able to see it. Celeste turned at the door and gave them both a steady look, but she said nothing. Charles seemed distracted, and he frowned as they set off into the city, his art materials in a leather satchel over his shoulder. He walked quickly, striding ahead so that Dimity struggled to keep up. She kept her eyes on his back, and watched as a dark fan of sweat spread slowly through his shirt. After a while, it seemed as though he was running from her, trying to leave her behind, and she hurried on, feeling a rising desperation that she couldn't quite define. Desperate to be kept, and not abandoned. Desperate to be loved, and drawn, and wanted. Her heart was full of him; the words he had said to her sang like prayers in her mind. *I'll do my best for you, Mitzy. She is perfect.* Had he said that? Called her perfect? She was sure he had. *Who knows what the future will bring?* And how he had looked after he said that, how deep in thought, lost in imagining; clearly the future he saw was different to the present. And he would not marry Celeste; he had good reason not to. A reason the girls weren't allowed to tell her. A reason that *was* her? *Perfect. For you, Mitzy. The new swan was the loveliest of all.*

Soon they were out of the city's bustling heart and on quiet streets running between clustered houses. Dimity was fighting for breath and her legs felt heavier with every step. She realised that their path had turned uphill, and felt a trickle of sweat run down her own spine. They must have walked right across town, and been climbing out of the valley, a long, long way from the guest house. The sun was rising to its highest point, sharp as a knife. They came to a place where the walls on either side of the alley were no more than two feet apart, and the shadow pooling between them was cool and deep. Unable to go on at such a pace, Dimity gave up and leaned back on the wall for a moment to catch her breath. Realising that her footsteps had ceased, Charles looked back at her. He still wore the same distracted frown.

'You need a rest, yes, of course,' he said. 'Thoughtless of me.' He came to stand opposite her, lit a cigarette and took a long pull.

'You're never thoughtless,' said Dimity. Charles smiled.

'You must be the only person who thinks that, and I fear you're being more loyal than truthful. The people close to an artist often lose out to the art itself. It's unavoidable. Sometimes, there just isn't enough room in my thoughts for everybody.'

'We all need time to ourselves. Time to breathe, and be left alone. Or we'd forget who we really are.'

'Yes! Exactly that. Time to breathe. Mitzy, you are a surprising girl sometimes. One could take you for the most untutored *naïf*, and then you come out with a simple truth that cuts to the core of human nature . . . Remarkable.' He shook his head, and drew again on his cigarette. Dimity smiled.

'Are you going to draw today?' she said.

'I don't know. I wanted to but . . . Celeste . . .' He shook his head. 'She is a force of nature, that woman. When she is stormy, it's hard to find calm.'

'Yes,' Dimity agreed.

She watched the pursing of his lips on his cigarette, the movement of his throat, the way he narrowed his eyes against the smoke. They stood facing each other, just a few inches apart; nothing between them but the warm, shady air. That space seemed to pull at Dimity, seemed to urge her nearer to him. Charles looked at her and smiled, and she stepped forwards, helplessly. She was no more than a hand's width from him, and the closer she got the more she knew that she needed this to live. Needed the touch of his body, his skin; needed to taste him, to be consumed by him. A craving she couldn't withstand for another second.

'Mitzy . . .' said Charles. There was a tiny furrow on his forehead, and in it she saw the echo of her own need, the strain of resisting what was pulling at them. She stepped forwards again, so that her body was touching his. Her breasts, her stomach, her hips and thighs; she shivered, felt the yearning grow even stronger, even more urgent. With shaking fingers she grasped his hand, put it on her waist and left it there, warm, solid. She felt his fingers move, tightening slightly, and looked up to find him staring at her. 'Mitzy,' he said again, softly now. She tilted up her chin, but given the difference in their heights, she could go no closer to him than this; nestled herself tighter to him. She shut her eyes, and then felt his mouth against hers; soft, scented with smoke, the rough brush of whiskers on his top lip so unexpected, so unlike Wilf Coulson's kiss. She felt the lightest touch of his tongue, the wet tip of it, brushing hers. Against her pelvis, he grew hard and swollen, and for a hung moment he leaned into her, reached his hands around her waist and pulled her tighter. The feeling was like her heart exploding; an unbearable ache of joy. Then his kiss vanished, and he pushed her away so abruptly that she stumbled back and hit the wall with a thump.

Dimity blinked rapidly, her desire disorienting her.

'No, Mitzy!' Charles raked his hands through his hair, then put one of them across his mouth and looked at her, turning his body awkwardly to the side. Desperately she reached out for him again, but he clasped her fingers and held them away. 'Stop. You're just a child . . .'

'I'm *not* a child. And I love you . . .'

'You don't . . . you don't know about love yet. How could you? It's a crush, nothing more. I should have seen it before now . . . Celeste did warn me. I'm sorry, Mitzy. I shouldn't have done that. I shouldn't have kissed you.'

'But you did!' Tears choked her. 'Why did you kiss me, if you didn't want to?'

'I—' Charles broke off and looked away again. His cheeks were flushed. 'Sometimes it's very hard for a man to resist.'

'I know you want me . . . I felt it.' Her tears were making her nose run, but she didn't care. She couldn't care; she could only try to think of ways to convince him, ways to feel again the bliss of kissing him.

'Dimity, please, stop now! It shouldn't have happened and it mustn't again. We can't . . . we can't just take what we want, when we want it. It's a cruel fact of life, but a fact nonetheless. It would be wrong, and I am not free to . . . Celeste and I . . .'

'I'd never tell, I swear it. Please, I do love you. I want to kiss you again; I want to please you . . .'

'Enough!' He slapped her reaching hands away. His teeth were gritted together and his nostrils flared, and she saw some great conflict within him, and prayed that he would lose. But he did not. He folded his arms and took a deep breath, blowing it out through his cheeks. 'Come now, let's go on, and talk no more about it. Someday soon you'll make some young lad very happy, and be a lovely wife to him. But it cannot be me, Mitzy. Put it out of your mind now.' He walked away along the alleyway, and it was some moments before Dimity could find her feet to follow. She ran her tongue over her lips to pick up every last trace of him, and inside her head she was numb and dishevelled, as though his kiss had shaken up the right order of her thoughts and made a blizzard of them.

The next day she awoke feeling dizzy and weak. She lay with the mattress pressing into her sweaty back and couldn't think of rising, or of breakfast. Delphine fussed around her for a while, and brought her water while Élodie watched from the doorway, flatly curious and unwilling to help. When Delphine had gone she walked over to Dimity, looked down at her.

'If you think by playing sick you'll get to spend the day with Daddy again instead of with us then you're quite wrong. He's gone off already, to meet with an artist friend who arrived in Fez last night. So you'll be stuck here on your own all day,' she said, coolly. Dimity stared at her, and Élodie stared back, and did not blink. Even if Dimity hadn't been feeling as ill as she was, she would not have given this dark, perceptive child the satisfaction of seeing her slough off a ruse, and get up. In the glance they exchanged was all the power Élodie now had, in guessing Dimity's heart, and all the will with which Dimity would resist her. Eventually Élodie smiled, as though she had won, turned and walked back to the doorway. 'Everybody knows, you know. You're so obvious about it,' she said, in parting. Dimity lay very still, and felt sicker than ever. The world seemed to tip, throwing her off balance; she had to hang on tight not to fall.

She lay in a trance for some hours, then, unsteadily, she got dressed and went onto the inner terrace to look down into the courtyard. There was no sign of anybody. She walked along the hall to Charles and Celeste's room, listened for a moment and then knocked softly. There was no reply, no sound of movement. She knocked again, louder, and still there was nothing. Her throat was parched and had a tight, raw feeling. Turning away, she paused, then in a heartbeat, without thought, she had opened their door and gone inside. The shutters were closed to keep the room cool during the heat of the day, and in the dim light creeping through Dimity looked around, taking in the clothes and shoes lying about; Charles's stack of drawings and small canvases, his books and boxes of pencils and brushes. She stood at the foot of the bed and tried to tell which side Celeste slept on, and which side Charles. The pillows still bore the slight indentations of their heads, and she found a long, black hair on one, so she crossed to the other, and ran her fingers lightly over the place where his head had lain. Slowly, she knelt down and lowered her face, inhaled in search of the scent of him. But the dye on the striped fabric was too strong, and was all she could smell. She tried to imagine what Charles would look like in sleep, and realised that she had never seen him like that. Never seen his face soft and vulnerable in repose; the flicker of dreams playing with his eyes behind their lids; the steady, regular depth of unconscious breathing. Imagining it gave her a pulling sensation, like something tearing softly inside her. She swam in the heavenly memory of his kiss, emblazoned across her mind.

In one corner of the room was a wooden table with a mirror on top and a small upholstered stool in front of it. Celeste had been using this as a dressing table, and its top was covered with her jewellery and hairbrushes, pots of face cream and powder. In a small, tightly lidded box was a soft plastic cup, the size of an eggcup meant for a bantam's egg. Its base was rounded so it wouldn't stand up, and Dimity stared at it for a minute, trying to think what it could be for. Eventually she set it aside and picked up some of Celeste's silver earrings, long ones with turquoise beads; she held them up to her ears, then fitted them to the lobes, screwing the backs tight to secure them. She gathered her hair into a knot behind her head to see the effect better, the way the beads swung around her jawline. Her pulse raced along with the guilt and temerity of trespass. There were necklaces too. She picked up her favourite, the one Celeste only wore in the evening, for dinner. A twisted rope of black and grey freshwater pearls, their lustre like the sheen on the Berber woman's skin, gleaming in the light from a candle flame. Dimity tugged the neckline of her kaftan further open, so that the pearls would sit, cool and heavy, against her own skin. There was an ornate carved wooden screen next to the dressing table, and Celeste had draped her chemise and several other items over it – the scarves she sometimes wore around her hair or her waist; the belts and sashes that fastened her robes. Dimity chose one carefully: a gauzy, diaphanous veil of pale cream silk with tiny silver coins sewn along the edges. She draped it over her head so that it covered her hair, and studied the effect in the mirror. In kaftan, jewels and veil she hardly knew herself. Hazel eyes lined with thick, dark brown lashes, clear skin, the shadows under her eyes from her restless sleep only seeming to add an extra delicacy, a vulnerability.

She stared at her softly lit reflection for a long time. She stared into the eyes of a young woman, a beauty, a mistress covered in the gifts of a lover.

'I am Dimity Hatcher,' she said, quietly, watching the way her lips moved, how full and soft they looked. She pictured Charles's lips touching them, imagined how they had felt to him. Her pulse beat between her thighs. 'I am Dimity Hatcher,' she said again. Then: 'I, Dimity Hatcher.' She paused, pulled the pale scarf a little lower over her brow, like a bride. The silver coins glinted. 'I, Dimity Hatcher, take thee Charles Henry Aubrey . . .' Her throat stung as she said the words aloud, and when she heard them her heart thumped so hard that it shook her. She cleared her throat carefully, and spoke a little louder. 'I, Dimity Hatcher, take thee Charles Henry Aubrey, to be my wedded husband . . .' There was a sharp gasp from behind her, and in dismay Dimity moved her eyes across the mirror and saw the reflection of Celeste, standing in the doorway.

There was a dreadful, electric pause as their eyes met; a frozen moment in which Dimity felt the blood drain from her face. Celeste's mouth hung a little open; her eyes went so wide that the whites gleamed. 'I was only—' Dimity started to say, but Celeste cut her off.

'Take off my things,' she whispered. Her voice was colder than midwinter. 'Take them off. Now.' With shaking hands, Dimity struggled to comply, but she was not fast enough. In three quick strides Celeste was upon her, pulling the scarf from her head so roughly that it took a clump of hair with it, fumbling at the clasp of the necklace, tugging at it so that it cut into the skin of Dimity's neck.

'Celeste, please! Don't – you'll break it!' she cried, but Celeste's face was alight with a fury she had never seen before, and she would not stop until the necklace came free. It snapped and flew apart, the pearls hitting the floor like hailstones.

'How dare you? How *dare* you?' she spat. '*Coucou! Coucou dans le nid!* You are a cuckoo child!'

'I didn't mean anything by it!' Dimity cried, tears of fear blurring her eyes. Celeste grabbed her by the wrist with a grip like a vice and put her face so close to Dimity's that she could feel the woman's breath, feverishly hot.

'Don't you lie to me, Mitzy Hatcher! Don't you *dare* lie to me! Have you fucked him? *Have you?* Tell me!'

'No! I promise, I haven't—' Without warning, Celeste slapped her hard across the face, flat-handed but with the full swing of her arm. Dimity had no time to brace herself and was flung from the stool, which clattered onto its side. She hit her head on the edge of the table and felt an explosion of tingling pain. She put her hands over her face and started sobbing.

'Liar!' Celeste screamed. 'Oh, I am a *fool*. How big a fool you must think me! Now, get up. Get up!'

'Leave me alone!' Dimity cried.

'Leave you alone? Leave you to watch him and covet him and tempt him away? Leave you to steal everything that is dear to me? No, I won't. Get up,' Celeste ordered again, and her voice was so dreadful that Dimity didn't dare disobey. She scrambled to her feet and backed away from the woman. Celeste was shaking from head to foot; her fists were clenched and her stare was like a thunderstorm.

'Now *go*! Get out of my sight – I cannot look at you! Get out!' she shouted. Blindly, Dimity fled. She stumbled down the stairs, almost falling; wrenched open the huge door and ran away down the dusty street, not daring to look back. In seconds the city had enveloped her, drawing her onwards, deep into its twisted heart.

9

There was rain dripping down the chimney, making little puffs in the cold ash piled in the hearth and shiny black splodges on the grate. Rare for that to happen – normally the rain came in off the sea, blown at an angle over the land, and was whisked over the cottage roof. Such straight, resolute, constant rain only came a few times in the year. Dimity stared at the drops as they landed, heard a dull note as each one struck; not a tune but a syllable, she realised. She strained her ears, waited fearfully. Three more came, closer together this time; unmistakeable. *Él-o-die*. She held her breath, hoping she was wrong and hadn't heard it. A single drip fell, all alone, and hope flared in her chest. But then three again. *Él-o-die*. With a cry Dimity turned abruptly away from the hearth, spinning around fast enough to see a shadow against the living room wall. Upside down; doing a handstand.

'Élodie?' she whispered, pulling her eyes from left to right, searching every corner of the room. Quick, sharp, clever Élodie. A wonder she hadn't come back before; a wonder she'd never found a way, until now. The charm in a chimney stack was no match for a determined child, one not easily fooled. A frown on a young, soft forehead, a daisy tucked into black hair. A pouting lower lip, a will to fight, to argue, to challenge.

Dimity fled from her. The shadow kicked its legs away from the wall, righted itself, came after her on light, careless feet. 'It wasn't me!' Dimity said, hurrying into the kitchen, casting the words over her shoulder. She was certain of this, and yet not. The words sounded right, sounded true, but underneath them Valentina was laughing, and there was a knowing look in her eye. And worse than that, far worse: a look of something like respect. A grudging, unvoiced respect. *But it wasn't me!* She flicked the switch on the kitchen wall but the darkness stayed; the bulb, covered in dust and spider dirt, was wholly lifeless at the end of its wire. Dimity caught her breath, fear shaking her fingers, turning her gut to water.

There she stood, in darkness, pressed up against the kitchen worktop with nowhere else to go, except outside. But out there, the storm and the cliffs and the sea were waiting. She stared out through the window at a night as dark as Élodie's hair. Faint white streaks of troubled water along the shore; rain clouds smothering the moon and stars. She saw headlights lancing down to Southern Farm, saw lights come on inside the house and then, not long afterwards, saw the car leave again. There were people close by, there was life, but it was another world, one where she did not belong. Outsiders always wanted to come further in than you invited them. They wanted to come all the way in, see everything, know everything. Spreading themselves into every corner like a smell. Like Zach, who'd brought memories of Charles with him. She'd risked everything to revel in them for a while, but that world was not hers any more. She'd left it a long time ago, for a prison of her own making – The Watch. But that prison had been a haven, for a very long time. A place filled with love, once Valentina had gone. *You're so stupid, Dimity!* said Élodie, using the patter of rain on the window for a voice. *It wasn't me,* Dimity told her, silently. A half-forgotten song crept into her throat, from a time and a place a lifetime ago. One she did not understand, one she never had; the tune as elusive as

a warm desert breeze. *Allahu akbar . . . Allahu akbar . . .*
This waking dream kept hold of her, all through the night.

Zach set off for The Watch slowly. He had been doing
everything slowly since his visit to Annie Langton, from
driving to eating to thinking, because everything was
smothered, half asphyxiated, by what he now knew. That
Hannah was the one who had been selling the pictures of
Dennis; that she had known about them all along, and lied to
him. He thought of the sheep pictures of hers that he'd seen
in her tiny, bare shop. They were good, but the Dennis
portraits were something else. Was she good enough to pass
a drawing off as an Aubrey? He shook his head impatiently.
But what, then? Where was she getting them? With a
seasick feeling inside, he thought about James Horne, and
the boat Hannah had been watching; her knowledge of the
coastline and its waters. Something occurred to him then, as
he thought about the payment he'd seen Hannah making to
James the same day she'd settled up her bar tab with Pete
Murray. He took out his phone and checked the date, then
stopped walking before he'd descended any further towards
the sea, where mobile phone signal disappeared entirely.
The Christie's sale had been four days ago. He texted Paul
Gibbons at the auction house.

*Did Dennis sell? Mind telling me how much for? Funds all
paid and cleared without hitch?* He waited impatiently for a
reply, sitting on a bench that looked out over the cliffs and
listening to his thoughts churn like the distant waves. Ten
minutes later, his phone beeped. *V curious about all the
sudden interest. Yes, sold – six point five. Buyer in Wales, all
funds cleared. Paul.* Six and a half thousand pounds. Zach
wanted to feel angry with her, because she had played him
for a fool. But instead he felt betrayed. He had thought that

he knew her. He had been falling for her. Now everything had changed, and it cut him to the quick.

Dimity Hatcher seemed too distracted to notice his distress, however. She was so agitated that he made the tea himself again, while she paced and sat and rose again, her skinny elbows waving as her fingers fiddled constantly, picking dirt from under her nails, picking at dead skin, scratching. In the end, even lost in thought, Zach couldn't ignore it.

'Dimity, are you all right? What's wrong? You seem . . . nervous today.'

'Nervous? Maybe, maybe,' she muttered. 'Check that hearth charm, would you?'

'What do you mean?'

'The one you hung up for me . . . I can't check it. I can't touch it – it was you that hung it, you that cast it. Just see if it's still there, see that it's safe,' she pleaded.

'All right.' He ducked into the inglenook and peered up the flue, where the misshapen heart was hanging. He wrinkled his nose. 'It doesn't smell too good, but it's there.'

'That don't matter, the smoke'll see to that before long. Just as long as it's there?'

'It's there.' Dimity frowned and chewed her lip for a moment.

'Then . . . she can't mean me no harm, can she?' she said quietly, sounding puzzled. 'She can't have come in anger, or that'd keep her out, wouldn't it?'

'Who can't have come, Dimity?' said Zach.

'The little one. She came back. She was here . . .'

'The little one?' Zach tried to think who she might mean. 'Do you mean Élodie?' At the mention of her name, Dimity froze. She stared at Zach with an intense expression that made him suddenly uneasy. 'I'll get the tea, shall I?' he said. He tried to walk past her to the kitchen but she caught his hands in hers, digging her thumbnails into the palms of his hands. He could feel the stiff, filthy wool of her red mittens, and his skin crawled away from them. A long strand of white hair fell across her eyes, but she ignored it.

'She's dead. Élodie's dead,' she whispered. Zach swallowed, and for a second, he almost thought he heard a question in the words, a plea for confirmation.

'Yes. I know,' he said. Dimity nodded quickly, and seemed to shrink back from him. She let go of his hand, and let her own fall lifelessly to her sides.

Zach escaped into the kitchen and took a deep, steadying breath as he poured the tea into two mugs. For the first time, he had the unsettling feeling that Dimity Hatcher was not quite in the same room as him. Not quite in the same world. There had been other times, earlier on, that he'd been sure she was lying to him. Just now, he'd also begun to doubt the things she clearly believed to be true. He shook the feeling off. Finding out about Hannah's duplicity had made him doubt everything and everyone in Blacknowle. He tried to smile as he went back into the sitting room.

'We'd have wed, if that little girl hadn't died. We'd have wed if she'd lived, I know it,' Dimity said, ignoring the tea he put beside her.

'Élodie's death . . . put everything on hold, did it? It must have been a very hard time for Charles . . . From what you've told me, and from what I've read, he was a devoted father. Loving, if slightly absent at times. Was it simply because of Élodie's death that he went off to war, in the end?' There was a long silence after Zach spoke, and then he thought he could hear a faint tune, the quietest of hummed songs, a wordless lament, coming from Dimity. 'It must have been . . . very upsetting,' he said. 'I know I've read somewhere how she died . . . was it flu? I can't remember now. Did children still die of flu in the 1930s?' he muttered, almost to himself, since Dimity's attention was still else-where.

'Flu?' she said, turning back towards him. 'No, it was . . .' She shut her mouth abruptly, moistened her lips with a quick flick of her tongue. 'Flu. Yes. That was it. Her stomach – gastric flu. Poor girl, poor girl; carried off . . .' She shook her head in dismay and sat still for a moment. 'She was sometimes cruel to me, was Élodie. She didn't like the fact that her father loved me. She was a jealous child, very jealous,' she said. 'Celeste's favourite, oh yes. A mother shouldn't have one, but she did. She did. Élodie took after her, you see. She was the spitting image of her mother. She would have been very beautiful, if she'd lived . . .' Dimity's voice trailed into the faintest of whispers, and Zach had to lean forwards to hear her.

'Is that why Celeste disappeared, after her death? Where did she go?'

'I don't know. Nobody knows. She blew away, on the breeze . . . he asked me, too; thought I might know. But I didn't – I don't. I *don't!*'

'All right, it's all right,' Zach said, soothingly. Dimity's eyes roamed the room, her mouth made the shape of unspoken words. Zach paused before speaking. 'How did Delphine cope? Were they close, the two sisters?' Dimity's eyes came to rest upon him, and they were awash with tears.

'Close?' she said, hoarsely. 'Close as only sisters can be.'

They were both silent for a long moment, and Zach pictured his portrait of Delphine, hanging next to her mother and Mitzy on the wall of his gallery. He had found one of the three alive and well, but the other two were still lost in the past, vanished like mist. He sighed. Blacknowle suddenly seemed deep and distant and full of secrets, and however much he wanted to solve its riddles, it didn't seem fair to harry an old lady to do so.

'You've known Hannah a long time, haven't you?' he said, carefully.

'Hannah?' Dimity cocked her head to one side, and then smiled suddenly, a knowing, almost cheeky smile. 'I've seen the pair of you together. Down on the beach, down at the farm,' she said. Zach felt the wintery edge to his own smile.

'I like her. That is . . . I thought I knew her, but . . .' He shrugged one shoulder, wondering how much he should say, what he should ask – if anything. But it was weighing too heavily on him, and he had to talk to somebody.

'I've known her since she was a child. Not well, not as friends exactly . . . but as neighbours. She's a good neighbour. She's a good girl.'

'Is she?'

'Yes. Why? What has she said to you?' Suddenly, Dimity sounded worried.

'Said to me? Nothing – that's the problem. I found out . . . I found out that she's been lying to me. About something very important.'

'Lying? No. I've never known her to do that.'

'Well, she has. Believe me,' said Zach, miserably.

'Not telling is not the same as lying, you know. Not the same at all,' Dimity said, intently.

'I found out that . . . Do you remember those pictures by Charles that I showed you, of a young man called Dennis?' Dimity clamped her mouth shut, and nodded convulsively. 'Well, I found out that it's Hannah who's been selling them. It's Hannah who . . . has them. Or is producing them,' he muttered. 'Or is fencing them,' he added, rubbing his thumb and forefinger across his tired eyes until spots danced across his vision. 'She's known all along that I was trying to find out about them – she knew all along. I must have sounded like such an idiot, with all my theories . . .'

After a moment, he realised that Dimity still hadn't

spoken. He'd been expecting her to defend her neighbour, or to be outraged that works by Aubrey were being sold in secret, under her nose. He looked up and frowned. Dimity sat perfectly still, her face a blank mask, her mouth still firmly shut. 'Dimity? Are you all right?' Zach asked.

'Yes.' She forced the word out; it crawled from between her reluctant lips. Zach took a deep breath.

'Dimity, did you . . . did you know about this?'

'No! And I'm sure you're wrong! Hannah's a good girl. She would never do anything that was wrong . . . or against the law. She wouldn't. I've known her since she was tiny . . . Known her family since before either of you were born!'

'Well, I'm sorry. But she *has* been selling them, and I can't think why she'd keep it so secret unless she knew she shouldn't be doing it! I always knew there was *something* not right about those drawings. At least now I know who to ask.' He broke off and looked at Dimity again, but she merely sat with a helpless look on her face, as if she had nothing else for him. 'I've got to go,' he said, getting to his feet. Dimity rose as well, and as she did there was a thump overhead and a fluttering sound, like a newspaper dropped onto bare floor. Dimity froze, and kept her eyes down as if determined not to react. Zach waited for another noise but the silence in the house was profound. The skin between his shoulder blades tingled, as though somebody was standing right behind him, close enough to feel them breathing.

'Dimity,' he said, softly. 'Who's upstairs?'

'Nobody.' The look in her eyes was firm, but underneath that was a plea he couldn't understand. 'Just rats in the thatch,' she said. Zach waited a while, but knew that he'd get nothing more.

Dimity followed him to the door, stood on the threshold as he stepped out into the light. There was a large bunch of dried seaweed hanging on a nail outside the door. It had long, thick fingers growing from a central stalk, and it rustled like soft paper when Dimity touched it, running her fingers down it.

'Rain later today,' she said, then saw Zach's quizzical expression and nodded. 'Sea belt. When rain's coming it draws in water from the air, and goes limp, like this.' Her smile faded away. 'Storm's coming. Be careful,' she said. Zach blinked, wondering if it was a warning, or a threat. 'Will you leave me the picture of Morocco? Will you leave that one with me?' she suddenly asked, catching his sleeve as he turned to go.

'Of course.' He took the printout from his bag and handed it to her, and she snatched it, eager as a child. Zach squeezed her arm briefly in farewell.

Halfway back along the track to the village, movement ahead caught Zach's eye and he looked up to see Wilf Coulson's bent and wizened figure retreating, turning away from him around the bend. Zach jogged until he'd caught up with the old man.

'Hello, Mr Coulson. Were you coming down to visit Dimity?' he said.

'That's none of your business,' Wilf Coulson pointed out. He was wearing a tweed waistcoat buttoned up beneath his old jacket, which was patched at the elbows; his hair was combed neatly to one side. Zach almost smiled.

'Spruced yourself up a bit for her, I see?' he said. Wilf paused for a second to glare at him.

'Like I said, it's no business of yours, what I do or she does or anybody else for that matter . . .'

'Yes, you're right. But that's the trouble with people, isn't it? We can't stand not knowing. Ignorance is intolerable.'

'Bliss for some people, or so I've heard,' said the old man, pointedly. 'What you been asking her?'

'Ah – you see, Mr Coulson? You have questions too.'

'The difference being it's at least partly my concern to know the answers.' The old man marched on, slowly, and Zach fell into step beside him.

'I know. Mr Coulson, do you remember how Élodie Aubrey died? The youngest Aubrey daughter?'

'They kept themselves to themselves. Nobody went asking.'

'Really? A nine-year-old girl dies, in a village this size, and nobody's interested?'

'Flu, the doctor said. Stomach flu, or some such thing. Natural causes, though there were some that said otherwise. But there wasn't an inquest, no questions asked, you see. People knew when to leave well alone, back in them days.'

'Who said otherwise? What did they say?' Zach asked, but the old man set his jaw, and didn't answer. 'And that was why Celeste left, and Charles Aubrey joined the army?' Zach went on.

'How should I know that? Can I see into people's hearts now?'

'No, of course not. But you were going down to see her, weren't you? I mentioned to Dimity last week that I'd met you . . . She said you were a good man.' The old man glanced at Zach.

'She said that about me?' His voice was low and sad.

'Yes. I think . . . I think she'd like to see you again, even though she made it sound very complicated. Water doesn't travel under the bridge very quickly around here, does it?'

'No. I suppose it doesn't, at that.' Wilf paused, turning to look back at The Watch with a frown.

'I've sometimes got the feeling, talking to Dimity, that . . . she's not giving me the full picture,' Zach said, carefully. At this, Wilf turned a scornful expression on him.

'I'm sure she's told you more than you've a right to

know, young man. Take it and be satisfied, would be my advice.'

'You're very loyal to a woman you knew so long ago and haven't seen in decades.'

'If you like.'

'Tell me, Mr Coulson – please. Just tell me – is Dimity Hatcher a . . . good person?' said Zach. They stopped walking, and Wilf turned to look out to sea, where a heavy bank of cloud was building.

'Just as much sinned against as sinning, was Mitzy,' he said at last. 'That's what people never seemed to see, even though I tried telling them often enough. It weren't her fault, how things turned out. And I'd have wed her still, after all of it. If she'd have had me. I'd have wed her still. But she wouldn't. She only had room in her heart for one man, and that man was Charles Aubrey, whether he was worthy of it or not. But he never loved her like I did. How could he have? I knew the bones of that girl; I knew where she came from. But she would not have me. So, there. That's all I'll tell you. Don't ask me anything more, for you'll get nothing.'

'All right,' Zach agreed. Wilf nodded briefly. 'But don't let the fact that I've seen you stop you . . . if you were going down to see her. I think she's lonely, down there. It's not good for a person, to be alone so much of the time.'

'No more it is, but it's her choice,' Wilf said, sadly. 'I have tried to see her, though not for a long time. Tried and been turned away. So, no. I think now is not the time, either.'

They carried on in silence to the top of the track, where Wilf turned off and took his leave with a faint nod of his head. Zach watched until he was just a distant, lonely figure; a dark shape against the narrow road, bent with the weight of all his memories. Zach carried on towards the pub, feeling lost and uneasy after his conversation with Dimity. At the door to the Spout Lantern, his phone buzzed, surprising him. He took it from his pocket, and saw one rare bar of signal. The text was from Hannah, and the sight of her name startled him. *Pub later? Lambing all done.* He pressed reply, and then paused. The prospect of seeing her caused him a bewildering mixture of feelings. It had been three days since he last had, and he missed her, but he couldn't ignore what he knew. He knew she wouldn't answer his questions, and would be angry and intractable when he confronted her. He wanted to take her into his arms and hold her tightly, and at the same time shake her until some answers fell out. *Sure* he replied, and left it at that for the time being.

Dusk came very early that evening. A veil of glowering clouds settled over the coast, and as Zach came down to the bar the first heavy drops of rain began to fall, just as Dimity had said they would. Zach had already finished his first pint when Hannah and Ilir arrived, leaving their wet, muddy boots by the door and padding over to him in thick socks. The sight of Hannah's small, strong face, her carefully controlled expression, gave Zach an uncomfortable ache, like despair. But with Ilir beside her, there could be no question of starting a row. Zach couldn't air his feelings so freely. Hannah bought them all a drink and sat down, smiling. She looked tired and preoccupied, but highly alert. That same underlying current of nerves that he'd noticed before. There was a strained pause before any of them spoke.

'So, how's everything? Any trouble with the ewes?' Zach asked. The pair of them shook their heads, and Zach thought he saw Hannah relax minutely.

'No trouble,' said Ilir, running his hands through the thick, damp thatch of his hair. The deep colour of his skin seemed to soak up the low light. 'Twins to finish with – two sets of twins. No wonder the sheep did not want to give birth. Hard work for them.'

'But that's good, isn't it? Two lambs for the price of one?'

'Sort of. You have to keep an eye on them though. One is always bigger than the other, and the littlest never does as well, or gets as fat,' said Hannah.

'But that's lambing done now, right? At least now you can get some sleep,' said Zach. Hannah and Ilir exchanged a quick, almost furtive look, and then agreed with him. Zach smiled with gritted teeth and raised his glass. 'To the new generation of Southern Farm Portlands,' he toasted.

'And to new beginnings,' Hannah added. They drank, and Zach glanced at Ilir in time to see a fleeting look of something near panic cross his face, a spasm of desperation that gripped him, and then passed.

'New beginnings,' Ilir echoed, heavily. Hannah put her hand on his arm for a second, and a sudden flash of intuition made Zach ask:

'Do you get homesick, Ilir?' The Roma man looked up at him appraisingly, and waited a heartbeat before answering.

'Yes, of course.' He shrugged. 'Some days more than others. Where you are born is always your home, even if it is not such a good place.'

'What's Kosovo like? I've never been . . . I mean, I don't think I even know anyone who's ever been. I suppose it's not really on the tourist map just yet,' he said, apologetically.

'Of course, for years people only hear of it because of the war. It is a young country with a very old heart. Great beauty there, but also great hardship. Troubles, still. Not enough work to go around. Not enough money, sometimes not enough electricity, even. And the people still fight each other. We are meant to be one nation, but it does not feel that way.'

'It sounds like a tough place to live,' said Zach.

'Tough compared to Dorset, for sure. And I would not want to go back, it is true. But I have left much behind to come here. I left many precious things behind.' For a second, Ilir's sorrow hung all around them, almost palpable.

'But it was the right decision,' said Hannah, staunchly.

'Yes. For my people, life there is even more hard. There are more problems, even less money, even less work. The Roma are not loved. England is a good country. A good place to live. I listen to the news here and sometimes I think you do not know how good it is.'

'Yes, I suppose you're right. But people will always find something to complain about. That's what my father used to say, and he was one of life's great optimists. Although, I think now that he might have been mostly talking about my mother. He used to say that if she went up to heaven, she'd be the first to let God know that the clouds were too soft.' He smiled, weakly, and Ilir nodded.

'I think your mother and mine would find much to talk about,' he said.

'Come on, enough of the doom and gloom. Drink,' Hannah commanded them, knocking the base of her glass against each of theirs.

Much later, when Ilir had pushed his way through the throng and gone up to the bar, Zach leaned over and kissed Hannah, holding her head in one hand in case she should pull away. She didn't, and he pressed his forehead against hers, shutting his eyes, enjoying the smell of her. Warm and earthy and richly animal. The beer was mixing with his tiredness, producing a languor that made it hard to think. When he let her go she was smiling, warily.

'What is this, Hannah?' he asked.

'What do you mean?'

'Is this just sex, to you? Am I just . . . a holiday fling?' She leant back from him and took a long swig of beer before answering.

'I'm not on holiday,' she said.

'You know what I mean. What happens when I leave here? Is that it, over?'

'Are you leaving?' she said. The question caught him off balance, and he realised he'd given no thought as to when, or whether he might be finished in Blacknowle.

'Well, I can't stay here in a room above a pub for ever, can I?'

'I really don't know, Zach,' she said, and he wasn't sure which of his questions she was answering. He drew his finger through several drops of beer on the table top, linking them up into a shape like a starfish.

'I know you're keeping secrets,' he said, quietly. Beside him, Hannah went very still in her seat. 'I know you're involved in . . . something.'

'I thought you were here to research Charles Aubrey, not me?' she said, her voice turning hard.

'I was. I am . . . and I think you know, the two have . . . closer links than we've discussed yet.' They locked eyes; Hannah didn't blink. 'Aren't you going to say anything?' said Zach, eventually. Hannah looked down at her hands, and gouged a strip of dirt out from under one thumbnail. She frowned.

'Don't push it, Zach,' she murmured.

'Don't push it?' he echoed, incredulously. 'That's all you've got to say to me?'

'Zach, I like you. I do. But . . . you have no idea what I'm involved in—'

'I might have more idea than you think—'

'No.' She shook her head. 'Whatever you think you

know, you don't know the full story. And I can't tell you, Zach. I *can't*. So don't push it, because if we can't be together without you having to know, then we can't be together. Do you understand?' She stared into his eyes, and her expression was sad, but tempered with steel. The flare of anger Zach had felt died down to nothing, melted into confusion.

'How can we be together if you won't let me in? Are you saying this is over?'

'I'm saying . . . trust me, if you can. Try to forget about it.'

'And if I can't?' he said, and in reply she only watched him with that adamant expression.

The sound of raised male voices from the bar interrupted them, and Hannah looked away with visible relief. One voice in particular, loud and aggressive, was rising above the rest. Hannah got to her feet.

'No, I'll be bloody well damned if I'll wait while you serve this piece of shit before me!' The man's voice had a note of outrage that carried throughout the room. Gradually, all other conversations in the pub quietened. 'I live here, mate – I *belong* here. Where the hell do you belong?'

'Oh, *good*. Our favourite xenophobic tosser has decided to drop by,' Hannah said, as loudly as she could. Zach cursed inwardly as she strode towards the bar. She was almost a foot shorter than all the men, but walked ten feet tall. They parted before her just like her flock of sheep did.

'Now, Hannah, there's no need for you to come wading in, making things worse,' said Pete Murray.

'Why don't you keep that rough tongue of yours still for once? I got here first and this Polish stooge of yours tried to barge me out of the way. Personally, I don't think he should be served in here at all.' The man speaking was about fifty years old, tall and bald with a soft, wide belly hanging over worn jeans. His skin and eyes were pink, his blood rising with alcohol and anger.

'Well, luckily nobody in here gives a shit what you think, Ed,' Hannah said, sweetly. Ilir was glowering at the other man, his face black with fury. He muttered something in his own language and Ed recoiled from him, and from the anger in the words.

'Hear that? I know a threat when I hear one, even if it comes from a monkey who can't even speak the language. Are you going to throw him out, Murray, or am I going to have to do it myself?'

Pete Murray looked from Hannah's livid face to Ed's, then he said to Ilir, unhappily, 'Perhaps you'd better call it a night, mate. Not worth the bother, eh?'

'No! Why should he have to go just because this drunken idiot says so?' said Hannah.

'Oh, hark at her, calling *me* a drunk! Go on, run back to the barn, dog.' The bald man waved his fingers at Ilir, oblivious to the hostile expressions aimed at him from around the room. There was a short, loaded silence. Zach thought about putting a placatory hand on Hannah's shoulder, but she was trembling with anger and he half suspected she might turn around and hit him. When nobody moved, Ed looked at Ilir again with spite and feigned surprise. 'Are you still here? Go on, get out before I call immigration.' The effect these words had on Ilir was visible. Blood rushed into his face, and his eyes widened. Zach heard Hannah take a sharp inward breath, and a wide smile broke out over Ed's ruddy face. 'Oh, really?' he said, gleefully.

Ed cast a staggering, unfocused glance around the pub, looking from face to face, trying to mark them. 'You all saw that, didn't you? Hit a nerve, did I? Is it possible that if PC Plod paid you a visit, your papers might not all be in order? Eh, sunshine?' He tapped Ilir on the chest with one finger, and Zach realised just how drunk he must be, to be so oblivious to the murderous look on the Roma man's face.

'Of course his papers are in order, you arsehole.' Hannah ground the words out.

'Well, then there won't be a problem if I give the fuzz a quick bell tomorrow and tell them to check, will there?' Ed's face was alight with triumph.

'Now, Ed, why not forget it and enjoy your drink? What goes around, comes around. No sense causing trouble for folk . . .' Pete said, weakly, putting a fresh pint on the bar for him. Ed grinned up at Ilir, snide and happy.

'You'd better pack your things tonight. I understand they don't give you much time before they whizz you off back home.' He turned away, picked up his glass and tried to drink without spilling it; and in the next second Ilir flew at him.

The first punch glanced from the side of Ed's head, and did little more than make him lurch and drop his pint. The beer exploded into a cloud of froth and glass splinters on the floor. Ilir stepped forwards and grabbed Ed by his shirt, pushing him back against the bar, teeth bared in pure fury. Zach heard Hannah gasp, and while he stared, dumbstruck, she rushed forwards and tried to pull Ilir away. Ed was the drunker, but he was taller than Ilir and had a longer reach, and he managed to drive his fist into the Roma man's eye before Ilir hit him again, a short-range punch to the stomach that forced the air from Ed's lungs but wasn't hard enough to double him up, or stop him.

'Ilir! Don't!' Hannah shouted. Several men came forward to grasp Ilir's arms, and then Ed's too as he came after his assailant, chin thrust out and eyes bloodshot, all clumsy belligerence. Ilir looked like he could kill the man, and as Zach stepped forward to stand beside Hannah, between the two of them, he was glad that their arms were being firmly held.

'*Hannah!*' Pete Murray shouted, leaning his hands on the bar, arms straight, as though he might vault over it and get involved.

'Yes! We're going!' said Hannah, tersely. A reddish bruise was blooming on Ed's cheek where the first punch had glanced from the bone.

'You all saw that! You all saw! He attacked me! Don't think I won't press charges, you illiterate shit! I've got witnesses!' Ed's voice was shrill with outrage.

'Now, just calm down, Ed. All sorts of things happen in the heat of the moment. I'm sure we're all too confused to remember who swung first, aren't we?' The landlord looked around at a few of his regulars, and got some curt nods in reply. Ed sneered, gasping for breath.

'You're pathetic! All of you!'

'Lucy, call a taxi for Ed, would you. He looks a bit under the weather. And you,' Pete jabbed a finger at Ilir, 'let it go, and get off home. Right now.' Ilir swore at length in his own language, pulled him arms free from the men holding them and stalked to the door, grabbing his boots as he passed. 'You too, Hannah. I think that's enough for one night.'

'Fine by me,' said Hannah. She glared at Ed, eyes snapping.

'Right, well . . . Night, all,' said Zach, following her out of the door.

Ilir was walking away up the middle of the lane, in the wrong direction for the farm, weaving slightly and with his boots on the wrong feet, crumpled awkwardly at the ankle.

'Ilir! Wait!' Hannah struggled with her own boots under the covered porch of the pub. The rain was coming down in grey waves. Ilir had nothing on his head, and in the wan glow of the streetlight his hair was shiny and slick. 'Ilir!' She ran after him, caught him up and gently took his arm. Zach watched, unsure what to do, hunching his shoulders against the damp night air. He could hear Hannah talking to the man, but couldn't tell what she was saying; and then, to his surprise, Ilir sank to his knees in the road. 'Zach!' Hannah called to him. With a curse, Zach jogged out into the rain. There was blood seeping from the corner of Ilir's right eye, mixing with the rain to drizzle down his face. The eye was closing, the lid swelling shut.

'Jesus – does that need stitches?' he said. There was rain on Hannah's hands as she cradled the man's face, examining it. Ilir shut his other eye. He was breathing hard, and kept swallowing convulsively.

'No, just . . . help me get him up, will you? Ed must have hit him harder than I thought.' They each took an arm, hauled Ilir to his feet, but his steps were spongy, legs like jelly.

'I'll get the car. Hold on.'

'Wait – how drunk are you?' said Hannah.

'Stone cold bloody sober after that little incident. And I'd be pretty unlucky to get breathalysed between here and the farm. Or would you rather try and walk him home like that?'

'All right, go on,' she said, as Ilir sat down again, putting his hands over his head in pitiful supplication. Hannah crouched down and put her arms around him, rested her chin against his streaming hair. A tender gesture unlike any Zach had seen her make before, and in spite of himself he felt jealousy needling him.

They managed to coax Ilir into the back seat of Zach's car, then Hannah climbed into the front and Zach pulled away, the steering wheel slipping through his wet hands. Focusing his eyes through the sheeting rain was difficult, and he was glad when they turned off the road onto the farm lane, and there was no chance of meeting any other traffic.

He pulled the car as close to the farmhouse as he could, but they still got drenched as they helped a shaky Ilir out again. The rain was implacable. Between them, Hannah and Zach half carried him through the kitchen and upstairs to his room, dodging piles of detritus and abandoned furniture. Opening the door was like walking into another house altogether. Ilir's room was spotlessly clean and tidy. The bed was neatly made up with sheets and blankets, tucked in tightly; the curtains were laundered and drawn to; no clothes or shoes lay around on the floor; a bottle of deodorant and a comb sat unobtrusively on the mantelpiece below the wall mirror, and the carpet was immaculately vacuumed. Hannah caught Zach's incredulous gaze.

'I know.' She threw up her hands, let them fall. 'Believe me, I told him he was welcome to tackle the rest of the house, but he says only this room is his, and the rest is not for him to interfere with.'

'I don't blame him.'

'No, he didn't mean it like that. He was being considerate. Tactful.' She sat down on the edge of the bed beside Ilir and wrapped the bottom of the blanket over his feet.

'I am not dead. Do not speak like I have gone,' Ilir muttered. Hannah smiled.

'Of course you haven't gone. We thought you'd passed out.' Gingerly, Ilir sat up a bit straighter and touched his fingers to the cut above his eye, which was still oozing blood.

'I will pass out if I do not have coffee,' he said.

'I'll make us some,' said Zach.

'And I'll get some cotton wool and wash that eye.'

'Don't nurse me, Hannah. I am not a baby.'

'Then don't act like one, and take your medicine,' she said, flatly.

Down in the kitchen Zach put the kettle on and watched Hannah digging around in cupboards and drawers for a glass bowl, salt, cotton wool.

'Is Ilir here . . . illegally?' he asked. Hannah scowled, and didn't look up.

'Technically. Maybe. But does he have a right to be here? You bet he does.'

'Can't he get a visa, or something?'

'Oh, gee, Zach, we hadn't thought of that. Look, if there was a quick and easy way to get the paperwork sorted out, we'd have done it, OK? He doesn't even have a passport.'

'Jesus, Hannah – what if that Ed bloke really does call the police? You could get in trouble, couldn't you?'

'*I* could get in trouble?' She turned, squared up to him fiercely. 'Ilir used to live in the Roma Mahalla in Mitrovica. His whole community was persecuted out of their homes after the war, and forced to live in refugee camps. The one where he was put was built on the spoil heaps of a lead mine. A *lead mine*, Zach. Cesmin Lug, it was called. It's shut now, but they left them living there for *years*. It killed his parents. The children there grow up with lead poisoning. Now the UN has rebuilt some of their homes in Mitrovica and is trying to move them back – to a city where they will still be discriminated against, and live in fear of racist attacks. To a city none of them have called home for a generation. And you're saying *I* could get in trouble, if he's sent back?' She shook her head incredulously.

'I just meant . . . Well, you can get a huge fine for employing an illegal.'

'An illegal? Doesn't he have a name any more?'

'That came out wrong . . . I didn't mean—'

'What are all our little fears, compared to what he faces if he gets deported?' she said. 'What does the price of my lambs matter, or you finishing your book, or putting a name to this *relationship*? How big is any of that, compared to what he'd have to live with?'

'Did he get you into it? Into whatever you're involved in? Smuggling . . . selling fake pictures . . . I guess he must have more contacts in that world than you would.' Hannah stared at him, dumbstruck for a moment, and then anger made her eyes blaze.

'Drop it, or leave right now. I mean it.' She raised her arm and pointed to the door, and Zach saw that the finger at the end of that arm was not quite steady. It trembled.

'All right,' he said, softly. 'All right. I'm just . . . I'm worried for you.' Hannah let her arm drop, gathered up the cotton wool and salt water.

'Don't be. I'm fine.' She turned and went back upstairs.

For a moment, Zach considered walking out. Setting off into the pounding rain, alone, thwarted. He tried to picture Hannah running after him, the way she ran after Ilir, but he knew it was far more likely that she'd let him go. He searched the kitchen for a pot of instant coffee, made three mugs and dumped sugar into each one when he couldn't find any milk he'd be willing to use. Was it just that he knew she was keeping secrets from him? Was that all that made him stay? In which case, he should leave. He should have nothing more to do with her, because to publicly pursue the authenticity of the Dennis pictures would be to expose Hannah. But then he pictured her, standing at the end of the stone jetty, staring out at the empty spread of the sea, all alone. The resolute set of her shoulders, the way she faced the world head on, with her jaw set, while at home, in private, everything was chaos and neglect. His head was aching, but he knew with total clarity that he didn't want to leave her. He shut his eyes for a moment, cursed, then took a swig of one coffee and picked up the other two, walking carefully back towards Ilir's room.

He heard their voices from about halfway up the stairs, low but distinct. The stairs didn't creak, didn't give him away. Unbidden, his feet slowed. He took one more step up and then froze, listening, hating himself.

'I haven't told him anything, I promise,' Hannah said. Zach's jaw clenched in protest.

'I know, I know. But what if the police come, Hannah? What if Ed calls them, like he said he would?'

'That pig was so drunk tonight he could barely stand . . . he won't even remember what went on tonight, or what he said.'

'But what if he does?'

'If he does . . . well. We just have to hang on till next Tuesday. That's all. Three more days, Ilir, then it's done! You can disappear . . . If the police come, you can hide. I'll say you ran away after what happened in the pub. I'll say I don't know where you are.'

'You can get in trouble for this, Hannah. You would do this for me?'

'Of course I would. We've come this far, haven't we?'

'Are you sure?'

'I'm sure. Everything will work out, you'll see. Three more days, Ilir. Three! That's no time at all.'

'I am sorry for before. For the pub. I should not have got angry. I should not have provoked him.'

'Hey — I never want to hear you apologise for punching Ed Lynch, OK? Every blow that man takes is a service to society.' Zach could hear a smile shaping Hannah's words.

'What will you tell Zach, when it is done?' said Ilir. Not wanting to hear more, Zach took three steps up, to stand in the doorway. Two sets of eyes swivelled to look at him.

'Yes, what will you tell me?' he said, woodenly. He

suddenly felt cold, and exhausted. A muscle twitched in Ilir's jaw, and the silence in the room resounded. He saw Hannah shrink slightly, as if surrendering to something inevitable. 'What's happening next Tuesday?' he said.

'Zach,' she said, but added nothing to that. A statement of his name, loaded with all the awkward weight of unspoken things, and with it Zach realised that it was impossible, that he had never had her, never truly known her. With the exaggerated care of someone unsure of their feet, he went back downstairs and left without another word.

Dimity slept fitfully, with Charles's picture of her in the desert beside her. She had wanted that image to inhabit her dreams; had wanted to open her inner eyes and be that maiden, that beautiful creature that Charles had created. But what came were visceral memories, not visions of lost beauty. The intoxicating press of Charles's body, his mouth against hers, the taste of him and the feel of his arms around her in the precious seconds before he pushed her away. The pain that blossomed in her head when she hit it on Celeste's dressing table, the way her face had burned, as if the woman's slap had been venomous, a scorpion's sting. She was at the mercy of these truths, as she slept, and a drawn-out refrain repeated itself over and over, and seemed to mock her. *Allahu akbar! Allahu akbar!*

The *muezzin* was singing, calling, high above her head. She looked up at the dizzying height of a minaret, a short way off and dazzling green against the bright sky. There was sweat running down her face, into her eyes, stinging; the dry air wheezed into her lungs. She had run for a long time. Blinking furiously, she sat down on a dusty doorstep, leaned back against the ancient wood and waited to catch her breath. The memory of Celeste's anger gave her a sick, unsteady feeling. The woman's fierce blue eyes, the quick, hard movements of her hands as she tugged at the scarf, the necklace. She had heard Dimity practising her wedding vows. Practising her pledge to Charles. *It was only a game* – that was what she would have to say. But it wasn't true, and Celeste knew it wasn't true – only that could explain her fury. Dimity could not face seeing her again, trying to apologise. The thought was unbearable and yet she could think of no way to avoid it. If she didn't go back to the guest house then they couldn't take her back with them, could not force her back to Blacknowle, but what use that, if Charles departed with them? Tears were hot on her face, hotter even than the sultry afternoon sun.

For a while she drowsed, drifting into dreams where Charles came searching for her, took her into his arms and kissed away her fears. The images made her ache inside. Voices startled her awake. Two women were standing in front of her, one draped in ashen robes, with only her eyes peering out, like coals; the other with that deep, black skin that so fascinated Dimity, her teeth when she spoke as white as the crest of a wave at night. The black woman smiled; added soft, muttered comments to the stream of words coming from the veiled woman. Dimity could not tell if the veiled woman also smiled, or if she was angry, or inquisitive. She was anonymous, blankly threatening. Dimity had no idea what they were saying, so she sat, and did not answer or move. Her heart began to thump. The women exchanged a glance, then the black one reached out, put her broad hand on Dimity's arm and pulled gently, beckoning to her to rise, to go with them. Dimity shook her head violently, all of Delphine's stories of white slaves suddenly coming back to her. The black woman tugged again, and Dimity lurched to her feet, yanked her arm away and fled, stumbling in her urgency, expecting to feel their hands on her again at any second.

She ran until her chest ached and she couldn't run any more. Her dragging feet kicked up sprays of dust and rubbish and she tripped over the cobbles from time to time. Either side of her the buildings of Fez were tall and unadorned; plaster crumbling from reddish walls. The windows were hidden by weathered shutters; no balconies here, no bustling people. Slowly, Dimity stopped, and a new fear crowded in on her. She had absolutely no idea where she was, or how to get back to the guest house, or even how to find the city gates, the edge of the maze. She turned in a slow circle, breathing hard. *Don't wander off on your own, will you, Mitzy?* The doors opening onto the street were huge and forbidding; the wood carved into ornate designs which trapped the desert sand and the street dust in their filigreed patterns. For a second, Dimity considered knocking on one, and asking the way, as if a familiar face might answer it, someone she knew from home. As if she would have been able to name the guest house, or the street it was on, and would understand the reply. Her legs were heavy with fatigue, and the heat dragged at her like an anchor. She could no longer hear the *muezzin*, and she hummed the only words of his song she had learnt, as though this would draw her back to the green tower which she knew wasn't far from the *riad*. *Allahu akbar, Allahu akbar* . . .

Beside her, a door creaked open and a thin man squinted out, eyes sharp with curiosity. Dimity gasped, stopped singing, shook her head at the startling barrage of words the man aimed at her. She turned again, walking back the way she had come, and when she looked over her shoulder the man was standing in the street, watching her every move. There was dust in her shoes, rubbing the skin raw around her heels and toes. She wiped the sweat from her face and felt sand on her fingertips, gritty against her eyelids. On she hurried, and with every step her panic grew, beating its wings in her chest, in her head, until she could hardly think. A labyrinth, Charles had called the old city, and even Dimity knew that meant it was a place you never escaped from, a place designed to trap you, and drive you mad. A place with blind turns, and dead ends, and monsters at its heart.

She marched for hours. She tried walking in a straight line, never turning, thinking that she would eventually reach the desert, but the city was never ending. She tried taking all the turnings to the right that she could, but ended up returning to the same small square again and again, where a starveling dog eyed her distrustfully. She tried turning alternately left and then right, zigzagging from one direction to the other, but she never saw a building she recognised, or a street she had been in before. She tried to remember which way she had come, but when she retraced her steps she always found herself somewhere different, as if the city was one of black magic and imps who moved the buildings and the walls when her back was turned. Her heart ached with fear and fatigue like the rest of her.

She came to a bustling bazaar, and hope flared until she realised it was far smaller than the central medina Charles had taken her to, and from there she returned to empty streets. She felt watched, as though something malevolent was just waiting, biding its time until she collapsed. Eventually, she came to the foot of a steep flight of stone steps. She paused to catch her breath and then climbed, dragging at her heavy legs, hoping to reach some vantage point, to be able to see a landmark she might recognise. But the steps ended in a high stone wall that she could not see over and yet another arched door that she could not go through. Helplessly, she banged on the door, finally deciding to throw herself on the mercy of whoever happened to live there. A kind woman, perhaps, who might give her something to drink and make enquiries on her behalf. She knocked for a long time, but nobody answered the door. Still she knocked, until she skinned her knuckles and they started to bleed, and she could not keep from sobbing as she slumped down against the heedless wall.

Her throat was parched. She had never been so thirsty in all her life, nor so lost or afraid. The sun was sinking slightly in the sky, but it was still so bright that it seemed to scorch her eyes, and made her head pound. She had no idea how long she waited at the top of the steps, but eventually she found the strength to rise and go back down them. Back into the labyrinth of streets and alleys, the endless twists and turns and archways and doors. She walked until her legs shook with every step, weak with exhaustion, and, eventually, she returned to streets where there were shops and people, hurrying along or standing together, deep in conversation.

This was at once a relief and an added worry. Dimity wished she had swathes of grey cloth to throw over her head, over her face, to shield her from the stares of passing men. Perhaps this was why the women veiled themselves, she thought, because the watching eyes were hard and thoughtful; hostile; questioning. Even if she had spoken their language she would have been too afraid to ask for their help. She was lost for ever, to wander the narrow streets like a ghost, a wraith. She fought hard not to show her panic, her vulnerability. Then she rounded a corner and came upon an elaborately tiled fountain, with water splashing down into a stone trough. With a cry of relief she stumbled towards it and drank messily from the brass spout, filling her cupped hands, easing her parched throat; so much water that her belly swelled. She rinsed her hands and wiped them across her filthy face and when she was done she turned, and found that a small semicircle of men had gathered behind her. Dimity froze. Their faces were expressionless, unreadable, mouths closed into flat lines, eyes simply watchful, arms hanging loosely at their sides. *Don't wander off on your own, will you, Mitzy?* Charles's words came back to her again; the subtle warning in them. *What would happen if a Christian were to go inside? It would be best not to find out.* She realised that they were blocking her from getting away, each man no more than an arm-span from the man beside him. Dimity thought of cows. Of Barton's cattle, back in Blacknowle, who the previous summer had circled a tourist walking her dog through their field. Just circled her, and held her there, watching like this. And when she tried to move away they closed ranks. Trampled her, broke her leg and her ribs, killed the dog.

Dimity's throat went dry again. Her stomach twisted, and she fought to keep the water she had just drunk from spewing back out of her mouth. She looked for an escape route in the other direction – past the fountain to the empty street behind it. There was a wooden barrier across it, but it was only a single bar and she realised that she could easily duck beneath it. In the massive wall further up the street were a set of huge, beautiful gates. High above, the green tower of the Karaouine Mosque blazed in the sun, watching it all. Dimity waited for as long as she could, fearing that if she moved, her legs would give way and she would not be able to run. Then she took a fluttering breath, stepped down from the fountain and bolted towards the barrier. At once there was uproar behind her, a sudden clamour of voices and scuffling feet. Dimity whimpered in terror. She got to the barrier and bent to duck beneath it, but her hair was in her face and she misjudged it, hit her head hard on the beam and was knocked from her feet, sent sprawling to the ground.

She struggled to get up, but the world spun around her and white flecks of light spangled across her vision, and a wave of nausea rose in her throat. The men closed around her in a circle, all talking at once; some angrily, waving their hands at her, some agitated, some almost anxious. All she could see were their faces, closing over her like stormy water, their voices blurring and booming in her ears. Something dribbled from her forehead into her eyes, and she blinked, and the world turned red. She thought again of the cows, of the trampled dog, and knew that she would die if she did not get up. She got to her hands and knees and began to crawl towards the empty street behind the barrier, but before she had gone even a yard she felt hands grasp her.

Dimity screamed. The men held her around her ankles and wrists; around her shoulders and upper arms; around her calves. She was lifted up, carried away from that empty street, from the freedom it seemed to promise. She struggled as hard as she could, twisting and turning her body until her joints flared red hot with pain and her muscles began to tear. She waited to feel hands on her mouth, on her throat, waited for them to choke the life from her, but then she realised that they did not mean to kill her, but to take her for their own use, for whatever wicked purposes they might have. A slave not only made to work, but used for sport, for gratification, for ruination. Through the red smear marring her vision she saw the sky, a bright and heedless stripe overhead, all but crowded out by the grimacing faces of her captors. She screamed for Charles, as their fingers dug into her skin and bruised her, and her head boomed with pain and terror, and in the last moments she even screamed for Valentina. Then the world shimmered into darkness, and she could not fight any more.

When she woke up she struggled to rise, but as she opened her eyes the sun lanced into them, impossibly bright, and it felt like a knife stabbing her skull. She shut them again and sank back with a groan.

'Mitzy? You're awake! How do you feel?' She felt a small, soft hand clasp her own, and with a surge of relief that was almost violent, she recognised Delphine. She tried to think what had happened, how she had got back to the *riad* and why her head was so painful, but the room was spinning sickeningly and her stomach roiled.

'I'm going to be sick,' she said, weakly.

'Here. I've got a basin. To your left,' said Delphine, and Dimity felt the cold touch of china to her chin. She lifted her shoulders a little, turned her head, and threw up. 'It's the knock on the head, most probably. I came off my pony a couple of years ago and hit my head, and that made me sick too,' said Delphine. 'Here – have some water.' Still with her eyes shut, Dimity felt a glass lifted to her lips, and she grasped at it clumsily. 'Just sip it – don't gulp, or it'll all come up again.'

'It's so bright in here,' she protested, her voice a croak. She heard a rustle as Delphine stood, and then the clonk of the shutters closing. Dimity opened her eyes cautiously, and in the softer light saw Delphine, kneeling down beside the mattress. She had plaited her hair into two braids which hung forwards over her shoulders, thick and shiny.

'Welcome back,' she said with a smile. 'Did you get lost? We were all really worried about you . . . we thought you might have been kidnapped!'

'Lost . . . yes. I thought I was . . . how did I get back here?'

'Daddy found you. He brought you back here. Hang on, actually – I better go and tell them you're awake. The doctor said if you didn't wake up by this evening we had to call him back again, so I'd better. You'll be all right, just for a moment?' she said. Dimity nodded mutely, and Delphine smiled again. 'You're safe now. But you've quite a bump on your head!' She got up and left the room, taking the basin of sick with her.

Dimity had never felt so ill in all her life. Her head was pounding; her body felt battered, bruised; weak as a kitten's. The room was still spinning and lurching, and though the hot, dry air prickled her throat she still shivered as if with cold. Her skin felt raw. There was a light knock at the door, and a creak as it opened. When she saw Charles, Dimity struggled to sit up, though the effort made her grimace.

'No, don't get up, Mitzy,' he said, coming to stand at the foot of her bed. Dimity moved gingerly to sit with her back against the wall. She looked down in dismay, and saw that she was still wearing her bloodied and dusty clothes. 'How are you feeling?'

'I think . . . I think I might be dying,' she whispered, miserably, as the movement of sitting up caused her brain to swill around like soup. Charles laughed softly, and came to sit beside her.

'You gave us quite a scare. Why on earth did you run off like that?'

'I . . . Celeste . . .' She gave up, could find no way to explain. Charles's face seemed to loom towards her, close enough to kiss her, and then recede again, swelling and shrinking like waves. 'How did you find me?' she said. She had dreamed that he would rescue her, and that dream had come true.

'With a great deal of difficulty, as it happens. I walked in circles around the house, getting further and further away each time. I'd been looking for *hours*, and then I heard all the hullaballoo . . .'

'I . . . I got lost,' she said, and looked up at him shyly. 'Were you worried about me?'

'Of course I was bloody worried! How did you cut your head? Nobody hit you, did they?'

'Oh, those men!' she gasped, remembering. 'I was trying to go underneath the barrier, to get away from those awful men, and I hit my head . . .'

'You tried to cross the barrier? Into the mosque?' Charles frowned.

'Well, I . . . I just wanted to get away . . . they were all shouting at me, and trying to catch me!'

'They were telling you that you shouldn't have been there, silly girl! And that street behind the barrier is completely forbidden to non-Muslims. Well, at this time of day it's forbidden to women too, let alone unveiled ones. So you just about took the biscuit, little Mitzy!' Charles sighed, and then smiled a little. 'No wonder they were in such uproar about it.'

'I didn't mean to! I didn't know!' Dimity cried. 'I thought they wanted to kill me!'

'Hush, hush, of course they didn't want to kill you, only to keep you from blaspheming. A misunderstanding then, but it must have been very frightening, I can see that.' Dimity bit her lip and tears welled in her eyes. She didn't try to hide them.

'I'm sorry to be such a bother. I'm sorry to have worried you.'

'Never mind that now. We're all just pleased you're back with us, safe and sound. Celeste and the girls were so worried as well . . .'

At the mention of Celeste, Dimity sank inside. She looked down at her filthy hands in her filthy lap. Charles cleared his throat diffidently. 'Mitzy, please tell me what happened. What was the row about?' he said.

'Hasn't Celeste said, then?'

'No. She won't tell me. She says it's between the two of

you and I wouldn't understand.' Dimity considered this, and was at once happy that Celeste hadn't told Charles, and suspicious of her decision not to. As though a secret kept gave her more power.

'I was . . . I was trying on some of her things. In . . . your room. Her jewellery . . . and a scarf. She came back and found me in there. Maybe she thought I was stealing . . . but I wasn't! I swear it! I didn't mean no harm!'

'That's all? She caught you trying on some of her things, and that was enough to send her into a rage?' Charles frowned as if he couldn't quite believe it. Dimity swallowed.

'I thought she was going to kill me,' she said, meekly.

'Now, don't be ridiculous. Celeste loves you.'

'Do you love me?'

'I—' Charles broke off and looked at her again, seriously, as if suddenly uncertain of something. Dimity held her breath. 'Yes, of course I do.' His voice was odd, strained. 'Like my own daughter, Mitzy. Black and blue as you are. It's coming up a treat, you know – it'll be purple by the morning. Feel.' He took her fingers and guided them gently to the egg-shaped swelling on her skull. She winced. 'Even Élodie will be impressed,' he said.

'I do doubt it.'

'Oh – damn. We've made it ooze. Here.' Charles took out his handkerchief and dabbed at the bloody cut on her head, gently cupping her chin with one hand to hold her head steady. Dimity leaned into his touch, could feel his breath on her skin and caught the scent of his body, his sweat. Tentatively, she put one hand on his forearm, the arm that was holding her face. Charles was looking at the cut, but at her touch his eyes flickered down to meet hers, and gradually they widened, as if seeing danger of some kind. He stopped dabbing at the cut and for a second, for a wonderful second, Dimity thought he was going to kiss her again. She could picture it perfectly – his head dipping forwards, the touch of his mouth. The speed of her heart made pain bloom in her head like scarlet roses, but she didn't care.

'Is it all right?' she said, softly.

'Is what all right?' Charles asked, uneasily, moving away from her.

'My head.'

'Oh, yes. We had the doctor come and look at you, just in case, but he says you just need to rest. Mind you,' Charles paused, and laid the backs of his fingers against her forehead, 'you do feel very hot. Have you caught a fever?'

'I don't know . . . I wasn't feeling well this morning, before Celeste . . .'

'Yes – look at you, you're shivering! Lie back down. You must rest, Mitzy,' Charles said, and Dimity obeyed him, feeling the sweetness of his concern like warm honey on her tongue.

Do you love me? Yes, of course I do. Dimity heard this, over and over, after he'd gone, the words like a charm that made the whole world sparkle. She fancied she could still feel him holding her, carrying her back to safety; could feel his fingers pressing into her ribs, the protective cage of his embrace as they went; and it felt completely right, completely *perfect*. But the pain in her head could not be ignored, and when she raised her fingers gingerly to the cut again, they also found a bump on her temple, from where Celeste had knocked her off the stool earlier on. Unbidden, the woman's fiery eyes flashed into her memory, and she cowered back against her pillow, trying to escape their all-seeing glare.

She was already dozing fitfully when Delphine came back into the room. The sun was sinking, darkening outside, and though Dimity knew Delphine was speaking, she didn't heed the words until she heard:

'Soon we'll be back home in England and all this will be forgotten.' And if Delphine had sought to comfort her friend, her words had the opposite effect. Cold, bleak despair engulfed Dimity, and she shook her head vehemently.

'No! I'll never forget it here, as long as I live. I want to stay for ever,' she said, desperately.

'You can't mean that! I mean . . . it's nice to go on holiday, of course, but it's not like this is home, is it?' said Delphine, sitting beside her in her pyjamas, arms wrapped around her knees. Behind her, Élodie's dark eyes were watching from her own bed, hard and glossy as bottle glass.

'It's better than home,' said Dimity. Delphine gave her a quizzical look, but Dimity couldn't speak any more, the effort was too great. She lay still and tried to think only of Charles, and of him saying, *of course I do*. But thoughts of him were hard to hold on to, and time and again she slipped into a nightmare from which she could not wake; a black terror made up of grasping hands and flashing blue eyes, of running, and falling, and being lost for ever. On and on the images came, rolling like sea swell as her body shivered and burned. Once, in the night, she thought someone was leaning over her and caught a trace of Celeste's perfume in her nostrils, deep and floral; she was surprised by the spike of fear it gave her, and by the flare of rage that followed.

The journey back passed in a blur of feverish lassitude for Dimity. She was aware only of movement, of being uncomfortable and exhausted. A sweep of desert landscape; the fresh touch of a sea breeze at the coast; the sickening motion of the boat again. She was too weak to despair even as she realised that Morocco was receding behind her, but she could feel the knowledge of it, lying in wait inside her. It was a thing like the dead creatures that sometimes washed up on the beaches of Blacknowle. Black and cold; mis-shapen, foul. It waited there for her to be well enough to mourn. She was delivered back to The Watch, and into Valentina's rough care, and she had no idea how long she had lain there, in her childhood bed, when she finally awoke with a clear head.

The angle of the sun told her it was afternoon, not morning, and for a while after she awoke she couldn't imagine why Valentina hadn't roused her sooner. She sat up, and though every muscle ached, and every bone seemed soft and fragile, her vision was steady and she had control of her body. She could smell a sickly, stale smell coming from herself, and her hair hung in greasy ropes around her face. She rubbed her hands over her face, and saw that there was dirt under her nails. Red-brown dirt; desert sand. There was a wrenching feeling in her gut, like it was tearing, and she clasped at it helplessly.

Dimity went downstairs slowly, and found Valentina in the kitchen, gutting mackerel into a bowl on the worktop.

'Back in the land of the living then, and about time, too,' she said.

'How long have I been here?' Dimity asked.

'Three days, doing nought but sweating and mumbling nonsense.' Valentina wiped her hands roughly on her apron, and came over to her daughter. She grabbed a fistful of Dimity's hair and pulled it back to examine the cut on her forehead. The wound was a straight dark line by then, the lump much reduced, the bruising faded to yellow and brown.

'Who gave you this?' she asked, poking it with her index finger so that Dimity winced.

'Nobody. I banged my head.'

'Well, that was a stupid thing to do, wasn't it?' said her mother. She looked Dimity in the eye, and for a second there was something there, something that made her pause. An echo of something unsaid, a trace of relief. Then she pressed her lips together and went back to the fish.

'Is there food? I'm starving,' said Dimity. Valentina flicked her eyes at her daughter, and scowled for a second before relenting.

'Bread in the crock, and Mr Brown brought us some of his wife's damson jam, over there.' She gestured with her bloodied knife. 'So, how was this far-off land you went to see?' The question was loaded with scorn, so loaded that Dimity wondered if it was a mask. A mask for what she couldn't quite tell. Not envy, surely?

'It was . . .' She stopped. She didn't know which words to use. How to convey that life had been so sweet, so rich with colour and discovery and Charles and ease and new things that the same old words she'd always used to describe things before were utterly inadequate for the job. 'It was very hot,' she said, in the end.

'Oh, well, sounds *wonderful*,' said Valentina. 'Did you make any extra money?' Dimity blinked. 'Did he try to touch you?'

'No,' she said at once, and then swallowed because the urge to blurt out what had happened, the need to make it real, suddenly produced a huge lump in her throat. Valentina grunted.

'Pity. I was almost sure he would. Away from home, all bets off and all that. Well, you obviously didn't try hard enough. Or perhaps you're just not his type, eh?' She smiled unkindly. Dimity took hold of the memory of their kiss, and his touch, and hugged it tightly to her. Used it as a shield against such barbs. *He would have made love to me*, she wanted to shout. *But for Celeste, he would have. He is not free to, that's what he said. But he would, he wanted to. He will.*

The power of this thought surprised her; almost put a smile on her face.

'I suppose not,' she said, calmly enough.

'When you've eaten, go and wash. You smell like old milk.'

Dimity tired easily in the first two days after her fever broke. There were dark circles under her eyes, and she moved cautiously, like an old woman. She wanted to be beautiful, the next time she saw Charles. She wanted to look as she must have done in the alleyway in Fez, with the sun's glow on her skin, and her eyes sparkling. So she waited, and noticed that Blacknowle was small and damp and dreary and pathetic. It had always been damp and dreary, in fact, but never before had she realised how inconsequential a place it was. What pitiful lives its people led, toiling and drudging with each day the same. No time or chance to lean over a balcony and feel the hot sun on the top of their heads, while an ancient city buzzed and breathed beneath them. Walking with their eyes on their own feet because there were no apricot-coloured mountains to see, no vast stretch of desert around to pull the eye, to dazzle and frighten and tempt them with a hot, thirsty breeze. Blacknowle was mono-chrome. It was still summer, but the colours looked dead. Like a newspaper photograph, with a sea mist to blur the outlines and nothing but shadow and shades of grey to show the shape of things. When Dimity shut her eyes she saw a river of scarlet blood running down a cobbled alleyway; she saw bright blue goatskins pegged out on a hillside; she saw a lemon-yellow scarf fluttering around a woman's ebony neck; and children like fancy little birds dressed in turquoise, and azure, and aquamarine. She saw herself, in a kaftan the bright pink of bougainvillea blossoms, standing in a shaft of copper sunshine that made her hair flame.

Then, a week after she had been delivered back to The Watch, Dimity decided she looked well enough to go up to Littlecombe, and see Charles. She did not dwell on the fact that nobody had been to seek her out. Not Charles, not Delphine. That was down to Valentina, she decided. Any respectable person who'd encountered her mother gave the cottage a wide berth thereafter. It was Valentina's fault, so Dimity didn't tell her that she'd be leaving soon. That when he left Blacknowle this time, Charles Aubrey would be taking her with him. *I'll do my best for you, Mitzy.* She walked slowly to Littlecombe, in spite of her eagerness, because she did not want to arrive sweating or out of breath. There were no signs of activity within the house, but the blue car was parked in the driveway, and the sight of it brought a smile to Dimity's face that stayed, irrepressible, as she knocked on the door with her spirits high and joyous inside her.

There was a long pause, and Dimity thought she heard movement inside, thought she saw a shadowy face in the darkness behind the kitchen window glass. Then Celeste opened the door, and Dimity's smile faltered, sinking away into nothing. The two women faced each other across the threshold, and neither spoke. Celeste looked tired, and strained. Her expression was flat and steady.

'You're well again, I see,' she said at last.

'I think so,' said Dimity. The woman's baleful gaze was scattering her thoughts into fragments, confusing her.

'Well, I am glad. Whatever has passed between us, I would wish you no harm.' Celeste crossed her arms, pulling her shawl tighter around her shoulders. She seemed taller, somehow; harder, like she was made of stone. Dimity could no longer stand to look Celeste in the eye, so she looked down at the ground between them. A yard of flagstone garden path, but suddenly that distance was wider than the

Channel. She teetered slightly, as if she might lose her balance. Her hands shook.

'Can I come in?' she said, breathlessly. Celeste shook her head gravely.

'It gives me no pleasure to say so, but you are not welcome here any more, Mitzy. I have explained it to my girls as best I can, and I have explained it to Charles. You and I, we both know the reason. Sometimes, things do not stay as they began. They change, and we must change with them. It would be better if you did not come here again.' Dimity's heart stuttered in her chest; a little hiccough, a momentary stoppage.

'I want . . . I want to see Charles,' she said. She had meant to say *Delphine*, but the truth, just then, fought its way out. Celeste leant towards her, her cheeks flushing with anger. She seemed huge, terrifying. She seemed the stuff of nightmares.

'*That* is why you will come here no more. Now, go. We will not be coming back next year – not if I have any say in our plans. Go away, Mitzy. You have ruined everything.' As Celeste turned away there was a sparkle in her blue-green eyes, the shine of unshed tears.

Dimity had no idea how long she stood, without moving, staring at the patchy paint and wood grain of Littlecombe's door. Time didn't seem to matter, didn't seem to move as it should; like she was still in the grip of some fever, and only half alive. She was shivering, though the day was mild, and when she eventually turned to go the ground seemed treacherous. Her feet caught in invisible snares, and she had to hold onto the gatepost for support. She felt eyes upon her, and thought at once that Charles was there, that he had come out to see her. But when she turned, searching for him, she saw only Delphine, standing at one of the upstairs windows. A shadowy figure with a sad face, who raised one hand to wave at her forlornly. Dimity did not wave back.

For three days, she looked everywhere for Charles. Everywhere but Littlecombe. She looked in the village, at the pub and the grocer's; she looked on the beach and the cliff path, and up at the ruined chapel on the hill. But she did not see him. Valentina noticed that her daughter had stopped bringing money back from her outings, and cornered her one day.

'Has he lost interest, then? You don't take his fancy no more?' She jerked her chin up aggressively as she spoke, and for a blinding second, Dimity hated her utterly.

'He loves me! He told me so himself!' she said.

'Oh, does he, now?' Valentina chuckled. 'Well, we've all heard that one before, my girl. Believe me. You tell him from me, it all costs. Love or no love. You hear?' Dimity fought to pull her arm free. 'And you, Mitzy – you need to bring in a wage. You're old enough, now. If he'll not pay for the privilege, then I know several that will. We could get enough for your maidenhead to see us right through the winter.' Her voice was as bleak as her face, and her words made Mitzy think of the men in Fez, with their dark faces and angry eyes, and their open mouths above her, hard hands holding her down, poised to take everything. She wanted to run from her mother, just as she had wanted to run from them. Like in a nightmare, she wanted to run with every ounce of her will, but she couldn't. She had nowhere to run to.

Dimity fantasised that Charles would come knocking on the door of The Watch with that hungry look in his eye that she'd seen, just for a second, in a narrow alley a whole world away. She conjured it so carefully, so intensely, it was almost a spell. She pictured going to London with him when he left; pictured Charles finding a flat for her, or letting her live in his studio where she could be his model, his lover. Perhaps she would not even have to stay hidden away like this – perhaps he would marry her and introduce her to everybody as his wife, kissing her hand and looking at her with such a fire in his eyes that nobody could mistake it for anything but the most powerful devotion. His artist friends, who she pictured as bearded men with beetling brows and mad habits, would be jealous of him for having such a young and lovely wife, and he would be proud of her, so proud, and the thirst of having to be decorous in public would only heighten the passion with which he would ravish her once they were back behind closed doors. In the night, these images kept her awake, aching with longing; made her hand reach down between her legs, desperate for release.

But it was Wilf Coulson she saw, not Charles. She saw him outside the Spout Lantern where, now aged sixteen, he had taken to drinking with the other men at the end of the working day. He came after her once or twice, walking behind her like he had in the past, so that she would know he was there, and could lead him somewhere private where they could talk. Lead him to Barton's barn to lie close in the straw, and touch each other amidst the stench of cattle. But this time she turned around and gave him such a furious look that he stopped in his tracks, bewildered. She did not want his fumbling attention, his gifts, his boyish kisses. So after a while he came to The Watch to look for her, and the knock at the door set her alight because she thought it might be Charles. When she saw Wilf, her face fell; seeing this, so did his.

'Will you walk out for a while, Mitzy?' he said, dipping his chin into his chest and scowling.

'I've the chores to do,' she said, numbly. Wilf looked up at her then with such hurt and anger in his eyes that it startled her. 'All right, then. Just for a little while.'

She led him down the steep path over the cliff edge and onto the stony beach below The Watch, walking always slightly ahead of him, hands clenched, picking her way expertly between the rocks. A fitful breeze pushed at them, and the sea was a deep, glistening grey. A desert of a different kind, rolling into the far distance. Dimity kept walking right to the far end of the beach, then climbed up onto the rock jetty and walked along it until it began to slide beneath the water. She looked down at her battered leather shoes, and thought about continuing in spite of them.

'Mitzy, stop!' said Wilf, still behind her. Dimity looked back at him, and saw that his eyes were red and shining. 'What's happened, Mitzy? Why don't you want to know me no more? What did I do?' He sounded so stricken that Dimity felt little prickles of guilt, and turned around to face him.

'You didn't do anything, Wilf.'

'What is it then? Aren't we even friends now?'

'Course,' she said, grudgingly. She doubted she would see Wilf again, once she'd gone to London with Charles. No more Wilf, no more Valentina. Or perhaps she might visit her mother sometimes – drive down to The Watch in a shiny motorcar, wearing a silk scarf over her hair, and high-heeled shoes and stockings with the seams perfectly straight running up the backs of her calves. Wilf broke into this pleasant fantasy.

'I missed you, when you were gone. It wasn't the same without you about. I even think your ma missed you – she had to come up to the village a couple of times, for this and that. Walked around with such a look in her eye that nobody dared go near her!' He smiled slightly, but stopped in the face of her silence. 'So . . . what was it like, where you went?' He seemed desperate for something to say, some way to make her talk.

'It was the best place I've ever been. Charles said he'll take me back there sometime. Next year, probably. We might take a holiday there every year.' She smiled vaguely.

'Charles? You mean Mr Aubrey?' Wilf screwed up his face in confusion. 'What do you mean, take a holiday?'

'Well, what do you think it means?' she snapped.

'You can't mean that you and he . . . that you're . . . with him now?'

'Can't I?'

'But . . . he's twice your age, Mitzy! More than twice . . . and he's got a wife!'

'No he hasn't! She's not his *wife*, they're not married!' She turned again to look out to sea. 'He's going to marry *me*. I'm going to be his wife.'

'Then why are you still at The Watch with your ma, while he's packing up Littlecombe with his family, ready to go back to London?'

'What?' His words physically rocked her, made the jetty seem to pitch like the deck of a ship. Something came bulging up in her throat and she thought for a second that she might scream. 'What?' she said again, and instead of a scream it was a whisper, half lost in the breeze. Wilf blurred in front of her, smearing out of focus to become a part of the sea, a part of the shore behind him.

'I heard him talking about it in the pub not half an hour ago, settling up his bill. Mitzy,' he said, stepping forwards to take her by her upper arms. She looked up, only now realising how tall he'd grown, how his shoulders had fanned out above his narrow hips, how his jaw was stronger and firmer. 'Mitzy, listen to me. He doesn't love you. Not like I do. I *love* you, Mitzy!'

'No.'

'Yes, I do! I love you like no other. Marry *me*, Mitzy. I'd be good to you . . . we'd have a good life, I swear it! We can even leave Blacknowle, if that's what you want. My uncle in Bristol has a job waiting for me, if I want it. At the shipping company where he works. You'd never have to see Blacknowle or The Watch or your ma again, if that's what you want. We could have a baby straight away, if you like. And we could take our honeymoon anywhere you wanted . . . Wales, or St Ives, or wherever!' He gave her a little shake and Dimity blinked. But she was too lost in her own misery to realise that he had been dreaming all this, just as she'd been dreaming life in London with Charles. That thoughts of her had been what kept him awake at night, what made his hand stray down low beneath the blankets. She pulled her arms away from him.

'Get off me!'

'Mitzy? Haven't you heard what I've said?'

'I heard you,' she said, dully. 'Wales? St Ives? Is that how big you think the world is? Is that as far as you can imagine?' Wilf frowned.

'No. But it's as far as I can afford to travel just yet. I'm not stupid, Mitzy. And I know I'm not as exciting to you as . . . some others might seem. But this is *real*, not some impossible dream. This is a real life I'm offering you. We can save up . . . I can start saving and take you overseas too. It don't cost too much to cross the Channel . . .'

'No.'

'No?'

'That's my answer, Wilf. I won't marry you. I don't want you.'

Wilf was silent for a while; put his hands in his pockets and seemed ready to wait, as if waiting might make her change her mind. Eventually he took a long, heavy breath.

'He won't marry you, Mitzy. I can promise you that an' all.'

'What do you know about it? You're just like everyone

here! Watching and chattering and thinking you know my business!' she said, anger flaring at his words.

'I know enough to know he won't marry you. He can't. He—'

'Just shut up! You know nothing about it! *Nothing!*' The words were ragged, savage; put tears in Wilf's eyes as he looked at her.

'I know enough. I *love* you Mitzy. I could make you happy . . .'

'You could not.' She turned away from him and folded her arms, and for a long time she could sense him there, standing behind her, waiting. She heard him sniffle a bit, blow his nose, clear his throat. At some point she realised that he'd gone, and could not say for sure when he'd left. She glanced over her shoulder and couldn't see him on the beach or on the path up through Southern Farm. For a second she felt panic grip her, but she ignored it, and took the inland path towards the village.

Wilf had said Charles was in the pub, so that was where she went. She walked right up to the window, nervous excitement making her teeth chatter. She caught the tip of her tongue between them, and tasted blood. The inside of the pub was shady and dim, but she could see that it was almost empty. Two men were seated at the bar, but neither one was Charles. She walked across to the village stores, and peered inside; then walked a short distance along each of the little lanes that made up the village centre. She could not think where else to look, could not think why Charles had not come to find her, to reassure her. She knew he must have some plan; some scheme by which they would soon be together. But she wished, how intensely she wished, that she could find him and hear what it was. Her need to see him was giving her a pain behind her eyes, a pain that built all the time. She gave up on the steep track that led to Northern

Farm, and came back down it into the village past the rear elevation of the pub. And then she saw him.

He was in one of the pub's upstairs rooms, she could see him through the little window, half buried in the tiled eaves. The view was restricted – through the cramped pane she could see his arm and shoulder, his lower jaw. *Charles!* Dimity wasn't sure if she had shouted aloud in elation, or if her throat was too tight to make a sound. She waved her arms above her head, but then she stopped, and let them fall. Charles was not alone. He was talking to somebody – she could see his mouth moving. And then that somebody stepped into view, and it was the tourist woman. *The one who has to touch herself each time she sees you.* Celeste's voice was so clear that Dimity whirled around in confusion, looking for her. *Milksop skin.* The words were in the hiss of the breeze. The woman appeared to be crying; she dabbed at her eyes with the cuff of her blouse. Dimity stared at her, tried to make her not exist. A vast, bottomless chasm had opened at her feet, and she saw no way that she would not fall. There was nothing to save her. Charles took the woman's hand and raised it to his mouth, pressing a linger-ing kiss onto the skin. *Have you ever seen them together?* Celeste whispered in her ear, and the pain in Dimity's skull spiked unbearably. She clasped her hands to the sides of her head, whimpering in agony, then, with a cry, she fled from the Spout Lantern.

She walked blindly, as the crow flies, across fields and tracks, through the coppice of beech and oak on top of the ridge and down the other side. She soaked her feet in runnels of water, splashed her trousers with reddish mud, got cov-ered in sticky buds, burrs, and gnat bites. She picked as she went, using her shawl as a sling; gathering familiar plants almost without thinking. Sorrel for salad; nettles for tea and kidney tonics, and to feed the blood; milk thistles and pig nuts for stewing; fern to kill tapeworms; dandelion for rheumatism; chicory for a bladder infection. The task was so familiar, had such a natural rhythm that it hypnotised her, silencing the turmoil inside her head.

She passed by the watery ditch at the edge of the woods where a thick patch of water hemlock grew. Cowbane, it was also called, since it killed the cows that browsed it by mistake. She crouched down amidst the tall, deadly plants, surrounded by their innocent-looking umbrellas of white flowers. Their roots wound down into the sandy soil at the bottom of the ditch; long, serrated leaves with the tempting smell of parsley. Water fleas scudded around her feet and a banded demoiselle flew in wide arcs above her head, watching curiously. Dimity wrapped her hand around one woody stem and pulled gently, careful not to bruise it, until the tuberose root came free from the ground. It would taste almost sweet, like parsnip, if eaten. She rinsed it off and laid the plant carefully in the sling, away from the others. Kept apart, reviled, not to be trusted. Separate from all the rest, just as she had always been. Dimity took a slow breath; her mind was quite empty. She went back to pull another stem.

Hours later, with her shawl heavy and cutting into her shoulder, Dimity was still walking. Her legs felt too long, and though everything she saw was familiar to her, still she felt as though she didn't know it, didn't belong to it. On the beach she kept bruising her toes and shins by walking into rocks, and could not work out why. Some way further along the shore she stopped walking altogether, and realised that it was night-time. She could not see to walk because the sky was as black as the inside of her mind, without a moon to light it. If this darkness was natural, or because the light had gone out of the whole world, she could not tell. She sat down where she'd been standing, feeling the stones prod her, cool and damp, through her clothes. There she stayed, in the dark, not hearing the waves because her own crying drowned them out; sobs tearing at her, convulsing her. And all the time she felt like she was falling, like she had stepped into that fathomless chasm, and would never reach the surface again. She did not sleep.

In the cold light of the morning the rising tide roused her, lapping at her feet with icy little ripples. Dimity scratched at her face, itchy with salt, and stood up shakily. She started walking again, with little idea where she would go; just following her feet like before until eventually they brought her to the top of Littlecombe's driveway. There she paused, and stared down at the regular, compact shape of it. There was no sign of the car in the driveway, no sign of anybody in the garden; the windows were all shut. Charles was there. This was where she had first seen him; where he had first drawn her. This was where he slept, where he ate. This was where he *had* to be. Dimity felt hollow, insubstantial, and a sudden lightness washed through her head, the lightness of joy tempered with something else. Something nameless and bleak; something that had come up from the depths of the chasm to be with her. She stumbled on her bruised feet as she walked down to the kitchen door.

She knocked loudly, with conviction. Charles would open the door, and gather her up; slide his arms around her waist like he had in the alleyway in Fez, and she would feel the firm touch of his mouth and the hardness of him, and she would taste him and fold into him and everything would be right. Nobody else would exist. When Celeste opened the door, frowning and wiping her hands on a towel, Dimity blinked, bewildered, and Celeste's face darkened.

'Dimity. Why have you come? Why do you persist?' she said. Dimity opened her mouth but there were no words within it. The air whistled in and out of her throat. 'Tell me, do you honestly think he would leave his daughters to be with you? Do you think that?'

Her voice was flat and angry. Dimity stayed silent. She felt faint, hazy; not quite real. 'He's not here, if that's what you were hoping. He's gone with the girls to Swanage, to ride the donkeys on the beach and to shop and play on the amusements.'

'I wanted to . . .' Dimity started to say, but she didn't know what it was that she had wanted. The woman in front of her was the sum of everything she would never have. In a hindquarter of her brain, Dimity gazed at Celeste, and despised her. 'I brought these for you. For all of you,' she said, putting a hand on the plants she had collected.

'There is no need.' Celeste tapped her toe against a basket on the doorstep, already full of leafy plants. 'Delphine went early this morning. Without you. She left me these herbs to make a soup for my lunch.'

'Oh.' Dimity struggled to focus her eyes, struggled to think. There was a shrill humming sound in her ears, and Celeste's voice seemed to come from a long way away. She squinted up at the Moroccan woman and wondered how she had ever thought her beautiful. Celeste was shadowy and cruel, a figure to be feared and loathed. A stubborn blight, an open sore that refused to heal.

'Now listen to me. No more of this.' Celeste sighed abruptly, through her nose. 'Leave us alone,' she said, and closed the door.

Dimity rocked slightly on her heels. The ground was a queasy blur at her feet and a sudden sickness filled her throat with a foul, acid taste. *If he was free, he would be with me.* She shut her eyes and pictured Charles rescuing her, saving her, as she lay on the ground, ready to be torn apart by wild men in Fez; she thought of his kiss in the alleyway, the touch of his hand as he helped her up; the flowers like a wedding bower arching over them as they had sat together at the Merenid Tombs. That desert place where everything had been as perfect and glorious as a dream. Dimity opened her eyes and looked down at Delphine's basket. She saw wild garlic and parsley; celery, lovage and caraway. It was a good forage, the leaves all young and tender, nothing picked that might have gone woody or bitter. And caraway was a rare find, a delicious one. Delphine had been an attentive pupil. Dimity stood and stared down at the herbs for a long time. She looked at her own collection, in the sling hanging at the end of her numb arm. The weight of it was suddenly too much and she set it down at her feet, bending low over it. *Garlic, parsley, celery, lovage, caraway.* The blood thumped in Dimity's head, painful and insistent. The greenery swam in front of her eyes, half hidden by her own trailing hair. *Garlic, parsley* . . . There was the water hemlock, the cowbane, in her own pile. Carefully kept apart, carefully bunched together; leaves, stems, sweet thick roots. Dimity could hardly breathe for the pain behind her eyes. She stood up at last and walked away with jerky, wobbling steps. And somehow the cowbane was no longer in her sling. It was in Delphine's basket.

10

Two days after Ilir had fought with Ed Lynch in the pub, Zach began to pack up all his things. A catalogue slipped from his fingers onto the floor, the spine cracked by the number of times he had looked at it so that it fell open at a picture of Dennis, the young man who'd brought him to Blacknowle in the first place. Dennis, and Delphine: the daughter who disappeared. He pictured her face, hanging on the gallery wall; all the hours he had spent studying it and coveting it. He'd been so sure, for a while, that he would find out what had happened to her. That Dimity Hatcher would know, and would tell him once he had fetched hearts for her, and charmed her with portraits of herself she had never seen before. Now he had to choose between Charles Aubrey and Hannah Brock, since Hannah was somehow involved in cheating the man to whom Zach felt a fierce, if nebulous, loyalty. Hannah who had shut him out, and lied to him, and possibly felt nothing for him. Soon, he would have to drive out of Blacknowle with a destination in mind. Soon, but not quite yet. He breathed a small sigh of relief as he gave himself this stay of execution.

The Watch was silent and lifeless, the windows blank, betraying not even a flicker of movement from within. Zach stood beneath the small window in the north end wall and stared up at it. This was the room from which the sounds of movement had always come. The glass pane was broken in one corner, a small hole at the centre of a starburst of cracks, as though somebody had thrown a pebble through it at some point. He could see pale curtains hanging inside, half open, half closed. One of them shifted slightly in the breeze, and the sudden movement made Zach jump, made him duck for cover nearer the wall, before he realised what it was. Was there something in that room that Dimity Hatcher wanted to hide? Something, or someone? Just then he heard the quiet, dry sound of paper sliding against paper, coming from the window. The turning of a page; the discarding of one piece from a pile. Zach's scalp crawled peculiarly, and he hurried away from the window.

He knocked several times on the door, but there was no answer. He couldn't think where else Dimity could be, except inside. He pictured the way her gaze drifted into the distance, the way she seemed to vanish into her thoughts. He thought of her oddness, her charms and spells. He thought of a kitchen knife in her hand and the way her light sometimes stayed on late into the night, as though she never slept. He thought of blood beneath her fingernails, staining her dishevelled mittens. Shivering slightly, he knocked again, more softly; suddenly almost afraid to rouse her. This time, he heard the lock moving within.

There was a pitch-black thing, crowding the room; swelling like a huge and deadly wave, waiting to break. Dimity cowered from it. It did no good to shut her eyes. When she shut her eyes she saw rats. Rats twisted up with their eyes bulging and their bodies twitching and jerking into death. Rats that had eaten Valentina's hemlock bait. She went from room to room, murmuring all the charms she knew, but the threatening darkness kept after her. *What happened to Celeste?* she heard Zach ask, and she spun around, wondering how he'd got inside, how long he'd been there, listening. But no, just another echo, the echo of a question he'd asked before. Recently, or a long time ago? She couldn't remember now. Time was behaving oddly; day and night had blurred. She could no longer sleep at night, only in fitful snatches during the safety of the daylight hours. Too many visitors, too many voices. Élodie doing handstands against the living room wall; Valentina laughing, mocking, waving her finger; Delphine's sad, sad eyes. And now this dreadful black thing too, which had no name, which refused to identify itself. But in the writhing rats, scrabbling in the corners of the room, Dimity understood what it was, and she feared it more than anything. It was the thing that she did. The awful thing.

She wanted to go upstairs to the closed room, she wanted to throw open the door and lie down and be comforted, but something stopped her. When she surrendered to that yearning, it would be for the last time. It would be an unrepeatable thing, the one final time, and after that she would be truly alone. It was instinct that told her this; intuition rather than rational thought. She could not face it; would not do it, not yet. She got halfway up the stairs at one point, to escape the black thing, but she made herself stop and go no further. Valentina was up in her room now, asleep, keeping out of it, leaving Dimity to face the thing alone. Earlier she had cocked an eyebrow at her daughter, just like she had in the summer of 1939. *That was a stroke of luck then, wasn't it?* she'd said, savagely. Now, as then, Dimity had no words to answer her. Valentina was never moved by tears; never once, not even when Dimity was tiny. Not even the time when she was five years old and she tripped over her feet and fell into a hollow packed with furze and nettles and bees, to emerge stung and scratched and howling. *Life's going to throw worse at you than that, my girl, so stop that racket*. And life had thrown worse at her. Valentina had been right about that.

There was a knocking at the door, loud and insistent, and Dimity stared at it in shock. It was almost dark outside. She

354

waited until she was no longer sure she'd heard anything at all, and then the knocking came again, for longer this time. She thought it could be a trick; it could be anyone, anything, waiting to be let in. Her heart fluttered like a moth. She crossed to the door and hesitantly laid her ear to it. All the voices of The Watch sounded louder that way, coming through the walls and the wood like the sea whispering through the caverns of a shell. Mutterings, accusations, laughter; the rough voices of Valentina's many, many visitors.

'Dimity? Are you there?' A voice so loud it made her yell and scuttle back from the door.

'Who is that?' she said, and found her eyes full of frightened tears.

'It's Zach. I've just come down to say hello.'

'Zach?' Dimity echoed, thinking hard.

'Zach Gilchrist – you know me. Are you all right?' She did know him of course. The one with all the pictures, whose voice had now joined all the others in The Watch, asking his incessant questions. Her first thought was to not let him in. She couldn't remember why she didn't want to, and only knew that she didn't; but he could be no worse than the black thing already inside with her, she decided. Perhaps he might make it subside for a while, might make it bide its time. Tentatively, Dimity opened the door.

Zach watched Dimity with consternation as she moved around the kitchen, ostensibly making them tea. She twitched and dithered, her eyes darting around the room as if searching for something. Her attention flitted like a mayfly, never quite alighting. She moved the mugs from one worktop to the next, poured the water from the kettle down the sink before it had boiled, and refilled it. At one point, as Zach was telling her about the fight at the pub, she whirled around with a cry and put her hand to her mouth. He thought for a moment that he had shocked her with the violence of the story, but then he saw that she was staring straight past him, at the kitchen window. He turned to look but there was nothing there, nothing outside, just the green hill, rolling down to the sea.

'What is it, Dimity? What's the matter?' he said. She flicked her eyes at him, and shook her head, and Zach saw how quick and shallow her breathing had become. He stood up, took her hands and drew her towards a chair. 'Come and sit down, please. Something's upset you.'

'They won't leave me alone!' the old woman cried, as she sank into one of the rickety kitchen chairs.

'Who won't, Dimity?'

'All of them . . .' She passed her hand in front of her eyes again, and took a deep breath. 'Ghosts. Just ghosts, that's all. Just an old woman's fancy.' She looked up and tried to smile, but it was a tremulous, unconvincing thing.

'You . . . see them, do you?' Zach asked, cautiously.

'I . . . I don't know. I think . . . sometimes . . . that I do. They want answers from me, just like you do.' She gazed at him, steady and desperate, and Zach sensed some vast sorrow inside her.

'Well . . . I won't ask you for any more answers. Not if you don't want to give them,' he said. Dimity shook her head, and tears dropped into her lap.

'I saw them together. I didn't tell you . . . but perhaps you've a right to know.'

'Saw who, Dimity?'

'My Charles, and your . . . grandma. I saw them kiss.' There was a note of despair in her voice, and Zach had an odd feeling, like something falling into place. Or perhaps out of place.

'So, you think he could have been—'

'I don't know!' Dimity cried abruptly. 'I don't know! But I saw them together, and I never told. I never told . . . Charles. Never told Celeste.'

'Jesus.' Zach leaned back in his chair, absorbing her words. Somehow he had always thought, deep down, that the rumour was just that – a rumour. He'd been quite prepared to believe Dimity before, when she'd denied any affair between them. Now, it seemed, he wasn't quite prepared to be told that there had been. 'So he . . . he betrayed you?' he said, softly. Dimity broke into sobs and Zach took hold of her hands. 'I'm sorry, Dimity. I really am.'

For a while, Dimity allowed herself to be comforted, but then she gripped his hands fiercely.

'Why are you here? Are you one of them? Have I dreamed you?' she said.

'No, Dimity.' Zach swallowed uneasily. 'You haven't dreamed me. I'm real.'

'Why are you here?' she said again.

'I came . . . well, I suppose I came to say goodbye.' He hadn't realised it until he said it. He took a deep breath, and looked hard into Dimity's eyes. 'Is there anything else . . . *any*thing else, you can tell me about that summer? About Dennis, or why Charles went off to war? About what happened to Delphine, and Celeste?' For a hung moment, neither of them breathed. Their eyes stayed locked together, and the moment seemed to spread out, to pause unnaturally. It was so still that Zach couldn't hear his watch ticking, or the kettle coming to the boil; he couldn't hear Dimity's laboured breathing, or the background song of the sea. For a second, he thought he heard a fretful wind, blowing through the dank little kitchen. A hot, dry wind, carrying strange perfumes. For a second he thought he heard the sound of hands clapping, and the voices of children, chanting along in time. He thought he heard the scratch of a pencil on paper and a man's chuckle, deep and energetic; captivating, infectious. Then he blinked, and it was all gone.

'No,' said Dimity, and for a second Zach could not remember what he'd asked. 'No. There is nothing more I can tell you.' Her voice was desolate.

'I want to ask you one more thing.'

'What?'

'May I draw you?'

To draw the same subject that Aubrey had once drawn — it was yet another pilgrimage, of a kind. Zach had no doubt that his would be poor work in comparison, but the fascination remained and he was no longer afraid to try. He had still never sketched Hannah. He wondered if he'd missed his chance now, and whether he'd have been able to draw everything that was wonderful and infuriating about her; from her toothy, wolfish smile to her hard-headedness; from her unabashed sensuality to the barriers she put up between herself and the world. Between herself and Zach. He wondered if he'd have been able to capture that nagging familiarity he sometimes saw, when she turned her head just so. Thoughts of her brought a cocktail of lust, anger, tenderness and frustration, so he tried determinedly to dispel them. He focused on his sitter, wearing a frown of concentration, and began.

He didn't work fast. They took breaks, and drank tea, and put the lights on when it got dark outside. But Dimity didn't seem in the least impatient. On the contrary, she grew still and serene under his scrutiny, as though waiting to be drawn came as naturally to her as breathing. He tried to capture the wisps of beauty hidden in her dishevelled face; tried to capture the way her irises, though surrounded by whites gone greyish yellow, remained a warm hazel colour, perfectly halfway between green and brown. When he finally finished there was cramp blazing in his pen hand, and his neck was aching. But when he looked at his drawing, it was Dimity Hatcher. Quite unmistakeably. It was the best work he'd done in years.

'Will you show me?' Dimity asked, with a dreamy half smile. At once, Zach's quiet satisfaction dissolved into anxiety. But he took a breath, and handed the picture to her. Her face fell into lines of dismay, and her hand rose halfway to her mouth before fluttering back into her lap. 'Oh,' she said.

'Look, it's not very good. I'm sorry – nothing like being drawn by Aubrey, I'm sure . . .'

'No,' she murmured softly. 'But it is good . . . it's good. But I thought . . . silly really . . . I thought I might see myself as I was. As I was in all these other pictures you brought me. I might be beautiful again.'

'You are, though. Far more beautiful than I've managed to draw you . . . Blame the artist, not the sitter, Dimity,' said Zach.

'But it is me. It's a good likeness. You're very talented,' she said, nodding slowly. Zach smiled, heartened by this verdict. 'Will you take a meal in payment for this picture?'

'You want to keep it?' said Zach.

'Yes, if I can. It'll be the last one, after all. Who else will draw me, before the end?' She smiled sadly, but Zach was pleased to see how much calmer she seemed now than when he'd arrived. As though being drawn had soothed her troubled spirit.

'All right, then. What's for dinner?'

It was late when he finally took his leave of Dimity, thanking her for dinner, which had been bacon, eggs and greens, and giving no answer when she asked when he would be back. It was dark outside, a greenish dark that he found he could see quite well in, after a while, even though he had no torch. In the field behind the house at Southern

Farm, the Portland ewes dotted the hillside with their lambs keeping close to their heels. From time to time he heard them call to one another, throaty and plaintive. He felt something like affection for them, something almost like pride. As though in helping with the lambing, in sleeping with their mistress, he had taken on some responsibility for them. *They're not your sheep and she's not your woman. That is not your life*, he told himself firmly. It was time to banish the pleasant daydream he'd been having, of Elise sitting at Hannah's kitchen table with a mug of hot chocolate in her hands. It was clearly never going to happen. In the dream the farm kitchen was clean, tidy, warm. No longer a wreck of a place, a shrine to Hannah's loss and grief. He excised the images from his mind as carefully as he could, but the process still cut him. The breeze slipped damp fingers down his collar, and he was hit by a sudden rush of loneliness. A tawny owl came to hunt the field in front of him, criss-crossing the pasture on silent wings. He envied its sense of purpose.

On a whim he walked down towards the cliffs. Saying goodbye again, he realised. He stood and listened to the invisible sea. There was a brisk wind blowing, and the waves against the rocks sounded hurried, impatient. By straining his eyes he could just about see their white crests as they frothed ashore, and then another light sparkled, like a jewel against the black. Zach blinked, and thought he'd imagined it. But then it came again, from beyond the beach, out on the water. No, not on the water, he realised. On the stone jetty. A torch beam, lancing out to sea. Zach's breath caught in his chest. He couldn't see the light's source, couldn't see a hand or an arm, only the glitter of the beam on the water, stretching out into the blackness. But he knew, he *knew*, it was Hannah. The sky was overcast with cloud, no stars to light the scene, no moon to make it glow. A cold, hard darkness, perfect for keeping secrets. It was Tuesday night.

A minute passed, then another. The wind blew Zach's coat open and parted around him coldly. He was riveted to the spot, his heart bumping uncomfortably. And then, another light appeared out on the water. Coming along the coast from the west; the single, larger beam of a boat's spotlight. It manoeuvred in a wide arc opposite the bay, then came in straight towards the torch beam, slow and steady, slightly to the left of the stone jetty. In the tiny spot of light from Hannah's torch Zach saw a man's large form, swathed in waterproofs; the white side of the boat, the orange flash of a life buoy. Then, as the boat reached the side of the jetty and stopped, both lights went out, and there was nothing more to see. Zach remained, listening hard. During a slight lull in the wind a minute later he heard the boat's engine gunning as it reversed, pulling away again; then he heard nothing more.

Zach's thoughts were rushing, tumbling along, and he was paralysed by the need to do something, to react in some way. But in what way, he had no idea. They had smuggled something in from the sea. Something paid for in secret that needed the cover of night, and as little light as possible. James Horne and his boat, and Hannah to know the way, to guide him in. Whatever they had brought was obviously illegal. *More pictures of Dennis*, he thought, or was that only one line of trade? Did they deal in worse things as well? He stood with the silent bulk of The Watch behind him and the invisible drop down to the ocean in front of him, and felt as though the whole of Blacknowle had shut him out. It had seemed for a while as though he might settle, as though he might be included there. He'd thought that Dimity Hatcher was his friend; that Hannah was his girlfriend. That he would be the one to put Blacknowle on the map with a wholly different book about Charles Aubrey. But now he saw that it had all been a misconstruction on his part. He'd been played along with to a point, and then brushed aside. Zach felt the pain of this rejection beneath a rising swell of anger. Below him the sea hissed in the dark.

He strode back towards the village at a rapid pace, so that he was out of breath by the time he got to the top of the track. He moved as though he had a purpose, when in truth he had no idea where his walk would terminate, and what he would do when it did. His anger was directionless, purposeless, just like his impatient speed. But in the next moment, both were abruptly curtailed for him. Seeing what was up ahead, at the top of the lane to Southern Farm, Zach's pace dwindled to nothing. He stood and stared. Three police cars were parked nose to tail, tucked into the hedge at the top of the lane. One had its lights on, its engine running softly. Uniformed officers either sat in their vehicles or waited in the road beside them; three stood in a tight knot nearest the running car, their dark clothing the perfect camouflage on such a dark night. They looked tense, alert. One looked over at Zach where he stood, stock still, in the middle of the road. The shock of that sudden scrutiny pushed Zach into motion again, and he carried on towards them with a prickle of misplaced guilt. He walked right past them, trying not to seem curious, and as he did there was a blast of static from a radio, and the officer who'd noticed him dipped his head towards the microphone.

'Copy that. We're in position, ready to go,' he said. Zach kept walking until he was sure the darkness had swallowed him, then he ducked left towards the hedge, vaulted over the gate into the field, and started running.

He didn't look back as he ran haphazardly down the hill, stumbling over rabbit holes and slipping in patches of sheep shit. It was frightening, electrifying; running so fast when he could not see the ground, could not see his feet. Thistles and long grasses whipped at his shins, and he saw pale shapes in the corners of his eyes as startled sheep hurried away from him. The lane was to his left, and at any moment he expected to see blue lights pouring down it, passing him, getting to her first. He ran faster than he'd run since child-hood; his lungs ached with the sudden rush of cold air. The night parted in front of him and closed behind him; he left no wake. There were two more gates between him and the yard, and he scaled them clumsily, landing badly after the last and turning his ankle. Swearing at the tearing pain, he staggered around to the front of the farmhouse where a light was on in the kitchen, blazing out into the night through the curtainless window. It seemed wantonly danger-ous, such a gaudy display. His mouth had gone completely dry and his heart was hammering, and he thumped loudly on the farmhouse door with both fists.

Hannah opened it cautiously, her eyes wide with anxiety. When she saw him relief flooded her face and Zach felt a rush of panic wash through him.

'Zach! What the hell are you doing here?' she said, holding the door ajar, not letting him in or letting him see past her.

'The police are coming – they could be here any moment. I saw them,' he gasped, fighting for breath. 'I saw them at the top of the lane. I wanted to warn you, to give you a chance to . . .' He trailed off, watching fear grip her as she digested this. Behind her he heard Ilir say something.

'The police? Here? Jesus . . . how did they know?' she said.

'I don't know. You don't have much time, so if there's something you'd rather they didn't find, you'd better get it out of sight now. Right now!' Hannah hesitated, then turned her head and spoke rapidly, quietly over her shoulder. There was a startled sound from Ilir and then sounds of movement, scuffling.

'God,' Hannah said, bleakly. 'Maybe Ed Lynch did say something to them. James said he thought he was being watched. And the last time I spoke to him on the phone there was a lot of interference . . . Fuck! I'm such an idiot!'

'I'm . . . sorry, Hannah.' Now that he had warned her, he didn't know what else to do. At that moment, Ilir appeared beside her in the doorway.

'You are sorry? *You* tell the police to come?' he said, yanking the door wide open and striding out, right up to Zach, with anger disfiguring his face. Zach took an uneasy step backwards.

'What? No! I just—'

'You are spying on us tonight?' Ilir jabbed a rigid finger into Zach's chest.

'Yes – well, no, not spying – I was on the cliffs, and I saw . . . the boat. And then I saw the police—' Ilir grasped Zach by the front of his coat, spun him around and shoved him hard against the wall of the house. His mouth twisted into a snarl, eyes alight with anger and something else besides. Something like fear, holding every one of the man's muscles tighter than steel.

'It is *your* fault they come!' he spat.

'No, I just wanted to warn you!' said Zach.

'You will be sorry.' Ilir drew back his right arm and slammed his fist into Zach's jaw. Pain and bright light bloomed behind Zach's eyes, and his head was flung back, hitting the wall hard.

'Ilir! *No!* Stop it!' Hannah was there behind Ilir, the wind whipping her hair into her eyes as she tugged at his arm, holding it on its second backswing, preventing the blow from landing. 'Ilir! We don't have time! Stop it! It wasn't Zach's fault! Go inside – go inside and get ready!' Abruptly,

Ilir dropped Zach, seeming to lose all interest in him. And now Zach could really see how frightened he was. The anger dissolved, and this fear was all that was left. He clasped his hands over his head and his eyes filled with tears.

'What will we do, Hannah?' he said, desperately. 'What can I do?'

'I'll think of something! Go inside, now,' she said, and once he had stumbled away towards the door she turned to Zach, who was rubbing his jaw and waiting for his head to clear. 'You came down to warn us, right?' she said. Zach nodded gingerly. 'So you want to be on our side, right? Right?'

'I . . . yes. I am on your side.'

'Then help us.' She stood in front of him with her arms hanging ready at her sides and the wind pushing at her; dark eyes harder than granite and every inch of her now calm and resolute. Zach realised that he would do anything for her.

'What do you want me to do?' he said.

'You saw me guide the boat in. You saw us bringing something ashore. Now I need you to take it somewhere else for me. If the police are coming, they can't find out what was on that boat. Do you hear?' Zach swallowed. She was making him part of it, he saw. Making him complicit; partly to have his help, no doubt, but also to have his silence from then on. He nodded uneasily.

'OK. But look, if it's drugs . . .' He shook his head. A disgusted expression creased Hannah's face.

'*Drugs?* You seriously think it's drugs?'

'I honestly have no idea.'

'You think I would risk everything to deal drugs? For fuck's sake, Zach! You want to know what I would risk everything for? Do you? Then come and take a look.' She grabbed him by the sleeve, towed him to the farmhouse door, up the steps and into the kitchen. She gave him a second to absorb the scene, and the sudden light hurt his eyes. 'Now do you get it?' she said. Zach stared in amazement.

'Jesus,' he murmured.

Dimity slept more deeply than she ever had before, for the rest of the day after Celeste had turned her away again. A dreamless sleep, like oblivion. She awoke just before sunset with a vague, heavy feeling of unease. She could not sit still, or settle to any household chore, so the stove sputtered out after she lit it, and the water in the kettle stayed cold, and the chickens kept their eggs a while longer, tucked into their warm and greasy feathers. She stole a glance through her mother's bedroom door. Valentina was sprawled across the mattress, her yellow hair matted and wiry, her face scrunched into the pillow. She was snoring softly, dead to the world; thinking back Dimity remembered the bang of the door, sometime after she returned. A visitor leaving; ducking out into anonymity. A faint, fishy smell lingered in the airless room. She shut the door again softly, and wondered at the sudden urge she felt to creep into bed beside her mother, to feel the warmth of her fusty, sleeping body. A yearning for safety and protection that she'd long ago learnt not to seek from Valentina.

Then, for just a minute or two, all her dreams came true. The sun was below the horizon; a velvety twilight lingered that made the sea seem to glow. She was looking out of her bedroom window as the blue car came down the track towards The Watch, travelling fast, kicking up dust and stones from its wheels. It slithered to a halt right outside, and Charles got out. Charles on his own, running his hands through his hair to tidy it, or so she thought; coming up to the door and pounding on it, urgently, carelessly. He had come to fetch her away, she thought, as she made her way downstairs, smiling dreamily. Fear had plagued her since she woke, though she couldn't trace the cause of it; all she knew was that she never wanted to go to Littlecombe again. But now he had come for her at last, and that fear melted away. She looked around the house as she went to the door, thinking that she might not see it again. That this would be the last time she would come down those stairs, cross those worn flagstones, pull the handle of the heavy oak door. Her smile widened when she saw him, and she let the love shine on her face; no more hiding, no more waiting.

'Mitzy – you must come right away. Right now! Please,' he said. She didn't notice that there was sweat on his forehead, misting his top lip; that his face was ashen, his hands shaking as he pushed them through his hair again.

'Of course, Charles. I've been waiting for you. I haven't packed my bag yet – is there time for me to do that? Just some clothes, and a few things?'

'What? No – there's no time! Please come at once!' He grabbed her wrist and began to pull her towards the car. 'Wait – is Valentina at home? Call her too – and fetch your medicines, any medicines you have. Bring them all!'

'Valentina . . . but why should you want to bring my mother? We do not need to—'

'Is she here?'

'She's sleeping.'

'Well wake her, goddamn it! Right now!' His sudden shout was so loud that she recoiled; so violent that a fleck of his spit landed on her cheek.

'I don't understand!' Dimity cried, and Charles glared at her, half mad with impatience. 'She won't be woken; she was occupied this afternoon—'

'Then you'll have to come alone. Celeste and Élodie . . . they're very ill. You have to help them.'

'But, I—' All protest was cut off as Charles pulled her

towards the car. She scrambled in obediently, but a sudden and dreadful terror was tying knots in her chest, and she found herself gasping for air.

Sure enough, Charles drove her to Littlecombe, the last place she wanted to go. Drove with reckless speed, almost hitting the baker's van as they burst out of the top of the track and onto the village street. Dimity shut her eyes and did not move when the car pulled up outside the house. Charles had to drag her out by her arm, his fingers digging into her, his teeth gritted.

'I've called two different doctors but both of them are miles away with other patients . . . they won't be here for at least an hour, they said. They said to keep giving them water to drink but . . . but they can't keep it down. They can hardly even drink it! You have to help them, Dimity. There must be something you can give them. Some herb . . .' he said. She had to run to stay on her feet as he towed her to the front door. On the threshold, she braced her hand against the doorframe and wrenched her arm free of him, making him pause. 'What are you doing? Come *on*!' he cried.

'I'm frightened!' she said. True enough, but she had no way to express how huge and ugly and confused that fear was. Suddenly the doorway to the house was like a hole into hell, or the den of some dangerous wild animal. Charles stared at her with eyes full of tears.

'*Please*, Dimity,' he said, in a desperate voice. 'Please help them.' She had no choice but to try.

They were in the big bedroom, both of them; on the bed. Celeste was sitting half propped up against the wall, with vomit all down her blouse and some of it caught in a bowl. A long, thick string of saliva was hanging from her chin, constantly renewing itself, never breaking off. Every few seconds she twitched, a sharp jolt like an electric shock passing through her. The stink in the room was horrible. Delphine was holding her mother's hand, crouching beside the bed with a look of profound anguish on her face. On the other side of the bed lay Élodie, her small body twisted and still.

'Élodie is worse. Go to her first,' said Charles, propelling Dimity towards her and rushing over to Celeste and Delphine.

'Oh! Please do something, Mitzy! You must know what to give them . . . you must know a cure! Please!' Delphine begged her, the words slurred with weeping.

'I . . . I don't know . . . what's wrong with them?' Dimity faltered.

'I don't know! Something they ate – it must be! Something I picked . . . I went picking on my own and I left some things for Mummy for her lunch, and she made a soup and Élodie had some too when we got home, but I didn't have any and neither did Daddy . . . I must have picked the wrong thing, Mitzy! I was sure I hadn't . . . I was sure I knew what I'd found, but I must have been wrong, mustn't I? I must have been!' She sobbed into her hand for a second, but stopped to grasp her mother's fingers as Celeste vomited again, a mouthful of yellow fluid that slid down her chin, and then she convulsed, her head flying back to crack against the wall, her arms straining, straight against the mattress. From the other side of the bed Dimity caught sight of her eyes. Black as night; black as a lie; black as murder. The pupils so vastly dilated that almost nothing of the blue irises was visible. Her eyes looked like open doors, wide enough for her soul to escape. Suddenly her mouth opened, and she spoke in rapid French, an unintelligible stream of noise more like the sound an animal would make, rather than a person. Delphine whimpered and tried to hold her mother's hands, but Celeste wrenched them away, staring around her with those wide black eyes as though she could see unimaginable monsters.

Dimity crouched down beside Élodie and took the girl's wrist, feeling for a pulse. It was there, weak and irregular. The child's whole body was arched backwards and rigid, every muscle as tight as a violin string. Her face was immobile, eyes fixed; every bit as wide and black as her mother's. A steady trickle of drool soaked into the mattress beneath her. She looked like a demon, she looked possessed. Dimity's skin crawled as she put her ear close to the girl's open mouth, and felt the slightest touch of air, moving in and out in minute amounts. Dimity's own head was as empty as their eyes. More than anything, she wanted to flee the room; wanted to be gone from this deathbed, since deathbed it was. They'd eaten the roots, that much was clear. Treacherously sweet, full of flavour. If they could be saved, it would not be by anything Dimity could give them. The doctor was their only chance, but even that depended on how long they would have to wait.

'When did it start?' she asked, woodenly. She felt sleepy, all of a sudden. She wanted to lie down and shut her eyes and dream.

'A . . . about two hours ago. Celeste had a stomach ache when we got back from town, and by the time she began to vomit, Élodie had eaten the soup too and was also sick . . . What can you give them? What can we do?' Charles stood with his arms hanging loose by his sides, chewing his lip as he stared at her, keen as a hawk. She saw that he expected her to make them well, expected her to save them, and she swallowed the sudden, mad urge to laugh. She shook her head instead, and saw his face crumple. It was too late. After two hours, the poison would be deep within their bodies, too deep to fetch it back out.

'There's nothing I can give them. The poison is too

strong. I have . . . seen it before.' Rats, rats in the corners of the room, twisting and twirling in death's dance. She started up to her feet, looking around at them in horror.

'So you know what it is? You know what they ate?' he said. Dimity could hardly keep the air in her lungs long enough to answer him. She nodded her head, felt Celeste's empty, ink spot eyes watching her. A flood of tingling horror washed down her back, and she swayed.

'Cowbane,' she said at last. 'Water hemlock.' *Hemlock*. They knew the name. Charles went paler still; Delphine gaped at her, her jaw hanging slackly open.

There was a long pause, filled only by the sound of Celeste's laboured breathing and the strange gurgling noise she made in her throat when another seizure gripped her. From Élodie there was no sound.

'You mean . . .' Charles cleared his throat, dragged his hands over his face. 'You mean they could *die* of this? They might die?' He sounded utterly incredulous, and ignored Delphine as she began to sob once more. Dimity met Charles's gaze and managed not to flinch. The room was crowded with shadows and devils; with contorted rats and black, black eyes; awash with a revolting sea of spittle and bile. Dimity felt as though her mind was going to fly apart.

'Yes,' she said. Charles stared at her, paralysed by the word. 'Take them to hospital. Straight away. They cannot wait for a doctor, or an ambulance – take them now. Dorchester. Tell the doctor there what they've eaten . . .'

'But you'll come with us – you'll come and help. Take Élodie. Delphine! Open the doors for us!' Charles wrestled Celeste's jerking body into his arms and carried her towards the door, and Delphine rushed ahead to clear the way, and Dimity was left to lift Élodie. She did it slowly, almost tenderly. The thin little body was like a peculiar wood, hard and unyielding and yet warm at the same time. No flicker of movement over her face, no change of expression at all as Dimity lifted her. And as she carried her down to the blue car, Dimity did not think she could feel the movement of air from her open mouth any more. There was nothing behind the black discs of her eyes. Dimity's skin crawled away from Élodie as she climbed into the car, and there she remained, trapped beneath her with no way to escape.

Zach stared in amazement at Hannah's cluttered kitchen table; or rather, at the figures seated around it. Ilir was standing four-square to the door, defensively, his face still wracked with fear and anger, and he was holding the hand of a tall, thin woman, who in turn had her arm wrapped tightly around a little boy of around seven or eight years of age. Zach stared at them, and they stared back at him. Their faces were pale with fatigue. The woman's hair was dark brown, long and straight, parted in the middle and tied back in a simple ponytail. Her forehead was lined with worry.

'Zach, let me introduce you to Rozafa Sabri, Ilir's wife, and their son Bekim,' said Hannah, standing beside him, her body still tense with emotion.

'Hello,' said Zach, woodenly. Ilir said something impatient in a language Zach couldn't understand, and Rozafa looked up at him anxiously.

'In English, Ilir?' said Hannah.

'They cannot stay here. Not even for one night.'

'I know. I'm sorry, Rozafa . . . there's been a slight hitch.' Zach felt all eyes turn to him, as if he were to blame. He was sweating beneath his jumper and coat, an uncomfortable prickle that made him fidget. 'Zach's going to take you somewhere safe. It seems that . . . that the police might be coming here shortly—'

'*Policija?*' said Rozafa, her eyes widening. The child beneath her arm did not react. He gazed distantly at Zach as if only half awake. When his mother stood up and pulled him up with her, he moved slowly, clumsily. Rozafa stooped, gathered him into her arms and looked from Hannah to her husband. Ready to run, Zach saw. However tired she might be, she was ready to take her child and run. They were plainly exhausted, badly in need of rest. With a guilty flush, he reminded himself how convinced he'd been that Hannah was smuggling art, or drugs, when it had been something far more precious, far more fragile.

'Now do you see? Why I couldn't tell you? Why this needed to be kept a secret?' Hannah asked him, intently.

'You could have trusted me. I would have understood.'

'I didn't know that. Not for certain. But I'm trusting you now. Take them somewhere else. Right now, before the police show up. OK?'

'Where . . . how should I take them? Should I take the jeep?'

'No – they'll see you go up the lane, and you can't drive off into the fields without headlights – you'll get killed. Go on foot – somewhere safe. Anywhere.'

'The Watch. I'll take them to The Watch,' he said. Hannah hesitated, frowning, and then nodded.

'Good. Keep out of sight. We'll just have to hope they don't think to look there.'

'Why would they?'

'Because . . . No, never mind. I'm sure it'll be fine. Go on – hurry!'

Glancing up the lane, which was sunk in darkness, Zach ran across the yard with Ilir and Rozafa close on his heels. *This is unreal*, he thought, in a quiet hindquarter of his brain that was staying well out of it, and watching to see what would happen. At the gate that led into the fields spreading up to The Watch, Ilir stopped. He spoke rapidly to his wife in what could have been Serbian, or Albanian, or Roma, and

Rozafa replied, her voice high with alarm, as Ilir turned to go. She put out her hand and grasped his sleeve.

'Isn't he coming with us? Aren't you coming with us, Ilir?' said Zach.

'Hannah might need me here, when they come. I will stay with her.'

'But, they might ask to see your passport . . .'

'If I leave, they will wonder where I am. Maybe they come looking,' said Ilir, resolutely. 'Now go – take them somewhere safe. Please.' He stared at Zach for a second, and Zach read the dread of their discovery in his face, and he nodded.

'Keep your mobile switched on,' Hannah shouted, as they hurried away.

They ran as quickly as they could up the dark hillside, which was steeper on that side of the valley. Tussocky grass tripped them, and it was almost easier to lean forwards and use hands, to scramble on all fours. When they'd gone two hundred metres or so they reached a fence and paused. Zach turned to look over his shoulder. The three police cars were pulling into the farmyard below them; no sirens, but their blue lights impossibly bright in the darkness.

'Down! Get down,' he said. Rozafa stared at him in incomprehension, and he realised that her English was not as good as her husband's. He pulled at her as he sank low to the chilly, wet hillside, and she copied him, crumpling herself over the little boy. He could hear her whispering gently to him, a stream of soft words that might have been a song, or a nursery rhyme. Zach could smell fear on their unwashed skin, and he swallowed, feeling the vastness of this responsibility settle onto him. Rozafa had no choice but to trust him, not only with her own fate but with that of her child. He turned to look up the hill, but could see nothing but darkness. Shreds of sheep wool surrounded them, hanging from the wire fence like garlands and dancing in the wind. The smell of them was greasy and rich. Below them six police officers, one leading a bounding Alsatian, climbed out of the cars and ran over to the house. Three peeled off and jogged around to the back, cutting off the exits. There was nothing in there for Hannah to hide, but Zach suddenly felt frantic at the thought of her trapped inside, under attack.

'God, I hope that dog only sniffs out drugs, not people,' he muttered. Rozafa's head came up at once when he spoke, eyes bright with adrenalin. 'Come on,' he said.

They hurried on up the hill, and after a short distance Zach turned and took the little boy from his mother, hoisting him up to ride piggyback, and hurrying on again. The child weighed almost nothing. A piece of driftwood, fresh in off the sea. Zach suddenly realised how dangerous it must be to cross the Channel in a small fishing boat at night; how long and uncomfortable and dark that journey must have been. Human jetsam, exhausted and on the brink; on the edge of disaster. He could not imagine risking what they had risked, could not imagine how frightened they must be. He tightened his grip on Bekim.

After ten minutes that felt like an eternity, Zach saw the white shape of The Watch looming faintly in the darkness up ahead. Gasping for breath, he led them to the front door of the cottage, passing the boy back to Rozafa as he knocked. He turned to look down the hill again, desperate to know what was happening at Southern Farm. There was nothing to see. The police cars still sat on the yard, one set of blue lights flashing. Zach knocked again, and thought about how confused and afraid Dimity had seemed when he'd turned up earlier in the day.

'Dimity, it's only me, Zach. I'm . . . back again. Please can we come in? It's very important . . . Dimity?'

'Zach?' Her voice came through the door, faint and croaky.

'Yes, it's me. Please let us in, Dimity. We need a place to hide.' The door cracked open, and the darkness within was even deeper than the night outside. The police lights flared on the old woman's pale skin, and in her wide eyes.

'Police?' she said, sounding bewildered.

'They're looking for these two. This is Ilir's wife and son. You know Ilir – Hannah's help on the farm? Can we come in?' Zach turned to look at Bekim, in Rozafa's arms, and saw that the child was fast asleep. His face was drawn and his mouth had dropped open, and his gums looked almost greyish. Zach had the sudden clear impression that the boy was not at all well. 'We need to hide here. Just for a little while. They're . . . very tired. They've been travelling for a long time.'

'Travelling?' Dimity said vaguely, and she stared at Rozafa in incomprehension. Rozafa accepted her scrutiny without blinking. Zach took a deep breath to quell his rising panic.

'Yes, travelling. They've just arrived from—'

'Ilir's people? The Romany?' Dimity interrupted him suddenly. The old woman blinked, and her expression seemed to pull into focus, as if some essence of her had returned from elsewhere. The gaze she turned on Zach grew sharper.

'Yes, that's right . . .'

'Come, come, come!' she said briskly, holding the door wider and ushering them in. 'His people are my people, after all. My mother was a gypsy, did I ever tell you that? Come in, come in, shut the door. This is a good place to hide . . .'

Zach was the last one in, and as he closed the door he saw headlights, up on the village lane. They lanced towards the cottage, and he caught his breath. He could think of no reason why they should come to The Watch, and yet Hannah had hesitated when he suggested it, as if not entirely sure it was safe. Perhaps they had been seen after all, fleeing across the fields. He grasped Dimity's arm gently to get her attention.

'I think . . . I think someone's coming down to the house . . . coming here,' he whispered anxiously. 'We need to hide them. Where can we go? No – don't!' he said, as Dimity reached for a light switch. 'It's late, better to pretend to be in bed.' The old woman clasped her hands tightly in front of her, an attitude almost like prayer. Their eyes were nothing more than faintly gleaming points in the dark. Dimity seemed caught in the grip of some impossible indecision. The police lights were still visible, sending eerie grey shadows careering around the walls. 'Dimity?' Zach pressed. 'They can't be found. Please – they'll be taken away if they're found.'

'Taken away? No, no. Upstairs is the only place. If they come here I'll turn them back. Go on upstairs, to the room on the left. The room on the *left*, you understand? The open door. On the left.' Just then, there was the sound of an engine outside the cottage, and headlights glared through the naked window.

'Make them put their ID cards through the letterbox before you open the door, Dimity! Go, go!' Zach hissed, propelling Rozafa towards the stairs. The Roma woman hurried up them on light feet, with Zach close behind. They shut themselves in a bedroom and crouched against the door, fighting to breathe silently, ears straining for any noise.

There was a knock at the door, and a long pause before Dimity answered. Muffled voices came up through the floor, but Zach couldn't make out what was said. Beside him, Rozafa's breathing grew steady and deep, and he wondered if she'd gone to sleep – surrendered all control of her situation and succumbed to exhaustion. Before long there was another smooth growl of engine noise from outside, and then everything went silent.

The air in the room was laden with peculiar scents: scents of mould and green plant life, paper, unwashed clothing; stale food of some kind; water, salt, soot, ammonia; another strong, chemical smell that Zach recognised at once. He could not imagine how that smell came to be in Dimity's cottage. However impatient he felt, he knew they shouldn't emerge until Dimity came to fetch them, just in case. He took out his phone and saw that he had a single bar of signal, now that he was upstairs. There was no missed call or text from Hannah, and he resisted the urge to call her until he knew the coast was clear. The silence stretched. Zach waited, and as he did so, he became aware of the touch of cold night air against his cheek. Puzzled, he turned to look for the source of the draught. Through the little window, the faint light of the sky was a patch of paler black, and he could see the broken pane of glass which was letting in the wind. It was the window he had stood beneath, and seen the curtains shifting within. The room to the left, Dimity had said. But Rozafa had led the way, and she wouldn't have understood the instruction. Zach went peculiarly cold all over. They were in the room on the right. The room from which quiet, unidentified sounds had often come, during his visits to Dimity.

Without moving, Zach strained his eyes to see into the corners of the room. They were lost in shadow. He could just about make out dark, crowding shapes against the unlit walls. He could not shape them into furniture, could not work out what they were. He struggled to keep his breathing steady, as if some sleeping thing in the room might wake at the sound. He felt watched; he felt as though there was some awareness in that room with him, other than the huddled forms of Rozafa and her son. He thought he heard the sound of something breathing; a slow, moist exhalation. Against all common sense, he felt a rising panic, a need for light, for clarity; a need to flee from that room with its secrets and its cold, creeping air. His phone beeped and he jumped. A text from Hannah, glowing into his eyes and ruining what night vision he'd had. *They've gone. On our way up to you.* Rozafa said something he didn't understand, her voice thin and tight with tension.

'It's OK,' he whispered. 'They're coming up here to get you.' He could tell, in the woman's silence, that she could not understand him. In the dim light from his phone her eyes shone above raw cheekbones. She stared at him in frustration for a moment, and then burst into French. '*Vous parlez français?*' Her accent was strange, but to Zach's surprise he understood her, and he dug about in his distant schoolboy French for the words to reply.

'*Hannah et Ilir . . . sont ici bientôt. Tout est bien.*' *All is well.* The words had a visible effect on Rozafa. She slumped back against the wall, clasping one hand around his forearm and shutting her eyes.

'*Merci,*' she said, so quietly he hardly heard her. Zach nodded, and wished he had the language to ask if Bekim was all right, if there was anything he could do for the limp, grey little boy.

Stiffly, he got to his feet, glad that Rozafa could not see his deep unease. With gritted teeth, he put out a blind hand, fingers splayed, and felt along the wall for the light switch. The plaster was soft, slightly damp. It came off on his fingers as a fine powder. He couldn't find the switch, and to his shame, he hardly dared take a step away from Rozafa to search further afield. Then something brushed against his neck and he yelped out loud. Rozafa was on her feet in an instant with an answering cry of alarm, as Zach scrabbled to find what had touched him. It was the light switch – a wooden toggle at the end of a string. He tugged at it savagely, and light came on overhead, a single bulb so bright that they were temporarily blinded. Through watering eyes, Zach squinted around the little room. Slowly, things swam into focus, and he realised what all the many dark shapes were. His mouth hung open in shock, in utter disbelief; so stunned that thought abandoned him.

Still cradling Élodie in arms that felt boneless, not like her own, Dimity struggled out of the car when it pulled up at Dorchester hospital. It was a towering, crenellated building of red brick walls and towers, built early in the previous century and taller even than the church spire in Blacknowle. Dimity felt it looming above her as she rushed along behind Charles. She felt the countless windows watching, recognising the thing in her arms for what it was. The thing she had done. Dimity stumbled. Her knees crumpled and for a moment she thought she would fall. The strength had gone out of her; bones turned to sand, and washed away. *The thing she had done*. Delphine was at her side, lifting her, helping her up.

'Hurry, Mitzy! Come on!' In Delphine's frantic tone Dimity heard the remnants of a dangerous hope. But there was no hope, and she wanted to scream it, wanted to shout it out loud so that she could put down the thing she was carrying. The little dead thing. Their footsteps echoed in the hallway of the hospital, and the light of many bulbs blinded them. Charles's voice echoed around, calling for help. Then, strong arms in white sleeves took Élodie from Dimity, and she sank to her knees in relief.

She was left alone, and she waited. For a while she knelt in the hallway, in the sudden quiet after the Aubreys, both well and sick, had been herded away by a knot of grim-faced people. She could have followed them, but felt too weak to move. Slowly she stood up, and she waited, and she tried not to think. There was a ringing sound inside her head, like the hum after a bell has sounded; deafening, deadening. The weight of something was pushing down on her inexorably. The weight of something undeniable, which once done could not be undone. In due course she let herself be led to a long, empty corridor where there were wooden pews against one wall. The person who led her was anonymous, faceless; a different species to her altogether, and wholly incomprehensible. A cup of tea was put next to her, but Dimity had no idea what she should do with it. She sat down and stared at the wall in front of her. Days passed, weeks, months; or just the space between one laboured heartbeat and the next – she could no longer tell the difference. It was night outside, and the light in the corridor was weak. Dimity heard echoes from time to time. Footsteps, soft snores, wordless shouts from a long way away. Disembodied sounds that drifted along the corridor like ghosts. There was sandy mud all over her shoes; dried and crumbling away. Sandy mud from the ditch where the cowbane grew. Dimity wished she didn't exist at all; she wished that she was just one more ghost who could wander the corridor, lost and all alone.

It was light outside when Charles appeared through a door, walking out into the corridor with his shoulders slumped and his head down. He moved like a sleepwalker, dull and unaware; when he saw Dimity he came to stand in front of her, and did not speak.

'Charles?' she said. He blinked, and raised his eyes to her, then he sat down beside her. His skin was grey, purple shadows under his eyes. He tried to speak but his throat was closed; he had to cough and try again.

'Celeste,' he said. The word sounded like an accusation, like a plea. 'Celeste will pull through, they think. They have given her something . . . Luminol, to stop the spasms. They are giving her drugs through a tube into her veins. I never saw such a thing before. But Élodie . . . my little Élodie.' The word collapsed into a sob. 'They have taken her away. She was not strong enough. There was nothing they could do.' The words were not his own, Dimity realised. They were words he had been told, and parroted now in place of words of his own, of which there were none.

'I knew she was dead,' Dimity said, breathlessly. Something was squeezing her chest, tightening painfully. 'I knew she was dead when I carried her. I knew it. I knew!' she gasped. Charles turned his head to look at her, and the look was one of incomprehension. He couldn't even see her, she realised. *I am a ghost, an echo. Let it be so.* She wanted to touch him, but to do so she would have to become flesh again. It would all have to be real. They sat in silence for a while then Charles got up and went back through the door, and Dimity, drawn along by the shackle around her heart, followed him.

There was another corridor, shorter this time, with tall, white doors opening off it. The stink of disinfectant was everywhere, sharper than cat's piss but not quite masking the smell of sickness, of death. There was no sign of Élodie. Gone already; gone as if she never was. Dimity shook her head at the impossibility of it. Celeste was lying back against a single pillow, her jaw slack and her hair smeared out around her, tarry and slick. There was a spidery contraption hanging over her, a needle and a cord attached to her arm; a bruise spreading down her forearm. Her lips were white, her eyes shut. She looked quite dead, and Dimity wondered if nobody had noticed, until she saw the shallow rise and fall of her ribcage. She stared and stared at the woman. Stared hard enough to see the flicker of a pulse through the thin skin of her neck.

'There will be consequences,' said Charles, and the words hit Dimity like an electric shock. She jerked her eyes to him but he was staring at Celeste. His voice was quite broken. 'The doctor says . . . she may never be the same again. Hemlock has side effects. She will have . . . some memory loss, of the days leading up to today. She will be confused. There will still be tremors. It will take time for these effects to fade, and she may never . . .' He paused, swallowing. 'She may never be her old self again. She may never be as she was before. My Celeste.'

On the other side of the bed sat a pitiful figure. A figure curled in on itself, as if trying not to be. It was doing such a good job that Dimity only gradually became aware of it. Delphine. She was crying without pause, even though she was near mute and her eyes were dry and dull, as if they'd run out of tears. Still she shook and quivered almost as much as her mother had done, before they'd come to hospital, and the sounds she made were terrible, like the repeated keening of a rabbit in a snare, but quietly – so quietly. Trying not to be. Dimity stared at her, and gradually Delphine looked up and met her gaze with eyes all red and bloody, and so swollen they had almost shut. But there was something in those eyes, besides grief, that took Dimity's breath away. It was unbearable to see, and she turned away, drifting a few paces to slump against the wall. She sank slowly to the floor. Nobody seemed to notice, or think it amiss. She put her fingertips in her mouth, and bit down on them till they bled, feeling nothing. Delphine's eyes were full of guilt. Utter, consuming, poisonous guilt.

A while later, Dimity was back on the pew in the

corridor. She didn't know how she'd got there. Voices roused her — men's voices, arguing in hushed tones by the doorway to the rooms. She rubbed at her eyes, and struggled to focus. Charles Aubrey and another man, tall and thin, with steel-grey hair. She recognised him as Dr Marsh, one of the doctors who made regular visits to Blacknowle to treat those too ill for any of Valentina's potions.

'It must be recorded, Mr Aubrey. Such things cannot be avoided,' the doctor said.

'You can write part of the truth, without writing the whole truth. And you must. My daughter . . . my daughter is tearing her own heart out. If you record the death as a poisoning, there will have to be an inquest, am I correct?'

'Yes.'

'Then for pity's sake, do not record it as such! She will carry this with her the rest of her days. If it is made public . . . if the whole world knows what she did, however accidentally . . . it will ruin her. Do you see? It will ruin her!'

'Mr Aubrey, I understand your concerns, but—'

'No! No buts! Doctor, I beg you — it will cost you nothing to record the cause of death as a gastric disturbance . . . but it will cost Delphine dearly if you do not. *Please*.' Charles gripped the doctor's arm, stared into his eyes. His desperation was written all over his face. The doctor hesitated. 'Please. We have suffered enough already. And we will suffer a great deal more as it is.'

'Very well.' The doctor shook his head, and sighed.

'Thank you. Thank you, Dr Marsh.' Charles released the man's arm and put his hand up to shield his eyes.

'But you should know . . . I was in Blacknowle last night, to see Mrs Crawford with her ulcer. I drank a glass in the pub afterwards, and there were those that were asking after you . . .'

'What did you tell them?' Charles asked, anxiously.

'I said it appeared to be a poisoning of some kind. Perhaps some plant, eaten by mistake. Forgive me. I was so shocked by the events that I spoke too freely. I will do as you ask, but you ought to be prepared for . . . rumours, in the village.'

'Rumours we can ignore. And we will leave Blacknowle, as soon as Celeste is well enough to travel. Then they can keep their rumours, and bother us no more.'

'It's probably for the best.' The doctor nodded. 'I am most terribly sorry for your loss,' he said, shaking Charles's hand and turning to walk away. As if reminded by these words, Charles rocked on his heels, seemed about to fall. Dimity rushed over to him, instinct seizing control of her body. As she reached him, Charles's legs buckled and he toppled, his arms flailing as though he was falling from a great height. Gladly, Dimity let him drag her down with him. She knelt and put her arms around him, and crooned to him gently as he sobbed and sobbed. She stroked his hair and felt his tears wetting her, and she let love light her up like the dawn breaking, strong enough, she hoped, to save her.

When she was asked, as asked she would be, she was to say *gastric flu*. Charles reminded her of this, two days later, when his tears had given way to a kind of dreadful, stony calm that was more like a state of wakeful catatonia; as though he'd been hypnotised. He moved like he was half stunned, and Dimity felt unsafe in the car as he drove her to the top of the track to The Watch, and left her there. Dimity nodded and did as she was told, though the only person who asked her was Valentina, who then studied her daughter, looked her deeply in the eye, and knew that a lie was being told. She extracted the true cause of death from her, by the sheer weight of her will and the subservience that she'd bred into her daughter, then she put her head on one side, considering.

'No cowbane within three miles of the village by my reckoning – not when the summer's this dry, and the farmers cut and burn it wherever they can. I wonder how the girl came by it? Hmm? I wonder if you might know how she came by it?' She gave an ugly cackle, and Dimity cowered away from her, shaking her head, saying nothing more. But she didn't need to. Her mother could read her mind sometimes, and her spiteful smile, her grudging respect, were bitter as bile to Dimity.

On the third day, Dimity saw the blue car creeping cautiously down the driveway to Littlecombe, as if carrying something precious and desperately fragile. She followed it down, a short and unhappy procession. Celeste was escorted into the house by Charles, who kept one hand around her waist and one hand in the air before them, as though to ward off any obstacle that might arise. In the September sunshine Celeste's face was transformed. Her complexion was grey, her cheeks drawn and hollow. Her eyes had a distant, haunted expression, and her hands shook constantly – sometimes just a tiny tremble, like a shiver, sometimes jerking convulsively like Wilf Coulson's grandma, who had the St Vitus dance. Dimity hung back as they went past her into the house. Delphine followed them, and did not look up. She was pale and looked older somehow; and as though she would never smile again. Dimity saw this, and could not believe that this was how things would be, from then on. Things could not be fixed, or changed. Things could not go back to the way they'd been. The thought turned her guts to water, and for a moment she feared she might mess herself. Something inside her was fighting to get out, but she felt that if she let it, it would kill her. So she fought with it as she followed them into the house and stood, and waited, and watched.

Nobody spoke to her. Nobody spoke at all. Nobody seemed to notice her until she put a cup of tea down next to Celeste, drawing her flat and lifeless blue gaze. 'I know you,' she said, frowning slightly. 'You are a cuckoo . . . a cuckoo child . . .' She brushed her hand down Dimity's cheek, but though her words froze Dimity's blood, suddenly Celeste smiled, just a tiny bit, just for a second. Then her eyes slid away to roam the room, as if she couldn't remember where she was, or why. Her arms twitched, shoulders hunching. Dimity swallowed, and looked around to see Charles standing behind her. He drew her to one side. 'I've told her about Élodie, but I don't know . . .' He paused, his face creasing into lines of anguish. 'I don't know if she realises what I've told her. I think I will have to say it again.' His dread at the prospect was audible. Behind him, Delphine's eyes were the only bright thing in the room; glazed and shining like polished stone.

Charles crouched down to tell Celeste, clasping one of her limp hands in both of his. It was a gesture that betrayed his own need for comfort; Dimity saw it and she longed to hold him. In the pause before he spoke, Dimity and Delphine stood so still they might have been statues.

'Celeste, my darling.' He lifted up her hand and pressed it to his mouth, as if to stop the words. 'Do you remember what I told you, last night?'

'Last night?' Celeste murmured. The faintest touch of a smile gave an apology, and she shook her head. 'You told me . . . I would be well soon.'

'Yes. And I told you . . . I told you something about Élodie. Do you remember?' His voice shook, and Celeste's smile vanished. Her eyes darted around the room.

'Élodie? No, I . . . where is she? Where is Élodie?' she said.

'We lost her, my darling.' After he spoke, Celeste stared at him, and her eyes filled with fear.

'What are you talking about? *Où est ma petite fille?* Élodie!' she called suddenly, shouting the word over Charles's head. He gripped Celeste's hand ever tighter; his knuckles were white. Dimity thought he might crack her bones.

'We lost her, Celeste. You and Élodie . . . you ate something that poisoned you. Both of you. We lost Élodie, my love. She is dead,' Charles said, and tears rolled down his face. When she saw them, Celeste paused. She stopped looking around for Élodie, stopped shaking her head in denial. She watched Charles weep and realisation spread across her face; the shadow of a loss so huge that it could not be contained.

'No,' she whispered. Beside Dimity, Delphine let out a whimper. She was watching her mother with a gaze so raw and tender it was like her heart had been torn wide open for all to see.

'We lost her,' Charles said again, lowering his head as if in submission, as if to accept whatever punishment she would give.

'No, no, *no!*' Celeste cried, the word rising to a howl that turned the air to ice. With a sob, Delphine ran across to her, and threw herself down beside her mother, wrapping her arms around her. But Celeste fought her, disengaged her arms and scrabbled to push her away. 'Get off me! Let me go!' Celeste told her.

'Mummy,' Delphine moaned, pleading with her. 'I didn't mean to.' But with a final effort Celeste shoved her back, so hard that Delphine fell from the couch to the floor. Celeste sat up as if she would rise, but did not have the strength.

'Élodie! *Élodie!*' She called the name over and over. It was a plea, a command, a wish. And on the floor beside her, Delphine could only huddle, a picture of abject misery, hugging her own knees for comfort. Charles neither moved nor spoke; he had nothing left. Inside, Dimity was falling. She was falling too fast for thought, for words, and at her feet a spatter of urine was spreading across the floor.

Delphine was sent away to school at the end of the week, the day after her sister's funeral. She went mutely, quietly, as though she had surrendered all right to an opinion, all right to free will. Dimity stood to one side as Charles hefted her trunk into the back of the car. Celeste emerged from Littlecombe, moving with the careful, small-stepping walk she had adopted since the poisoning; as though she no longer trusted her feet. She was draped in a loose robe, one of her lightweight kaftans, but it hung from her now. She was thinner, the sensual curves of her body carved away. She took no trouble to tie a sash around her waist, or arrange her hair, or put on jewellery. Her skin had not regained its glow; her eyes were always red rimmed. This creature seemed like the ghost of Celeste; as though she had died along with Élodie. She stood motionless when Delphine kissed her cheek and put careful arms around her, and did not return these signs of affection. Charles watched this awful exchange with a distraught expression.

'Goodbye, Mitzy,' Delphine said to Dimity, pressing her marble cheek to Dimity's. 'I'm glad . . . I'm glad you're here. To look after them. I wish . . .' But she did not say what she wished. She swallowed, and then an eager light kindled in her eyes. 'Will you come and visit me? At school? I don't think I could bear it if nobody did.' Her voice was high, manic with need. 'Will you? I could send you the train fare.' Her fingers gripped Dimity's arm tightly.

'I . . . I'll try to,' said Dimity. She found it hard to talk to Delphine, hard to look at her. It was near impossible to keep mind and body together when she did.

'Oh, thank you! Thank you,' Delphine whispered, hugging her tightly. She got into the car then, keeping her eyes down, her shoulders slumped. *Celeste can't forgive Delphine for what happened*, Charles told Dimity later, once Celeste was asleep. *Even though she knows it wasn't deliberate, she can't forgive her. Élodie was the littlest, you understand, still her baby, in some ways. And so like her. So like her. My little Élodie*. Dimity made him a pie for his dinner, and he didn't seem to notice that she was always there, where she did not belong.

In the night Dimity dreamed dark dreams, and every morning she sat up in bed, quite still, and waited for them to subside. But what remained, what was real, was worse than her nightmares, and inescapable. She was careful to empty her mind of thought before she rose, because without an empty head she could not breathe, let alone walk or talk or cook or take care of Charles. Her dreams were of vast black eyes and the stink of vomit. Her dreams were of hearts cut out and left on the floor, with blood seeping from them to stain the boards. Her dreams were of Élodie coming back, coming to The Watch, pointing her finger and shouting *you you you!* Her dreams were of their broken faces and of Delphine's quiet implosion; and of the way a part of each of them had gone. A part of Charles, even. It had gone wrong. She'd almost shouted it out the day before, having watched him for a full half an hour, thumbing through sketches of his daughters with a broken look on his face. *It had all gone wrong*. She had meant to free him – free him to love her and be with her and take her away, but instead Charles was more trapped than ever. It was only by keeping her carefully empty head that Dimity did not shout out things like this.

Truths like this. It was only by keeping an empty head that she did not hit the bottom of the abyss she was falling through, and break apart like glass.

The autumn rolled on in gentle warmth, with dry breezes to shake and scatter the tiny black seeds from the poppy heads amidst the golden crops and parched lawns. Outside the shop and the pub there were mutterings of war, rumours of dark clouds looming in the east; of Poland; of trouble coming; but Dimity paid no attention. Nothing like that mattered, not in Blacknowle. Nothing penetrated this far from the rest of the world; that wide, distant world Charles had promised to show her. She had only to wait, she told herself. She had only to wait a little longer and real life would begin – this limbo state would end.

She found Celeste in the garden in a deckchair one day, her legs splayed inelegantly as though she'd been casually discarded there and hadn't bothered to correct her pose. The sun had no power to warm her, to light her. Her hair was clean and combed, but still she looked half-dead. The tendons running down her neck made ridges beneath the skin; she looked raw, denuded. It was easy to think that she was unaware, that she could be ignored. Dimity made a sweep of the house and found Charles not at home, and was about to leave again when Celeste caught her hand with surprising strength.

'You. Mitzy Hatcher. You think I have lost my memory, and it is true, some things are lost to me. But not all things. When I see you there is a feeling in my gut, like a warning. Like looking down from a high place and feeling myself slipping. *Danger*, that is what I feel when I see you. I feel I am in danger.' She kept hold of Dimity's hand, kept her eyes fixed upon her. Dimity tried to twist her arm free but couldn't. Celeste's touch was like iron, cool and hard. 'It was you, wasn't it?' she said, and Dimity went cold all over; a sudden, electrifying clench of fear.

'What? No, I—'

'Yes! You are to blame! I saw you, watching Delphine bear it all, while you stayed silent. I saw you, letting her take all of the blame. But without you, she would never have gone picking wild things. Without you, she would never have thought to do so. And without your betrayal of my girls, your pursuit of their father, she would never have had to go alone, and pick the wrong thing. As much as she made this mistake, it was you who caused her to make it. Do not think you can carry on your life without sharing that burden with her. You *must* share it with her!' She threw Dimity's hand back at her and Dimity felt tears sliding down her face. They were tears of relief, but Celeste misread them and looked oddly satisfied. 'There. That is better. I have not yet seen you weep for Élodie, but at least now I see you weep, even if it is for yourself.'

'I never meant to hurt Élodie,' said Dimity. 'I never meant for it to happen!'

'But it did happen. My baby is dead. My little Élodie is never coming back . . .' Her voice failed her, and for a while the only sound was her ragged breathing, and the distant hiss of the sea. 'How I wish . . .' she said softly, some minutes later. 'How I wish we had never come here, to this place. How I wish it. Help me up.'

Dimity did as she was told, and took Celeste's arm as she rose from the deckchair; she walked with her out of the garden and across the grassy fields towards the sea. 'Take me right to the edge. I want to look at the ocean,' said Celeste, and Dimity obeyed her. She walked with a steady step now, and the tremors in her body were far fewer, far gentler. Dimity soon realised that Celeste needed no help to walk, but she kept a firm hold on Dimity's arm nonetheless, her fingers gripping tightly, her gaze straight ahead, determined. Suddenly Dimity was uneasy, though she could not say exactly why. *Danger*, just as Celeste had said. Some instinct made the hairs at the back of her neck stand on end. They walked towards the cliff edge, to a point in the path where the beach was some sixty feet below them. Dimity stopped on the path, but Celeste snapped at her. 'No! Closer. I want to look down.' Closer they went, until their toes were inches from the blowy air of the edge. Dimity's throat was so tight she could no longer swallow.

Side by side they stood, and looked down at the beach below where a handful of holidaymakers were swimming and lounging, their children playing. Celeste pointed to a dark-haired little girl who was digging in the sand near the water's edge. 'There! Look! Oh, couldn't that be her? Couldn't that be my Élodie, safe and alive and playing in the sand?' She took a long, shuddering breath and then gave a low moan. 'If only it was. If *only*. Oh, wouldn't it be easier to just step off, Mitzy?' she said. 'Wouldn't it be easier not to live at all?' Dimity tried to step back but Celeste wouldn't move.

'No, Celeste.'

'Don't you think so? Do you feel no guilt, then, for what has happened? You are quite happy to live on, with her gone? I think it would be easier to step off, to fall and to go with her. Far easier.' She gazed at the distant little girl with an awful intensity, her mouth open, an unhealthy sheen on her skin.

'Come away, Celeste! You still have another daughter! What about Delphine?'

'Delphine?' Celeste blinked, looking across at Dimity. 'She is my daughter, still, but how can I love her as I loved her before? How can I? She meant no harm, but she has done harm. Great harm. And she never needed me, not like Élodie did. She always loved Charles better.'

'She loves *you*,' said Dimity, and then gasped because something speared into her empty head, as it always did when she thought of Delphine. Something so painful that she swayed, tipping precariously towards the empty air in front of them. Celeste saw this change in her, and for a second it seemed as though she might smile.

'You do see, don't you? How much easier it would be.' And for a second, Dimity did see. All the long years of her life stretched out in front of her, and this emptiness would have to be her constant companion because the pain would never go. Things could not be undone. Her dreams would always be dark; the wide world would always be a distant, imagined thing. She would have Valentina's scorn for company, and nobody else. Charles was not free, and perhaps he never would be. But it was the thought of him that saved her. Rushing through her blood like a drug, like magic.

'No! Let me go!' She used all of her weight to pull free from Celeste, staggering back a few paces to sit down on the turf with a bump. There she sat, and watched. Celeste was still right at the edge. The violence with which Dimity had pulled away made her teeter, and fight for balance. She put out her arms, like fragile, fledgling wings. Wings that could never save her, if she fell. She wobbled, her toes tipping over the edge, breaking the lip of the cliff, and as she turned to look at Dimity the wind caught her hair, and lifted it around her face; a dark veil, a veil of grief. *Go then, if you want to*, thought Dimity. She stayed still, she watched; she felt the reassuring solidity of the ground beneath her, curled her fingers into the grass, hung on. The wind circled Celeste, and tempted her with the promise of flight. But then her wide eyes settled on Dimity, and they hardened, and she stepped back. Dimity realised she'd been holding her breath, and this time Celeste did smile; a thin smile with no amusement in it, no pleasure.

'You are right, Mitzy. I have another daughter. And I have Charles. And my life is not over, though part of me might wish it was. Yet I remain. I will remain.' Her words were a slamming door, and Dimity's crowding thoughts, her chaotic feelings, made her stupid and slow. 'Perhaps you would prefer me dead, and that is the warning I feel when I look at you. But soon it will be all the same. I will not stay here. This place is like an open grave.' She stood over Dimity but did not seem to see her. She cupped her hands, raised them to her face and inhaled; an odd, alien gesture. '*Je veux l'air de désert, où le soleil peut allumer n'importe quelle ombre,*' she said, so softly that the words were almost lost on the breeze, and only one was clearly heard. *Désert.* Dimity did not rise for a long time, and when she did Celeste was already halfway back to the house, a thin, upright, lonely figure, walking onwards without her help.

Celeste was as good as her word. Two days later Dimity was walking through the village when Charles came bursting from the shop and ran right into her. He gripped her by her upper arms and shook her before he'd even spoken.

'Have you seen her?'

'What? Who?'

'Celeste, of course, you foolish girl!' He gave her another little shake and she could not understand his expression, or his tone. Anger, fear, frustration, scorn. He was muddled, overcrowded.

'No, not since Monday! I swear it!' she cried. Abruptly, he dropped her and pushed his hands through his hair. It was a gesture he made frequently now, when she'd never seen it before that summer. 'Has she gone away?' she said.

'I don't know . . . I don't know where she's gone. She was so strange on Monday . . . when I got back from town she was so strange. She said she had to leave right away. I said we had to wait for a few days, until she's a bit stronger . . . she said she couldn't wait. I said . . . I said she had to. And now she's gone and I don't know where and I can't find her anywhere! Did she say anything to you? Anything about where she wanted to go?' Dimity thought about Celeste at the edge of the cliff, arms outstretched, hair swirling around her; ready to take flight, ready to fall. She shook her head, not trusting herself to speak. *This place is an open grave*. 'Mitzy! Are you listening to me?'

'This place is an open grave.' It was true. Blacknowle was a place to die. Her home was a place in which to die.

'What?'

'That's what she said. She said, "This place is an open grave."' Charles went still.

'But . . . but she can't go back to London on her own! Where will she stay? How would she even get to the station? She's too weak . . . anything could happen to her . . . She's not well enough yet.' His lips were dry and cracked; shreds of skin clung to them and Dimity wanted to brush them off with her fingers, and gently kiss his questions away. She pictured Celeste walking away from the cliff without her, slow but resolute. She was strong enough to travel alone. Celeste was strong enough for anything. 'And you're sure she didn't say anything else? No clue as to where she would go – did she mention any names, friends in London, anybody?' Dimity shook her head again. There was the one word she had understood. Charles would think of it, eventually. But she would not prompt him. She would give Celeste a head start, a chance to disappear. *Desert*. A quiet word, full of longing. *Desert*. *Let her go*; she sent the thought silently to Charles. *Let her go*.

Charles was quiet for a long time, as they walked slowly back to Littlecombe. 'She's right, isn't she?' he said at last.

'This place is full of death. I can't . . . I can't . . .' He trailed off as a sob clenched his throat. 'This place . . . it's so different now,' he muttered, almost to himself. 'Can't you feel it? It's like everything good and right went with her, and only the bad, the corrupt, was left behind. Such a heavy, lonely feeling. Do you feel it too?'

'Every time you leave,' she said, but Charles didn't seem to hear.

'I think . . . I will never come back here, after today. I think there are too many terrible memories . . .'

'Then we'll go away! Anywhere you want to . . . I'll go wherever you want to go, and we can start our new life. A fresh life, with no ghosts, no death . . .' Dimity stepped closer to him, took his hand and placed it on her heart; she gazed up at him intently, but Charles snatched his hand away. His eyes went wide, and stormy.

'What are you talking about?' He laughed suddenly, an ugly, barking sound. 'Don't be ridiculous. Don't you see? Everything is ruined! I am ruined. I can't draw; I can't sleep or think since . . . since Élodie died. Only dark, horrible thoughts.' He shook his head abruptly, and his face collapsed into itself. 'I miss her. I miss her so much. And now I've lost Celeste as well. My Celeste.'

'But . . . you love me! In Fez you . . . you saved me. You kissed me. I know you love me, as I love you! I *know* you do!' Dimity cried.

'Enough! I do not love you, Mitzy! Perhaps as a friend, almost as a daughter, at one time . . . but that was then, and this is now. And I should never have kissed you. I am sorry for that, but you have to forget about it now. Do you hear me?'

When Dimity spoke, her voice was little more than a whisper, because the sting of his words, the cruelty of them, took her breath away.

'What are you saying?' She shook her head. 'I don't understand.'

'For pity's sake, girl, have you quite lost your mind? Don't keep on with this nonsense! Can you think of nobody but yourself, Mitzy?'

'I only think of you,' she said, numbly. There was only him in the world, she realised. He was the only solid thing, and behind and around him the world dissolved into shadow. 'Just you.' She grasped the front of his shirt in her fists. She had to keep hold of him, in case she became nothing but shadow too.

'I won't stay here another second. I have to find Celeste. The world's rotten, Mitzy. Rotten and foul. I can't bear it! If you see Celeste . . . if she comes here after I've gone, be kind to her, please. Tell her I love her and . . . tell her to wait here until I come for her. She can always telephone me, or send a letter . . . please. Will you do that for me, Mitzy? Promise to look after her, if she comes here?'

'Please, don't go. Please don't leave me,' Dimity begged.

'Don't leave you? What are you talking about? None of this has anything to do with you.'

'But . . . I love you.'

Charles looked at her strangely then, with an expression Dimity had never seen before. It looked like anger, like disgust. But it could not be, so she did not recognise it. He turned away from her and strode over to the car. She followed him, kept close behind him. Had hold of the handle of the passenger-side door when the car lurched forwards with a violent jerk that bent her fingers back, and broke all the nails. Blood seeped out from under them. When the car vanished from sight she looked down at her body, checking it here and there, wondering if she were bleeding because it felt as though the life was draining out of her and into the stony ground.

A week after Charles went up to London in search of Celeste, war was declared and travel curtailed. Word of it swept over the country, even to Blacknowle, like the first cold wind of winter. But that wind died down; nothing much seemed to happen. If anything was happening, people said, then it was happening a long way away. Domed, concrete lookouts appeared along the coast; strange, bristling ships passed up and down the Channel. Some of the farming lads answered the call of duty; went to Dorchester and signed their lives away. Dimity was scarcely aware of any of it. She only had room in her head for thoughts of Charles, and of how, when he came back, she would heal all his sorrows with her love for him; fill him up with it, and make him see that it was better that Celeste had gone. She was a constant reminder of terrible things. He would love her back and finally, finally, the nightmare would be over and they would be united. Together, as man and wife, with no more whispers about her, or about them. No more rumours or scandal; they would be wed and there was nothing to stop it now. Élodie, Delphine, Celeste; all had gone. The autumn was cold and this thought alone kept her warm. He would come back, and be with her. He would come back.

II

Zach was still standing in the little room upstairs at The Watch, staring all around, when Hannah came up to stand beside him. Squinting in the light, she put her hand on his arm, and he felt her fingers clench tightly. She drew breath as if to speak, but stayed silent.

'Are these . . . what I think they are?' he said at last. Dimity had been climbing the stairs behind them, but when she saw that the door was open she froze, and a low wail rose from her throat; a startling lament of pure grief. Rozafa rushed to the old woman as she crumpled down onto the stairs, asking questions in her own language and glancing up at Zach in fright. Dimity stared at the open door, weeping, and Ilir joined Rozafa, weaving their lyrical, incomprehensible language around the old woman as if to comfort her. Hannah exhaled a long, steady breath.

'Aubrey pictures. Yes.'

'There must be . . . thousands of them.'

'Well, not thousands, perhaps, but a good few.' Zach tore his eyes from the contents of the room to give Hannah an astonished look.

'You knew about this?' he said. Hannah pursed her lips, and nodded. She looked away uncomfortably, but there was no trace of guilt on her face.

'How did you get in here?' she asked.

'It was a mistake. Dimity said to go to the left but . . . Rozafa didn't understand.' Zach looked around the little room again, letting his eyes sweep slowly over everything. He couldn't quite believe what he was seeing. Hannah followed his gaze, and he felt a shudder pass through her. She clasped her arms tightly across her chest, but Zach was too distracted by what he was seeing to ask what troubled her.

There was the little window in the far wall, opposite the door, with the broken pane of glass and the pale, shifting curtains. To the right of that a narrow bed sat against the wall, covered with greyish, rumpled sheets and blankets, and with a scooped indentation in the pillow as though somebody had only just risen from it. To the left of the window was a long wooden table with a simple, hard chair pulled up to it. The table was covered with papers and books, jars of pencils and brushes. The floorboards were dusty and bare save for a small, faded rag rug by the bed. Odd sheets of paper also lay scattered about the floor, and in a draught from the window, one shifted suddenly. Lifted itself up and scudded a few inches towards Zach. He jumped at the movement, nerves jangling. And all over the walls, pinned up and leaning against it, on almost every available bit of space, were pictures. Predominantly drawings, but some paintings too. Beautifully, unmistakeable, the work of Charles Aubrey.

'This is not possible,' said Zach, to nobody in particular.

'Well, that's all right then. We've got nothing to worry about,' said Hannah, with deadpan humour.

'Do you have any idea . . .' he said, but stopped. Awe had stolen the words he needed to finish the sentence. He walked slowly to the southern wall of the room, where most of the larger pieces were leaning, lifted the top ones and looked at those behind. There were lots of Dennis. Both the Dennis he knew, the tantalisingly ambiguous young man whose portrait had recently sold several times over, and of other Dennises. Dennises who were wholly different – different face, different clothes, different stature. A wide variety of young men, all bearing the same name. Zach frowned, and tried to think what it could mean. Behind him he heard Dimity suddenly shout.

'Is he there? Is he in there?' There was a kind of wild hope in the question, and Zach looked over his shoulder as she appeared in the doorway with Hannah trying to hold her, to contain her.

'There's nobody here, Dimity,' he said. The old woman's face sagged into dismay. Her eyes scanned the room, as though not wanting to believe him. And then she knelt down on the floor, and hugged her arms tightly around herself.

'Gone, then,' she said softly. 'Truly gone, and for ever.' There was such sorrow in the words that Zach felt it cool his excitement; felt it slow and sadden him.

'Who's gone, Dimity?' Zach asked. He crouched down beside her and put one hand on her arm. Her face was wet with tears, and her eyes roamed the room as if still searching for someone.

'Charles, of course! My Charles.'

'So . . . he was here in this room? Charles Aubrey was here? When was that, Dimity?'

'When? When?' She seemed bewildered by the question. 'Always. He was always here with me.' Zach looked at Hannah in confusion, and saw the way she kept her mouth firmly closed when she clearly had things to say. He turned back to the old woman.

'Charles went off to fight in the Second World War, Dimity. He went off to fight, and was killed near Dunkirk. That's right, isn't it? You remember?' Dimity looked at him with a slightly scathing expression, and when she spoke there was a trace of pride, and of defiance.

'He went off to war, but he didn't die. He came back to me, and he stayed with me for the rest of his life.'

'That's just not possible,' Zach heard himself say, but

even as he did so his eyes were drawn up to Hannah's, and she nodded.

'It's true,' she said, quietly. 'He died six years ago. Here. He died here.'

'You mean . . .' Zach's mind whirled, fighting to keep up, to understand the implications of what he was being told. 'You mean . . . you saw him? You *met* Charles Aubrey?' He almost laughed, it sounded so outlandish to his own ears. But Hannah didn't laugh.

'I saw him, yes. But we didn't meet. He was . . . he was already dead, the only time I saw him.'

'Dead,' Dimity whispered, and her face sank again, her body seeming to fold in on itself, limp and boneless. Zach stared at her and then at Hannah, and then at the little narrow bed with the stained sheets and the head-shaped hollow in the pillow.

'I think . . . I think I need somebody to explain all this to me slowly and clearly,' he said, shaking his head in amazement.

Dimity sang 'Bobby Shaftoe', over and over. *He'll come back and marry me, bonny Bobby Shaftoe*. The song became a chant, a tuneless, repetitive mantra, beating to the rhythm of her questing feet as she walked, and watched, and waited. Valentina heard her, and tried to beat the idea out of her. *He's gone, don't you get it? He's not coming back*. But Dimity insisted that he would. That Charles would not leave her in Blacknowle. Forgotten about, cast aside. And slowly, the words of the song trickled deeper and deeper into her mind, and became the truth. *He'll come back and marry me . . .* It became the truth; it became what lay in store for her, because the alternative was unbearable. The alternative was that crushing span of lonely time she had suddenly glimpsed, standing on the clifftop with Celeste. She knew she would not survive it so she kept on singing, and believing.

But the next person to come looking for her, as the first frosts bit the air and the last apples were packed away in barrels, was not Charles Aubrey. It was a tall, elegant woman with chestnut hair combed into an immaculate twist at the back of her head. She wore a green twill coat and white kidskin gloves; her mouth a slick of scarlet lipstick. A taxi was parked behind her, its engine idling, and she stood on the doorstep of The Watch with a stern, unhappy expression on her face. When Dimity opened the door she felt grey eyes sweep her from feet to face in quick appraisal.

'You're Mitzy Hatcher?'

'I am. Who are you?' She studied the woman, and tried to guess. She was perhaps forty years old, not beautiful but handsome. Her face had the smooth, sculpted look of a statue.

'Celia Lucas. I was told in the village to come and talk to you . . . Delphine Aubrey has run away from school again. She's been gone a week already, and they're getting worried. I was told you were most likely to have seen her, if anyone had. If she'd come back this way, that is.' The woman looked around her, from the cliffs to the woods and the cottage, as if she couldn't understand why anybody would. She spoke with cut-glass vowels.

'I have not seen her,' Dimity replied. She tried to take a deep breath, but her lungs felt like they'd shrunk. She tried again, and her head began to spin. 'Where's Charles? Why didn't he come to look for her himself?' Celia's gaze sharpened at once, and she stared into Dimity's eyes for a moment.

'Don't tell me you're another one of his?' Her mouth pursed bitterly. Defiantly, Dimity nodded. 'Well, well. They get younger all the time.' She spoke casually, but Dimity saw the way her hands gripped each other, so tightly that they shook. 'And to answer your question, Charles didn't come to look for her because the damn fool of a man has joined the army and gone off to fight in France. What do you make of that?' She arched her eyebrows, and beneath her sangfroid was the panic of a trapped animal. Dimity recognised it; she felt it too.

'Gone off to fight?' she echoed, breathlessly.

'Yes, quite my reaction too. A lifetime of pacifism and high rhetoric about the evils of war, and at the first sign of a painful situation, off he trots.'

'To the war?' said Dimity. Celia frowned at her, and seemed to wonder how much more to say.

'Yes, dear, to the war. So whatever plans you thought he might have for you, I'm afraid you're on your own,' she said, blandly. 'And I, it seems, must chase around the country looking for one of his bastard offspring. Poor child, indeed, but if the mother couldn't be bothered to look after her, I find it somewhat hard that I should be expected to.' She pulled the lapels of her coat tighter together, her breath steaming damply in the frigid air.

'Are you . . . Delphine's teacher?' Dimity asked, after a pause. She was fighting to understand, struggling to make sense of what she'd been told. The woman's face registered irritation, impatience.

'No, child, I am Charles's *wife*. So help me.' She looked out to sea, squinting at the horizon. 'For how much longer I shall remain his wife, however, who can say?' Dimity stared at her. Her words were nonsense. The calm inside her head grew so profound that nothing could disturb it. The cut-glass vowels slid away from her like snowmelt. 'Look, if you do see Delphine, call me and let me know, would you? Here's my card. I'll . . . I'll write down Charles's regiment and company on the back, so you can . . . look out for news of him. Or write to him, if you like. Odd that he didn't let you know. But then, Charles is very odd these days. When I last saw him he could hardly string a sentence together.' She pressed her lips crisply, took out a pen and wrote something on an oblong of card before putting it into Dimity's limp hand. 'Good luck to you. And try to forget about him. Difficult, I know, but for the best.' She turned and walked back to the waiting taxi cab.

Later on, a song Dimity had known from childhood burst into her head and went around and around, like a caged thing, echoing in the empty spaces there. *I heard a fair maid making loud lamentation, singing Jimmy will be slain in the wars I be feared . . . Jimmy will be slain in the wars, I be feared.* The line rolled over and over, like wavelets breaking ashore. Charles had gone off to war. He was a hero now, a brave soldier, and she the poor wife left at home to worry. Neatly, seamlessly, Dimity wrote herself into this narrative. She was so tired that she took to her bed at four in the afternoon, and could neither sleep nor rise. She lay, and she hummed the words of that old song, and when Valentina came up to find out why there was no dinner, she found the smart, embossed card on the nightstand by the bed. *Celia Lucas Aubrey.*

'Who's this then? Where's this come from?' she demand- ed, sitting down on the edge of the bed. Dimity ignored her, watching the way the light from the bulb overhead made her fingertips glow. Valentina gave her a shake. 'What's the matter with you? Is this who came to the door earlier? Some relative of his?' She frowned at the card. It bore his name, or at least part of it. 'Not . . . his wife?' she ventured. Dimity stopped singing and glared at her. Something scratched at the back of her eyes, at the back of her mind. Something with sharp little claws, which left stinging scratches. A rat?

She sat up abruptly, checked the corners of the room. There were rats on the floor, twisting and writhing and bent backwards in pain. With a loud shriek Dimity clapped her hands over her eyes.

'No!' she shouted, and Valentina tipped back her head to laugh.

'His bloody wife came looking for him, didn't she?'

'No!'

'Will you forget it now, eh? He's not coming back, and even if he did, he's married. He's not going to marry you.' For a second, as Valentina looked at her daughter, something almost like kindness softened her face. 'Let it go, Mitz. There'll be others. No point turning yourself inside out over it.'

'He'll come back for me. He's coming back for me!' Dimity insisted.

'Have it your way, then.' Valentina stood abruptly. 'You're a bloody fool.'

Dimity waited out the winter; she waited out the spring. She fled the house when Valentina tried to introduce her to a grey-haired man, shifty and thin, who looked at her with such naked hunger in his eyes that his gaze felt bruising. She stayed out for two days and two nights that time, hardly eating, hardly sleeping. She sang her songs, she emptied her mind. She told herself over and over that Charles would come back to her. And so, eventually, he did.

It was close to summer before he made it. As dusk fell Dimity stood on the rise above Littlecombe; stood for so long that her legs were tingling with pins and needles and her feet were aching from it. She stared for so long that she forgot why she was staring. By then, it was taking a long time for things to penetrate her calm – the things her mother said, the people she saw in the village; Wilf Coulson, who talked to her in a staccato rattle of sound that made no sense, and irritated her ears, so that she turned and drifted away whenever she saw him. And so it was only after half an hour, rooted to the spot, that she realised what she was looking at. A light, gleaming out of an upstairs window at Littlecombe. A light that spoke of every wish coming true, and every prayer answered. Dimity walked steadily down to the house. She did not need to rush. This time, he would stay. This time, he would not leave her, and they had all the time in the world. She let herself into the house, climbed the stairs and pushed open the bedroom door. And there was Charles Aubrey, waiting for her, just as she'd known he would be.

The smell of him was everywhere. As she entered the room this smell rose to greet her even though Charles did not. He was sitting in a small chair by the bed, his chin drooping to his chest, his hands clasped in his lap, his feet side by side like a schoolboy's. His clothes were ruined, filthy and misshapen. A duffel jacket that was far too big; cord trousers torn at the knees; cracked boots with no laces. Underneath them he was thinner, more angular. His bones were sharp at shoulder and elbow, knee and jaw. His hair was matted with dirt, his cheeks covered by straggling whiskers. There was a cut along his right cheekbone, the blood from it still black and caked on the skin below. It looked deep, and angry – Dimity thought she saw the ghastly grey of bone showing through. *Comfrey*, she thought at once. Salt water to clean it and then comfrey to soothe it, once it was stitched. She went to him, knelt down and laid her head in his lap. The smell was of shit and piss, of sweat and infection, of fear and death. Dimity didn't care. She felt the press of his thigh bone through his trousers, and everything was perfect.

'I got away,' he said, after this long, suspended moment.

Dimity looked up at him, and touched her fingertips to his ravaged face. Her whole heart was his, and beat only for him. She wanted to gather him up, never let him go. There was a strange, flat light in his eyes; a gleam she had never seen before. He looked as though he had seen things that he could never un-see. He didn't say her name, or seem surprised to see her. 'I got away,' he said again. Dimity nodded, and bit back a storm of quick, happy sobs. He was free then, finally.

'You did, my love. And I am going to look after you now . . . I need to go back to The Watch to get some things for that cut on your face. I need a needle and thread, and salt to clean it . . .' He snatched at her wrist as she began to stand. As quick as a snake.

'Nobody must know! I can't go back . . . I can't go back, do you hear?' His voice was ragged with fear.

'Well, they can't make you, can they?'

'They can . . . they can send me back. And they will! I can't go!' His fingers were bruising her arm, the grip like an animal bite, hard and instinctive. She didn't try to pull away, and only soothed him, stroking his hair and murmuring to him until he was calm again.

'I'll hide you, my love. Nobody will know that you're here, with me. I will keep you safe, I promise.' Gradually, his grip loosened and then fell away, and he stared at the floor again, blank as a new canvas.

'You will come back, won't you?' he said, as she went at last to the door. Dimity felt stronger than she ever had; more certain, more complete. As softly and easily as snow-fall, everything fell into its right place around her. She smiled.

'Of course, Charles. I'm only going to find a coat to warm you, and cover you as we go down to The Watch.'

*

'Well, he can't stay here, can he?' said Valentina, pinching her nose shut, eyes narrowed against the smell. Dimity ushered her mother out of her room, where Charles was lying down on the narrow bed, and shut the door softly behind her.

'He is staying here. He is my man, and I will look after him.' She stared at her mother, and Valentina stared back. Dimity took a short breath and let her arms hang loosely at her sides, sleeves pushed up, ready for battle. Her heart thumped, slow and deep.

'He's not staying here. Got it? Harbouring a deserter? People round here would jump at the chance to cause trouble for us. Don't you get that? How long do you think you can keep him hidden, eh? People know everything around here. Someone'll see him . . .'

'The only visitors we have are yours,' Dimity muttered.

'And don't I bloody know it, girl! And let's not go forgetting that it's those visitors that keep this roof over our heads and food on the table, and scarce enough for two let alone with a useless man to feed as well.'

'They keep cider in your blood perhaps, but the food I'll take some credit for!' Dimity was ready for the slap. She caught her mother's hand before it could land and held it mid-air, both of their arms shaking with the tension. Valentina curled her lip.

'So, I've finally found something you'll fight for. That wreck in there? *Really?* The one that stinks of his own shit and jumps at the sound of a footstep? That's what you'll fight me for, after all these years?'

'Yes!' Dimity didn't hesitate.

'You love him, or you think you do. I can see that. More fool you, when you've never even lain with the man – and there's scant enough of novelty there, believe me. But I'll tell you this so you'd better listen – this is my house, not yours, and there's no place for a man in it. Least of all one who can't earn and will get us all arrested. You hear me? He's *not* staying here.'

'He is.'

'He's not and you'd better get that through your thick head! Take yourself off to Littlecombe with him, if you want. You'll be no great loss around here.'

'We can't live there . . . people would notice for sure. The rent would have to be paid, people in the village would see the lights on . . .'

'Well, I don't count that amongst my problems. God knows I have enough, but that man is not one of them. Do what you want with him, but he has to go.'

'Ma, *please* . . .' Dimity felt the words half strangling her. She knew how futile it was to beg, and only desperation made her try it now. Her insides curled. She hated it. She tried to grasp her mother's hands, tried to make her see. '*Please*—' But Valentina snatched her hands away, raised an index finger in warning. The stained nail looked like a curse.

'He's gone by the morning – him or the pair of you, I don't mind which. Or I'll turn him in myself. You got that?'

The night was long, and pitchy black. Dimity did not sleep. She bathed Charles from top to toe, with basin after basin of warm water and every flannel and cloth in the house. She washed the mud and grease from his hair, took a fine comb and cleared as many of the lice and eggs as she could. She smoothed the blood from the cut on his cheek and stitched it as neatly as possible. Charles didn't wince when the thick needle pierced his skin. She cleaned every trace of dirt and stink from his skin, feeling a blush light her cheeks when she took off his trousers, and saw his naked body for the first time. Charles seemed to find nothing amiss in this, and accepted her attentions calmly, obediently. She cut his toenails, and scrubbed the dirt from under his fingernails with a small brush. A tremor ran through his arms and hands, constant, shuddering. It brought with it a memory of Celeste which Dimity carefully ignored. Her own hands were steady, entirely sure of themselves. His clothes would have to be burnt, and new ones found for him. Straight away she knew which washing lines she could pinch them from, easily and discreetly. Eventually Charles slept, as naked as the day he was born, with the blanket tucked around him tightly. Dimity gazed at him for a long time, and ran her fingers softly down the contours of his face. She did not notice that he was too quiet; that there was an emptiness behind his eyes that hadn't been there before. She did not notice that the fire that had once lit him, the quickness and surety of his movements and words, had burnt out. She knew only that he was there, with her.

Eventually she left him to sleep. There was no room for two in her bed, but she didn't want to lie down anyway. She couldn't remember when she'd last felt as awake as she did then. She tidied up the detritus of Charles's extended bath, taking his clothes out into the backyard and dropping them onto the burning heap. It was close to dawn. A faint grey glow was seeping across the black sky. Almost midsummer, and the nights were short, sweet. The year was rising to its apex, and about to peak. An auspicious time, a time of change. Dimity felt it in her blood; in her bones. The Watch was silent, and she felt it watching. Thatch and plaster, wood and stone. And Valentina, the hard heart of the place. Sharp as a barking dog, watching her all the time. She poured herself a glass of milk, drank it slowly, then rinsed the glass and went up to her mother's room.

Valentina was deeply asleep with her arms thrown back above her head and her hair straggled out across the pillow. She had enough pillows for two people, as though the bed was always half empty and just waiting to welcome another occupant. Pale dawn light made her mother's face silvery, made her hair shades of grey and white. She was almost beautiful, Dimity saw. Her cheekbones rose delicately beneath her eyes, her nose was fine and feminine, her lips still full. But even with her face slack and relaxed in sleep, the marks of her habitual expressions remained, etched into her skin. The furrow of her frown between her eyes; the scathing lines across her brow; the bitter brackets either side of her mouth; fine lines along her upper lip where she puckered her mouth around cruel words. Her chest rose and fell with perfect rhythm. Dimity looked down at her and thought how small she looked, how vulnerable. Never something she had thought about Valentina before, but there it was now, with sudden clarity. *Vulnerable*. Valentina had always been there; the bitter kernel at the centre of life. *You have always been there, to make things worse*, Dimity told her, silently. Her mother's chest rose and fell, her breath swept in and out, in and out. Dimity watched, and soon her own breathing moved to the same rhythm. For that short time, they existed in perfect harmony. But when she left the room a while later, with her fingers aching peculiarly, Dimity's breath was the only song still singing.

Dimity hid Charles when the police came. She coaxed him out of her bedroom, down to the backyard, and sat him on the wooden seat of the privy. At first he didn't seem to understand who was coming, why exactly he should hide. Then, when she explained, he thought that the police were coming for him, and that he would be taken back to the war. He was shaking all over when she left him, pressing a long kiss of reassurance onto his lips.

'They won't find you. They're not looking for you. I promise,' she told him. Sweat beaded his brow and ran down at his temples. With her heart aching for him, Dimity shut and latched the door, went back inside and waited for PC Dibden to arrive. PC Dibden was a young man whose mother knew Valentina well, although perhaps not as well as his father had known her, before he'd died of a heart attack scant hours after a particularly strenuous evening three years previously. The young man was awkwardly fascinated by her corpse, and kept glancing at it as he took Dimity's statement and waited for his superiors to arrive.

Valentina lay in the same position in which she'd been sleeping – on her back with her arms flung up – and Dimity also glanced at her as she told the policeman that Valentina had had a visitor the night before but that she hadn't seen his face, only the back of his head as he'd gone into the bedroom. She glanced at her mother to be sure that her chest remained still, that her breath had not returned. That her eyes were still shut. She did not trust Valentina to make anything easy for her. She gave a description of the man she'd supposedly seen. Medium height and build; short brown hair; wearing a dark coloured jacket of the kind every man within a fifty-mile radius possessed. PC Dibden wrote all this down dutifully, with an expression on his face that told her how useless it would be in finding the killer. There were no fingermarks on Valentina's neck, no signs of violence. It was possible, said the policeman, that Valentina had died of natural causes and that her visitor had run off in panic. Dimity agreed that it was quite possible. She gnawed at her thumbnail until it bled, but even this could not bring tears to her eyes. *Shock*, said PC Dibden to the undertaker, as they took Valentina out later that morning and the police dusted the bedroom and the banister for fingerprints. There would be hundreds, Dimity knew. Hundreds and Hundreds.

The funeral was quick, and sparse. PC Dibden came along, and stood a respectful distance from Dimity. Wilf Coulson was there, and his father, which came as a surprise to Dimity. None of Valentina's other visitors had dared to show their faces. The Brocks from Southern Farm stood close together, hands clasped respectfully. Still Dimity did not cry. She cast the first handful of earth over the coffin, after the vicar had read a short sermon, and found herself praying that Valentina would stay down there. A sudden storm of fear swept through her, and she stumbled; stooped for another handful of earth and threw it after the first. If no one else had been there to see, she might have fallen to her knees and clawed the whole mound back in with her bare hands. *Buried, buried. Gone*. She clenched her fists for calm, and met nobody's eye as she walked back to The Watch. No conversations, no wake. No words of sympathy. PC Dibden trotted up behind her and tried to give her an update on the case, but in truth there was nothing to update. He assured her they were doing all they could to find out who had been with her mother that night, but the apologetic look in his eye told her otherwise. They held out little hope of finding him, because they weren't really looking all that hard. There were other, more important cases to solve. They weren't even sure that a murder had been committed. Valentina's suffocation could have been accidental, during whatever activity she'd been engaged in. And, in the end, the police didn't really care. Valentina was no huge loss to the community, other than to her visitors, and they were content to stay silently anonymous. *She got what was coming to her*, Dimity thought, and knew she wasn't the only one to think so.

When she got back to The Watch, and rounded the corner of the cottage, out of sight of any onlookers, she pushed her shoulders back and straightened her spine, and a joyous smile broke out across her face. Charles wept with relief when she let him out of the privy, and told him that it was all over, nobody else would be coming. He clasped her tightly and sobbed like a child.

'You must hide me, Mitzy! I can't go back,' he mumbled. Dimity held him and sang to him until the fit passed, then they went back into the house together, slowly, like the walking wounded, and she shut the door behind them.

'But . . . I heard somebody moving around in here. I heard it! I'm sure I did . . . you heard it too, right, Dimity?' said Zach. He waited for a reply from the old lady but she seemed lost in her own mind; her gaze settled on him when he took her hand but it was diffuse, absent. Hannah shook her head.

'You know how old houses move around and creak. Plus the window's been broken for ages. I offered to get it fixed for her but she point-blank refused. Because it meant opening the room, I guess. But the wind's been blowing through here for months, shifting the papers around, making the floorboards damp . . .'

'No, I heard a person. I'm *sure* of it,' Zach insisted. Hannah threw up her hands and let them fall to her sides.

'You can't have, Zach. Unless you believe in ghosts now.' She meant it as a throwaway remark, but Zach noticed Dimity's eyes flicker as she said it, and then follow Hannah as she paced the room restlessly. Zach took a deep breath, and wondered what surreal world he had stumbled into that night. An odd other world where he fled from place to place through a dark night, smuggling people, avoiding the law; where huge collections of art lay hidden, like buried treasure, left by a man who had lived far beyond his own death. None of it seemed quite real.

It was late, and Zach and Hannah sat at the kitchen table with cups of tea going cold in front of them. Ilir was in the living room, keeping vigil over his wife and son. Bekim was fast asleep, laid out on the sofa with a moth-eaten blanket draped over him. Rozafa sat by the child's head with one hand on his shoulder, her head tipped back, also sleeping. Ilir curled his body over them protectively, as though now he had them back he would let nobody near them, and no distance come between them. Zach wondered how long Ilir had been in Dorset; how long it had been since husband and wife had seen each other. Dimity was still upstairs in the little room full of pictures. Zach had taken her some tea, but the old woman was quiet and still and would not come downstairs. Uneasily, he'd noticed the way her chest rose and fell, quick and shallow. Sipping at the air as if she couldn't quite reach it.

'Tell me how you saw him. How he was. What happened that night,' said Zach. Hannah sighed, and got up.

'We need something stronger than tea,' she muttered, and pulled open kitchen cupboards until she found an ancient, sticky bottle of brandy. She poured a good measure into two mugs and brought them over to the table, sliding one to Zach. 'Cheers.' She knocked hers back in one, then rolled her lips over her teeth in protest and shuddered slightly. 'Mitzy came down to the farm late one evening. It was in the summer and it had only just got dark, so it must have been ten or half ten. She was confused, panicking. She asked for my grandmother at first, and didn't seem to remember who I was until I explained. I knew something was up at once. She hadn't come knocking on our door for . . . well, for as long as I could remember, anyway. She asked me to come back with her, and wouldn't say why. Practically towed me out of the house. "I can't do it by myself", was all I could get her to say. And so I went with her, and she brought me here, and up to that room, and there he was.' She exhaled heavily.

'Dead?'

'Yes. He was dead,' she said. 'Mitzy said we had to get rid of him. Hide the body. I asked her why . . . why we couldn't just call an undertaker. But she was convinced that the police would come, if anybody knew; and she was probably right. Sudden death and all that, and he wasn't even supposed to be here. He wasn't supposed to exist. I gathered this slowly, as she told me who he was.'

'But . . . he must have been *ancient*,' said Zach.

'Almost a hundred. But then, he'd lived a very . . . sheltered life. The latter part of it, anyway.'

'And you had no idea before that that anybody was living here with her? All those years and you didn't suspect a thing?'

'All those years. Not so surprising when you consider how cut off her cottage is. The farm is the only place that looks onto it, and we never made a point of looking. And besides, he never came out of this room. I can count on the fingers of one hand the number of times I'd been inside The Watch before that evening, and I'd never been upstairs, not once. How would anybody have known?'

'Did you . . . Did you know who he was?'

'Not at first, no. But when Dimity told me . . . I'd heard of him, of course. My grandmother used to talk about him all the time. And then I saw the pictures, and I knew it had to be true. It had to be him.'

'But . . . how the hell did he *get* here? His body was buried on the Continent – it was found, identified, his death was recorded, and he was buried . . .'

'*A* body was found. *A* body was identified. *A* body was buried. I don't know how much you know about the retreat to Dunkirk?'

'I've . . . seen films. Documentaries.'

'It was chaos. Thousands and thousands of men on the beach, waiting to be evacuated, and hundreds of small boats coming over from England to help. Fishing boats, charter yachts and pleasure boats, cargo ships. Charles got on one of those small ships. It brought him all the way back to

England, and then he . . . slipped away. Made his way back to Blacknowle somehow.'

'You mean he deserted?'

'Yes. AWOL. Dimity told me . . . she told me he was quite happy to stay here. Very happy. That he insisted he couldn't go back. He wouldn't go back. Hiding for the next sixty-odd years might seem a bit extreme, but it sounds to me like he had a breakdown of some kind. Post-traumatic stress, or something. And I guess once you've been hiding for a certain length of time, it stops feeling like hiding and starts to just feel like . . . the way you live.'

Hannah got up for the brandy bottle and topped up both their mugs, even though she was the only one who had emptied hers. Zach tasted it and grimaced.

'I can't believe any of this,' he said, shaking his head. 'How did he get back here? Who was buried in France if it wasn't Charles?'

'Who was buried? Can't you guess?' said Hannah. Zach thought hard, but could make no sense of it.

'No. Who was it? Who did they bury in 1940, thinking it was Charles?' Hannah studied him for a moment, her eyes switching rapidly back and forth across his face.

'Dennis,' she said, eventually. 'They buried Dennis.'

Charles told Dimity about it in one of his outpourings – his rare outpourings. Usually he would only talk about his drawings, or request art supplies, or tell her the odd food cravings he would get. Cherries one day, French onion soup the next. Once he wanted smoked salmon, and Dimity fretted and fussed and took days building a smoking barrel in the backyard, since there was none to be had in the shops and she could never have afforded it if there had been. The result was a tough and overdone trout, the flesh almost leathery, but Charles swallowed it down without complaint, smiling appreciatively. Dimity wondered then if she'd needed to bother – if she could have given him fresh herring and told him it was smoked salmon, and he would have eaten it with as much relish. But she would never try such a deception. She would always strive to give him whatever he asked for. Making him happy was all she could do for him; and all she could do for herself. Protecting him assuaged the feeling of falling that she still woke up with, every single day.

But sometimes he had nightmares, and his shouts woke her and sent her rushing in to comfort him, both for comfort's sake and in case, just in case, there was anybody outside to hear him. He would be up from the bed and pacing the room, clasping at his hair or wiping his hands down his body as though there was something on them that appalled him. She followed him and held him, even when he pushed her away, until he slowed and then sat down, the weight of her too much to resist. She tethered him back to the earth, to the Dorset coast, to where he was. Held him down until he could feel the sea booming through the bones of the house, and his body went limp. Then he would tell her what he had seen, and who had been to visit him in the darkness of sleep. A torrent of words, an outpouring like a purge. As necessary to healing as draining the poison from a wound.

And as often as not, it was Dennis he'd seen. The naked, charred remains of a young British soldier. The blast that killed him had burnt the clothes from his body and left only his boots, which still smouldered. He was lying in the long grass a good thirty feet from the crater, and Charles tripped over him as he made his dogged and desperate way north, to the coast. No trace of his uniform and almost none of his skin. He was so badly burnt that his eyelids were gone, as were his lips. His teeth ringed a mouth that sat slightly open, so that he appeared mildly surprised by his own death. One eyeball was charred black and ruined, but the left side of his face, which must have been turned away from the blast, was more intact. The iris was exposed, and watchful. A rich brown colour in a white stained yellow by the smoke. Charles stared into it and was reminded, grotesquely, of crème caramel. The man's flesh was scarlet and orange and black; cracked, weeping, sticky and raw. Flies had already begun to settle on him. Charles stayed with him for half an hour or more because he could not look away from that one startled, piteous eye. The rest of Charles's unit had moved away. He lay hidden, and felt the dread and panic of being left behind mingling with the terror of going forwards.

Gradually, things grew quieter, and a glint of colour caught Charles's eye. The sun, coming out from behind clouds and smoke, shone onto the green and red discs of the dead man's identity tags. They had been flung around to his less-burnt side, and lay against the top of his shoulder, still threaded onto a charred leather thong. There was nothing else to identify him. No badges, no papers. Charles ran his eyes the length of the man, and guessed their heights to be roughly similar. He reached out to lift the tags, to read the man's name, but they were stuck to his burnt flesh. Nestled into it. He had to claw at the man's shoulder with his finger-nails, and pain and horror shot through his own body like electricity as he did so, because he could feel how much it must hurt.

He was whimpering by the time he got the tags free, and wiped the mess from them with his thumb to read the name. *F. R. Dennis*. Beneath the twin holes where the tags had been, a whitish gleam of bone showed though the black and red. Charles lifted the bald, leathery skull to get the thong over it, then took off his own tags and put them around Dennis's neck. He fitted them into the holes in his shoulder, covering the exposed bone. Then he put on Dennis's tags and backed away, and felt something clinging to his hands and caught beneath his fingernails. It was shreds and chunks of Dennis's burnt skin and flesh, and he wiped them frantically on the long grass, whimpering, and then vomited until he fainted. When he made it to the beaches, to the chaos and the fire and the thronging men, he was bundled onto a small ship by an officer he didn't know. *Careful with this one*, the officer said, to someone else on board. *I don't know what happened to him, but I think he's gone wackers.*

'F. R. Dennis? So . . . all these years the body lying in Charles Aubrey's grave was in fact this F. R. Dennis?' said Zach. Hannah nodded. 'I've been to his grave. I paid my respects – I took flowers. I almost prayed, for God's sake!'

'I'm sure Mr Dennis appreciated it,' said Hannah, quietly. Zach tapped agitated fingernails on the tabletop, thinking rapidly.

'This is . . . this is incredible. That such an important man lived on for so long when the whole world thought he was dead . . .' He shook his head, and the scale of that secret made his pulse pick up. 'It's incredible . . . And the pictures?'

'All his work from the last sixty years of his life. Well, all except three or four pictures, that is.'

'The ones that were sold?' Zach asked. Hannah nodded. 'You sold them for her?'

'For her, and for me. When we needed the money.'

'For you?' Zach stared at Hannah for a second and thought about this. 'You mean . . . she gave you drawings, and you sold them?'

'Not exactly.'

'You *took* drawings?' Hannah said nothing. 'Because if Dimity wanted it all kept secret, then I guess that gave you the leverage to take whatever you wanted, right? How could you do that?'

'It wasn't like that! I . . . I had every right to. Besides, she needed the money too, and she couldn't have sold them without me.'

'I hardly think dealing with the auction house for her gives you the right to—'

'I'm not talking about that. I'm talking about . . . making the pictures saleable. Making them viable.' Zach shook his head in incomprehension, and Hannah fidgeted slightly. It was the first time he had ever seen her look guilty. She sighed suddenly. 'A lot of them we couldn't let anybody see because they were of Dimity, but obviously later on in her life, when he supposedly couldn't have known her, since he was meant to be dead. And a lot of them are scenes of war, so obviously they couldn't be seen either. That left some of Dennis, and some of Dimity while she was still young but . . . He never dated any of them. None of the pictures he did after he came back from the war were dated.'

'Why not?'

'Because, I suppose, he had no idea what the date was.'

'Christ. And you . . .'

'I wrote the dates on them,' she said. Zach drew in a steadying breath.

'I knew it! I *knew* the dates weren't right!'

'You were right,' she said, solemnly, and Zach's moment of excitement faded. They sat in silence for a minute.

'You do a good mimic of his handwriting,' Zach told her, not sure how to feel. 'You have a talent for that.'

'Yes. I know.'

Again they sat in silence for a while, each lost in thought. Outside, the wind had got up and it started to rain. It made a lonely sound, and Zach felt the sudden need to gather Hannah close to him, and warm her. But the shadows in the corners were too deep, too distracting. Years of lies and hidden things left so long that they'd hardened, ossified. Beside him, Hannah reached behind her head and pulled her hair out of its ponytail, and the familiar scent of it gave him a sharp, unhappy pang.

'You had no right, you know,' he said, quietly. Hannah looked at him, and her gaze hardened.

'I think I did.'

'Those pictures don't belong to you. They don't even belong to Dimity! She was never his wife . . . she never had his child. Keeping somebody prisoner for sixty years doesn't make you their common-law wife, if that's what you've been thinking . . .'

'Prisoner? He was never a prisoner! If he'd wanted to leave, he could have.'

'So it was OK that she let the world think he was dead? That she let his family think he was dead?' Hannah pursed her lips; answered him in a clipped tone.

'If that's what he wanted. Yes,' she said. Zach shook his head and Hannah seemed to wait. Waiting for his next attack, his next argument.

'Those pictures belong to Charles Aubrey's next of kin,' he said, and to his surprise, Hannah smiled.

'Yes, I know that. And you're looking at her.'

'I'm *what*?'

Dimity could hear them speaking downstairs, but she couldn't understand their words so she stopped trying, and let them wash over her like the blurred sounds of the wind and rain outside. None of it mattered any more. The room was empty. Charles was gone. No way to explain to them that keeping the door closed had kept her heart beating. No way to explain that as long as she couldn't see that he'd gone, she could dream he was still there. The shifting of the house that sounded like his footsteps, the breeze moving his papers that sounded like him working. She had come to believe it, over the last few years. Come to feel like he had not gone, and the long, happy years she had spent looking after him still continued. The sudden emptiness of the house was as cold and deep as death. She could hardly find the breath to go on living. The chill of his absence crept closer all around her, leeching the warmth from her blood and bones. Every limb felt heavy, every breath was a labour. Her heart was as vast and hungry as the sea; as empty as a cave. Life was just a burden, with the room upstairs sitting empty. The long debate of the young man and woman downstairs kept the other voices of The Watch quiet, at least. The living were louder than the dead. But there was a new face in the shadows; come to see her at last, come to haunt her. A silent reprimand of wide eyes, full of anguish. *Delphine*.

She came to The Watch one day. Out of nowhere, on a still, yellow autumn morning tangy with the smell of dew and dead leaves. The war went on, all unobserved. Charles had been with her for over a year and they had settled into their strange new life together, finding a rhythm to it, the comfort of habit. And for Dimity, the joy of having everything she ever wanted. A person to love, and be loved by; to be needed by.

'Hello, Mitzy,' said Delphine, with a cautious smile, and all at once the ground yawned open at Dimity's feet again, vertiginous as the cliff edge, just ready for her to teeter and fall. Delphine looked older. Her face was longer, and thinner. Her jaw followed an elegant curve, her hair was parted to one side, and swept back in gentle waves, soft and shiny. Her brown eyes were deeper than they'd been before. As deep as the earth; they seemed far older than the rest of her. 'How are you?' she asked, but Dimity couldn't answer her. Her heart was beating too hard, her thoughts clamoured, and no words would come. Delphine's smile faltered, and she fiddled with the clasp of her handbag. 'I was . . . just hoping to see a friendly face. A familiar face, you know. And I . . . I wanted to make sure you know about . . . Father's death. Last year. They sent me a telegram at school. Did you know?' she said, in a rush. Delphine's eyes flooded with tears as Dimity nodded. 'Well, I thought I should check. I thought you ought to know. Because . . . well, you loved him too, didn't you? I didn't like it at the time, when Mummy told me. But why shouldn't you love him too, just because we did?'

'I . . . I loved him,' Dimity said, with a tiny nod of her head.

They faced each other across the step for a while, and Delphine seemed undecided about what to do or say next.

'Listen, I . . . Could I come in, for a while? I'd like to talk to you about—'

'No!' Dimity shook her head rapidly, as much in refusal as in denial – in response to the small voice at the back of her mind that was telling her that of all the wrong things she had done, turning Delphine away would be one of the worst. She buried the voice, stood firm.

'Oh,' said Delphine, taken aback. 'Oh, right. Of course . . . Will you come out for a walk then? Down to the beach? I don't want to go just yet. I don't . . . know where to go next.' Dimity stared at her for a moment, and felt her careful emptiness deserting her; felt the falling start. But Delphine's eyes were meek, imploring, and in the end she could not refuse her.

'All right. To the beach then,' she said.

'Just like old times,' said Delphine. But it wasn't, and neither of them smiled.

They went down the valley, through Southern Farm's fields, then onto the shore. They walked westwards into the late season sun, weaving through the boulders to the shingle by the water's edge. It was a flat sea that day, all silvery and pretty, as though the world was a calm and safe place. The two young women, as they walked, knew otherwise.

'How is your mother?' Delphine asked. 'I think back a lot, you know. Over the time we all spent here. I think back and I can see, now, how hard it must have been for you, for us to just come and go. And I can . . . guess, now, how hard a time your mother must have given you. All the bumps and bruises you always had . . . I was so blind, at the time. I'm sorry, Mitzy,' she said.

'She's dead now,' Dimity said, hurriedly. She could not bear to hear Delphine apologise.

'Oh, I'm so sorry.'

'Don't be. I don't miss her. Maybe that's not what I should say, but it's the truth.' Delphine nodded a little, and didn't ask anything else about Valentina.

'But aren't you a bit lonely now, up there all by yourself?'

'I'm not . . .' Dimity's heart gave a jolt. She had been about to say that she wasn't alone; she had been about to give herself away. She had to learn to think faster, to say less. 'I'm not lonely,' she managed, her voice uneven because her blood was buzzing like insect wings. Delphine glanced at her and frowned, not believing her.

'When the war is over, things will be different,' she said. 'When the war is over, you'll be able to go wherever you want, do whatever you want.' She spoke with certainty, and Dimity stayed silent, wondering how on earth a bright girl could still think things like that.

They had come to a wide stretch of sand, smoothed by the tide, immaculately flat and even. Delphine stopped, and stared at the place with a frightening intensity.

'There – can't you just see her?' she whispered.

'What? See who?'

'Élodie. Wouldn't she have just loved this spot? She'd have written her name in the sand, or drawn a picture.'

'She'd have done cartwheels,' Dimity agreed, and Delphine smiled.

'Yes, she would. She'd have complained that we were walking too slowly, and that she was hungry.'

'She'd have told me I was a stupid know-nothing.'

'But she'd have listened to you, all the same. To your stories, and your folklore. She always listened, you know. She was just jealous of you – of how grown-up you were, and how free. And that Mummy and Daddy took to you so.'

'I was never free. And Élodie never liked me,' Dimity insisted.

'She was too young to know why not, though. It wasn't your fault, or hers.' Delphine stared at the buff-coloured sand, the silver waterline. 'Oh, Élodie!' she breathed. Her eyes shone with tears. 'When I think of all the things she'll never do, and never see . . . I can hardly bear it. I can hardly breathe.' She pressed her fists into her ribs. 'Have you ever felt like that? Like you'll just stop breathing, and die?'

'Yes.'

'I dream about her sometimes. I dream that it's Christmas, and she's all grown-up. I dream about how beautiful she would have been, how smart and sharp. She would have broken hearts, Élodie would. But I dream that she comes to me at Christmas, and we stand and talk beneath this huge tree, all covered with lights. She's all lit up by fairy lights, in her eyes and in her hair. She wears a silver dress, and her hair is blacker than jet beads. We have a glass of champagne, and we laugh and swap secrets, and gossip about her newest beau. And I . . .' Delphine trailed off, gripped by a silent sob that stole her voice. 'And I . . . wake up so happy from those dreams, Mitzy. So happy.' Delphine put her face in her hands, and wept. And Dimity stood beside her, and could not breathe, and felt like she would die.

For a long time they said nothing. They simply stood, and the sea broke quietly against the shore, unperturbed. Delphine stopped crying, and lifted her wet face to the horizon. She looked as calm as the waters, numb and untouchable.

'Have you heard from Celeste?' Dimity asked, unsure if she wanted the answer. Delphine blinked, and nodded.

'She wrote to me, after I sent a telegram to *Grandmère*. She wrote me a terrible letter. I keep it with me, and I keep reading it in the hope it'll say something different. It never does, of course.'

'What does it say?'

'She says she loves me, but she misses Élodie too much to see me. But what it really says, underneath, is that she blames me. She won't see me because she blames me. And she's right, of course. I am to blame – I killed my sister, and I nearly killed my mother, too.' She shook her head violently. 'I was so sure! I was *so sure* I'd picked the right things! How can I have made such a mistake? How?' She looked at Dimity, desperate, mystified. Dimity stared at her with her mouth fallen open. The truth hovered there, on her tongue, waiting. Wanting to be spoken. *I had gone black inside*, she wanted to say. *My heart had stopped. I wasn't me*. But she stayed silent. 'I thought I knew what I was doing. I thought I knew as much as you. I thought I was so clever.' Delphine's voice was heavy with self-loathing.

'Why did you come back here?' said Dimity. It was an accusation, a plea for her to go. Delphine tore all the wounds wide open, wider than ever.

'I . . . I just wanted to . . . be where they had been. Mummy and Daddy, and Élodie. I've left school now, you see. I wasn't sure where to go, or . . . any of it, really. I went to London but our house was . . . bombed out. Ruined. Like everything else. This was the last place I saw them. I was hoping . . . they might still be here. In some way.' Tears splashed onto her cheeks again, and Dimity wondered that she had any left to cry. 'I wish I could remember what it felt like, back then. What life felt like, when we came here and played and messed about, and Father drew, and Élodie argued with Mummy, and you and I wandered around picking herbs and catching crabs. We're the only ones left who knows how good things were then. You and I. What did it feel like? Do you remember?' She stared at Dimity with an awful hunger, but didn't wait for an answer. 'What did we do wrong that our lives should be ruined like this? Ruined or finished, so soon? Why are we being punished like this?' she murmured. Dimity shook her head.

'Why don't you go to your mother?'

'I . . . can't. Not when she doesn't want me.' Delphine paused, and wiped her eyes with the back of her hand. 'I can't believe she left me behind, Mitzy. I can't believe it. I never meant to hurt Élodie . . . she must know I never meant to.'

'If Celeste saw you, she would love you again. You should go to her,' Dimity urged. But Delphine shook her head.

'Well, I can't, even if she wanted me to. Not with the war on. I don't know what to do next, Mitzy.' She looked up then, her face a plea, but Dimity only knew that she could not stay in Blacknowle. She could not, because being calm, being happy, not letting the black tide and the rats take her over, would be impossible if Delphine was near. 'Perhaps . . . do you think I could stay with you for a while, Mitzy? Now that your mother is . . . gone. Just for a short time, while I think about where to go, and what to do next?'

'No! You can't stay here. Don't stay here. Too many memories.' Dimity spoke in a clipped, alien voice. Delphine stared at her in dismay, and the hurt on her face burnt like cigarette ash on Dimity's skin. 'You can't!' she gasped. 'It's . . . *unbearable* to have you here!'

'Of course. I'm sorry.' Delphine blinked, and looked towards the sea. 'I'm sorry. I shouldn't have asked. I might go for a walk, now. Before I leave. I'd like to . . . see some more of the places where we went, before. I'd like to remember how it was, for a while. How life was, when everything seemed so safe, and we were all so happy that we didn't even realise how happy we were.' She sniffed, and took a handkerchief from her pocket to blow her nose.

'Then you should leave here. This place will catch you, otherwise. It's a trap, and it'll keep you here, if it can. So go soon, before it gets a grip on you,' said Dimity. She wanted to grab Delphine and propel her away, far from Blacknowle. She could not have her friend near and live in peace, that much was clear.

'I understand,' said Delphine, though Dimity didn't see how she possibly could. With another flash of excruciating clarity, she saw that Delphine had come to expect rejection, to expect to be unwanted.

'Don't stay here, Delphine. Start over, somewhere new.'

'Yes, perhaps you're right. It does no good, when those times are gone. But a walk, perhaps. To see them all again, one last time.' She took Dimity's hand and squeezed it, then pulled her close and hugged her. 'I wish you happiness, Mitzy Hatcher. You deserve some.' Delphine was walking away before Dimity could answer her, and Dimity was grateful for that.

She went back to The Watch at a steady pace, careful not to trip or stumble, careful not to startle herself in case she flew apart like a flock of sparrows. She went up to Charles's room, where he was sketching the face of a young man, shut the curtains and put the light on for him. He didn't seem to notice. He didn't know that his daughter had been at the door; that the warmth of her embrace still lingered on Dimity's clothes. Again Dimity stood, and the truth was so heavy that she was sure it would drip from her mouth. *His daughter. His daughter.* A young woman who needed her father more than anything. *But her father is dead,* Dimity reassured herself.

'No one can know that you're here,' she said, and Charles's head came up from his drawing, quick and frightened.

'No one. *No one* can know that I'm here,' he whispered, eyes as wide as a child's in a nightmare.

'No one will know, Charles. I'll keep you hidden, my love.' He smiled when she said this, so grateful, so relieved. Dimity took a step back from the edge, felt his smile soothe and warm her. She breathed more easily, and went downstairs.

All the rest of that day she watched from the windows, looking out for Delphine. She scanned the cliffs and the visible part of the beach, and had only just begun to relax, and think her gone, when she saw her, late in the afternoon, crossing the far paddock and into the yard at Southern Farm; knocking on the farmhouse door. From a distance she looked even less like a girl any more – she looked like a woman, willowy, tall and thin as a whip. She saw Mrs Brock step out and hug Delphine. She hugged her for a long time, and then she drew her into the house. And Dimity remembered the way Christopher Brock had always looked at Delphine, the way he'd smiled and dropped his gaze, abashed, and she knew with dreadful certainty that Delphine would never leave. The trap had closed, and she would always be there, like a wound that wouldn't heal, to remind

Dimity of what she had done, and what she should have done. To make the threat of Charles being discovered more pressing, more real. If Delphine found him, she would claim him. But she would never find him, Dimity resolved there and then. Delphine would never set foot inside The Watch, and Charles would never set foot outside it. She stood for a long time, staring down at the farm and knowing that she would not see Delphine leave. It was full dark before she finally roused herself, and realised that she could no longer see out through the window. She shook herself, took a deep breath; tried to remember what she had been so sad about, earlier that day, what had frightened her so. She shrugged it off, since it couldn't have been important. Nothing was, apart from Charles. She hummed an old song as she began to prepare his dinner.

Zach stared at Hannah in complete amazement. She waited patiently for him to speak.

'I always said . . . I always felt that I recognised you. From the first moment I met you.'

'Yes you did. I thought it was a line.'

'No, it wasn't a line. I *did* recognise you – you look like Delphine. But I only saw it at certain angles, because I only really know Delphine from certain angles. From the picture of her that I have, that I love . . . I've spent so long studying it, looking at it.' He shook his head incredulously. 'Delphine was your grandmother?'

'She was. She came back to Blacknowle during the war, when she finished school. She ended up marrying the farmer's son, Chris Brock, and the pair of them never left.'

'Nothing was ever written about her. Nobody ever mentioned what happened to her.'

'Well, I expect nobody really cared. She wasn't a famous artist after all – and Aubrey was dead. Delphine was only a teenager when the war broke out. I expect nobody was interested in finding her, or talking to her.'

'Is she . . . still alive?' For a moment, the thought of meeting the girl whose picture he had studied and loved so intensely made Zach's mouth go dry, but Hannah shook her head.

'No. She died when I was still young. She was only just in her sixties, but she had cancer.'

'Oh. I'm sorry. Do you remember her? What was she like?'

'Of course I remember her. She was lovely. Always very kind, thoughtful. And softly spoken – I never once heard her raise her voice. But she was solemn too. I hardly ever heard her laugh.'

'Well, her sister had died, and then she thought her father had too, and her mother left her . . . Losses like that will leave a mark on you, I guess. Weren't you angry when you found out that Aubrey had been alive all this time? Your great-grandfather? God, I still can't believe it! It's . . . unreal . . . But weren't you angry? He was your family, after all.'

'No,' said Hannah, lightly, as though the thought hadn't occurred to her. 'I never knew him. I lost nothing when he died.'

'But, on your grandmother's behalf . . .'

'Yes, I suppose I should have been. Poor Delphine – she did always miss him, I know that much. But what's the point of anger when something can't be undone? No good can come from punishing people so long after the event – Delphine had been dead nearly twenty years before her father followed.'

'Did she ever talk about her mother? About Celeste? Did you ever meet her?'

'No. As far as I know, she never saw her again; certainly

not after I was born – as far as I know. She never talked about her either. It was like she'd died in the war, same as her father.'

'So . . . the pictures belong to you. As Charles Aubrey's great-granddaughter. They belong to you now,' said Zach, looking up at Hannah and trying to work out what he felt. He was exhausted. He was overloaded, bewildered, excited. Hannah nodded slowly.

'What will you do?' he asked. At once, Hannah looked uneasy.

'Much more to the point, Zach, what will *you* do?' Puzzled, Zach didn't answer.

The night seemed to have started years before, decades even. After a while, Zach went back upstairs to the small bedroom, where all the pictures were waiting. He looked at each and every one of them. Two hundred and seventeen finished works in total. There were pictures of Dimity in her twenties and thirties; in middle age; in old age. The slow, steady passing of her years, recorded a piece at a time in Aubrey's vibrant sketches and paintings. There were scenes of violence and devastation, of chaos and the brutal, confusing ugliness of war, the likes of which Zach had never known Aubrey produce before. Aubrey, a man inspired above all else by beauty. Already he was cataloguing them in his mind, arranging them into an exhibition, drafting the explanatory biographical notes that would accompany each piece. The art world had never known a story like this one, he realised. Everyone would want to come and see these pictures, and hear this story. And he knew, in that instant, that he wanted to be the one to tell it. But of course, that wasn't up to him. It was up to the owner of all the pictures. And if she wanted to lock this room and never open it again, then that was her right. The thought gave him a crushing feeling.

There were portraits of Dennis with a multitude of different faces, and Zach studied them all, under the weak light from the solitary bulb overhead. He looked at all of Aubrey's possessions, the scattered items on the desk, touching each thing gently, reverently. Tubes of oil paint and a bottle of turpentine – the chemical smell that had been so instantly recognisable to him as he'd sat in the darkness earlier, with Rozafa. Beneath some loose papers he found a startling thing. Military ID tags, still threaded onto a stiff and twisted leather bootlace. British, not made of metal like American ones would have been. A round red disc and an octagonal green one, made of some tough fibre, with the name *F. R. Dennis*, and his regimental details, stamped clearly onto the surface of each. Zach ran his fingertips over the lettering. *Dennis. I've finally found you. You get to have a story now too.* There was bound to be a photo of him, somewhere. In some old family album. Zach would be able to see the face that Aubrey had so struggled to imagine.

'Dimity told me once that he never forgave himself,' said Hannah. Zach hadn't even heard her come into the room.

'For what?'

'Stealing that soldier's identity. He used him to get home, to get away from the war and make a break for it. Ruined his name by deserting, and denied his family a body, a burial. He had nightmares about it all the time. About the war, and about Dennis.'

'Why are all the Dennis pictures of different men?'

'They're not. They're all of him. It was Aubrey's way of . . . giving him his life back. He never knew what he looked like, you see. Dennis was already dead when Aubrey found his body, and switched their tags. Dead and so badly injured that he had no idea what the lad had looked like in life. This was his way of . . . paying him back, I think. He tried to give him back his face.'

'The pictures of Dennis that have come up for sale lately . . . they were so similar, but I knew . . . I *knew* there was something different about each one.'

'Yes.' Hannah nodded. 'You're the only one who looked closely enough to see it, it seems. I picked the ones in which he looked most alike. Where Charles had clearly got an image in his mind, and had drawn it several times before it shifted. But he never got it one hundred per cent the same because . . .'

'Because it was a fantasy. He had no model.'

'Yes. It was a risk, putting them up for sale, but they were the only ones that wouldn't have . . . raised questions.'

'Why take the risk?'

'We needed money. Dimity to live on, me to . . . to help Ilir, and his family.' Zach considered this for a second.

'That most recent Dennis picture, the one that sold the week before last. That paid for Rozafa and the boy to come over, didn't it?' he asked, already knowing the answer when Hannah nodded.

'Ilir has been working for me for years, and saving up what I could afford to pay him. He sent some of it to them in France, as well. But when the French authorities started to break up the Paris camps at the beginning of the month, it was too soon. We hadn't got enough between us. We needed more.' Her eyes were wide and calm, but they were searching too. She was trying to see how he felt about it all, trying to explain all the secrets, and the lies. To explain her part in it. 'I never actually lied to you, Zach,' she said, as if reading his thoughts.

'You wrote fake dates on his pictures, Hannah. That's forgery. You denied all knowledge of Dennis, and the new pieces that were sold. You lied to me and to the whole bloody world,' he said, realising only then how much it hurt.

'It wasn't forgery! The pictures *are* by Charles Aubrey.'

'Yes. The lie you told the world wasn't as big as the one you told me,' he said. Hannah pressed her lips together unhappily, but she did not say sorry.

'What did you do with his body? You never did say. Does Charles Aubrey have a true grave that I could go and see?' Zach asked. He had a sudden dark vision of an exhumation, of relocation to hallowed ground. Of soil caught in grinning teeth and insects hiding in bony eye sockets. Hannah had been fingering the fine bristles of a paintbrush standing in a jar on the desk. She dropped her hand guiltily, as though he'd slapped her wrist.

'No. There's no grave.'

'But . . . Don't tell me you . . . burnt the body? Jesus Christ, Hannah . . .'

'No! Not that. You have to understand . . . Dimity was near hysterical when I got here. With grief and with fear. She was *adamant* that if people found out he'd been here all this time she'd be in some kind of awful trouble. She kept going on and on about secrets and bad things . . . she was hardly making sense. It wasn't long after . . . after I lost Toby. I wasn't in a clear and logical place myself . . . And he'd been dead a while, you understand. I think . . . I think she'd been in denial, or maybe she just wanted to be with him for as long as possible. But he was . . . he was starting to smell.' She broke off, swallowing hard at the memory. 'It was night-time and there was this dead body – my second dead body that year – and Mitzy was sobbing and chattering and going on and on, so I . . . I went along with what she suggested.' She looked up at him, still with those wide eyes; expectant now, ready for his reaction. On any day before that day he'd have been happy to see that vulnerability on her face.

'Which was?'

'We gave him to the sea.'

The night he died was blowy and dry, the breeze a restless whisper, like a song. Dimity's back was aching from scrubbing the kitchen floor. For years she'd supported herself and Charles by cleaning houses; riding the bus to the homes of people outside Blacknowle, newcomers, people resettling after the war. People for whom the name Hatcher had no connotations. And as soon as she could draw her pension she did so, stopping work and spending the whole of each day with Charles at The Watch. The cottage no longer felt like a prison, but a home. A sanctuary. A place where she was happy and her heart was full. But that night her bones were aching, right through to the marrow, and after a while the hairs on the back of her neck began to prickle, and an awful, sick feeling gathered under her ribs. She hummed and she sang and she went about her chores, and made a dinner of lamb chops and mint sauce, but she put off taking it up to him for as long as she could. She knew; she *knew*. But she didn't want to see, to have it proven. Each step of the stairs was a cliff face, each push of her muscles a marathon. She forced herself up to his room when the chops had long gone cold and the fat from them had congealed in a ring around the plate.

The room was in darkness and she put the tray carefully on the desk before crossing to the switch. The hand she raised to pull it was leaden; weighed more than all the rocks on the beach combined. And there he was, fully dressed but lying on the bed with his legs under the sheet, arms across his middle, tidy and organised. His head was nestled into the centre of the pillow and his eyes were shut but his mouth was not. It sagged open slightly, just enough for her to see his lower teeth, the swell of his tongue. A tongue that was no longer pink, but greyish pale. And then, in that second, the world stopped turning and everything seemed to fade to shadows; nothing was real or solid any more. The air wasn't fit to breathe, the light burned her eyes and the ceiling pressed down on her until her knees buckled. The house, the world and everything in it turned to ashes, and she tottered to the bedside, gasping at the pain. His skin was cold and dry, the flesh beneath it too firm, inhuman. The white wisps of his hair were soft and clean when she put trembling fingers up to touch them. The years had given him sunken cheeks and gaunt sinews to garland the length of his neck but when she looked at him all she saw, all she had ever seen, was her Charles, her love. For a long time she lay crumpled there, with her cheek pressed to his still, silent chest.

New faces, new voices, came to fill the grey hollow where Charles had been. They were indistinct at first; they kept their distance. They were suggestions of movement, voices too quiet to hear. But then, almost a week after Charles had left, she caught a flash of blond hair in the hallway mirror as she passed it. Dyed yellow hair, long and coarse and split at the ends. *Valentina*. And then that evening a seizure gripped her, a shudder taking over her arms and shoulders that was not hers, but Celeste's. The dead were drawn to their own, she knew, like wasps to a murdered comrade. Death was in the air at The Watch, the smell of it was spreading, getting stronger, tempting others to come and look, to come visiting. She ran up to his room in terror, and held his cold hands for comfort. They were soft again now, but in a wrong way. His whole body seemed to be sinking, settling lower into the mattress. His eyes had drawn back into his skull, his cheeks were even deeper and the strands of his neck even looser.

The tongue nestling between his teeth had darkened, blackened. His skin was waxen and yellow. 'Hawthorn,' she murmured to him in anguish, as the day got old and the sun went down. 'You smell like may flowers, my love.'

Delphine opened the farmhouse door. For a moment Dimity accepted this, and then she was startled because it could not be. She had seen Delphine carried out, years before. It was not Delphine but the girl, the dark-haired one who had sometimes come knocking on the door of The Watch when she was small, to ask for sponsorship for Red Nose Day, or to sell raffle tickets for the Brownies. A small, angular thing with scraped elbows and knees, she had been, but now here she was, grave and solemn and lovely. Her breath was ripe with alcohol, her gaze scattered and bewildered. But Dimity took her hand and pulled her back to The Watch. She could not lift him by herself. The cottage was roaring with the voices of the dead, but Hannah didn't seem to hear. They stirred Dimity into a frenzy of fear and desperation. They had to go, they all had to go, and take their secrets with them. Secrets that had to be kept; too many of them, and too grave, for even one to be spoken – the pebble that would start the landslide. No police, no undertaker, nobody else but the two women and the dead man. Hannah put her hand over her mouth as they went into Charles's room, and gagged. Her eyes were darkly alight with horror.

Between them, they lifted him off the bed. Heavier than he looked; a tall man with good, strong bones. They carried him out of The Watch and down to the cliffs. Not above the beach, but behind the cottage, to where the land dropped vertically down into the inlet. The tide was high, Dimity knew. She knew it so well she didn't even have to think to know; the currents too, the tow that would pull him under and take him far out to sea. The wind was buffeting, lifting white crests to beat against the rocks. It carried away the smell of hawthorn blossom; it carried away the sound of her sobs. They swung him back and forth, once, twice. Released him on the third. And for a second, just for a second Dimity almost followed him down. She wanted to keep hold of him, to go with him, for there seemed little point in staying on without him. But her body had other ideas, some gut instinct to live, and her hands let him go, and he flew into darkness. Swallowed by the surging water; gone. She stayed on the cliffs for a long time afterwards. The girl stayed with her; with her sweet, whisky-scented breath, her hair fluttering and the sure grip of her hands, as though she understood what Dimity might do otherwise. Where she might go. Then later she was back at The Watch, with no memory of moving, and the place was as dim and quiet as a grave.

12

Morning woke Zach, who had been dozing with his head on Dimity's kitchen table. Sharp sunlight needled his eyes, and he lifted his head cautiously. It was thick with lack of sleep and the weight of his thoughts. His skull felt like an eggshell, liable to crack with all the new things crammed into it in the past twenty-four hours. He was alone in the kitchen, surrounded by cold, sticky mugs that stank of sour milk and brandy. He filled the kettle and put it on, drank a whole pint of water and then went through to the living room. When he'd last seen Hannah she'd been asleep in an armchair, curled up opposite the Sabris family with her jumper pulled down over her hands and her mouth pursed so sweetly that he'd fought the urge to kiss it. Now the room was empty. Zach scrubbed at his eyes and tried to wake up.

'Hannah? Ilir?' he called up the stairs, but there was no reply. Then he heard a noise outside, and opened the front door.

Hannah's jeep was sitting in front of the cottage with its engine running and the doors open. Rozafa and Bekim were already in the back seat, and Hannah was swinging two canvas holdalls into the boot. 'Hey! What's going on?' said Zach, shivering with fatigue in the cool of the early morning. Hannah looked over at him with a momentary flash of alarm.

'I'm taking them to the station. I didn't want to wake you,' she said, dropping the bags into the boot and striding over to him with her hands in her pockets. Zach raised a hand to shade his eyes.

'Is it safe to? Won't the police still be watching?'

'I don't think so. I spoke to James. They searched his place last night too, and came away with nothing. He doesn't think they're still hanging around. They even apologised to me, last night. Apologised profusely, when they didn't find anything.' She flashed him a quick smile.

'Will you be long?'

'No. We're just going to the station at Wareham. Ilir is taking them north, to Newcastle. He has friends there – well, somebody he knows from home, anyway. Someone who can give them a place to stay and help get them settled, and my brother-in-law is a doctor there. He's going to help with the asylum application, and start Bekim's chelation treatment . . .'

'His what?'

'Look, there's no time to explain it all now, we have to catch a train in forty minutes. They were going to stay with me for a few days' rest before moving on, but after last night we thought it better not to wait,' she said. Zach took her hand, held it open in his and studied it. Small and scarred, the nails broken off short and grubby at the cuticles, calluses on her palms, at the base of each finger. Tough, outdoor hands; hands that inhabited an entirely different world to his.

'Do you want me to come with you?' he said.

'No, there's no need. Stay with Dimity. Look at the pictures,' she said, in an odd tone of voice.

'OK. See you when you get back then.'

'I'll be back as soon as they're away. An hour and a half or so. We'll talk then.' She turned and walked back to the car, and Ilir appeared in front of him.

Zach waited nervously to hear what the Roma man would say. His jaw still ached from the punch he'd been given the night before. Instinctively, he put up his hand to rub it, and felt how tender the bruise was. Ilir smiled slightly.

'I'm sorry for punching you, Zach,' he said. 'But you understand, I was very afraid.'

'Don't mention it.'

'No, I must. You have helped us . . . I am grateful.' Ilir's face was tired and bruised, but he looked happier than Zach had ever seen him look. A radiant kind of inner peace, as though the absence of his wife and child had always gnawed at him; a nagging pain that was now gone, in spite of the precariousness of their situation.

'Please. It was the least I could . . . I'm glad they're safe.' He offered his hand to shake and Ilir took it and pulled him into a brief, rough embrace. They'd had no time to wash or change, and the man still wore the stink of last night's stress and turmoil.

'Ilir, come on. We haven't got time,' Hannah called from the car.

'Be kind to her,' said Ilir, in a low voice. 'Now I am gone . . . she seems strong but she needs people. More than she will admit. She will need your friendship now I am gone. She is difficult sometimes, but she is a good woman.'

'I know,' said Zach. 'Good luck.' Ilir clapped him on the shoulder, nodded, then turned and climbed into the passenger seat. With a cough of blue diesel smoke, they were gone.

Zach waited on the step for a while, sweeping his gaze to take in the view from the watery horizon to the green swell of the ridge inland. Part of him was desperate to go back upstairs and look through all the pictures again; start making some notes on subject and tone. But he hesitated, startled to find that it didn't feel right to, not with Hannah gone and Dimity so upset. The pictures, however intently he had hunted them down, did not belong to him. And there was something else on his mind, something that Hannah's revelation about her grandmother had made him think about. He waited for a while, chewing his lip as he thought, trying to tell himself it didn't matter. But it did, there was no denying it. He went upstairs on soft feet.

'Dimity?' he called. He'd last seen her the night before, huddled by the doorway of the small empty bedroom where Charles Aubrey had lived, but she wasn't there now. Zach knocked gently on the door of the other bedroom, and peeped through it. 'Are you awake?' he said softly. There was no answer from the small figure curled on the bed. Her knees were pulled up in front of her, her hands clasped to her stomach in their grubby red mittens. Seeing them, Zach felt a sudden tug of affection for the old woman, and admiration too. Few people could have protected a secret with such steady faith, and such success, for so many years. He thought back over all the hours he'd spent talking to Dimity, studiously recording her tales of Charles Aubrey from the 1930s, when all the time she'd been guarding this huge and unimaginable truth. She'd always seemed to be holding something back; always seemed half afraid of letting something slip, or giving away too many clues. It must have loomed large in her mind. Dimity didn't answer his call, and her breathing was soft and even, but as Zach retreated he had the strongest feeling that she was not sleeping.

Zach avoided talking to Pete Murray as much as he could, even though the publican was keen to gossip about the police presence in the village the night before. Zach shrugged and denied all knowledge. He was impatient to be moving, to see the one person who could settle something that was clamouring for his attention, louder all the time. On the two-hour drive north, he fought to concentrate on the road. He rehearsed in his head what he would say, how he would finally find out, once and for all, a truth that had been deliberately veiled all his life.

His grandmother lived in a tiny Victorian almshouse in a market town near Oxford. Neat little brick and flint cottages, joined together in a U-shape around an immaculate lawn carefully fenced from wandering feet. The last of the late season roses showed their faded colours in the borders. Zach gave his name to the warden, and made his way to the middle of the terrace. He knocked and opened the door, to save his grandma the trouble of getting up.

'Hello, Granny,' he said, and she stared at him with a small frown, only smiling when he bent to kiss her cheek.

'Dear boy,' she said, clearing her throat. 'How sweet of you to come. Which one are you?'

'I'm Zach, Granny. I'm your grandson. David's son.' At the mention of his father's name, his grandma smiled with more conviction.

'Of course you are. You look just like him. Sit down, sit down. I'll make some tea.' She began to struggle out of her chair, her thin arms wobbling as they deployed two cane walking sticks.

'I'll get it, Granny. You stay put.'

From the tiny kitchenette, Zach studied his grandma. It had been four months since he'd seen her last, and she seemed less substantial every time. A wisp of a woman, her hair like the ghost of the curls she'd once had, her body the bare bones of what was once a neat, vigorous figure. Here she was, fading by degrees every day, and he had been too caught up in his own troubles to notice. With a prickle of guilt, he realised that he should have brought Elise to visit before she went to America. He vowed to do so, without fail, the next time his daughter was in the UK. He could only hope that his grandma would be alive to see her, but it seemed highly likely. She was frail, but her eyes were bright.

Zach took in the tea, and they chatted about family and his work for ten minutes or more.

'Well, go on and ask me,' she said, after a silence had fallen between them. Zach glanced up at her.

'Ask you what, Granny?' She fixed him with those bright eyes, and looked amused.

'Whatever it is you're so desperate to ask. I can see it hanging over you like a cloud.' She smiled at his guilty expression. 'Don't worry, dear. I don't mind why you've come to visit, it's just lovely that you have.'

'I'm sorry about this, Granny. But I need to ask about . . . about Charles Aubrey.' He'd thought she might smile, or blush, or get that happy, secretive look in her eye, like she'd always used to, but instead she sat further back in her chair, and seemed to sink slightly, to retreat from him.

'Ah,' she said.

'You see, when I was little, it always seemed to be hinted at . . . to be suggested that perhaps . . . Charles Aubrey was actually my grandfather.' Zach's pulse quickened. Putting this long-thought but never spoken thing into words felt outrageous.

'Yes. I know,' was all she said. Her expression was troubled, and Zach wondered about that. Her husband, Zach's grandfather, had died eleven years previously. The truth could no longer hurt him.

'Well, I've been down in Blacknowle these past few weeks—'

'Blacknowle? You've been in Blacknowle?' she interrupted him.

'Yes. I've been trying to find out more about Aubrey's life and work there.'

'And have you?' She leant forwards in her chair, eagerly.

'Oh, yes. That is . . .' Zach hesitated. He'd been about to blurt out everything he'd found. But he couldn't, he knew.

The secret that Dimity had kept so carefully for a whole lifetime could not be so casually betrayed. Not even to another woman who'd loved Aubrey all her life. 'I've found something down there. Something that makes it very important for me to know . . . to know whether or not I am actually a descendant of Charles Aubrey. Whether I am his grandson, or not.'

The old woman sat back again, and crimped her lips together. Her bony hands clasped the arms of her chair, and in the overheated room Zach felt sweat prickling under his arms. He waited, and for a while it seemed like he wasn't going to get an answer. His grandmother's eyes were looking into the past, just like Dimity Hatcher's did, but eventually she spoke.

'Charles Aubrey. Oh, he was wonderful. There's no way you can know, now, how wonderful he was.'

'I can see how wonderful his pictures were,' said Zach.

'Any fool can see that. But you would have to have met him, to have known him, to really know—'

'But don't you see,' said Zach, feeling a sudden rush of irritation. 'Don't you see what that did to Grandpa? And to my dad?' His grandma blinked, and frowned at him a little. 'My father, your son David, grew up with a father who didn't love him, because he didn't think he *was* his father!'

'Any decent kind of man would have loved the boy regardless,' she snapped. 'I offered to leave him. I offered to take my son, and set him free. He wouldn't have it. The scandal, he said. Always so concerned with what other people thought, he was. Too concerned that we should be respectable to care if we were happy.'

'And were you?'

'Were we what, dear?'

'Were you respectable? Was your husband the father of

your son, or was my dad an illegitimate . . . love child?' At this, his grandmother laughed.

'Oh, dear boy! You sound just like your grandpa! So pompous.' She patted his hand. 'But I'm impressed that someone, after all these years, has finally got up the courage to actually *ask* me. But what does it matter, now? Try not to dwell on it. Everyone is allowed secrets, especially a woman . . .'

'I have a right to know,' Zach insisted.

'No, you don't. You grew up with a caring father, and you were well loved and looked after. Why go digging around for something less than that? For something worse than that?'

'Because . . . Because *my* father didn't grow up with a loving father, did he? He grew up knowing he was never quite good enough. Never quite what was wanted. He grew up as a disappointment, under the shadow of Charles Aubrey!' Zach took a steadying breath. 'But that's not the point. Well, it is the point, but it's not why I'm here. I've met a woman, down in Blacknowle, who *is* related to Aubrey. She's his great-granddaughter. The granddaughter of Aubrey's daughter Delphine. Remember her?'

'Delphine? The older girl?' His grandma tipped her head to one side. 'I saw them, briefly, from time to time. But I never spoke to them, really. Not to either of his daughters, or to the other one.'

'What other one?'

'The little village girl who used to follow them everywhere.'

'Dimity Hatcher?'

'Was that her name? Quite a beauty, but always dressed in rags and hiding behind her hair. I wondered if she was simple.'

'She wasn't simple. And she's still alive,' Zach said, before he could stop himself. 'She's been telling me all about the summers that the Aubreys spent there . . .'

'Has she really? Well, then, you hardly need me to—'

'Granny, *please*. I have to know. This woman that I've met . . . Aubrey's great-granddaughter. It's . . . very important that I know whether or not we're related. Whether or not I'm actually Aubrey's grandson. Please, just tell me. No more hints and shrugs.'

'You mean the pair of you are courting?' she said, with keen intuition. Zach nodded. His grandma's fingers patted the arms of the chair in agitation. She grasped and released, grasped and released, and her face reflected a powerful dilemma. Zach took a deep breath.

'Well?' he said. The old woman scowled at him.

'Well. If you demand to know then I shall tell you. And perhaps we shall both be the poorer for it. The answer is no. No. Your grandpa was your grandpa. I never had a love affair with Charles Aubrey.'

'You never even had an affair with him? It was all made up?' Zach was incredulous, and a storm of relief and disappointment blew through him.

'I did not make anything up, young man! We had . . . a liaison. And I loved him. I loved him from the first moment I set eyes on him. And perhaps I would have betrayed your grandpa . . . but Charles wouldn't have me.' She pressed her lips together again, as if she'd stung herself. 'There. I've said it, so I hope you're happy.'

'He . . . turned you down?'

'Yes. He was the more honourable one, in the end. He came and found me in the room above the pub where we'd been staying. I thought he'd come to seduce me! But he'd come to break it off with me. Not that it had really started; just . . . the possibility. Just the enchantment. But he broke it off instead, and broke my heart into the bargain.' She laid her fingertips lightly on her chest, and sighed. 'He said that . . . he wasn't free to take what he wanted. To do what he wanted. He said he'd got into trouble already that summer, for doing just that, and that he had a family to think of.'

'Celeste and the girls . . . and he must have meant Dimity. He must have meant Dimity, when he said he'd been in trouble already. They had an affair, that summer.'

'Dimity? The little village girl? But she was only a child! I can hardly believe he would . . .'

'Perhaps that's what he meant by "trouble".'

'But are you sure, Zach? Are you *sure* they had an affair?'

'She certainly insists that they did,' he said, and his grandma smiled sadly.

'Ah, but don't you see? So did I. Until today, so did I.'

Zach left the almshouse a short while later, promising to return again soon. His grandmother's words echoed in his head. *So did I.* What did it mean, then? That Dimity hadn't been having an affair with him either? But something must have happened for Aubrey to tell his grandmother about it. *Trouble.* That was how he described the love affair that Dimity had been reminiscing about all these weeks? But then, when he went AWOL during the war, it was Dimity he sought out, Dimity he stayed with, all the long years afterwards. Or was it just that Dimity was the only person left? The only person there when Charles got back, damaged and vulnerable and in need of shelter. But no – there was also Delphine. Living less than a mile away and thinking all the while that her father had been killed in action. Zach's head ached. Dimity had kept her enormous secret, even from Delphine, the man's own child. That had been a terrible thing to do. Zach drove with the knuckles of one hand pressed into his lips. And his own family, his father, his grandfather, had lived with a ghost of Aubrey that was only that. A ghost. Nothing real, nothing substantial. Had Aubrey really been so powerful that even the suggestion of him could live on like that? Clearly, he had. And Zach's artistic streak was a quirk of fate, not an inheritance. He felt something slip away from him then, something he'd been holding on to, carefully, for many years. He thought he would miss it, but instead he felt lighter.

Zach drove straight down to The Watch. It was getting late in the afternoon, and when there was no answer to his knock, he tried the door. It was unlocked, and he let himself in uneasily. Dimity locked it, normally. He'd always heard the rattle of bolts before she opened it. For the second time that day, he went upstairs calling her name, with a head so full of thoughts he was having trouble addressing any one of them clearly. He only knew he had things he wanted to ask her; accusations, almost. Dimity hadn't moved. She still lay on her side, on the bed, and this time Zach rushed over to her with a jittery feeling, sighing with relief when he heard her breathing. Her eyes were open, staring at nothing. She blinked when Zach crouched down beside her. He gave her a gentle shake.

'Dimity, what's wrong? Are you all right?' Without a word, Dimity swallowed, and struggled to rise. Zach helped her sit up. Her legs, as he guided them over the edge of the bed, were bone thin. 'Should I call a doctor?'

'No!' she said suddenly, and then coughed. 'No doctor. I'm only tired.'

'It was a strange night,' said Zach, carefully. She nodded, and looked down at the floor, her expression desolate. 'I'm sorry,' he said. He didn't know quite how to explain what he was sorry for. For discovering her secret, when she'd kept it so long. For taking it from her, he supposed.

'He was dead these past six years. I knew, but I . . . I

dreamt that I didn't know. I wished it,' she said. Tears swelled in her eyes and splashed onto her cheeks.

'You really did love him, didn't you?' Zach murmured. Dimity looked up at him, and the pain in her eyes was tangible. One by one, the questions in Zach's mind came loose, and drifted away. She owed him nothing.

'More than life,' she said. She took a deep breath. 'And I'd have done anything for him. Done anything to make it up to him.'

'To make what up to him, Dimity?' Zach frowned. Two more tears dropped onto her clasped hands.

'What I did,' she breathed, so quietly that he hardly heard her. 'What I did.' She shook as a sob ran through her. Zach waited to hear more, but she was silent. Something Wilf Coulson had said to him came into his mind. 'Now everyone will know. People will come, and they'll know he was here. They'll know I hid him. Won't they?' She looked at him again, grief and fear scoring her face. Zach shook his head.

'They don't have to, Dimity. If you don't want me to tell anyone, I won't. I promise.' Disbelief made her eyes grow wide.

'Do you mean it? Do you swear it?' she whispered.

'I swear it,' said Zach, feeling the weight of the promise circle his heart tightly. 'The secret you and Charles kept is still yours to keep. And the pictures are Hannah's property. She hasn't betrayed you for them yet, and I'm sure she won't now,' he said. Dimity nodded, and shut her eyes.

'I'm so tired,' she said, lying back down on the faded sheets.

'Rest then. I'll . . . come back and see you tomorrow.'

'Rest? Yes, perhaps. But they'll be coming for me, you know,' she said, her voice small and fearful.

'Who will, Dimity?' Zach frowned.

'All of them,' she whispered, and then her face went slack

in sleep. Zach pulled the blanket up over her, and touched his fingers to one grubby red mitten in brief farewell.

Troubled, and still in two minds as to whether or not he should call a doctor to visit Dimity, Zach drove into the village and was about to take the lane to Southern Farm when he saw a familiar figure, sitting on a bench with a small dog at his feet, and looking out to sea. Zach pulled up alongside and lowered his window.

'Hello, Mr Coulson, are you well?' he said. Wilf Coulson clasped his hands around the whippet's lead, and nodded with the minimum of good manners. 'I know you told me not to ask you anything else about Dimity . . .'

'That's right. I did,' said the old man, warily.

'I've just been down to see her and she said something . . . Well, it reminded me of something you'd said and I wanted to ask you about it? Please?' Wilf Coulson gave him a complicated look – curiosity mixed with sadness and belligerence.

'What, then?'

'I asked you what little Élodie Aubrey died of, and you said natural causes but that there were some that said otherwise. I was wondering . . . what you might have meant by that?'

'Was it unclear?'

'No . . . but, who were these people? And what did they say? I won't use this information, you understand. I mean, not for my book. I'm just trying to understand what Dimity's going through . . . Will you tell me what you meant?' Wilf seemed to consider this, his jaw working slightly, cheeks moving in and out. But in the end he wanted to talk, Zach could see. He wanted to unburden himself.

'The doctor was in the pub, right after it happened. Dr Marsh, who'd been at the hospital with them, earlier. I was there too, so I heard him talking. He reckoned she'd got food poisoning. The older girl was often out picking things from the hedges, with Dimity.'

'The older girl? Delphine?'

'That's her, that married the Brocks' boy in the end. The doctor talked about the symptoms and I saw some looks exchanged, over his head. There were plenty in there that knew what it sounded like.'

'And what was that?'

'Cowbane,' Wilf said, shortly. 'Hemlock.'

'Jesus . . . you mean, Delphine picked it by mistake, and . . . and Élodie ate some?'

'Either that or . . .'

'Or what?'

'It's hard to come by. Water hemlock. Farmers pull it up wherever they find it, since it'll kill livestock. She'd have to have gone a long way and get damned unlucky to find any.'

'So . . . what are you saying? That it was deliberate?'

'No. I'm not saying that. Why would the one sister poison the other? And risk poisoning the whole house? Why would she profit from it?'

'Well, she wouldn't . . .' Zach trailed off, because a chill had slid down his spine. He looked down towards The Watch. 'Delphine wouldn't profit from it,' he murmured.

'Dimity weren't herself late on that summer. When they came back from Africa. And what were they doing, taking a girl like Mitzy to Africa, anyway? What good can it have done? She weren't herself. I tried talking to her, but she weren't her right self.' Wilf clamped his lips together, and shook his head angrily. 'There, now. Let that be enough for you. Let it lie,' he said, gravely. Zach noticed that the old man's knuckles had gone white, gripping the lead so hard. Zach paused for a moment, and understood his fear.

'I won't tell her that you've told me. I give you my word,'

he said. Wilf Coulson sat back a little, though his expression did not change.

'I'd have married her still, after all of it,' he said, in a strained voice. 'I'd have married her still, but she would not have me.' He took out a threadbare handkerchief and blotted his eyes, and Zach's heart ached for him. He wished he could tell Wilf why Dimity wouldn't have him – why she couldn't. She'd had Charles to think about, and to love, and to hide. And to redeem herself to.

'Thank you, Mr Coulson. Thank you for talking to me. I think . . . I think Dimity is getting rather tired. I think . . . that if you did want to visit her, then sooner rather than later might be best.' Wilf gave him a quick, startled glance, and then nodded.

'I understand you, boy,' he said. 'Now leave me be.'

Hannah let him in wearing an expression that Zach couldn't read. There were shadows under her eyes, and her lips were pale.

'You've started to clear up,' said Zach, as he sat down at the long kitchen table. There were gaps in the detritus on the worktops, and the paperwork on the table seemed to be shifting into piles, into some kind of order. Two bulging black sacks sat near the door, ready to be taken out. Hannah nodded.

'I . . . suddenly felt like it. It felt like the end of an era, with Ilir gone.'

'Did they make it to Newcastle OK?'

'Yes.' She nodded. 'Yes, they're fine. Well . . . as fine as they can be. Bekim needs to start treatment for lead poisoning as soon as possible . . .'

'That's the chelation you were talking about?'

'Yes. To draw the lead out of his system.'

'Is it really that bad, then? I mean, I noticed that he was groggy, but I thought he was just exhausted . . .'

'It's worse than you know. He'll be living with the effects for the rest of his life. How old would you say he is?'

'I don't know – a bit older than Elise. Seven or eight?'

'He's ten. Coming up eleven. The lead stunts growth and development . . .'

'Christ. Poor kid,' said Zach. 'I understand . . . I understand why you wanted to help them. Give them a new start.'

'Of course.' She busied herself at the worktop, with the kettle and mugs and teabags. She seemed unwilling to meet his eye. 'I thought you'd gone,' she said eventually.

'What do you mean?'

'Well, you got what you came for.' She turned around to face him, folding her arms defensively. 'You found out where the Aubrey pictures were coming from. You found out what happened to Delphine, and who Dennis was.'

Zach studied her for a while, and noticed that though her voice was angry, her eyes looked fearful. He shook his head, stood up and walked over to her.

'So you thought I'd just take off, with all this new-found knowledge? And do what with it?'

'I don't know.' She shrugged. 'Write a book. Break the story. Cause a splash.'

'Wow. You really don't have much faith in people, do you?' He smiled, and put up one hand to brush her cheek. Hannah knocked it away impatiently.

'Don't play games with me, Zach. I need to know . . . I need to know what you're going to do.'

'I'm not going to do anything,' he said.

'Nothing at all?' she said, incredulously. She shook her head and went back to making tea. 'So, where did you go?'

'I went to see my grandma.'

'Oh? Spur of the moment?'

'Yes. I finally got her to admit whether or not she had an affair with Aubrey. Whether or not I am actually Aubrey's grandson.' Hannah paused, and took a deep breath.

'Because if you are, then all those pictures belong to you,' she said, stonily. Zach blinked.

'I hadn't even thought of that. But yes, that would be the case, wouldn't it?'

'It would, yes,' she said, scathingly.

'Hannah, come on. I swear that's not why I went. I went because if I am his grandson, then you and I would be related. I'd be your great uncle, or something.'

'Second cousin.'

'What?'

'If you were his grandson, we'd be second cousins. But only half, because I'm descended from Celeste, and you from your grandmother.'

'Half second cousins? You worked it out already?' Zach smiled at her, and Hannah's cheeks coloured, ever so slightly.

'Weeks ago,' she said. 'When we first slept together. You'd already told me about your family rumour. So, what's the verdict? Are we kissing cousins? Are you Aubrey's heir?'

'No,' Zach said, still smiling. 'No, not at all. My grandpa was my grandpa. Granny let us think otherwise all these years because . . . well, because she'd married a man she didn't love, and she wanted it to be true, I guess.' Hannah stopped what she was doing and hung her head for a moment, shutting her eyes.

'Good,' she said, at last. Zach gave her a quizzical look. 'It would have made things very complicated, if you'd suddenly wanted to claim your inheritance. All those pictures.'

'No. Those are your pictures. Your inheritance.'

'Mine to do what I like with.'

'Yes.'

'And if what I want is to leave them there, with Mitzy?' she challenged him.

'Then so be it,' said Zach. Hannah blinked, taken aback.

'You mean you're fine with that? You don't mind? You can keep a secret like that?'

'I just swore to Dimity that I would. And I will.'

'Well,' she said, and turned away again. She put her hand on the kettle as if to make tea, but she'd forgotten to put it on to boil. She paused, and said nothing more. Zach took her by the shoulders and gently turned her to face him. There were tears in her eyes which she blinked away angrily.

'What is it?' he said.

'Nothing. I'm fine. I just thought . . . I thought . . .'

'You thought you had another battle on your hands. With me,' said Zach. Hannah nodded.

'It's been a . . . a stressful few months. You know?' She blew her nose messily on a piece of newspaper, leaving a smudge of newsprint on her top lip.

'I only want to help you,' Zach said, gently. 'You must know that by now?'

They finished making the tea, and once they'd drunk it Hannah went out of the room for a moment. She came back with a small envelope in her hand.

'What's this?' Zach asked, as she handed it to him. Hannah sat down opposite him.

'Open it.' Zach frowned at the front of the letter. The address was written in extravagant handwriting, all loops and lazy slopes, and quite hard to decipher; the addressee was Delphine Aubrey. Zach glanced up at Hannah. 'I found it in my grandma's things, after she died. It was the only one. The only letter from Celeste, that is. She kept it all those years. I thought it might . . . interest you,' said Hannah.

'Oh, my God,' Zach murmured. He brushed his thumb reverently over her name. *Delphine*. Abruptly, Hannah stood up.

'I'm going for a swim. I need to . . . clear my head. Come and find me, once you've read it.' Zach nodded his head distractedly, already opening the letter and starting to read.

Delphine, chérie, my daughter. I miss you so much. I hope you do not miss me as much, but this is a pointless thing to hope. You were always loving, and loyal. You were always a good child, and a good sister to Élodie. Help me — writing her name is like cutting myself. My poor Delphine, how can you know? How can you know the pain I feel? It hurts you to lose her, to lose your sister, but to lose a child is more than a person can stand. It is more than I can stand. Your father will look after you, I know it. His heart is like a cloud in the summer sky. It drifts and is blown about, it chases the wind, and the sun. It is inconstant, in some ways. But love for a child does not lie in the heart — it is in the soul, it is in every bone of your body. He cannot be inconstant to you. You are part of him, as you are part of me. And Élodie was a part of us too, and since she died I am no longer whole. I will never be whole. I am like a child again myself, no longer a mother. I don't know how to live any more. I am with my mother, and she cares for me.

When I started to write this letter, it was to tell you to come to me, here, when the war is over. If you wanted to. But the thought of seeing you fills me with fear. A terrible, terrible fear. When I think of seeing you, I think only of not seeing Élodie. Of that gap by your side, of that gap in all our lives. And it is not fair and it is cruel and unjust, and it was not meant to be so. But still, I fear it, and I cannot bear it. So instead I say: do not come. Please do not. And do not tell your father where I am. Though I will always love him, I am trying every day to cut that love from my heart. It does no good, to love a man like

Charles. And I see Élodie in him of course. I see her there too. I see her everywhere, even in my father's eyes, which were passed on to her. How can it be that she is dead? Nothing makes sense to me now.

You more than anybody did not deserve this fate, Delphine. Try to be happy. Try to start a new life. Try to forget about me. Try to forget what you did. My life is over, I am nothing but shadows. But there is time for you, perhaps. You are young enough to start again, and to forget. Try to forget, my Delphine. Tell yourself that your mother is dead, for the best of me surely is. Your heart is good. Your heart was always good, ma chérie. *Be happy if you can. I will not write again.*
C.

Zach read the letter three times, and tried to imagine how much it must have hurt Delphine. For a second he caught a glimpse, and sadness came like dark clouds. His throat was painfully dry, and he swallowed as he folded the paper and slid it back into its envelope. He sat for fifteen minutes or more with his head in his hands and his heart breaking for a girl he had never met. *Try to forget what you did*. The line repeated itself in his head, and he thought about what Wilf Coulson had told him earlier that day. Suddenly, he was flooded with dread, as though the truth would spill out, unbidden. He thought of Dimity, of her face full of fear and tears in her eyes. He thought of the way she'd looked at the ceiling when they'd heard sounds above. Full of desperate hope, he saw it now. He swallowed again, and vowed that he would never share his suspicions about Élodie's death with anybody. Perhaps not even with Hannah, and certainly not in his book. The thought caught him off guard. Was there still a book? He could not publish it in Dimity's lifetime, that much he knew. Zach stood up and ran his hands through his hair. He thought about what he would do next, about what mattered, and it was suddenly brilliantly simple, perfectly obvious. The future wasn't a brick wall, it was a blank page.

Zach jogged down the track to the beach, and saw her straight away. The pale glow of her skin against the dark blue water, her red bikini on, curly hair shifting in the wind. Standing at the end of the jetty with the waves coming up to her knees and her arms loose at her sides, as if the sea was the only thing keeping her there, the only thing to curb her. Zach kicked off his shoes, rolled his jeans above his knees and set out towards her, splashing impatiently. She heard him coming; turned and folded her arms across her ribs. Still defensive, still unsure of him. In that instant, Zach knew that he loved her. It was as clear as the sky that day.

'Poor Delphine,' he said, after they'd exchanged a long look. Hannah nodded. 'Of all the futures, of all the lives I imagined for her, standing in front of her portrait, I never imagined she'd had to deal with such pain.'

'Yes.'

'And you still think it was better that she never knew her father was alive?'

'I don't know. Who can know? But perhaps it . . . did help her to forget. To move on in life. Perhaps a dead father, a memory to treasure, was better than a lifetime with a broken father.'

'But she didn't forget. How could she have? And she kept that letter her whole life.'

'Yes. I saw her reading it, from time to time. When I was little, and we'd been out all day on the farm, and she'd been in the house by herself. I would come in and find her reading it, all alone. She would try not to let me see that she'd been crying.' Hannah wiped at her eyes and shook her head. 'Do you see, now? Do you see that it's not just about pictures by a famous artist? These are people's lives. These are the things they have lived through.'

'Yes, I do see. But I want to say . . . if, sometime in the future, perhaps when Dimity's . . . gone. If you ever do decide to exhibit the pictures, I want to be the one to help you. We could even exhibit them here – turn one of the barns into a gallery. And I do want to write this story. I think I will write it, now, because it feels too big to keep in. But I won't do anything with it until I have your permission. I promise.'

'Won't revealing all those new works devalue them, anyway? I thought scarcity was part of what put an artist's prices up?'

'Theoretically, yes. But in a case like this? No way.' Zach shook his head. 'The provenance, the story . . . it's like nothing people have seen or heard before. If you wanted to, you could make a lot of money. If you wanted to.'

'I want to make money as a sheep farmer, not by selling my inheritance.'

'I thought you might say that,' said Zach, with a smile.

'What will you do now?' Hannah asked.

'Close the gallery. Formally close it, I mean. It's been closed all these weeks; I just . . . didn't want to admit it. I'll sell all the stock, and my pictures of Celeste and Dimity. That should pay back the book advance and give me something to live on for a while. But I won't sell Delphine. I'll always keep my drawing of your grandmother.'

'I'd like to see it,' said Hannah.

'Of course you'll see it. I'll bring it here.'

'Here?' She frowned.

'Closing the gallery rather makes me homeless, you see. The lease is for the whole building, and if I'm not open for business, then I can't afford to keep it. I was thinking I might . . . stay in Blacknowle. For a while.'

'Zach . . .' Hannah shook her head, and looked troubled.

'Don't panic. I'm not suggesting I move in with you.

But . . . I want to keep seeing you. I want to help you, if I can. Maybe you could give me a job on the farm.' He grinned.

'And spoil those lovely soft hands of yours? Never.'

'Hannah. When I came here I thought I was looking for Charles Aubrey. I thought I was looking for . . . for the reason my life had gone the way it had. The reason my marriage had ended, and my business was failing. I thought I was looking for a pay cheque, and for answers. But now I know I was wrong about all of that. I think that when I came here, I was looking for you.'

'What are you trying to say? That you're in love with me?'

'Yes! I think I am. Or I could be, if you gave me half a chance. And I know that . . . after the way you lost Toby it might seem a lot safer to be by yourself, and to have nothing to lose. But I know you're braver than that.'

'Zach—' She splayed the fingers of one hand, let them drift up in front of her eyes.

'No, let me finish. I don't know what will happen next. I'll get a job of some kind, and I'll do sketches at the weekends to send to my daughter. But I want . . . I want to do that here. With you. That's what I'm trying to say. The only thing I want right now is to be where you are, Hannah.'

Hannah kept watching him, steadily. The breeze lifted a few locks of her hair and brushed them into her eyes, and the sunshine made her squint. She was as hard to read as ever, and Zach wanted to take her face in his hands, keep it still until he could decipher what was written there. After a long silence he realised that she wasn't going to answer him. That she probably couldn't answer him; not with words. So he battled on, stepped forwards and bent to kiss her. There was salt on her lips, and on her skin, and her mouth was warm. She stood still, as taut as a bowstring, but she didn't step away. And then he let go of her, and he waited. The light and shade of the sky was fleet across her face. He longed to draw her.

'I . . .' She broke off, cleared her throat. 'I was about to swim, if you fancy it.' Zach looked down at himself, and smiled.

'But . . . my clothes . . .'

'Diddums,' she said, and smiled. 'They will dry again you know, city boy.'

'City boy, still? Am I always going to have that hanging over my head?'

'Probably,' she told him, airily.

'All right then. Clothes and all.' Hannah took his hand, and there was conviction in her fingers as they laced through his, and held on tightly. A grip that would survive the pull of the water, of the tide. They moved forwards, felt for the edge of the jetty with their feet and then dived in, head first, together.

Dimity watched them from the clifftop. They were so caught up in each other, so riveted, that they didn't look up to notice her. She was tired, but she had wanted to come out onto the cliffs, wanted to look down at the sea. At the place where Charles was, somewhere. His bones were in the white crests of the waves; there were traces of his skin in the sand. He had been taken in, made a part of it. She watched Zach and Hannah dive in together, and she was jealous. She wanted to swim in him, too. She wanted to feel his spectral touch; a hand on her midriff, holding her afloat. Instead the wind circled her gently, uncaringly, and made her eyes sting. Below her, the beach blurred, and she blinked furiously to see again. There were figures on the beach, and she knew, before she could see them properly, who was there.

She knew, and the next breath she took felt like glass splinters in her chest.

Delphine and Élodie were playing on the sand. Delphine was standing, neat and decorous, with her yellow cardigan buttoned up and her hair in plaits, conducting her sister in a wild dance. Élodie leapt and spun, her footprints making a circle in the sand around Delphine; long strips of kelp in her hands that she twirled like streamers. The wind lifted up from the shore, and carried the sound of their voices to her. Élodie laughing, high and gleeful; Delphine instructing her, patiently, kindly. Letting her play, letting her be a child. *Always a child.* The voice was close to her ear and she turned to find Celeste standing beside her, looking down at her daughters with a smile of pride and love. Celeste, with her glorious eyes and her beauty shining like light all around her; no trace of a tremor in her body, no trace of grief in her face. The kelp in Élodie's hands fluttered and snapped like pennants. Dimity struggled to breathe. There was a pain in her side, in her heart; more than she could bear. She gasped like a landed fish, clasping her right hand to the left side of her ribs, to the wound she felt there, gaping, letting in the cold wind. She wanted to stay with them, with Élodie and Delphine. She wanted to see their faces bright with smiles; the faces of children who were loved, and whole, and carelessly happy. She wanted to see Élodie's black hair flying out all around her. But they faded. The water swept in, and washed away their footsteps. *Delphine!* She called out, but no sound came from her mouth. Celeste studied her gravely, staying on the cliffs as Dimity turned, and walked back to The Watch on slow, unsteady feet.

The Watch was crowded – far too crowded, because they followed her there. Élodie was lying on the sofa, kicking up her heels, and Delphine sat next to her. They were different now. They weren't happy any more, these shades. They were waiting. Celeste was walking in wide circles around the house, trying to find a way in, and Valentina scrutinised her every move with narrowed eyes. There were accusations in their eyes; echoes of things so secret that Dimity could barely remember them now. Things so secret she had made herself forget. But the Aubrey girls hadn't forgotten, and neither had Celeste, or her mother. Dimity searched the house desperately, the pain in her chest getting worse, but Charles was not there. The one she wanted to see, the one she longed for. Of him there was no sign. She stumbled to the foot of the stairs, and started to climb.

His room was lit by the afternoon sun, and the door had been left open. So carelessly, so thoughtlessly. It had never once stood open like that, not since he'd come back to her. He liked it to be closed; liked that security, that privacy. Sometimes, he looked up sharply when she came in, checking to be sure it was her. That instant of fear in his eyes before he recognised her – it had made her heart ache for him, every time. Other times he hadn't seemed to notice she was there. Now, she went over to his bed, the bed that had been hers in childhood, and gazed down at it as though he might still be lying there. Her fingers trembled. She could almost feel the soft texture of his hair, the hard bars of his ribs. *Old maid*, Valentina whispered spitefully in her ear. And it was true. Charles couldn't stand her being too close to him. It seemed as though her touch almost hurt him. The times she'd tried to lie down next to him he'd got a confused, panicked look in his eyes and she'd quickly relented. Sometimes she stole kisses when he slept; just the lightest touch of her lips to his, too soft to wake him. She was ashamed of herself, but could not help herself either, because in those moments she was a girl again, and they were in the alleyway in Fez where he had put his arms around her and kissed her deeply and the world had been bright and complete and startlingly wonderful.

This was Charles's room, the one place she might still find him. She put her hand on his pillow, just where his head had lain, and felt her heart slow in response, in recognition. She hadn't stood by his bed since the night they took him out, and now it felt like that night again. The six years since had been a frightening, fitful dream; now it was time to wake up. To follow him, like she should have done all along. She lay down on the bed, careful not to disturb the sheets. She wanted everything to be as he had left it, as he had last touched it. Wanted her body to touch each place his had touched. She put her head into the hollow in the pillow and crossed her arms over her middle, just as he had done. Lying in the last space he had lain, and yearning to feel him there. *Come back to me, my love. Come back and take me with you this time*. She breathed as slowly, as quietly as she could, and she waited. Waited to feel him take her hand and show her which way. And soon, softly, he came. She caught her breath in a gasp as she felt it. Just him, just them, alone in the little room where for more than sixty years he had dwelt, and she had loved him, and lived only for him. The others slipped away through the walls – she felt them go. Élodie, Delphine, Celeste, Valentina. Finally, they all let her be. They left her alone with Charles, which was all she had ever wanted. Her heartbeat was slow and tired; she felt so cold and heavy that she didn't think she would ever get up from that bed again. She didn't ever want to. And then he was there. She heard him clearly; and the joy of it was a vivid pain right through her, so sweet, so sharp. *Mitzy, don't move*. And she didn't. Not even to breathe.

Acknowledgements

I am immensely indebted to the whole team at Orion for all their excellent work; and most especially to my editor, Sara O'Keeffe, for all her great advice, vision and support. My thanks also to my wonderful agent, Nicola Barr, for her help, encouragement and expertise.

My thanks to Jane Kallaway at Langley Chase Farm, for meeting me and introducing me to her flock; and to Richard Heaton CB for his insights into the workings of the art world. All and any inaccuracies regarding either sphere – art or organic sheep farming – are entirely my own.

Finally, my love and gratitude to Mum, Dad, Charlie, Luke and all my friends who have been, as ever, generous with their support and enthusiasm as I write.

A Half Forgotten Song

Forgotten Song

Reading Group Notes

About the Author

Katherine Webb was born in 1977 and grew up in rural Hampshire before reading History at Durham University. She has since spent time living in London and Venice, and now lives near Bath. Having worked as a waitress, au pair, personal assistant, book binder, library assistant, seller of fairy costumes and housekeeper, she now writes full time. *A Half Forgotten Song* is her third novel. Her first two novels, *The Legacy* and *The Unseen*, were both bestsellers and *The Legacy* was a Channel 4 TV Book Club pick for 2010 and won the popular vote for Best Summer Read.

The Story Behind *A Half Forgotten Song*

The first seed of the idea for this novel was planted by a summer job I had during my university years. The job was in the bindery department of a printing works, which produced high quality art books and periodicals. For two weeks, I hand-collated a book about the artist Augustus John, and saw, again and again, his glorious portraits, which were often of the women in his life. I was captivated by them. I took a copy of the book home with me, and learned a bit more about the man – one of Britain's foremost twentieth century artists.

He lived in a very unconventional way for the late Edwardian era, with wife Ida, mistress Dorelia, the children of both women, and sometimes Dorelia's sister too, all under one roof. He was said to have tremendous allure, and to be a great lover of women – so much so that it was joked that he would pat the head of any passing child in the street – just in case it was his. His portraits are strikingly sensuous. He manages to convey mood, expression, and atmosphere with just a few strokes of his pencil, and often worked quickly, spontaneously, to capture a moment. There's a photograph of Augustus, Ida and Dorelia, with several of their children, enjoying a picnic on a cliff top in Dorset, where they lived for several years. When I saw it, I started to wonder – what must the residents of a quiet place like Dorset, in the early part of the twentieth century, have made of such Bohemian living arrangements?

So the character of Charles Aubrey was born, inspired by but not based upon Augustus John. And the character of Dimity also came to me – a girl who had never known anything but the village and house where she grew up, and whose experience of life to date had been one of exclusion and hardship. How would she react when confronted by the warm, open, extended family of a great artist? How would she react when she was invited into that circle? How would she adjust? Would it be too much for her? The most rural parts of any country are the slowest to change, and in the 1930s, the era I decided to set the story, a lot of houses in rural England would have remained unmodernised, without indoor bathrooms or telephones; in some cases even without electricity. The pace of life was slower, and still shaped by the farming calendar. Many people still spent their whole lives within reach of the village where they were born.

Dorset remains one of the most beautiful parts of England, and one that, for me, epitomises the joy of the British seaside. It has a stunning coastline, and rolling hills inland. In the summer, it's flooded with holidaymakers for these very reasons. When I was a child we took our summer holidays in Devon, rather than Dorset; but since then I have visited the county many times, and come to love it. I jumped at the chance to try to capture the landscape and feel of the place – how wild and lonely, as well as lovely, the coast there can be. To an outsider, just coming to visit, it's the picturesque scenery that gives the lasting impression. But I could well imagine that to have grown up there, in an earlier time, might have been a difficult and insular experience.

The nature of Dimity's upbringing – in near poverty with

a neglectful single mother – means that she has had to fend for herself, and often feed herself, a lot of the time. Dimity is an expert in the kind of wild food and foraging lifestyle that has recently come back into fashion! But I wanted to show that if you had to forage to survive, it would be a very different thing – knowledge would be passed down from parent to child, and it would become a necessity, even a chore. I have long been interested in lost herb lore, wild food, and hedge pharmacy. A low-income family in the 1930s, before the days of the National Health Service, would not have been able to see a doctor for every minor, or even major, ailment that they suffered. Home remedies were still very much in use, for everything from liver disease to piles, birth control and beauty treatments; and again, such recipes were passed down in families, and shared with neighbours. I really wanted Dimity to be perfectly adapted to her environment in this way – to have all this knowledge, which to the Aubrey family is something of a novelty, but to her is a means to survive. It would have been a hard way to exist, and when Dimity is shown an alternative way of life by the Aubrey family, she is captivated by it.

So the stage was set for two different worlds to collide – Dimity's poor, traditional, lonely one; and the Aubreys' cosmopolitan, expansive, exuberant one. Neither side will be the same again, once the consequences of their meeting have fully played out. The intense and flattering attention of the artist, as he repeatedly sketches the rustic Dimity, is like nothing she has experienced before, and once she has tasted it, she cannot let it go. I'm sure we can all remember crushes we had during our adolescence, and just how powerful and all-consuming they could be. I suddenly wondered, as I thought of Dimity, just how destructive such an obsession might be, given an extraordinary set of circumstances; how, with the carelessness of happy, privileged people, the Aubrey family might push Dimity past reason to a stranger, darker place.

The story also touches on memory, and the way it can play tricks on us. Or rather, the way we can wilfully use it to play tricks on ourselves. How often, when something happens that we are ashamed of, do we deliberately forget about it, or tweak the events to exonerate ourselves somewhat? At the extreme end of this scale there are cases of people whose minds have entirely suppressed memories that are too painful or too traumatic for them to cope with. Given a lifetime to reflect, and bury, and build her own cover-story, would Dimity manage to entirely expunge those memories of the Aubreys that were hateful to her? Would she be able to rewrite her own history, or, towards the end of her life, would the memories bubble up, and refuse to stay silent? Would they come back to haunt her, like ghosts, and not rest until she had confronted them?

A Half Forgotten Song became a story about the precarious balances we live with – how so many things can be both wonderful and destructive; both beautiful and savage – from love to landscape, from art to childhood. That the apparent kindness of welcoming a stranger into your home can in fact be cruel; that trying to fit in where you don't really belong can make you lose yourself. It's about what can happen to us when we're put into a situation for which we are wholly unprepared, and how careful we all ought to be with the lives and feelings of others.

In Conversation with Katherine Webb

Q *Which character in* A Half Forgotten Song *reminds you most of yourself?*

A I think they all have at least one trait I can relate to, or see a little of in myself. I have some of Hannah's practicality and stubbornness, and also some of her self-reliance. But I also have some of Zach's self-doubt and uncertainty, and I can be a bit of a fantasist, just like Dimity.

Q *Silence or music while you write? If music – who do you listen to?*

A Silence – if there's any music, I listen to it and stop working!

Q *Do you like Zach?*

A I do, very much – he's genuinely kind-hearted, and honest, even if he's not perfect. He's sometimes uncertain, and slow to act – not exactly an action hero! But I sympathise a great deal with the nagging feeling he has that he ought to be doing better than he is. People often expect an awful lot of themselves, and give themselves unrealistic deadlines and milestones to reach – *by the age of thirty I*

will have . . . etc. I'd like to sit Zach down and tell him not to beat himself up so much! He's doing his best, which is all any of us can do.

Q *Which authors do you admire and why?*

A I find something to admire in pretty much every book I read – and I read a lot. I know how difficult writing a novel is, so I appreciate the hard work of others! The writers I really enjoy are the ones whose books hold me completely captivated, and so immersed that I forget that I'm reading and feel like I am actually inside the story; who make me care so deeply about their characters that I develop genuine feelings for them, be they positive or negative. Some favourites include Ian McEwan, Jim Crace, Margaret Atwood, Helen Dunmore, Kate Atkinson, Sir Terry Pratchett, Tad Williams and Rose Tremain.

Q *Like Ilir, is your home where you were born?*

A For me, I would say yes. Not the exact town, perhaps, but the country. However much I moan about the weather, the overcrowding, the politicians, the prices and the weather (again), I'm not sure I'd want to live anywhere else but England. If I did move away, I'd be homesick for it – and nowhere else serves a proper cup of tea! But I have friends who have cut all ties with the UK completely and never looked back, so I think it's a very individual thing.

Q *How did you physically write* A Half Forgotten Song, *and why?*

A I write directly into my laptop. I have a workbook full of scribbled notes which I have to have open beside me, even if it's no help at all – it gives the illusion of planning and forethought when, to a large degree, I'm never quite sure exactly what I will write until I write it! I work from a good outline of the plot, but from scene to scene the books evolve very organically. It's better that I type – my hand writing is atrocious. Half the time I can't read my own notes.

Q *How do you hope your readers will feel about Dimity?*

A I'm always interested in the grey areas of human behaviour and morality – the fact that good people sometimes do bad things, and vice versa; and that none of us really knows what we might be capable of doing under extreme circumstances. With Dimity I wanted readers to be able to see why she ended up the way she did, and perhaps understand how desperate she had become and why. I personally feel that she did an inexcusable thing, but given that she spent the rest of her life punishing herself for it, perhaps readers might be able to forgive her in the end.

Q *What's your most treasured possession?*

A My two cats, Erik and Pole. Always there to wake me up when I oversleep, and to destroy my house with claws and muddy feet. I love cats – they maintain such a perfect balance of affection and indifference! I also have a ring that was my grandmother's which is very special to me. The band has worn almost right the way through, and I like to think of all the many times she must have worn it. Grandma was a fantastically stylish, charming and self-possessed woman. Whenever I'm feeling nervous before some important occasion, I put on her ring and try to 'channel Grandma'!

Q *Why did you call the novel* A Half Forgotten Song?

A The idea for the title came from all the little musical snippets and childhood songs through which Dimity was transported back into her recollections. Then I realised it perfectly described her flawed memories as well – the way her version of events, and the stories she tells Zach, don't quite tally with reality. I think that happens a lot – an invented version, or rose-tinted ideal, gets more and more deeply entrenched until it completely obscures the actual, less appealing reality. It's a way of protecting ourselves that I'm sure we're all guilty of sooner or later, to some extent.

Q *Did an actual artist inspire Charles? Did real paintings inform your description of his work?*

A Yes. The character of Charles Aubrey was inspired by the life and work of Augustus John. He's a fascinating figure, and one of Britain's greatest twentieth-century artists. He drew such beautiful, sensuous pencil portraits of his wife, his mistress, his children . . . I find them utterly captivating, and I tried to describe that magnetic quality when I was describing Charles Aubrey's work. Augustus John was also rumoured to be a tremendous philanderer . . .

Q *What single thing about you would surprise us the most?*

A Not much! I'm a fairly straightforward sort of person, I think; no extreme hobbies or weird habits. Perhaps, given that the stories I tell are often quite tragic, and that I don't give all my characters happy endings, it might be surprising that I'm generally a very cheerful and upbeat person! Also, I get completely paralysed when I'm asked to write a dedication in a book, or a witty something in a birthday card – I can never think of *anything* to write, which is a bit embarrassing for an author.

Q *Was the plot of* A Half Forgotten Song *worked out before you began writing, or did it develop as you went along?*

A It was pretty much all worked out. I wrote a comprehensive synopsis for my editor before I got going, which I don't like doing and found very hard indeed, but which did hammer out a few plot holes before I'd written my way into them! I always know where my characters need to end up in a story; I work out how to get them there once I'm underway.

Q *What's your most vivid memory?*

A   Memory is a funny thing. Some seemingly significant things have already blurred into the background, and some seemingly banal things I can remember with crystal clarity. Who knows why? The little things that stay with us must be significant in ways we can't immediately decipher. I remember the squashed, desiccated frog I found in the road when I was five; and sitting at the kitchen table practising my letter 'e's. I remember in excruciating detail a social faux-pas I made at a dinner party eight years ago, but I can't really remember what I did on my sixteenth birthday. I remember the exact moment I heard that I'd got a publishing deal, and in what order I then called my friends and family to let them know; but I can't really remember my graduation day at university. Moments of real fear or anxiety stay with me – probably because, happily, there have been so few of them.

Q   *The settings in the novel feel very real – how do you go about creating the feel of real places?*

A   I always try to give as much of a multi-sensory picture to readers as I can – rather than giving a detailed description of the layout or exact situation of a place, I try to show what the light is like there, what the smells are, what the weather is doing, what you would hear if you were there. Those are the things you'd notice if you were actually there, and those are the things that make one place so different from another. Obviously, it helps if you've been to the place you are setting your story, and spent enough time there to build up an impression of all these things, which you can then relay to readers. I think writers and artists are often very observant for this reason – the urge is always there to recreate that place, that feeling, that atmosphere.

Q *Any clues about your next novel – any snippets for us?*

A It's set in Bath in 1820. It's about a girl who vanished – a girl who meant a great deal to a disparate group of people, but was not loved by them all. The story follows the unravelling of her disappearance . . .

For Discussion

❧ 'Sometimes things were too big, Zach suddenly thought. They were too big to step back and look at them all at once.' Zach is pondering restarting painting here, but is that all he's thinking about?

❧ 'What was it that made children love the seaside so? And made adults feel more alive?' What is it do you think? Do you feel the same?

❧ 'I think we only stay children if people let us.' Is this your experience?

❧ 'Nobody ever really starts a *new life*, or anything like that. You take the old one with you. How can you not?' Seems to make sense, yet people try to all the time – is it possible?

❧ To what extent is *A Half Forgotten Song* about the nature of memory?

❧ 'She believed in a watching fate that took pleasure in punishing those who went too lightly into danger.' What does this tell us about Hannah?

❧ 'Can't something man-made, also be a thing of beauty?' The need to ask the question says a lot about Charles and his attitudes doesn't it?

❧ 'That is the key to happiness. Realising where you are, and what you have right now, and being grateful for it.' Do you agree? Is Charles happy?

❧ '"I mean, I want to know everything about you." He smiled. "Nobody ever knows everything about a person, Zach," she said solemnly.' What does this say about Zach?

❧ 'What's for you won't go by you.' True, do you think?

❧ How has the author created the two contrasting worlds of Blacknowle and Morocco?

❧ 'Where you are born is always your home.' Do you agree with Ilir?

❧ 'She would always strive to give him whatever he asked for. Making him happy was all she could do for him; and all she could do for herself. Protecting him assuaged the feeling of falling that she still woke up with, every single day.' When you reached the end of the novel, what were your feelings about Dimity? How had they changed as you read?

Suggested Further Reading

Atonement by Ian McEwan

Confinement by Katharine McMahon

The Forgotten Garden by Kate Morton

Never Let Me Go by Kazuo Ishiguro

The Memory Keeper's Daughter by Kim Edwards